MERICAN STORIES II

FICTION FROM THE

ATLANTIC MONTHLY

AMERICAN STORIES II

FICTION FROM THE

ATLANTIC MONTHLY

C. Michael Curtis, Editor

Chronicle Books • San Francisco

Copyright © 1991 by Chronicle Books. All rights reserved.
No part of this book may be reproduced in any form
without written permission from the publisher.

Introduction copyright © 1991 by C. Michael Curtis

Pages 273 to 274 constitute a continuation of the copyright page.

Printed in the United States of America

Library of Congress Cataloging in Publication Data available.
American stories II : fiction from the Atlantic monthly / edited by C.
    Michael Curtis.
        p.   cm.
      ISBN 0-87701-894-4
        1. Short stories, American.   I. Curtis, C. Michael.   II. Atlantic
    (Boston, Mass. : 1981)   III. Title: American stories 2.   IV. Title:
    PS648.S5A495   1991
813'.0108—dc20   91-14724
                                                                    CIP

Book and cover design: Herman + Company
Composition: **T:H** Typecast, Inc.

Distributed in Canada by Raincoast Books,
112 East Third Avenue, Vancouver, B.C. V5T 1C8

10 9 8 7 6 5 4 3 2 1

Chronicle Books
275 Fifth Street
San Francisco, CA 94103

 *printed on recycled paper*

This one is for Jean, who wanted a long story, and got one, and for our children, Christopher, Hilary, and Hans.

Table of Contents

Introduction

WHAT *IS* A SHORT STORY? AND WHY IS ONE "BETTER" THAN ANOTHER? One might as easily inquire into the nature of "goodness," or the meaning of "progress." Most writers and critics set the question aside as needlessly academic, or formalistic in some gratuitous sense, or simply as impossible to answer with anything like convincing precision. When pressed for an explanation, a cornered critic usually reaches for identifying characteristics loose enough to satisfy literary anarchists, instrumental in ways likely to pacify literalist scholars. These critics concede that a story might well include a series of events (some insisting that they be causally linked), and almost all admit a liking for some sort of point to this enterprise—a conclusion, a clarifying insight, a sudden understanding or illumination, what one writer imaginatively refers to as an ax "for the frozen sea within us."

One conclusion to draw from all this uneasiness is that a short story can be pretty much what we want it to be. To put it another way, a "short story" has no quantity of its own, no fixed properties in the sense that a molecule of water can be said to require absolute proportions of hydrogen and oxygen. The more interesting question is what we have in mind when we describe something as a "short story" and why we call it, whatever it is, a short story rather than blank verse, or recollection, or a lie.

C. MICHAEL CURTIS

But does even that question need to be answered in the first place?

Surely the answer is no, and that is why story collections appear with introductions saying something like, "here are the ones I liked," and very little more, or at least nothing more that could be described as curious or definitive where form is concerned. In general, critics willing to commit themselves on the matter fall into three rough categories.

The first group believes it can, more or less, say what a story *is*. Thus armed, it can also say why Story A is better than Story B. This kind of critic, or literary gatherer, often admires stories that resonate with "authenticity," "humane concern," or "openness to experience," and are free of ideology, are illuminating, are morally or psychologically acute, are concerned with real life, and are artistically suggestive in some enterprising way. These standards are recognizable, and respectable, not so esoteric or idiosyncratic as to be threatening, even vaguely; they also pay homage to the possibilities of intuitive connection or stylistic experiment.

The second group of critics or anthologists is either indifferent to, or suspicious of, an approach that seems to them formulaic. These critics are alarmed by the idea that a story or a writer "ought" to do anything, but are not prepared to throw the baby out with the bath. They duck the problem by attending to the *effect* of a story, rather than its intention or form. Good stories, assessed from this perspective, do what they want to do, using standards of their own. They touch the heartstrings; they amuse; they educate; they reveal eternal passion; they ask questions. Take your pick. The important point is that neither these stories nor their authors are or should be held accountable to any predetermined standard. Stories, in this view, have a momentum of their own and either touch us or don't. This allows, of course, for a great deal of range, and its openness is admirable. As a guide for anthologists, however, it is hopelessly nonspecific, and it leads to collections that seem, and are, guided by nothing more systematic than the anthologist's gut response—or are chosen within the framework of literary values the anthologist privately, even subconsciously, subscribes to but is reluctant to prescribe across the board. Critics who follow this path are appealing because of their modesty and apparent tolerance, and because they aren't looking for a fight.

The third group is. These writers and critics respond fiercely to the idea that a story ought to be "about" anything at all, though some of their stridency seems to me a sort of protocol, offered on behalf of quite a different question: the imperatives of *artfulness*. In the minds of these critics, anyone can put together a working definition of an art form, using language that is appropriate and trustworthy. But art simply *is*, and its successes sometimes defy lucid explanation and often resist conventional critical interpretation. Conventional stories are not harmful, in the eyes of these critics, but conventional standards may be. What is needed is a sublime openness to aesthetic possibility, a willingness to view each artifact as something with intentions and conventions of its own. What we have, in this unpredictive universe, are simply stories—and our reactions to them. In practice, the work admired by even these extreme critics can be shown to contain elements familiar to good readers everywhere, though they are often discrete, or truncated, or unpredictable in their arrangement. Even an artist who flatly declares that his/her work has no "meaning" can usually be said to have something in mind, a phenomenon that ought to alert us, yet again, to the difference between the meaning words have in and of themselves, and the meaning we provide for them, that we intend, when we use them.

Given these alternative views, each powerful and yet dissatisfying, I wonder how persuasive a case can be made for what a story *is*, and why one is better than another. At *The Atlantic* this question is not academic, since in an average year some twelve to fifteen stories must be culled from a body of twelve thousand submissions in a manner that is not utterly capricious or foolishly limiting.

For better or worse, we rely on the distinction between *stories* and *story-telling*. Story-telling is not the same as image-making, or language play, or fantasizing about other worlds or obscure sensibilities. All of those things can be artful and entertaining, even instructive. But they are not story-telling. Story-telling is a sort of controlled catharsis, a review of historical evidence, a rehearsal of imagined tomorrows. Story-telling allows us to look for connections between injuries of the past and uncertainties of the present. At its best it establishes a context for problem-solving, and for problem identification. Story-telling is our way of reminding ourselves who we are or want to be or might have been. It helps us to make sense of behavior that thrills or alarms us. Story-telling *does* instruct, whether we intend that or not. It *does* help us to distinguish the real from the fraudulent, and it *does* make bearable the otherwise dismaying range of our disappointments and frustrations. At its best, story-telling has to do with recognizable voices, characters, and situations that lead us to conviction or direction. Artificial crises, by contrast, tend to lead us to amusement or indifference. We look for closure because our lives are full of tensions that seek resolution, decisions that have to be made, fears that must be put to rest. We look for heroes because we need them, because we yearn for convincing illustration that love has consequences, that courage pays, that patience will earn us more than heedless insistence.

Writing, per se, need not intend or accomplish any of these things, and it often doesn't. But when *Atlantic* editors speak of short stories, we usually have in mind some or all of the elements of story-telling outlined above. And *Atlantic* editors, of necessity, are even more stringent in their preconceptions.

The truth is we *like* stories that reflect life's apparent realities, that permit (even encourage) characters to learn, that have unified structure, that lead to resolution, to change, to a rethinking of mood or situation. Among other things, successful stories remind us of our own moral uneasiness, the difficulty of our own life choices. We *like* finding characters who seem to us "realistic" because they are afflicted with uncertainties like our own, are fully capable of decency or malevolence, are as perplexed as we are by the apparently unending abundance of life's paradoxes. To say that stories with this sort of content or intention are the ones we prefer—provided the language and vision that delivers them seems to us wise, and fresh, and imaginative—is not to say they are the only stories that matter or that stories meeting this sort of standard can safely be judged superior to others. These fairly conventional criteria, however, probably explain why some stories endure in our hearts and imagination, why we hand them down, from anthology to anthology, from writing class to writing class, why we know they matter, why we know they fully and honorably represent the art form from which they evolved.

The stories in this collection have emerged from that tradition, though many, of course, were chosen by earlier *Atlantic* editors. My own connection with these stories begins with Joyce Carol Oates' "In the Region of Ice," her first story in a major general magazine and an eventual First Place selection in the 1966 *Prize Stories; O. Henry Awards* collection. Most of the stories that follow in the chronological sequence were stories I lobbied for and edited. A good many of the writers have reputations of substance. Others still await the larger reading public they deserve. All of these stories have depths of moral meaning, language, and characters that are recognizable, a sense of "event," and other virtues. They are also, in ways that elude succinct analysis, magical and surprising, or unsettling, or disarming, or confounding. They do not so much resist interpretation as survive its scrutiny. They take us where we haven't been or point us to what we missed while we were there. They please us in the way of unexpected kindness, or alarm in the way of unwelcome self-discovery. They are what they want to be, and we need them.

Gold Is Not Always

WHEN THEY DREW NEAR THE COMMISSARY, LUCAS SAID: "YOU WAIT HERE."
"No, no," the salesman said. "I'll talk to him. If I can't sell it to him, there
ain't a—" Then the salesman stopped. He did not know why. He was
young, not yet thirty, with the slightly soiled snap and dash of his calling,
and a white man. Yet he stopped and looked at the Negro in battered overalls, whose face showed only that he was at least sixty, who was looking at
him not only with dignity but with command.

"You wait here," Lucas said. So the salesman leaned against the lot fence
in the bright August morning while Lucas went on up the hill and mounted
the gnawed steps beside which a bright-coated young mare with a blaze
and three stockings stood under a heavy comfortable saddle, and entered
the commissary, with its ranked shelves of tinned food and tobacco and
patent medicines, its hooks from which hung trace chains and collars and
hames, and where, at a roll-top desk beside the front window, his landlord
was writing in a ledger. Lucas stood quietly looking at the back of the white
man's neck until the other looked around. "He's done come," Lucas said.

Edmonds swiveled his chair about, back-tilted. He was already glaring
at Lucas before the chair stopped moving; he said with astonishing violence: "No!"

"Yes," Lucas said.

"No!"

"He done fotch the machine with

WILLIAM FAULKNER

him," Lucas said. "I seed hit work. I buried a dollar in my back yard this morning' and it went straight to whar it wuz and found it. He just wants three hundred dollars for it. We gonter find that money tonight and I can pay it back tomorrow morning."

"No!" Edmonds said. "I tell you and tell you and tell you there ain't any money buried around here. You've been here sixty years. Did you ever hear of anybody in this country with enough money to bury? Can you imagine anybody in this country burying anything worth as much as two bits that some of his kinfolks or friends or neighbors or acquaintances ain't dug up long ago?"

"You're wrong," Lucas said. "Folks finds it all the time. Ain't I told you about them two strange white men that come in here after dark one night three years ago and dug up twenty-two thousand dollars and got out again before anybody even seed um? I seed the hole whar they had done filled it up again. And the churn hit was buried in."

"Hah," Edmonds said. "Then how do you know it was twenty-two thousand dollars?" But Lucas only looked at him. It was not stubbornness. It was an infinite, an almost Jehovah-like patience, as if he, Lucas, were engaged in a contest, partially for the idiot's own benefit, with an idiot. "Your paw would a lent me three hundred dollars if he was here," he said.

"Well, I ain't," Edmonds said. "You've got damn near three thousand dollars in the bank. If I could keep you from wasting any of that on a damn machine to find buried money, I would. But then, you ain't going to use any of your money, are you? You've got more sense yourself than to risk that."

"It looks like I'm gonter have to," Lucas said. "I'm gonter ask you one more time—"

"No!" Edmonds said, again with that astonishing and explosive violence. Lucas looked at him for a time, almost contemplative. He did not sigh.

"All right," he said.

When he returned to the salesman, his son-in-law was there too—a lean-hipped, very black young man with a ready face full of white teeth and a ruined Panama hat raked above his right ear.

The salesman looked once at Lucas's face and hunched himself away from the fence. "I'll go talk to him," he said.

"No," Lucas said. "You stay away from there."

"Then what you going to do about it?" the salesman said. "Here I've come all the way from St. Louis—and how you ever persuaded them to send this machine out without any down payment in the first place, I still don't see. And I'll tell you right now, if I got to take it back and turn in an expense account for this trip and no sale, something is—"

2

"We ain't doing no good standing here, nohow," Lucas said. The other two followed him, back to the gate and the highroad, where the salesman's car stood. The divining machine rested on the rear seat and Lucas stood in the open door, looking at it—an oblong metal box with a handle for carrying at each end, compact and solid, efficient and businesslike and complex with its knobs and dials, and Lucas standing over it, sober and bemused. "And I seed hit work," he said. "I seed hit with my own eyes."

"Well?" the salesman said. "What you going to do? I've got to know, so I can know what to do, myself. Ain't you got three hundred dollars?" Lucas mused upon the machine. He did not look up yet.

"We gonter find that money tonight," he said. "You put in the machine and I'll show you whar to look, and we'll go halves on hit."

"Ha, ha, ha," the salesman said harshly. "Now I'll tell one."

"We bound to find hit, cap-tin," the son-in-law said. "Two white men slipped in here three years ago and dug up twenty-two thousand dollars one night and got clean away wid hit fo' daylight."

"You bet," the salesman said. "And you knew it was exactly twenty-two thousand dollars because you found where they had throwed away the odd cents."

"Naw, sir," the son-in-law said. "Hit mought a been even more than twenty-two thousand dollars. Hit wuz a big churn."

"George Wilkins," Lucas said, still half inside the car and still without turning his head.

"Sir," the son-in-law said.

"Shut up." Now Lucas turned and looked at the salesman; again the salesman saw a face quite sober, even a little cold, quite impenetrable. "I'll swap you a mule for it."

"A mule?" the salesman said.

"When we find that money tonight I'll buy the mule back for your three hundred dollars." The son-in-law had begun to bat his eyes rapidly. But nobody was looking at him. Lucas and the salesman looked at one another—the shrewd, suddenly attentive face of the young white man, the absolutely impenetrable face of the Negro.

"Do you own the mule?"

"How could I swap hit to you ef'n I didn't?"

"Let's go see it," the salesman said.

"George Wilkins," Lucas said.

"Sir," the son-in-law said. He was still batting his eyes constantly and rapidly.

"Go up to my barn and get my halter," Lucas said.

EDMONDS FOUND THE MULE WAS MISSING AS SOON AS THE STABLEMEN brought the drove up from the pasture that evening. She was a three-year-old, eleven-hundred-pound mare mule named Alice Ben Bolt, and he had refused three hundred dollars for her in the spring. But he didn't even curse. He merely dismounted and stood beside the lot fence while the rapid beat of his mare's feet died away in the darkling night and then returned, and the head stableman sprang down and handed him his flashlight and pistol. Then, himself on the mare and the two Negroes on saddleless mules, they went back across the pasture, fording the creek, to the gap in the fence through which the mule had been led. From there they followed the tracks of the mule and of the man who led her in the soft earth along the edge of a cotton field, to the road. And here too they could follow them, the head stableman walking and carrying the flashlight, where the man had led the unshod mule in the softer dirt which bordered the gravel. "That's Alice's foot," the head stableman said. "I'd know hit anywhar."

Later Edmonds would realize that both the Negroes had recognized the man's footprints too. But at the time his very fury and concern had short-circuited his normal sensitivity to Negro behavior. They would not have told him who had made the tracks even if he had demanded to know, but the realization that they knew would have enabled him to leap to the correct divination and so save himself the four or five hours of mental turmoil and physical effort which he was about to enter.

They lost the tracks. He expected to find the marks where the mule had been loaded into a waiting truck, whereupon he would return home and telephone to the sheriff in Jefferson and to the Memphis police to watch the horse-and-mule markets tomorrow. There were no such marks. It took them almost an hour to find where the tracks had vanished on to the gravel, crossing it, descending through the opposite roadside weeds, to reappear in another field a hundred yards away. Supperless, raging, the mare which had been under saddle all day unfed too, he followed the two shadowy mules at the backstretched arm of the second walking Negro, cursing the darkness and the puny light which the head stableman carried, on which they were forced to depend.

Two hours later they were in the creek bottom four miles away. He was walking too now, lest he knock his brains out against a limb, stumbling and thrashing among brier and undergrowth and rotting logs and branches where the tracks led, leading the mare with one hand and fending his face with the other arm and trying to watch his feet, so that he walked into one of the mules, instinctively leaping in the right direction as it lashed out at him with one hoof, before he discovered that the Negroes had stopped.

4

Then, cursing out loud now and moving quickly again to avoid the invisible second mule which would be somewhere to his left, he discovered that the flashlight was now off and he too saw the faint, smoky glare of the lightwood torch among the trees ahead. It was moving. "That's right," he said rapidly. "Keep the light off." He called the second Negro's name. "Give the mules to Dan and come back here and take the mare." He waited, watching the light, until the Negro's hand fumbled at his. Then he released the reins and moved around the mules, drawing his pistol and still watching the moving flame. "Hand me the flashlight," he said. He took the light from that fumbling hand too. "You and Oscar wait here."

"I better come wid you," the Negro said.

"All right," Edmonds said. "Give Oscar the mules." He didn't wait, though from time to time he could hear the Negro behind him, both of them moving as quietly and rapidly as possible. The rage was not cold now. It was hot, and there was an eagerness upon him, a kind of vindictive exultation as he plunged on, heedless of brush or log, the flashlight in his left hand and the pistol in his right, gaining rapidly on the moving torch, bursting at last out of the undergrowth and into a sort of glade, in the centre of which two men stood looking toward him, one of them carrying before him what Edmonds believed at first to be some kind of receptacle of feed, the other holding high over his head the smoking pine-knot. Then Edmonds recognized George Wilkins's ruined Panama hat, and he realized not only that the two Negroes with him had known all the time who had made the footprints, but that the object which Lucas was carrying was not any feedbox and that he himself should have known all the time what had become of his mule.

"You, Lucas!" he shouted. George flung the torch, arching, but the flashlight already held them spitted; Edmonds saw the white man now, snap-brim hat, necktie, and all, risen from beside a tree, his trousers rolled to the knees and his feet invisible in caked mud. "That's right," Edmonds said. "Go on, George. Run. I believe I can hit that hat without even touching you." He approached, the flashlight's beam contracting on to the metal box which Lucas held before him, gleaming and glinting among the knobs and dials. "So that's it," he said. "Three hundred dollars. I wish somebody would come into this country with a seed that had to be worked every day, from New Year's right on through to Christmas. As soon as you niggers are laid by, trouble starts. I ain't going to worry with Alice tonight, and if you and George want to spend the rest of it walking back and forth with the damn thing, that's your business. But I want that mule to be in her stall by sunup. Do you hear?" Edmonds had forgotten about the white man until he appeared beside Lucas.

5

"What mule is that?" he said. Edmonds turned the light on him for a moment.

"My mule, sir," he said.

"I've got a bill of sale for that mule," the other said. "Signed by Lucas here."

"Have you now," Edmonds said. "You can make lamplighters out of it next winter."

"Is that so?" the other said. "Look here, Mister What's-your-name—" But Edmonds had already turned the light back to Lucas, who still held the divining machine before him.

"On second thought, I ain't going to worry about that mule at all," he said. "I told you this morning what I thought about this business. But you're a grown man; if you want to fool with it, I can't stop you. But if that mule ain't in her stall by sunup tomorrow, I'm going to telephone the sheriff. Do you hear me?"

"I hears you," Lucas said.

"All right, big boy," the salesman said. "If that mule is moved from where she's at until I'm ready to move her, I'm going to telephone the sheriff. Do you hear that too?" This time Edmonds jumped, flung the light beam at the salesman, furious and restrained.

"Were you talking to me, sir?" he said.

"No," the salesman said. "I'm talking to him. And he heard me." For a while longer Edmonds held the light beam on the other. Then he dropped it, so that only their legs and feet showed, planted in the pool and its refractions as if they stood in a pool of dying water. He put the pistol back into his pocket.

"Well, you and Lucas have got till daylight to settle that. Because that mule is to be back in my barn at sunup." He turned and went back to where Dan waited, the light swinging and flickering before him; presently it had vanished.

"George Wilkins," Lucas said.

"Sir," George said.

"Find that pine-knot and light it again." George did so; once more the red glare streamed away in thick smoke, upward against the August stars of more than midnight. "Now grab a holt of this thing," Lucas said. "I got to find that money now."

But when day broke they had not found it, the torch paling away in the wan, dew-heavy light, the white man asleep on the wet earth now, drawn into a ball against the dawn's wet chill, unshaven, his dashing city hat, his necktie, his soiled shirt and muddy trousers rolled to his knees, and his mud-caked feet whose shoes gleamed with polish yesterday. They waked him. He sat up, cursing. But he knew at once where he was, because he said: "All right now. If that mule moves one foot out of that cotton house, I'm going to get the sheriff."

"I just wants one more night," Lucas said. "That money's here."

"What about that fellow that says the mule is his?"

"I'll tend to him in the morning. You don't need to worry about that. Besides, ef'n you try to move that mule yourself, the sheriff gonter take her away from you. You leave her whar she's at and lemme have one more night with this-here machine. Then I kin fix everything."

"All right," the other said. "But do you know what it's going to cost you? It's going to cost you just exactly twenty-five dollars more. Now I'm going to town and go to bed."

He put Lucas and George out at George's gate. They watched the car go on down the road, already going fast. George was batting his eyes rapidly. "Now whut we gonter do?" he said. Lucas roused.

"Eat your breakfast quick as you can and come on to my house. You got to go to town and get back here by noon."

"I needs to go to bed too," George said. "I'm bad off to sleep too."

"Ne'mine about that," Lucas said. "You eat your breakfast and get up to my house quick." When George reached his gate a half hour later, Lucas met him, the check already written out in his laborious, cramped, but quite legible hand. It was for fifty dollars. "Get it in silver dollars," Lucas said. "And be back here by noon."

It was just dusk when the salesman's car stopped again at Lucas's gate, where Lucas and George, carrying a long-handled shovel, waited. The salesman was freshly shaved and his face looked rested; the snap-brim hat had been brushed and his shirt was clean. But he now wore a pair of cotton khaki pants still bearing the manufacturer's stitched label and still showing the creases where they had been folded on the store's shelf. He gave Lucas a hard, jeering stare as Lucas and George approached. "I ain't going to ask if my mule's all right," he said. "Because I don't need to. Hah?"

"Hit's all right," Lucas said. He and George got into the rear seat beside the divining machine. The salesman put the car into gear, though he did not move it yet.

"Well?" he said. "Where do you want to take your walk tonight? Same place?"

"Not there," Lucas said. "I'll show you whar. We was looking in the wrong place. I misread the paper."

"You bet," the salesman said. "It's worth that extra twenty-five bucks to have found that out—" The car had begun to move. He stopped it so suddenly that Lucas and George, squatting gingerly on the front edge of the seat, lurched forward before they caught themselves. "You did what?" the salesman said.

"I misread the paper," Lucas said.

"What paper? Have you got a letter or something that tells where some money is buried?"

"That's right," Lucas said.

"Where is it?"

"Hit's put away in the house," Lucas said.

"Go and get it."

"Ne'mine," Lucas said. "I read hit right this time." For a moment longer the salesman sat, his head turned over his shoulder. Then he looked forward. He put the car in gear again.

"All right," he said. "Where's the place?"

"Drive on," Lucas said. "I'll show you."

It was not in the bottom, but on a hill overlooking the creek—a clump of ragged cedars, the ruins of old chimneys, a depression which was once a well or a cistern, the old worn-out fields stretching away and a few snaggled trees of what had been an orchard, shadowy and dim beneath the moonless sky where the fierce stars of late summer swam. "Hit's in the orchard," Lucas said. "Hit's divided, buried in two separate places. One of them's in the orchard."

"Provided the fellow that wrote you the letter ain't come back and joined it all up again," the salesman said. "What are we waiting on? Here, Jack," he said to George, "grab that thing out of there." George lifted the divining machine from the car. The salesman had a flashlight himself now, quite new, thrust into his hip pocket. He didn't put it on at once. "By God, you better find it first pop this time. We're on a hill now. There probably ain't a man in ten miles that can walk at all that won't be up here inside an hour, watching us."

"Don't tell me that," Lucas said. "Tell hit to this-here three hundred and twenty-five dollar buzz-box I done bought."

"You ain't bought this box yet, big boy," the salesman said. "You say one of the places is in the orchard. All right. Where?"

Lucas, carrying the shovel, went on into the old orchard, the others following. The salesman watched him pause, squinting at trees and sky to orient himself, then move on again, pause again. "We kin start here," he said. The salesman snapped on the light, handcupping the beam on to the metal box which George carried.

"All right, Jack," he said. "Get going."

"I better tote it," Lucas said.

"No," the salesman said. "You're too old. I don't know yet that you can even keep up with us. Get on, Jack!" So Lucas walked on George's other side, carrying the shovel and watching the small bright dials in the flashlight's contracted beam as they went back and forth across the orchard. He was watching also, grave and completely attentive, when the needles began to spin and jerk and then quiver. Then he held the box and watched George digging into the light's concentrated pool and saw the rusted can come up at last and the bright cascade of silver dollars about the salesman's hands and heard the salesman's voice: "Well, by God! By God!" Lucas squatted also; they faced each other across the pit.

"I done found this much of hit, anyhow," he said. The salesman, one hand upon the scattered coins, made a slashing, almost instinctive blow with the other as if Lucas had reached for the coins. Squatting, he laughed harshly at Lucas across the pit.

"*You* found? This machine don't belong to you, old man."

"I bought hit," Lucas said.

"With what?"

"A mule," Lucas said. The other laughed at him, harsh and steady across the pit. "I give you a billy sale for hit."

"Which never was worth a damn. It's in my car yonder. Go and get it whenever you want to." He scrabbled the coins together, back into the can. He rose quickly out of the light, until only his legs showed in the new, still-creased cotton pants. He still wore the same low black shoes. He had not had them shined again—only washed. Lucas rose also, more slowly. "All right," the salesman said. "This ain't hardly any of it. Where's the other place?"

"Ask your finding machine," Lucas said. "Ain't it supposed to know?"

"You damn right it does," the salesman said.

"Then I reckon we can go home," Lucas said. "George Wilkins."

"Sir," George said.

"Wait," the salesman said. He and Lucas faced each other in the darkness, two shadows, faceless. "There wasn't over a hundred here. Most of it is in the other place. I'll give you ten per cent."

"Hit was my letter," Lucas said. "Hit ain't enough."

"Twenty. And that's all."

"I wants half," Lucas said. "And that mule paper, and another paper to say the finding machine belongs to me."

"Tomorrow," the salesman said.

9

"I wants hit now," Lucas said. The invisible face stared at his own invisible one. Both he and George seemed to feel the windless summer air moving to the trembling of the white man's body.

"How much did you say them other fellows found?"

"Twenty-two thousand dollars," Lucas said.

"Hit mought a been more," George said. "Hit wuz a big—"

"All right," the salesman said suddenly. "I'll give you a bill of sale for the machine as soon as we finish."

"I wants it now," Lucas said. They went back to the car. While Lucas held the flashlight, they watched the salesman rip open his patent brief case and jerk out of it and fling toward Lucas the bill of sale for the mule. Then they watched his jerking hand fill in the long printed form with its carbon duplicates and sign it and rip out one of the duplicates.

"You get possession tomorrow morning," he said. "It belongs to me until then. O.K.?"

"All right," Lucas said. "What about them fifty dollars we done already found? Does I get half of them?" This time the salesman just laughed, harsh and steady and without mirth. Then he was out of the car. He didn't even wait to close his brief case. They could see him half running back toward the orchard, carrying the divining machine and the flashlight both.

"Come on," he said. "Bring the spade." Lucas gathered up the two papers, the bill of sale which he had signed for the mule, and the one which the salesman had signed for the divining machine.

"George Wilkins," he said.

"Sir," George said.

"Take that mule back whar you got hit. Then go tell Roth Edmonds he can quit worrying folks about her."

LUCAS MOUNTED THE GNAWED STEPS BESIDE WHICH THE BRIGHT MARE stood beneath the heavy saddle, and entered the commissary, with its ranked shelves of tinned food, the hooks from which hung collars and trace chains and hames and ploughlines, its smell of molasses and cheese and leather and kerosene. Edmonds swiveled around from the roll-top desk. "Where've you been?" he said. "I sent word two days ago I wanted to see you."

"I was in bed, I reckon," Lucas said. I been had to stay up all night for the last three nights. I can't stand hit no more like when I was a young man."

"So you've found that out at last, have you? What I wanted to see you about is that damn St. Louis fellow. Dan says he's still hanging around here. What's he doing?"

"Hunting buried money," Lucas said.

"What?" Edmonds said. "Doing what, did you say?"

"Hunting buried money," Lucas said. "Using my finding box. He rents it from me. That's why I been had to stay up all night. To go with him and make sho' I'd get the box back. But last night he never turnt up, so I reckon he's done gone back wherever it was he come from."

Edmonds sat in the swivel chair and stared at him. "Rents it from you? The same machine he sold you?"

"For twenty-five dollars a night," Lucas said. "That's what he chawged me to use hit one night. So I reckon that's the regular rent on um. Least-ways, that's what I chawges." Edmonds stared at him as he leaned against the counter with only the slight shrinkage of the jaws to show that he was an old man, in his clean, faded overalls and shirt and the open vest looped across by a heavy gold watch chain, and the thirty-dollar handmade beaver hat which Edmonds's father had given him over forty years ago above the face which was not sober and not grave but wore no expression whatever. It was absolutely impenetrable. "Because he was looking in the wrong place," Lucas said. "He was looking up there on that hill. That money is buried down there by the creek. Them two white men that slipped in here that night three years ago and got clean away with twenty-two thousand dollars—" At last Edmonds got himself out of the chair and on to his feet. He was trembling. He drew a deep breath, walking steadily toward the old Negro leaning against the counter, his lower lip full of snuff. "And now that we done got shut of him," Lucas said, "me and George Wilkins—" Walking steadily toward him, Edmonds expelled his breath. He had believed it would be a shout, but it was not much more than a whisper.

"Get out of here," he said. "Go home. And don't come back. Don't ever come back. When you need supplies, send your wife after them."

November 1940

Two Rivers

HIS FATHER'S VOICE AWAKENED HIM. STRETCHING HIS BACK, ARCHING against the mattress, he looked over at his parents' end of the sleeping porch. His mother was up too, though he could tell from the flatness of the light outside that it was still early. He lay on his back quietly, letting complete wakefulness come on, watching a spider that dangled on a golden, shining thread from the rolled canvas of the blinds. The spider came down in tiny jerks, his legs wriggling, then went up again in the beam of sun. From the other room the father's voice rose loud and cheerful:—

"Oh I'd give every man in the army a quarter
If they'd all take a shot at my mother-in-law."

The boy slid his legs out of bed and yanked the nightshirt over his head. He didn't want his father's face poking around the door, saying, "I plough deep while sluggards sleep!" He didn't want to be joked with. Yesterday was too sore a spot in his mind. He had been avoiding his father ever since the morning before, and he was not yet ready to accept any joking or attempts to make up. Nobody had a right hitting a person for nothing, and you bet they weren't going to be friends. Let him whistle and sing out there, pretending nothing was the matter. The whole business yesterday

WALLACE STEGNER

was the matter, the Ford that wouldn't start was the matter, the whole lost Fourth of July was the matter, the missed parade, the missed fireworks, the missed ball game in Chinook were the matter. The cuff on the ear his father had given him when he got so mad at the Ford he had to have something to hit was the matter.

In the other room, as he pulled on his overalls, the bacon was snapping in the pan, and he smelled its good morning smell. His father whistled, sang.

"In the town of O'Geary lived Paddy O'Flannagan,
Battered away till he hadn't a pound,
His father he died and he made him a man again,
Left him a farm of tin acres o' ground. . . ."

The boy pulled the overall straps over his shoulders and went into the main room. His father stopped singing and looked at him. "Hello, Cheerful," he said. "You look like you'd bit into a wormy apple."

The boy mumbled something and went outside to wash at the bench. It wasn't any fun waking up today. You kept thinking about yesterday, and how much fun it had been waking up then, when you were going to do something special and exciting, drive fifty miles to Chinook and spend the whole day just having fun. Now there wasn't anything but the same old thing to do you did every day. Run the trap line, put out some poison for the gophers, read the Sears Roebuck catalogue.

At breakfast he was glum, and his father joked him. Even his mother smiled, as if she had forgotten already how much wrong had been done the day before. "You look as if you'd been sent for and couldn't come," she said. "Cheer up."

"I don't want to cheer up."

They just smiled at each other, and he hated them both.

After breakfast his father said, "You help your Ma with the dishes, now. See how useful you can make yourself around here."

Unwillingly, wanting to get out of the house and away from them, he got the towel and swabbed off the plates. He was rubbing a glass when he heard the Ford sputter and race and roar and then calm down into a steady mutter. His mouth opened, and he looked at his mother. Her eyes were crinkled up with smiling.

"It goes!" he said.

"Sure it goes." She pulled both his ears, rocking his head. "Know what we're going to do?"

13

"What?"

"We're going to the mountains anyway. Not to Chinook—there wouldn't be anything doing today. But to the mountains, for a picnic. Pa got the car going yesterday afternoon, when you were down in the field, so we decided to go today. If you want to, of course."

"Yay!" he said. "Shall I dress up?"

"Put on your shoes, you'd better. We might climb a mountain."

The boy was out into the porch in three steps. With one shoe on and the other in his hand he hopped to the door. "When?" he said.

"Soon as you can get ready."

He was trying to run and tie his shoelaces at the same time as he went out of the house. There in the Ford, smoking his pipe, with one leg over the door and his weight on the back of his neck, his father sat. "What detained you?" he said. "I've been waiting a half hour. You must not want to go very bad."

"Aw!" the boy said. He looked inside the Ford. There was the lunch all packed, the fat wet canvas waterbag, even Spot with his tongue out and his ears up. Looking at his father, all his sullenness gone now, the boy said, "When did you get all this ready?"

His father grinned. "While you slept like a sluggard we worked like a buggard," he said. Then the boy knew that everything was perfect, nothing could go wrong. When his father started rhyming things he was in his very best mood, and not even breakdowns and flat tires could make him do more than puff and blow and play-act.

He clambered into the front seat and felt the motor shaking under the floorboards. "Hey, Ma!" he yelled. "Hurry up! We're all ready to go!"

THEIR OWN ROAD WAS A BARELY MARKED TRAIL THAT WIGGLED OUT OVER the burnouts along the east side of the wheat field. At the line it ran into another coming down from the homesteads to the east, and at Cree, a mile inside the Montana boundary, they hit the straight section-line road to Chinook. On that road they passed a trotting team pulling an empty wagon, and the boy waved and yelled, feeling superior, feeling as if he were charioted on pure speed and all the rest of the world were earth-footed.

"Let's see how fast this old boat will go," the father said. He nursed it down through a coulee and onto the flat. His fingers pulled the gas lever down, and the motor roared. Looking back with the wind-stung tears in his eyes, the boy saw his mother hanging to her hat, and the artificial cherries on the hat bouncing. The Ford leaped and bucked, the picnic box tipped over, the dog leaned out and the wind blew his eyes shut and his ears straight back. Turning around, the boy saw the blue sparks leaping from the magneto box and heard his father wahoo. He hung onto the side and leaned out to let the wind tear at him, tried to count the fence posts going by, but they were ahead of him before he got to ten.

The road roughened, and they slowed down. "Good land!" his mother said from the back seat. "We want to get to the Bearpaws, not wind up in a ditch."

"How fast were we going, Pa?"

"Forty or so, I guess. If we'd been going any faster you'd have hollered 'nuff. You were looking pretty peaked."

"I was not."

"Looked pretty scared to me. I guess Ma was hopping around back there like corn in a popper. How'd you like it, Ma?"

"I liked it all right," she said, "but don't do it again."

They passed a farm, and the boy waved at three open-mouthed kids in the yard. It was pretty good to be going somewhere, all right. The mountains were plainer now in the south. He could see dark canyons cutting into the slopes, and there was snow on the upper peaks.

"How soon'll we get there, Pa?"

His father tapped the pipe out and put it away and laughed. Without bothering to answer, he began to sing:—

"Oh, I dug Snoqualmie River,
And Lake Samamish too,
And paddled down to Kirkland
In a little birch canoe.

"I built the Rocky Mountains,
And placed them where they are,
Sold whiskey to the Ind-i-ans
From behind a little bar."

It was then, with the empty flat country wheeling by like a great turntable, the wheat fields and the fences and the far red peaks of barns rotating slowly as if in a dignified dance, wheeling and slipping behind and gone, and his father singing, that the strangeness first came over the boy. Somewhere, sometime . . . and there were mountains in it, and a stream, and a swing that he had fallen out of and cried, and he had mashed ripe blackberries in his hand and his mother had wiped him off, straightening his stiff

15

fingers and wiping hard. . . . His mind caught on that memory from a time before there was any memory, he rubbed his finger tips against his palm and slid a little down in the seat.

His father tramped on both pedals hard and leaned out of the car, looking. He swung to stare at the boy as a startled idiot might have looked, and in a voice heavy with German gutturals he said, "Vot it iss in de crass?"

"What?"

"Iss in de crass somedings. Besser you bleiben right here."

He climbed out, and the boy climbed out after him. The dog jumped over the side and rushed, and in the grass by the side of the road the boy saw the biggest snake he had ever seen, long and fat and sleepy. When it pulled itself in and faced the stiff-legged dog he saw that the hind legs and tail of a gopher stuck out of the stretched mouth.

"Jiminy!" the boy said. "He eats gophers whole."

His father stopped with hands on knees to stare at the snake, looked at the boy, and wagged his head. "Himmel," he said. "Dot iss a shlange vot iss a shlange!"

"What is it?" the mother said from the car, and the boy yelled back, "A snake, a great big snake, and he's got a whole gopher in his mouth!"

The father chased the pup away, found a rock, and with one careful throw crushed the big flat head. The body, as big around as the boy's ankle, tightened into a ridged convulsion of muscles, and the tail whipped back and forth. Stooping, the father pulled on the gopher's tail. There was a wet, slupping noise, and the gopher slid out, coated with slime and twice as long as he ought to have been.

"Head first," the father said. "That's a hell of a way to die."

He lifted the snake by the tail and held it up. "Look," he said. "He's longer than I am." But the mother made a face and turned her head while he fastened it in the forked top of a fence post. It trailed almost two feet on the ground. The tail still twitched.

"He'll twitch till the sun goes down," the father said. "First guy that comes along here drunk is going to think he's got D.T.'s." He climbed into the car again, and the boy followed.

"What was it, Pa?"

"Milk snake. They come into barns sometimes and milk the cows dry. You saw what he did to that gopher. Milk a cow dry as powder in ten minutes."

"Gee," the boy said. He sat back and thought about how long and slick the gopher had been, and how the snake's mouth was all stretched, and it was a good feeling to have been along and to have shared something like that with his father. It was a trophy, a thing you would remember all your life, and you could tell about it. And while he was thinking that already, even before they got to the mountains at all, he had something to remember about the trip, he remembered that just before they saw the snake he had been remembering something else, and he puckered his eyes in the sun thinking. He had been right on the edge of it, it was right on the tip of his tongue, and then his father had tramped on the pedals. But it was something a long time ago, and there was a strangeness about it, something bothersome and a little scary, and it hurt his head the way it hurt his head sometimes to do arithmetical sums without pencil and paper. When you did them in your head something went round and round, and you had to keep looking inside to make sure you didn't lose sight of the figures that were pasted up there somewhere, and if you did it very long at a time you got a sick headache out of it. It was something like that when he had almost remembered just a while ago, only he hadn't quite been able to see what he knew was there. . . .

BY TEN O'CLOCK THEY HAD LEFT THE GRADED ROAD AND WERE CHUG-
ging up a winding trail with toothed rocks embedded in the ruts. Ahead of them the mountains looked low and disappointing, treeless, brown. The trail ducked into a narrow gulch and the sides rose up around them, red-dish gravel covered with bunch grass and sage.

"Gee whiz," the boy said. "These don't look like mountains."

"What'd you expect?" his father said. "Expect to step out onto a glacier or something?"

"But there aren't any trees," the boy said. "Gee whiz, there isn't even any water."

He stood up to look ahead. His father's foot went down on the low pedal, and the Ford growled at the grade. "Come on, Lena," his father said. He hitched himself back and forward in the seat, helping the car over the hill, and then, as they barely pulled over the hump and the sides of the gully fell away, there were the real mountains, high as heaven, the high slopes spiked and tufted with trees, and directly ahead of them a magnificent V-shaped door with the sun touching gray cliffs far back in, and a straight-edged violet shadow streaming down from the eastern peak clear to the canyon floor.

"Well?" the father's voice said. "I guess if you don't like it we can drop you off here and pick you up on the way back."

The boy turned to his mother. She was sitting far forward on the edge

17

of the seat. "I guess we want to come along, all right," she said, and laughed as if she might cry. "Anything as beautiful as that! Don't we, sonny?"

"You bet," he said. He remained standing all the way up over the gentle slope of the alluvial fan that aproned out from the canyon's mouth, and when they passed under the violet shadow, not violet any more but cool gray, he tipped his head back and looked up miles and miles to the broken rock above.

The road got rougher. "Sit down," his father said. "First thing you know you'll fall out on your head and sprain both your ankles."

He was in his very best mood. He said funny things to the car, coaxing it over steep pitches. He talked to it like a horse, patted it on the dashboard, promised it an apple when they got there. Above them the canyon walls opened out and back, went up steeply high and high and high, beyond the first walls that the boy had thought so terrific, away beyond those, piling peak on peak, and the sun touched and missed and touched again.

The trail steepened. A jet of steam burst from the brass radiator cap, the car throbbed and labored, they all sat forward and urged it on. But it slowed, shook, stopped and stood there steaming and shaking, and the motor died with a last, lunging gasp.

"Is this as far as we can get?" the boy said. The thought that they might be broken down, right here on the threshold of wonder, put him in a panic. He looked around. They were in a bare rocky gorge. Not even any trees yet, though a stream tumbled down a bouldered channel on the left. But to get to trees and the real mountains they had to go further, much further. "Can't we get any further?" he said.

His father grunted. "Skin down to the creek and get a bucket of water." The boy ran, came stumbling and staggering back with the pail. His mother had already climbed out and put a rock under the back wheel, and they stood close together while the father with a rag made quick, stabbing turns at the radiator cap. The cap blew off and steam went up for six feet and they all jumped back. There was a sullen subterranean boiling deep under the hood.

"Now!" the father said. He poured a little water in, stepped back. In a minute the water came bubbling out again. He poured again, and the motor spit it out again. "Can't seem to keep anything on her stomach," the father said, and winked at the boy. He didn't seem worried.

The fourth dose stayed down. They filled up the radiator till it ran over, screwed the plug in, and threw the pail in the back end. "You two stay out," the father said. "I'll see if she'll go over unloaded."

18

She wouldn't. She moved two feet, strangled and died. The boy watched with his jaw hanging, remembering yesterday, remembering when something like this had happened and the whole day had gone wrong. But his father wasn't the same today. He just got out of the car and didn't swear at all, but winked at the boy again, and made a closing motion with his hand under his chin. "Better shut that mouth," he said. "Some bird'll fly in there and build a nest."

To the mother he said, "Can you kick that rock out from under the wheel?"

"Sure," she said. "But do you think . . . Maybe we could walk from here."

"Hell with it," he said cheerfully. "I'll get her up if I have to lug her on my back."

She kicked the stone away and he rolled backward down the hill, craning, steering with one hand. At the bottom he cramped the wheels, got out and cranked the motor, got in again, and turned around in the narrow road, taking three or four angled tries before he made it. Then his hand waved, and there was the Ford coming up the hill backwards, kicking gravel down from under its straining hind wheels, angling across the road and back and up, and the motor roaring like a threshing engine, until it went by them and on up to the crest and turned around with one quick expert ducking motion, and they got in and were off again.

"Well!" said the mother in relief. "Who'd have thought of going up backwards."

"Got more power in reverse," the father said. "Can't make it one way, try another."

"Yay!" the boy said. He was standing up, watching the deep insides of the earth appear behind the angled rock, and his mind was soaring again, up into the heights where a hawk or eagle circled like a toy bird on a string.

"How do you like it?" his mother shouted at him. He turned around and nodded his head, and she smiled at him, wrinkling her eyes. She looked excited herself. Her face had color in it and the varnished cherries bouncing on her hat gave her a reckless, girlish look.

"Hi, Ma," he said, and grinned.

"Hi, yourself," she said, and grinned right back. He lifted his face and yelled for the very pressure of happiness inside him.

THEY LAY ON A LEDGE HIGH UP ON THE SUNNY EAST SLOPE AND LOOKED out to the north through the notch cut as sharply as a wedge out of a pie. Far below them the golden plain spead level, golden-tawny grass and golden-green wheat checkerboarded in a pattern as wide as the world. Back of them the spring they had followed up the slope welled out of the ledge, spread out in a small swampy spot, and trickled off down the hill. There were trees, a thick cluster of spruce against the bulge of the wall above them, a clump of twinkling, sunny aspen down the slope, and in the canyon bottom below them a dense forest of soft maple. The mother had a bouquet of leaves in her hand, a little bunch of pine cones on the ground beside her. The three lay quietly, looking down over the steeply dropping wall to the V-shaped door, and beyond that to the interminable plain.

The boy wriggled his back against the rock, put his hand down to shift himself, brought it up again prickled with brown spruce needles. He picked them off, still staring out over the canyon gateway. They were far above the world he knew. The air was cleaner, thinner. There was cold water running from the rock, and all around there were trees. And over the whole canyon, like a haze in the clear air, was that other thing, that memory or ghost of a memory, a swing he had fallen out of, a feel of his hands sticky with crushed blackberries, his skin drinking cool shade, and his father's anger—the reflection of ecstasy and the shadow of tears.

"I never knew till this minute," his mother said, "how much I've missed the trees."

Nobody answered. They were all stuffed with lunch, pleasantly tired after the climb. The father lay staring off down the canyon, and the sour smell of his pipe, in that air, was pleasant and clean. The boy saw his mother put the stem of a maple leaf in her mouth and make a half-pleased face at the bitter taste.

The father rose and dug a tin cup from the picnic box, walked to the spring and dipped himself a drink. He made a breathy sound of satisfaction. "So cold it hurts your teeth," he said. He brought the mother a cup, and she drank.

"Brucie?" she said, motioning with the cup.

He started to get up, but his father filled the cup and brought it, making believe he was going to pour it on him. The boy ducked and reached for the cup. With his eyes on his father over the cup's rim, he drank, testing the icy water to see if it really did hurt the teeth. The water was cold and silvery in his mouth, and when he swallowed he felt it cold clear down to his stomach.

"It doesn't either hurt your teeth," he said. He poured a little of it on his arm, and something jumped in his skin. It was his skin that remembered. Something numbingly cold, and then warm. He felt it now, the way you waded in it.

"Mom," he said.

"What?"

"Was it in Washington we went on a picnic like this and picked blackberries and I fell out of a swing and there were big trees, and we found a river that was half cold and half warm?"

His father was relighting his pipe. "What do you know about Washington?" he said. "You were only knee-high to a grasshopper when we lived there."

"Well, I remember," the boy said. "I've been remembering it all day long, ever since you sang that song about building the Rocky Mountains. You sang it that day, too. Don't you remember, Mom?"

"I don't know," she said doubtfully. "We went on picnics in Washington."

"What's this about a river with hot and cold running water?" his father said. "You must remember some time you had a bath in a bathtub."

"I do not!" the boy said. "I got blackberries mashed all over my hands and Mom scrubbed me off, and then we found that river and we waded in it and half was hot and half was cold."

"Oh-h-h," his mother said. "I believe I do. . . . Harry, you remember once up in the Cascades, when we went out with the Curtises? And little Bill Curtis fell off the dock into the lake." She turned to the boy. "Was there a summer cottage there, a brown shingled house?"

"I don't know," the boy said. "I don't remember any Curtises. But I remember blackberries and that river and a swing."

"Your head is full of blackberries," his father said. "If it was the time we went out with the Curtises there weren't any blackberries. That was in the spring."

"No," the mother said. "It was in the fall. It was just before we moved to Redmond. And I think there was a place where one river from the mountains ran into another one from the valley, and they ran alongside each other in the same channel. The mountain one was a lot colder. Don't you remember that trip with the Curtises, Harry?"

"Sure I remember it," the father said. "We hired a buckboard and saw a black bear and I won six bits from Joe Curtis pitching horseshoes."

"That's right," the mother said. "You remember the bear, Brucie."

The boy shook his head. There wasn't any bear in what he remembered. Just feelings, and things that made his skin prickle.

His mother was looking at him, a little puzzled wrinkle between her eyes. "It's funny you should remember such different things than we remember," she said. "Everything means something different to everybody, I guess." She laughed, and the boy thought her eyes looked very odd and

21

bright. "It makes me feel as if I didn't know you at all," she said. She brushed her face with the handful of leaves and looked at the father, gathering up odds and ends and putting them in the picnic box. "I wonder what each of us will remember about today?"

"I wouldn't worry about it," the father said. "You can depend on Bub here to remember a lot of things that didn't happen."

"I don't think he does," she said. "He's got a good memory."

The father picked up the box. "It takes a good memory to remember things that never happened," he said. "I remember once a garter snake crawled into my cradle and I used it for a belt to keep my breechclout on. They took it away from me and I bawled the crib so full of tears I had to swim for shore. I drifted in three days later on a checkerboard raft with a didie for a sail."

The boy stood up and brushed off his pants. "You do too remember that river," he said.

His father grinned at him. "Sure. Only it wasn't quite as hot and cold as you make it out."

IT WAS EVENING IN THE CANYON, BUT WHEN THEY REACHED THE MOUTH again they emerged into full afternoon, with two hours of sun left them. The father stopped the car before they dipped into the gravelly wash between the foothills, and they all looked back at the steep thrust of the mountains, purpling in the shadows, the rock glowing golden-red far back on the faces of the inner peaks. The mother still held her bouquet of maple leaves in her hand.

"Well, there go the Mountains of the Moon," she said. The moment was almost solemn. In the front seat the boy stood looking back. He felt the sun strong against the side of his face, and the mountains sheering up before him were very real. In a little while, as they went north, they would begin to melt together, and the patches of snow would appear far up on the northern slopes. His eyes went curiously out of focus, and he saw the mountains as they would appear from the homestead on a hot day, a ghostly line on the horizon.

He felt his father twist to look at him, but the trance was so strong on him that he didn't look down for a minute. When he did he caught his mother and father looking at each other, the look they had sometimes when he had pleased them and made them proud of him.

"Okay," his father said, and stabbed him in the ribs with a hard thumb. "Wipe the black bears out of your eyes."

He started the car again, and as they bounced down the rocky trail toward the road he sang at the top of his voice, bellowing into the still, hot afternoon:—

"I had a kid and his name was Brucie,
Squeezed black bears and found them juicy,
Washed them off in a hot-cold river,
Now you boil and now you shiver,
Caught his pants so full of trout
He couldn't sit down till he got them out.
Trout were boiled from the hot-side river,
Trout from the cold side raw as liver.
Ate the boiled ones, ate the raw,
And then went howling home to Maw."

The boy looked up at his father, his laughter bubbling up, everything wonderful, the day a swell day, his mother clapping hands in time to his father's fool singing.

"Aw, for gosh sakes," he said, and ducked when his father pretended he was going to swat him one.

June 1942

Mademoiselle O

I HAVE OFTEN NOTICED THAT AFTER I HAD BESTOWED ON MY CHARACTERS some treasured item of my past it would pine away in the artificial world where I had so abruptly placed it. Although it lingered on in my mind its personal warmth, its retrospective appeal, had gone and presently it became more closely identified with my novel than with the folds of my former self where it had seemed to be so safe from the intrusion of the artist. Houses have crumbled in my memory as soundlessly as they did in the silent films of yore, and the portrait of my old French governess whom I once lent to a youthful hero of mine is already hardly discernible, now that it is engulfed in the description of a childhood entirely unrelated to my own. The man in me revolts against the fictionist, and here is my desperate attempt to save what is left of poor Mademoiselle O.

This "O" oddly enough is by no means the abbreviation of something beginning with an "O." It is not the initial of Olivier or Oudinet, but actually the thing itself: a round and naked name which seems about to collapse without a full stop to support it; a loose wheel of a name rolling downhill, hesitating, wobbling; a toothless yawn; a melon; an egg; a lake. What lake? The lake near which she had spent most of her life, for she was born in Switzerland, of wholly French parents, as she proudly would add. But this did not improve matters. Very soon, as soon as she had rashly imparted to us

VLADIMIR NABOKOV

the power of speaking her language, looping the loop of her name became the means of enraging her beyond measure. We squeezed every drop out of that vulnerable vowel; we inflated it till our cheeks all but cracked; we punned it, we punted it; we bounced it like a ball that leaves planet-like spots on the ceiling; we imagined Mademoiselle's father arriving in some watering place and people exclaiming: *"Oh! O au' eaux!"* In her favorite book, the squat, salmon-pink Larousse dictionary (with that red-curled maiden blowing the fluff off a dandelion on the cover), the first name listed under "O" happened to be that of "Francois, Marquis d'O, b. and d. in Paris, Superintendent of Finances under Henry III"; him we elected for Mademoiselle's ancestor, and she would have gladly adopted the legend herself had we not scoffed at the paradox of a nought handling millions.

A large woman, a very stout woman as round as her name, Mademoiselle rolled into our existence as I was about to be eight. There she is. I see her so plainly: her abundant dark hair which is covertly graying, the three wrinkles on her austere forehead, her beetling brows, the steely eyes behind a black-rimmed pince-nez, that vestigial mustache, that blotchy complexion which in moments of wrath assumes a purple flush in the region of the third and amplest chin, so regally spread over the frilled mountain of her blouse. And now she sits down, or rather she tackles the job of sitting down, the jelly of her jowl quaking, her prodigious posterior, with the three buttons on the side, lowering itself warily; then at the last she surrenders her bulk to God and to the wicker armchair, which, out of sheer fright, bursts into a salvo of crackling.

The winter she came was the only one of my childhood that I spent in the country. It was also a particularly severe one, incidentally producing as much snow as Mademoiselle O might have expected to find in the hyperborean gloom of remote Muscovy. When she alighted at the little station from which she still had to travel half a dozen miles by sleigh to our country house, I was not there to greet her, but I do so now, as I try to imagine what she saw and felt at that last stage of her fabulous journey. Her Russian vocabulary, I know, consisted of one short word—the same solitary word which seven years later she was to take back to Switzerland. This word, which in her case may be phonetically rendered as "giddy-ay," meant "Where?" And that was a good deal; uttered by her like the raucous cry of some lost bird, it accumulated such interrogatory force that it sufficed for all her needs. "Giddy-ay? Giddy-ay?" she would wail, not only to find out her whereabouts but also to express an abyss of misery: the fact that she was a stranger, shipwrecked, penniless, ailing, and that she was searching for the blessed land where at last she would be understood.

I can see her as she stands in the middle of the platform, and vainly my ghostly envoy offers her an arm which she cannot see. The door of the waiting room opens with the shuddering whine peculiar to nights of intense frost; a cloud of hot air rushes out almost as profuse as the steam from the great funnel-shaped stack of the panting engine; and now our coachman is attending to Mademoiselle: a burly man in sheepskin with the leather outside, his huge gloves protruding from his scarlet sash into which he has tucked them. I hear the snow crunching under his felt boots while he busies himself with the luggage, the jingling harness, and then his own nose, which he blows by means of a dexterous flip of finger and thumb as he trudges back round the sleigh. Slowly, with grim misgivings, Mademoiselle climbs in, clutching at her helper in mortal terror lest the sleigh move off before her vast form is securely encased. Finally she settles down with a grunt and thrusts her fists into her skimpy plush muff. At the juicy smacking of their driver's lips the horses strain their quarters, shift hoofs, strain again; and then Mademoiselle gives a backward jerk of the torso as the heavy sleigh is wrenched out of its world of steel, fur, flesh, to enter a frictionless medium where it skims along a ghostly road that it seems barely to touch.

For one moment, thanks to the sudden aura of a lone lantern at the turning, a grossly exaggerated shadow, also holding a muff, races beside the sleigh, climbs a billow of snow, and is gone, leaving Mademoiselle to be swallowed up by what she will later allude to with awe and gusto as "the Steppe." There, in the endless gloom, the changeable twinkle of remote village lights seems to her to be the yellow eyes of wolves. She is cold, she is frozen stiff—frozen "to the center of her brain," for she soars with the wildest hyperbole when not clinging to the safest old saw. Every now and then she looks back to make sure that, always at the same distance, like those companionable phantoms of ships in polar seas, the second sleigh bearing her trunk and hatbox is following. And now I notice that I have quite forgotten the moon; for surely there must be a moon, that full incredibly clear moon that goes so well with our lusty frosts—and with Mademoiselle's name. So there it comes, steering out of a medley of small dappled clouds which it tinges with a vague iridescence; and as it sails higher it glazes the runner-tracks left on the road where every sparkling lump of snow is emphasized by a swollen shadow.

Very lovely, very lonesome. But what am I doing here in this stereoscopic dreamland? Somehow those two sleighs have slipped away; they have left me behind on the blue-white road. No, even the vibration in my ears is not their receding bells, but my own blood singing. All is still, spellbound, enthralled by that great heavenly "O" shining above my Russian wilderness. The snow is real, and as I bend to it and scoop up a handful, thirty-five years crumble to glittering frost-dust between my tingling fingers.

AN OIL LAMP IS BROUGHT INTO THE GLOAMING. GENTLY IT SOARS AND comes down; the hand of memory, now in a servant's white cotton glove, places it in the center of a round table. The flame is nicely adjusted, and a rosy silk-flounced lamp shade crowns the light.

A warm, bright room in a snow-muffled house, soon to be termed *le château*; built by my great-grandfather, who, being afraid of fires, had the staircase made of iron, so that when the house was burned to the ground during the Revolution, those fretted steps remained standing, still leading up. But this is neither here nor there: such a number of things fade away, while and because their owners grow, change, and forget them, that it would be unfair to lay all the blame on civic convulsions.

Some more about that room, please. The oval mirror. Hanging aslant on taut cords, its pure brow inclined, it strives to retain the falling furniture and a slope of sheeny floor that keep slipping from its embrace. The chandelier pendants. These emit a delicate tinkling whenever anything is moved in an upstairs room. Colored pencils. That tiny heap of emerald pencil dust on the oilcloth where a penknife has just done its recurrent duty. We are sitting at the table, my brother and I and Miss Jones, who now and then looks at her watch: roads must be dreadful with all that snow; and anyway, many professional hardships lie in wait for that vague French person who will replace her.

Those colored pencils—how I loved them. The green one by a whirl of the wrist could be made to produce so simply a ruffled tree or the smoke of a house where spinach was cooking. The blue by drawing a single horizontal line invited a distant sail. Somehow or other the brown was always broken, whereas the little purple chap, a special favorite of mine, had got worn down so short as to become scarcely manageable. The white one alone, that lanky albino among pencils, kept its length, or at least did so until I realized that, far from being a fraud, leaving no mark on the page, it was the ideal tool because I could imagine whatever I wished while I scrawled.

Alas, these pencils too have been distributed among the characters of my books to keep fictitious children busy; they are not quite my own now. Somewhere, in the apartment house of a chapter, in the hired room of a paragraph, I have also placed that tilted mirror, and the lamp, and the chandelier-drops. Few things are left, many have been squandered. Have I given away that old brown dachshund fast asleep on the sofa? No, I think he is still mine. His grizzled muzzle, with that wart at the puckered corner of the mouth, is tucked into the curve of his hock, and from time to time a deep sigh distends his ribs. He is so old and his sleep is so thickly padded with dreams (about chewable slippers and a few last smells) that he does not stir when faint bells jingle outside and a pneumatic door heaves and clangs in the vestibule. She has come after all; I had so hoped she would not.

In our childhood we know a lot about hands since they live and hover at the level of our stature; Mademoiselle's were unpleasant because of the froggy gloss on their tight skin besprinkled with brownish liver spots. Before her time no stranger had ever stroked my face. Mademoiselle, as soon as she came, took me completely aback by patting my cheek in sign of spontaneous affection. Later on this gesture went through a natural evolution, producing varieties which she classified according to their degree of strength as flick, slap, smack, and finally what may be translated as "the Great Volley" and which, indeed, resembled the backhand smash of a tennis ace.

All her mannerisms come back to me when I think of her hands. Her manner of peeling rather than sharpening a pencil, the point held towards her stupendous and sterile bosom swathed in green wool. The way she had of inserting her little finger into her ear and vibrating it very rapidly. The ritual observed every time she gave me a fresh copybook. Always panting a little, her mouth slightly open and emitting in quick succession a series of asthmatic purrs, she would open the copybook to make a margin in it; that is, she would trace a vertical line with her thumbnail, fold in the outer edge of the page, press, release, smooth it out with a final pat, after which the book would be briskly twisted around and placed before me ready for use. A new pen followed; she would moisten the glistening nib with susurrous lips before dipping it into the baptismal ink font. Then, delighting in every limb of every limpid letter (especially so because the preceding copybook had ended in utter sloppiness), with exquisite care I would inscribe the word *Dictée* while Mademoiselle hunted through her collection of spelling tests for a good hard passage.

MEANWHILE THE SETTING HAS CHANGED. HOARFROST AND SNOW HAVE been removed by a silent property man. The summer afternoon is alive with steep clouds breasting the blue. Eyed shadows move on the garden paths. Lessons are over and Mademoiselle is reading to us on the veranda where the plaited chairs smell of vanilla in the heat. The sun is everywhere—on the steps, on the mat, on the white window sills, where it repeats the hues of the stained glass. This is the time when Mademoiselle is at her very best.

What a number of volumes she read through to us on that veranda! Her slender voice sped on and on, never weakening, without the slightest hitch or hesitation, an admirable reading-machine wholly independent of her sick bronchial tubes. We got it all: the so-called "Pink Library"— inventive Jules Verne, bombastic Hugo, romantic Dumas the Elder. There she sat distilling her reading voice from the still prison of her person. Apart from the lips, one of her chins, the smallest but real one, was the only mobile detail of her Buddha-like bulk. The black-rimmed pince-nez reflected eternity. Occasionally a fly would light on her stern forehead and the three wrinkles would instantly leap up together like three runners over three hurdles. But nothing whatever changed in the expression of her face—that face which I so often tried to sketch, for its impassive and simple symmetry offered an almost voluptuous temptation to my furtive pencil.

Presently my attention would wander still further, and it was then perhaps that the rare purity of her rhythmic voice accomplished its true purpose. I looked at a creamy cloud and years later was able to visualize its exact shape. The gardener was pottering among the peonies. A wagtail took a few steps, remembered something, and then strutted on. Coming from nowhere, a comma butterfly settled on the threshold, basked in the sun with its fulvous wings spread, suddenly closed them just to show the tiny initial chalked on the under side, and as suddenly darted away. But the most constant source of enchantment was the rhomboids of colored glass inset harlequin-wise in the crisscross panes of the side windows. The garden when viewed through these magic panes grew strangely still and aloof. If one looked through the blue glass the sand turned to cinders while inky-black trees swam in a tropical sky. The yellow one led to Cathay and tea-colored vistas. The red made the foliage drip ruby dark upon a pink-flushed footpath. The green soaked greenery in a greener green. And when after such richness one turned to a little square of normal savorless glass with its lone mosquito or lame daddy longlegs, it was like taking a draught of water when one is not thirsty, and one saw the first withered leaf lying on yonder bench and the blandly familiar birch trees. But of all the windows this is the pane through which parched nostalgia would long to peer now.

Mademoiselle never found out how potent had been the even flow of her voice. The claims she later put forward were quite different. "Ah," she sighed, "didn't we love each other! Those good old days in the château! The dead wax doll we once buried under the oak! (No—a golliwog in red pants!) And that time you ran away and left me stumbling and howling in the depths of the forest! (The grove just beyond the old tennis court!) My, what a spanking you bad boys got! (Not I—*I* managed to escape and find Mother!) And the Princess, your aunt, whom you struck with your little fist because she had been rude to me! (I don't remember.) And the way you whispered to me all your childish troubles! (Never!) And the cozy nook in my room where you loved to snuggle because you felt so warm and secure!"

Mademoiselle's room, both in the country and in town, was a weird place to me—something like a dim hothouse sheltering a thick-leaved plant imbued with a heavy, queerly acrid odor—and although next to ours, it did not seem to belong to our pleasant, well-aired home. In that sickening mist, reeking among other effluvia with the brown smell of oxidized apple peels, the lamp burned low, and strange objects glimmered upon the writing desk: a lacquered box with licorice sticks, black segments of which she would hack off with her penknife and put to melt under her tongue; a picture postcard of a lake and a castle with prismatic spangles sublimating its windows; a bumpy ball of tightly rolled and compressed bits of silver paper that came from all those chocolates she used to consume at night; photographs of the nephew who had died, of his mother who had signed hers "Mater dolorosa," of a certain Monsieur de Marante who had been forced by his family to marry a rich widow.

Lording it over the rest was one in a noble frame incrusted with garnets; it showed in three-quarter view a slim young brunette clad in a close-fitting checked dress, with a liquid glint in her eye and a great roll of hair burdening her pale graceful neck. "A braid as thick as my arm and reaching down to my ankles!" was Mademoiselle's melodramatic comment. For this had been she—but in vain did my eyes probe and dig into her familiar form to try to extract the exquisite creature it had engulfed. Such discoveries as I did make merely increased the difficulties of my task; and the grownups who during the day beheld only a densely clothed Mademoiselle O never saw what we children saw when, roused from her sleep by one of us shrieking himself out of a bad dream, disheveled, candle in hand, a gleam of gilt lace on the blood-red dressing gown that could not quite wrap her quaking mass, the nightmare Jézabel of Racine's absurd play stamped barefooted into our bedroom.

All my life I have been a poor go-to-sleeper. No matter how great my weariness, the wrench of parting with consciousness is unspeakably repulsive to me. I loathe Somnus, that black-masked headsman binding me to the block; and if in the course of years I have got so used to my nightly ordeal as almost to swagger while the familiar axe is coming out of its great velvet-lined case, initially I had no such comfort or defense, nothing—save a door left ajar into Mademoiselle's room. That meek line of light was something I could cling to, since in absolute darkness my head would swim, just as the soul dissolves in the blackness of sleep.

Saturday night used to be a pleasurable prospect because that was the night Mademoiselle indulged in the luxury of a weekly bath, thus granting a longer lease to my tenuous gleam. But then a subtler torture set in. The bathroom was at the end of a Z-shaped corridor some twenty heartbeats distant from my bed, and between apprehending Mademoiselle's return and envying my brother's stolid snore, I could never really put my additional time to profit by deftly getting to sleep while a chink in the dark still bespoke a speck of myself in Nirvana. At length they would come, those inexorable steps, plodding along the passage and causing some little glass object, which had been secretly sharing my vigil, to tinkle in dismay on its shelf.

Now she has entered her room. A brisk interchange of light-values tells me that the candle on her bed table takes over the job of the lamp on her desk. My line of light is still there, but grown old and wan, and flickers whenever Mademoiselle makes her bed creak by moving. For I still hear her. Now it is a silvery rustle spelling "Suchard"; now the trk-trk-trk of a fruit knife cutting the pages of *La Revue des deux mondes*; I hear her panting slightly. And all the time I am in acute distress, desperately trying to coax sleep, opening my eyes every few seconds to check the faded gleam, and imagining paradise as a place where a sleepless neighbor reads an endless book by the light of an eternal candle.

The inevitable happens: the pince-nez case shuts with a click, the review shuffles onto the marble of the bed table, and gustily Mademoiselle's pursed lips blow; the first attempt fails, a groggy flame squirms and ducks; then comes a second lunge, and light collapses. In that pitchy blackness I lose my bearings, my bed seems to be slowly drifting, panic makes me sit up and stare; finally my dark-adapted eyes sift out, among entoptic floaters, certain more precious blurrings that roam in aimless amnesia until, half-remembering, they settle down as the dim folds of window curtains.

How utterly foreign to the troubles of the night were those exciting St. Petersburg mornings when the fierce and tender, damp and dazzling arctic spring bundled away broken ice down the sea-bright Neva! It made the roofs shine. It painted the slush in the streets a rich purplish-blue shade which I have never seen anywhere since. Mademoiselle, her coat of imitation seal majestically swelling on her bosom, sat on the back seat of the landau with my brother next to her and me facing them, joined to them by the valley of the velvety rug; and as I looked up I could see, strung on ropes from house to house high above the street, great semitransparent banners billowing, their three wide bands pale red, pale blue, and merely pale—deprived by the sun and the flying shadows of any too blunt connection with a national holiday, but undoubtedly celebrating now, in the city of memory, that spring day, that drive, the swish of the mud, and the ruffled exotic bird on Mademoiselle's hat.

THE UNUSUAL ASPECT OF HER LIMBLESS AND BONELESS NAME MAY HAVE had something to do with the morbid touchiness that was perhaps her main characteristic. Being absolutely Russian-proof, she fortunately remained unaware of what native servants did to that name; but whenever she was being introduced to a guest and it rolled out, sounding somewhat like a terminal interjection in a doggerel rhyme, her look was a mixture of defiance and anxiety. Her obesity was another reason for her always being on the defensive, as if she were living among cannibals who licked their chops behind her back.

And as though nature had not wished to spare her anything that makes one super-sensitive, she was hard of hearing. Sometimes at table we boys would suddenly become aware of two big tears crawling down Mademoiselle's ample cheeks. "Don't mind me," she would say in a small voice, and she kept on eating till the unwiped tears blinded her; then with a heartbroken hiccough she would rise and blunder out of the dining room. Little by little the truth would come out. The general talk had turned, say, on the subject of the warship my uncle commanded, and she had perceived in this a sly dig at her Switzerland that had no navy. Or else it was because she fancied that whenever French was spoken the game consisted in deliberately preventing her from directing and bejeweling the conversation. Poor lady, she was always in such a nervous hurry to seize control of intelligible table talk before it bolted back into Russian that no wonder she bungled her cue.

"And your Parliament, sir, how is it getting along?" she would suddenly burst out brightly from her end of the table, challenging my father, who, after a harassing day, was not exactly eager to discuss troubles of the State with a somehow unreal person who neither knew nor cared anything about them. Thinking that someone had referred to music, "But Silence, too, may be beautiful," she would bubble. "Why, one evening in a desolate valley of the Alps I actually *heard* Silence." Sallies like these, especially when growing deafness led her to answer a question none had put, resulted in a painful hush instead of touching off the rockets of a sprightly *causerie*.

And, really, her French was so lovely! Ought one to have minded the shallowness of her culture, the bitterness of her temper, the banality of her mind, when that pearly language of hers purled and scintillated, as innocent of sense as the alliterative sins of Racine's pious verse? My father's library, not her limited lore, taught me to appreciate authentic poetry; nevertheless something of her tongue's limpidity and luster has had a singularly bracing effect upon me, like those sparkling salts which are used to purify the blood. That is why it makes me so sad to imagine now the anguish Mademoiselle O must have felt at seeing how lost, how little valued was the nightingale voice which came from her elephantine body. She stayed with us long, much too long, obstinately hoping for some miracle that would transform her into a kind of Madame de Rambouillet holding a gold-and-satin salon of poets, princes, and politicians under her brilliant spell.

She would have gone on hoping had it not been for Leonidas Orlov. He was a Russian tutor, with mild blue eyes and strong political opinions, who had been engaged to coach us in winter and play tennis and ride with us during the summer holidays. He taught mathematics entrancingly, lost his stirrups, and lobbed every ball into the lilac bushes. While venerating my father, he could not quite stomach certain aspects of our household, such as footmen and French, which last he considered an aristocratic convention of no use in a liberal statesman's home. On the other hand Mademoiselle decided that if Orlov answered her point-blank questions only with short grunts (which he tried to Germanize for want of a better tongue), it was not because he could not understand French, but because he wished to insult her in front of everybody.

I can see and hear Mademoiselle requesting him in dulcet tones, but with an ominous tightening of the lips, to pass her the bread; and likewise I can hear and see Orlov unflinchingly going on with his soup; finally with a slashing "Pardon, Monsieur," Mademoiselle would swoop right across his plate, snatch up the breadbasket, and recoil again with a "Thank you, sir" so charged with irony that Orlov's downy ears would turn the color of geranium. "The brute! The cad! The Nihilist!" she sobbed later in her room— which was no longer next to ours though still on the same floor.

If Orlov happened to come tripping downstairs while, with an asthmatic pause after every ten steps or so, she was working her way up (for the little hydraulic elevator would constantly, and rather insultingly too, refuse to function), Mademoiselle maintained that he had viciously bumped into her, pushed her, knocked her down, and we already could see him trampling her prostrate body. More and more frequently she would leave the table, and the chocolate ice or *gâteau d'Artois* that she would have missed was diplomatically sent up in her wake. From her remote room she would write a sixteen-page letter to my mother, who, hurrying upstairs, would find her dramatically packing her trunk. And then one day she was allowed to go on packing.

BECAUSE OF THE WAR SHE HAD SOME TROUBLE IN REACHING SWITZERLAND. "The Germans," she wrote with her usual emphasis, "stripped me to the skin, searching me for some secret message which, *bélas!* they did not find." Nor have I—at least up to this point of her life story. But some ten years later, in the middle twenties long after our correspondence had fizzled out, by some fluke move of life in exile I chanced to pass through Lausanne—so I thought I might as well look up Mademoiselle O if she was still alive.

She was. Stouter than ever, but quite gray and almost totally deaf, she welcomed me with a tumultuous outburst of affection. Instead of the Château de Chillon picture there was now one of a gaudy troika. She spoke warmly of her life in Russia as if it were her own lost homeland. Indeed I found in the neighborhood quite a colony of such old Swiss governesses ousted by our Revolution. Clustering together in a constant seething of competitive reminiscences, they formed a small island in the midst of a country which had grown alien to them. One is always at home in one's past, no matter what its color, which partly explains those pathetic ladies' posthumous love for another land that they never really had known and where most of them had been continuously unhappy.

As no dialogue was possible because of Mademoiselle's deafness, I decided to bring her next day the appliance which I gathered she could not afford. No sooner had she adjusted the clumsy thing than she turned to me with a dazzled look of moist wonder and bliss in her eyes. She swore she could hear every word, every murmur of mine. She could not, for I had not spoken. Was it silence she heard, that Silence she had talked about in the past? No, she had been lying to herself then; now she was lying to me.

BEFORE LEAVING FOR BASLE AND BERLIN, I FOUND MYSELF SOMEHOW OR other walking along the lake in the clammy and misty night. At one spot a lone arc light dimly diluted the darkness. In its nimbus the mist seemed transformed into a visible drizzle. *"Il pleut toujours en Suisse"* was one of those casual comments which formerly had made Mademoiselle weep. Below, a wide ripple, almost a wave, and something vaguely white happened to attract my eye. As I came quite close to the lapping water I saw what it was—an aged swan, a large and uncouth creature, making ridiculous efforts to hoist himself into a moored boat. He could not do it. The heavy, impotent flapping of his wings, that scaly, slippery sound against the rocking and plashing boat, the gluey glistening of the dark swell where it caught the light—all seemed for a moment laden with that strange significance which sometimes in our dreams is attached to a finger pressed to mute lips and then pointing to something we have not time to discern before waking with a shudder. But although I soon forgot that dismal night it was, oddly enough, that night, that compound image—shudder and swan and swell—which first came to my mind when a couple of years later I learned that Mademoiselle had died.

She had spent all her life in feeling miserable; this misery was her native element; its fluctuations, its varying depths, alone gave her the impression of moving and living. What bothers me is that a sense of misery, and nothing else, is not enough to make a permanent soul. My enormous and morose Mademoiselle O is all right on earth but impossible in eternity. Have I really salvaged her from fiction?

Just before the rhythm I hear falters and fades, I catch myself wondering whether, during the years I knew her, I had not kept utterly missing something in her that was far more she than her name or her chins or her ways or even her French—something perhaps akin to that last glimpse of her, to the radiant deceit she used in order to have me depart pleased with my own kindness, or to that swan whose agony was so much more real than a drooping dancer's white arms; something in short which I could appreciate only after the things and beings that I had most loved in the scrutiny of my childhood had been turned to ashes or shot through the heart.

January 1943

35

The Man Who Shot Snapping Turtles

IN THE DAYS WHEN I LIVED IN HECATE COUNTY, I HAD AN UNCOMFORTABLE neighbor, a man named Asa M. Stryker. He had at one time, he told me, taught chemistry in some sooty-sounding college in Pennsylvania, but he now lived on a little money which he had been "lucky enough to inherit." I had the feeling about him that somewhere in the background was defeat, or frustration, or disgrace. He was a bachelor and kept house with two servants—a cook and a man around the place. I never knew anyone to visit him, though he would occasionally go away for short periods—when, he would tell me, he was visiting his relatives.

Mr. Stryker had a small pond on his place, and from the very first time I met him, his chief topic of conversation was the wild ducks that used to come to his pond. In his insensitive-sounding way he admired them, minutely observing their markings, and he cherished and protected them like pets. Several pairs, in fact, which he fed all the year round, settled permanently on the pond. He would call my attention in his hard accent to the richness of their chestnut browns, the ruddiness of their backs or breasts, their sharp contrasts of light with dark, and their white neck-rings and purple wing-bars like the decorative liveries and insignia of some exalted order, the cupreous greens and blues that gave them the look of being expensively dressed.

Mr. Stryker was particularly struck by the idea that there was

EDMUND WILSON

something princely about them—something which, as he used to say, Frick or Charlie Schwab couldn't buy; and he would point out to me their majesty as they swam, cocking their heads with such dignity and nonchalantly wagging their tails. He was much troubled by the depredations of snapping turtles, which made terrible ravages on the ducklings. He would sit on his porch, he said, and see the little ducks disappear, as the turtles grabbed their feet and dragged them under, and feel sore at his helplessness to prevent it.

As he lost brood after brood in this way, the subject came, in fact, to obsess him. He had apparently hoped that his pond might become a sort of paradise for ducks, in which they could breed without danger; he never shot them even in season and did not approve of their being shot at all. But sometimes not one survived the age when it was little enough to fall victim to the turtles.

These turtles he fought in a curious fashion. He would stand on the bank with a rifle and pot them when they stuck up their heads, sometimes hitting a duck by mistake. Only the ducks that were thus killed accidentally did he think it right to eat. One night when he had invited me to dine with him on one of them, I asked him why he did not protect the ducklings by shutting them up in a wire pen and providing them with a small pool to swim in. He told me that he had already decided to try this, and the next time I saw him he reported that the ducklings were doing finely.

Yet the pen, as it turned out later, did not permanently solve the problem, for the wild ducks, when they got old enough, flew out of it, and they were still young enough to be caught by the turtles. Mr. Stryker could not, as he said, keep them captive all their lives. The thing was rather, he finally concluded, to try to get rid of the turtles, against which he was coming, I noted, to display a slightly morbid animosity, and, after a good deal of serious thought, he fixed upon an heroic method.

He had just come into a new inheritance, which, he told me, made him pretty well-off; and he decided to drain the pond. The operation took the whole of one summer: it horribly disfigured his place, and it afflicted the neighborhood with the stench of the slime that was now exposed. My own place adjoined Stryker's, and in the heavy days of August, when the draining had become complete, my house became uninhabitable and I was obliged to go away for weeks.

Stryker, however, stayed and personally attended to the turtles, cutting off their heads himself; and he had men posted day and night at the places where they went to lay their eggs. At last someone on less friendly terms with him than I complained to the Board of Health, and they made him fill up his pond. He was indignant with the town authorities and declared that he had not yet got all the turtles, some of which were still hiding in the mud; and he and his crew put in a mad last day combing the bottom with giant rakes.

THE NEXT SPRING THE TURTLES REAPPEARED, THOUGH AT FIRST THERE were only a few. Stryker came over to see me and told me a harrowing story. He described how he had been sitting on his porch watching "my finest pair of mallards out with their new brood of young ones. They were still just little fluffy balls, but they sailed along with that air they have of knowing that they're somebody special. From the moment that they can catch a water-bug for themselves, they know that they're the lords of the pond. And I was just thinking how damn glad I was that no goblins were going to git them any more.

"Well, the phone rang and I went in to answer it, and when I came out again I distinctly had the impression that there were fewer ducks on the pond. So I counted them, and, sure enough, there was one duckling shy!" The next day another had vanished, and he had hired a man to watch the pond. Several turtles were seen, but he had not succeeded in catching them. By the middle of the summer the situation seemed as bad as before.

This time Mr. Stryker decided to do a better job. He came to see me again and startled me by holding forth in a vein that recalled the pulpit. "If God has created the mallard," he said, "a thing of beauty and grace, how can He allow these dirty filthy mud turtles to prey upon His handiwork and destroy it?"

"He created the mud turtles first," I said. "The reptiles came before the birds. And they survive with the strength God gave them. There is no instance on record of God's intervention in the affairs of any animal species lower in the scale than man."

"But if the Evil triumphs there," said Stryker, "it may triumph everywhere, and we must fight it with every weapon at our command!"

"That's the Manichaean heresy," I replied. "It is an error to assume that the Devil is contending on equal terms with God and that the fate of the world is in doubt."

"I'm not sure of that sometimes," said Stryker, and I noticed that his little bright eyes seemed to dim in a curious way as if he were drawing into himself to commune with some private fear. "How do we know that God isn't getting old? How do we know that some of His lowest creations aren't beginning to get out of hand and clean up on the higher creations?"

He decided to poison the turtles, and he brushed up, as he told me, on his chemistry. The result, however, was all too devastating. The chemicals he put into the water wiped out not only the turtles but also all the other animals and most of the vegetation in the pond. When his chemical analysis showed that the water was no longer tainted, he put back the ducks again, but they found so little to eat that they presently flew away and ceased to frequent the place. In the meantime, a number of new ones that had come there had died from the poisoned water.

One day, as Asa M. Stryker was walking around his estate, he encountered a female snapping turtle unashamedly crawling in the direction of the pond. She had obviously just been laying her eggs. He had had the whole of his place closed in with a fence of thick-meshed wire which went down a foot into the ground (I had wondered why he didn't have the pond rather than the whole estate thus enclosed, but he had said that this would have made it impossible for him to look at the ducks from the porch); but turtles must have got in through the gate when it was open, or they must have been hiding all the time. Stryker was, as the English say, livid, and people became a little afraid of him because they thought he was getting cracked.

THAT AFTERNOON HE PAID A FEVERED VISIT TO A MAN NAMED CLARENCE Millbank, whose place was next to Stryker's on the other side from mine. Millbank came from Virginia, and he worked in the advertising business. When Asa Stryker arrived, he was consuming a tall Scotch highball, unquestionably not his first; and he tried to make Stryker have a drink in the hope that it would relieve his tension. But "I don't use it, thanks," said Stryker, and he started his theological line about the ducks and the snapping turtles. Clarence Millbank, while he was talking, dropped his eyes for a moment to the wing collar and large satin cravat which his neighbor always wore in the country and which were evidently associated in his mind with some idea, acquired in a provincial past, of the way for a man of means to dress. It seemed to him almost indecent that this desperate moral anxiety should agitate a being like Stryker.

"Well," he commented in his easy way when he had listened for some minutes, "if the good God can't run the universe where He's supposed to be the supreme authority so as to eliminate the forces of Evil, I don't see how we poor humans in our weakness can expect to do any better with a few acres of Hecate County, where we're at the mercy of all the rest of creation."

"It *ought* to be possible," said Stryker. "And I say it damn well *shall* be possible!"

"As I see it," said Clarence Millbank,—again, and again unsuccessfully, offering Stryker a drink,—"you're faced with a double problem. On the one hand, you've got to get rid of the snappers; and, on the other hand, you've got to keep the ducks. So far you haven't been able to do either. Whatever measures you take, you lose the ducks and you can't kill the snappers. Now it seems to me, if you'll pardon my saying so, that you've overlooked the real solution—the only and, if you don't mind my saying so, the obvious way to deal with the matter."

"I've been over the whole ground," said Stryker, tightening and becoming slightly hostile under pressure of his pent-up passion, "and I doubt whether there's any method that I haven't considered with the utmost care."

"It seems to me," said Clarence Millbank in his soothing Virginian voice, "that, going about the thing as you have been, you've reached a virtual *impasse* and that you ought to approach the problem from a totally different angle. If you do that, you'll find it perfectly simple"—Stryker seemed about to protest fiercely, but Millbank continued in a mellow vein of alcoholic explaining: "The trouble is, as I see it, that up to now you've been going on the assumption that you ought to preserve the birds at the expense of getting rid of the turtles. Why not go on the opposite assumption: that you ought to work at cultivating the snappers? Shoot the ducks when they come around, and eat them—that is, when the law permits it,"—Mr. Stryker raised a clenched fist and started up in inarticulate anger,—"or if you don't want to do that, shoo them off. Then feed up the snappers on raw meat. Snappers make right good eating, too. We make soup out of 'em down in my part of the country."

Mr. Stryker stood without speaking for such a long moment that Clarence was afraid, he told me afterwards, that his neighbor would fall down in a fit; and he got up and patted him on the shoulder and used all his tact and charm to prevent anything serious happening. "All I can say," said Stryker, as he was going out the door, "is that I can't understand your attitude. Right is Right and Wrong is Wrong, and you have to choose between them!"

"I've never been much of a moralist," said Clarence, "and I dare say my whole point of view is a low and pragmatical one."

STRYKER SPENT A TROUBLED AND RESTLESS NIGHT—SO HE AFTERWARDS told Clarence Millbank; but he got up very early, as he always did, to hunt for breakfasting turtles, which he baited with pieces of steak. He now scooped them up with a net, and he paused for a moment over the first one he caught before he cut off its head. He scrutinized it with a new curiosity, and its appearance enraged him afresh: he detested its blunt and sullen visage, its thick legs with their outspread claws, and its thick and thorny-toothed tail that it could not even pull into its shell as other turtles could. It was not even a genuine turtle: *Chelydra serpentina* they called it, because it resembled a snake, and it crawled around like a lizard.

As he held the turtle up in his net, in the limpid morning air which was brimming the day like a tide, it looked, with its feet dripping slime, its dull shell like a sunken log, as fetid, stagnant, and dark as the bottom of the pond itself; and he was almost surprised at the gush of blood when he cut away the head. What good purpose, he asked himself in horror, could such a creature serve? Underground, ugly and brutal—with only one idea in its head, or rather one instinct in its nature: to seize and hold down its prey. The turtle had snapped at the hoop of the net, and even now that its head was cut off, its jaws were still holding on.

Stryker pried the head off the net and threw it into the water; another turtle rose to snatch it. Then why not turn the tables on Nature? Why not prey on what preyed on us? Why not exploit the hideous mud turtle, as his friend from the South had suggested? Why not devour him daily as soup? But one would get sick of turtle soup every day. Why not sell it to the public, then? Let the turtle earn money for him! He snickered at what seemed to him a fantasy; but he returned to Clarence Millbank's that day in a mood of amiability that rather gave Clarence the creeps.

"Nothing easier!" cried Millbank, much amused—his advertising copy irked him, and he enjoyed an opportunity to burlesque it. "You know, the truth is that a large proportion of the canned turtle soup that's sold is made out of snapping turtles, but that isn't the way they advertise it. If you advertise it frankly as snapper, it will look like something brand-new, and all you'll need is the snob appeal to put it over on the can-opening public. There's a man canning rattlesnakes in Florida, and it ought to be a lot easier to sell snappers.

"All you've got to do up here in the North to persuade people to buy a product is to convince them that there's some kind of social prestige attached to it—and all you'd have to do with your snappers would be to give the customers the idea that a good ole white-haired darky with a beaming smile used to serve turtle soup to Old Massa. All you need is a little smart advertising and you can have as many people eating snapper as are eating [he named a popular canned salmon], which isn't even nutritious like snapper is—they make it out of the sweepings from a tire factory.—I tell you what I'll do," he said, carried away by eloquence and whiskey, "you organize a turtle farm and I'll write you some copy free. You can pay me when and if you make money."

Asa M. Stryker went away, scooped out two of the largest snappers, and that evening tried some snapping-turtle soup, which seemed to him surprisingly savory. Then he looked up the breeding of turtles, about which, in the course of his war with them, he had already come to know a good deal. He had turtles brought in from all around and his duck-pond was presently thick with them. It didn't cost much at first, though he did have to feed them, as he and his gardener did all the work.

Clarence Millbank helped him launch his campaign and wrote the copy for it, as he had promised. At that time there had already appeared in advertising a new angle on animal food, of which Clarence had been one of the originators. This was the device of representing the animals as gratified and even gleeful at the idea of being eaten.

You saw pictures of manicured and beribboned porkers capering and smirking at the prospect of being put up in glass jars as sausages, and of steers, in white aprons and chefs' hats, that offered you their own sizzling beefsteaks. Clarence Millbank converted the snapping turtle into a genial and lovable character, who became very familiar to the readers of magazines and the riders on subway trains. He was pictured as always smiling, with a twinkle in his wise old eye, and he had always some pungent saying which smacked of the Southern backwoods, and which Clarence had great fun writing.

As for the plantation angle, that was handled in a novel fashion. By this time the public had been oversold on Old Massa with the white mustaches, so Clarence Millbank invented a listless Southern lady, rather like Mrs. St. Clare in *Uncle Tom's Cabin*, who had to be revived by turtle soup. "Social historians tell us," one of the advertisements read, "that more than 70 per cent of the women of the Old South suffered from anemia or phthisis [here there was an asterisk referring to a note, which said "Tuberculosis"]. Turtle soup saved the sweethearts and mothers of a proud and gallant race. The rich juices of the Alabama snapping turtle, fed on a special diet handed down from the time of Jefferson and raised on immaculate turtle farms famous for a century in the Deep South, supply the vital calories that are lacking in the modern lunch or dinner."

The feminine public were thus led to identify themselves with the lady in the advertisement, who was distinguished by a slim and supercilious chic, and to feel that they could enjoy a rich soup and yet remain slim and superior. The advertisement went on to explain that many women today suffered from anemia and t.b. without knowing it, and that a regular consumption of turtle soup could prevent these diseases from becoming serious.

Deep South Snapper Soup became an immense success; and they presently stimulated the demand by putting on the market three kinds: Deep South Snapper Consommé, Deep South Snapper Tureen (Extra Thick), and Deep South Snapper Medium Thick with Alabama Whole-Flour Noodles.

Stryker employed more helpers and eventually built a small cannery on his place out of sight of the house. The turtles were raised in shallow tanks, where they were easier to catch and control.

MR. STRYKER, WHO HAD NOT WORKED FOR YEARS AT ANYTHING BUT HIS struggle with the turtles, turned out to be startlingly able as a businessman and industrial organizer. He kept down his working crew, handled his correspondence himself, browbeat a small corps of salesmen, and managed to make a very large profit. He went himself to the city relief bureaus and shrewdly picked out men who seemed capable and willing to work but not too independent or intelligent, and he put over them his gardener as foreman.

He would begin by lending these employees money, and he boarded and fed them on the place—so that they found themselves perpetually in debt to him. As secretary he employed a former teacher, who had lost her job in the high school. A plain woman of middle age, she had suddenly had a baby by an irresponsible character who worked in the local garage. Stryker boarded the mother and agreed to pay board for the baby at a place he selected. As the business began to prosper, this secretary came to handle an immense amount of correspondence and other matters, but he never let her feel she was indispensable.

Mr. Stryker had managed to accomplish all this without ever seeming himself to be particularly preoccupied with the business; yet he had always followed everything done with a keen and remorseless attention that masked itself under an appearance of impassivity. Every break for a market was seized at once; every laxity of his working staff was pounced upon. And his attitude toward the turtles themselves had now changed in a fundamental fashion: he had come to admire their alertness and toughness. When he would take me on a tour of his tanks, he would prod them and make them snap at his stick, and then laugh proudly at their refusal to let go when he would bang them against the concrete.

Clarence Millbank himself, who had invented Snapper Tureen,

presently began to believe that he was a victim of Stryker's sharp dealing. At the time that the business had begun to make money, they had signed an agreement which provided that Clarence should get ten per cent; and he now felt that he ought to have a bigger share—all the more as his easygoing habits had been fatal to his job at his agency. He had been kept on for the brilliant ideas which he had sometimes been able to contribute, but he had lately been drinking more heavily and he had been told that he was about to be fired. He was not the kind of Southerner who stands transplanting well.

Not that Clarence would have made much of a career for himself anywhere. But in the South his dissipation and his reckless behavior would have fallen into place in the landscape. In Hecate County he was always a foreigner. Yet he was much too deeply rural in the feudal Virginian way to enjoy the life of club and office, and he had bought, on the strength of the boom of the twenties, an extensive country place, which he was now finding it hard to keep up. He was also getting lonely and morbid, as a married lady whom he had expected to divorce her husband and marry him had decided that it was too much trouble and that Clarence drank too much. Lately he had been brooding on Stryker, whom he had been finding it rather difficult to see, and had come to the conclusion that the latter was misrepresenting the amount of profit he made.

Finally, one Sunday afternoon, Clarence got suddenly up from a succession of solitary gin fizzes, cut straight through his grounds to the fence which divided his property from Stryker's, climbed over it with inspired agility, and made a beeline for Stryker's house, declining to follow the drive and stepping through the flower beds. Stryker came himself to the door with a look that seemed hostile and apprehensive; but when he saw Clarence, he greeted him with a smile and a special cordiality, and ushered him into his study. With his highly developed awareness, he had known that something of the kind was coming.

This study, which Clarence had never seen, as he went rarely to Stryker's house, was a disorderly and darkish place. It was characteristic of Stryker that his desk should seem littered and neglected, as if he were not really in touch with his affairs; and there was dust on the books in his bookcase, large and unappetizing volumes on zoological and chemical subjects. Though it was daytime, the yellow-brown shades were pulled three-quarters down. On the desk and on the top of the bookcase stood a number of handsome stuffed ducks that Stryker had wished to preserve.

Stryker sat down at his desk and offered Clarence a cigarette. Instead of protesting at once that Clarence's demands were impossible, as he had done on previous occasions, he listened with amiable patience. "I'm going to go into the whole question and put things on a different basis as soon as business slackens down in the spring. So I'd rather you'd wait till then, if you don't mind. It was all we could do to fill orders even before this strike began, and now I can hardly get the work done at all. They beat up two of my men yesterday, and they're threatening to make a raid on the factory. I've had to have the whole place guarded." (The breeding ponds and the factory, which were half a mile away, were enclosed by a wire fence.)

Clarence had forgotten about the strike, and he realized that he *had* perhaps come at rather an inopportune time. "I can't attend to a real reorganization, which is what we've got to have at this point, till our labor troubles are settled and things have slowed up. There ought to be more in this business for both of us," he concluded, "and I'll take into account your cooperative attitude when we make our new arrangement in the spring."

The tension was thus relaxed, and Stryker went on to address Clarence with something like friendly concern. "Why don't you have yourself a vacation?" he suggested. "I've noticed you were looking run-down. Why don't you go South for the winter? Go to Florida or some place like that. It must be tough for a Southerner like you to spend this nasty part of the year in the North. I'll advance you the money, if you need it."

Clarence was half tempted, and he began to talk to Stryker rather freely about the idiocies of the advertising agency and about the two aunts and a sister whom he had to support in the South. But in the course of conversation, as his eye escaped from Stryker's gaze, which he felt as too intent between the sympathetic smiles, it lit on some old chemical apparatus, a row of glass test-tubes and jars, which Stryker had presumably carried along from his early career as a teacher; and he remembered—though the conclusion he drew may not have been a just one—the several deaths, at intervals, of Stryker's well-to-do relatives. His eye moved on to the mounted ducks, with their rich but rather lusterless colors.

Clarence had always been conscious with Stryker of his own superior grace of appearance and manner and speech, and had sometimes felt the other admired it; and now as he looked at Stryker at ease in his turbid room, upended, as it were, behind his desk, with a broad expanse of waistcoat and a rubbery craning neck, regarding him with his small bright eyes set back in the brownish skin beyond a prominent snoutlike formation of which the nostrils were sharply visible—as Clarence confronted Stryker, he felt first an uncanny suspicion, then an overpowering abhorrence, then a freezing fright.

Unhurriedly he got up to go and brushed away Stryker's regret that—since it was Sunday and the cook's day out—he was unable to ask him to dinner. But his nonchalance now disguised panic: it was hideously clear to him why Stryker wanted him to take this trip. He wouldn't take it, of course, but what then? Stryker would try to get him just the same. In his emotion he forgot his hat and did not discover it till they had reached the porch. He returned to the study and on a sudden impulse took down from its rack on the wall the rifle with which Stryker had shot turtles. Clarence came from a part of the country where men quickly take action for themselves, and years of suppressed distaste and pride secretly nourished on liquor were, I suppose, coming to a crisis in this moment. He went out on the porch and shot Stryker.

THE COOK WAS OUT; ONLY THE GATES WERE GUARDED; AND CLARENCE had cut back through the grounds. Nobody heard the shot. The suspicion all fell on the foreman, who had his own long-standing grudges against Stryker and had actually organized the strike. He had had to go into hiding to escape from Stryker's thugs, and after the murder he disappeared.

Clarence Millbank decided very soon that he would sell his Hecate County place and take a trip to Europe, which he had always wanted to see. But just after he had bought his passage the war with Hitler started, and prevented his getting off—an ironic misadventure, as he said, for a man who had encouraged breeding snapping turtles.

He had dissociated himself from the soup business, and he went to live in Southern California, where, on his pitifully dwindled income, he seems to be drinking himself to death. He lives under the constant apprehension that the fugitive foreman may be found by the police, and that he will then have to confess his own guilt in order to save an innocent man—so that Stryker will get him in the end.

August 1943

The Unspoiled Reaction

IN THE THEATER LOBBY EVERYONE AT FIRST MISTOOK HER FOR ANOTHER patron (a grandmother, perhaps), though the fact that she wore an unstylish close-fitting hat, antique earrings, and no coat and had a generally anxious, false, and flustered air should have announced her status: she was a hostess, or, rather, one of those *entrepreneuses* masquerading as hostesses who are inevitably associated with benefits, club luncheons, lectures, alumnae teas, with all gatherings whose intention is not primarily pleasure.

Here, in the theater, on a rainy Monday morning, she was an anomaly, for in New York, in the Times Square neighborhood, relations between the management and customers are, by common consent, austerely professional. Consequently her intervention at the door came as a perceptible shock to each parent and child; it demanded a slight adjustment of focus. "Haven't we seen you before?" She addressed the child, and the face that turned up to her in each case showed bewilderment and pleasure. Only a moment before, the child had been an anonymous consumer bent on mass gratification; this magic question turned him back into his human self, and the child, unless he were totally hardened, blushed.

"What is your name?" the lady continued, and now even the parent was drawn in and smiled tenderly, sharing for an instant with this unknown but plainly intuitive person the holy miracle of his child's iden-

MARY McCARTHY

tity. Sometimes the children answered, speaking their own names softly, with reverence; more often, shyness and delight held them tongue-tied, and the parent supplied the information. "It's for Sunny," the lady added, in a sort of whispered nudge at the parent, who came to himself with a start. The explanation, if it told him nothing else (who or what was Sunny, anyway?), told him unmistakably that he had been a fool just now—he ought to have suspected the utilitarian motive. Angry and disillusioned, he passed into the poorly lit auditorium, the remnants of the smile, the fond, fatuous smile, still tugging at the corners of his mouth.

But at once the sight of so many empty places (hardly twenty persons were seated in a cluster down in front) brought a sentiment of pity for the woman outside. Clearly, these puppeteers were in a bad way; not even the rain, not even Monday, not even the too high price of admission, could explain or palliate the smallness of the house. An air of failure hung over the whole undertaking, infecting the audience itself with the poison of financial sickness, so that even the most healthy, the most fortunate parents and children, sitting there in little groups in the bad light, with the dismal smell of damp wool and dead cigarettes all about them, had the look of derelicts huddled together.

So strong indeed was the sense of misery that the more sensitive parents felt an impulse to remove their children from this house of death and were only prevented by the practical difficulties (how to explain?) and by the habit of chivalry toward the poor and ill-favored. If the rat does *not* leave the sinking ship, his only recourse is to identify himself with its fortunes; so the parents, having committed themselves to this unhappy enterprise, immediately experienced the symptoms of solidarity. They began to tell themselves that the attendance could have been worse (after all, it *was* Monday and it *was* raining), to clock off each new arrival with a feeling of personal triumph, and finally to lean forward in their seats and will people into the theater as passengers in a decrepit car lean forward to will the car up a long grade.

These exercises in kinesthetic magic, in which, from their clenched fists and closed eyes, one would say nearly the whole audience was engaging, were cut short by another woman, younger and more openly managerial than the first, a progressive school teacher in genus if not in actuality, one accustomed to giving orders in the form of requests. "Will you please take an outside seat?" she said, leaning over and tapping the surprised parents on the shoulder.

Some mothers and fathers did as they were bid at once, almost apologetically. Others were slow and showed even a certain disposition to stand on their rights. Still others (the most well-fed and polished) pretended not to hear. "This does not apply to me," their deaf backs declared.

When it became plain that she was not going to be obeyed without further explanation (for her little air of authority had stirred up latent antagonism in an audience which had disposed itself to pity but not to be ruled by her), she walked down an empty row and took hold of the back of a seat, in a manner of an informal lecturer. "We like to have the children together in the middle," she announced with that excess of patience that suggests that patience is really out of place. "These puppet plays are intended for *children*. We want to reach the children as a group. We want them to be free of adult influences. We want an unspoiled reaction."

This fetched even the most stubborn, for it hinted to every adult in the audience that he was the snake in this paradise of innocence, that there was something intrinsically disgusting in the condition of being grown-up. There was a great shuffling of coats, hats, and handbags. Mothers dropped packages on the floor, a little girl cried, but at length the resettlement was accomplished, and the sheep were separated from the goats.

Whenever a new party came in, the earlier arrivals would, out of a kind of concerted malice, allow the parent to get herself well lodged in the center block of seats before breaking it to her that she was out of place. Indeed, the greater part of the audience was disinclined to make the revelation at all; its original feelings of mistrust had returned; it saw something ugly in this arbitrary manipulation of the natural order of seating, this planned spontaneity. Though it looked forward to the confounding of the newcomer, it would not take the side of the management; in an attitude of passive hooliganism it waited for the dark.

But disaffected as it was, the audience contained the inevitable minority of enthusiastic cooperators who rejoice in obeying with ostentatious promptness any command whatsoever, who worship all signs, prohibitions, warnings, and who constitute themselves volunteer deputies of any official person they can find in their neighborhood. These cooperators nudged, tapped, poked, signaled, relayed admonitory whispers along rows of children, until every misplaced adult became conscious of the impropriety of his position and retreated, in confusion, to the perimeter of the house. By the time the curtain went up, the adults formed three sides of a box which contained the children but left the cover open to receive the influences of the stage.

ALMOST AT ONCE THE OBJECT OF THE FIRST LADY'S QUESTION BECAME apparent. Laboriously, the curtains of the miniature stage parted and an unusually small puppet, dressed as a boy, was revealed, bowing and dancing in a veritable tantrum of welcome. This was Sunny. "Hello, boys and girls," he began in the shrieky voice that is considered *de rigueur* for puppets and marionettes. "Welcome to our theater." "Hello, Sunny," replied a self-assured child, patently the son of one of the cooperators. He had been here before, and he did what was expected of him. "Hello, John, how are you today?" the puppet screamed in answer, and now he passed from child to child, speaking to each by name.

The children, for the most part, looked at each other in wonder and astonishment. They were at a loss to account for the puppet's knowing them; they did not relate cause and effect and doubtless had already forgotten the question and answer in the lobby. After the first consternation, the voices that answered the gesticulating creature grew louder and firmer. The children were participating. Each one was anxious to show himself more at home than his neighbor, and soon they were treating the puppet with positive familiarity, which he encouraged, greeting every bold remark from the audience with peals of shrill artificial laughter. Before the actual play began he had drawn all but the very youngest and shyest into an atmosphere of audacity.

Along the sides of the human box, the parents were breathing easier. Gladly they divested themselves of their original doubts. It was enough that the children were entering into the spirit of the thing. That reciprocity between player and audience, lost to us since the medieval mysteries, and mourned by every theoretician of the drama, was here recovered, and what did it matter if the production was a mockery, a cartoon of the art of drama? What did it matter that the children's innocence had been taken advantage of, that the puppet who seemed to know them knew only their names? And as for the seating arrangements, perhaps in the modern world all spontaneity had to be planned; as with crop control and sex, the "unspoiled reaction" did not come of itself; it was the end-product of a series of maneuvers.

The curtains closed on Sunny, with the children yelling, "Good-bye." The main attraction, "Little Red Riding Hood," was about to begin, when a party of late-comers made its way down the aisle. There were eight or ten children and a dispirited-looking young teacher. They took places in the very first row and were a little slow getting seated. The children kept changing places, and the teacher was either ineffectual or a principled anti-disciplinarian, for she made no real effort to interpose her authority.

The curtains on the stage above them moved, as if with impatience, and a human hand and then a face, grotesquely enlarged to eyes adjusted to the scale of puppets, appeared and then quickly withdrew. This apparition was terrifying to everyone but those for whom it was intended, the school children in front, who had as yet no standard of comparison and continued their bickering unperturbed. The face had come and gone so abruptly that nobody could be sure whether it belonged to a man or a woman; it left the audience with a mere sense of some disembodied anger—a deity was displeased. Could this be Sunny? the parents wondered.

At length, the party in the front row composed itself. Little Red Riding Hood and her basket were revealed as the curtains lurched back. To the left of the puppet stage, a little box opened, and there was Sunny, ready with a prologue, adjuring the children to watch out for Little Red Riding Hood as if she were their own little sister. The box closed, the action began, and the children took Sunny at his word. From the house a series of warnings and prophecies of disaster followed the little red puppet out its door. "Look out," the children called. "Don't obey your Mummy." "Eat the basket yourself."

In all these admonitions none were louder than the party in the front row. These children, indeed, appeared to be the ideal audience for Sunny and his troupe; they were the unspoiled reaction in test-tube purity. While other boys and girls hung back, murmured their comments, or simply parroted the cries of the bolder children, the ones down in front were inventive and various in their advice—so much so that it seemed hardly possible that the play could go on without the actors' taking cognizance of what these untrammeled children were saying, and one almost expected Little Red Riding Hood to sail off from her lines into pure improvisation, and a kind of *commedia dell' arte* to ensue. But the puppets kept rigidly to the text, oblivious of interruptions and suggestions, and the usual situation was reversed—it was not the audience which was unresponsive but the players.

By the middle of the second scene, when the wolf had made his appearance, the whole theater was in a condition of wild excitement. Some children were taking the side of the wolf, urging him to make a good dinner, and some, traditionalists even in unrestraint, remained loyal to the grandmother. The contest on the stage was transported into the pit.

AT THE END OF THE SECOND SCENE, SUNNY CAME OUT ONCE MORE, AND now the boldness of the children perfectly matched the provocations of the puppet. Saucy answer met impudent question. Sunny was beside himself; from time to time, a witticism from the house would capsize him altogether and he would lie panting on the stage, gasping out the last exhausted notes of the hee-hee-hee. Liberty and equality reached such a pitch of frenzy that it seemed the most natural thing in the world that a boy from the front row should climb up onto the stage to speak directly to Sunny.

The audience watched him go without the slightest sense of breach of decorum. The puppet, however, drew back into his box at the approach of the child. Slowly, his cloth body began to wiggle and twist in an uncanny pantomime of distaste and fear. The child put out his hand to touch the puppet, and now the doll was indubitably alive. A shudder ran through it; it shrank back against the curtains and doubled itself up, as though to leave no intimate surface exposed to the violator's touch.

As the hand still pursued and it seemed as if no power on earth could prevent the approaching indignity, the puppet cried out. But its voice had changed; the falsetto shriek had become a human scream. "Sunny doesn't like that," called an agonized woman's voice from behind the curtain. The note of hysteria struck home to the boy, separating him from his intention. He leaped back, stumbled toward the stairs, slipped on them, and fell into the orchestra pit. Two of the fathers rushed forward. The teacher joined them, peering anxiously over the brink. The child was retrieved, unhurt, and firmly put back into his seat. In the commotion, Sunny had disappeared.

Fortunately, the children hardly missed him. For the moment, they were more interested in the mechanics of the little boy's fall than in its cause. "What is an orchestra pit?" they called out to the mothers who had tried to explain, and some got out of their seats, proposing to investigate. "Afterwards, afterwards," the mothers' voices ordered. "The show is going to begin again."

But was it? The parents, glancing at each other, wondered. Had they not witnessed, just now, one of those ruptures which are instantly and irrevocably permanent, since they reveal an aversion so profound that no beginning, i.e., no cause can be assigned to it, and hence no end, no solution can be predicted? Like guests sitting around a dinner table which the hostess has just quitted to pack her trunk in a fury, the parents fidgeted, waiting for a sign which would tell them that it was not really necessary to go home to meet again the emptiness of their own devices, yet knowing perfectly well that the only thing to do was to go and go at once, before anything else happened. But inertia, the great minimizer, provided them with the usual excuses. They told themselves that they were letting their imaginations run away with them, that nothing of any consequence had happened—an incompetent teacher had let her charge misbehave.

And as the minutes passed and the curtains did not move, the sentiment of the audience turned sharply against the teacher. "Damn fool of a woman," murmured the father of a boy to the pretty mother of a girl. "I certainly wouldn't send a child to *her* school," replied the mother, brightening up. As if aware of the whispers of criticism, the teacher stiffened in her seat and stared blindly forward, feigning unconsciousness.

In the middle of the house, the children were also turning the experience over, clumsily trying to fix the blame, but they were not so adroit, so practiced as their parents, and small frowns of dissatisfaction wrinkled their brows. "Was that little boy naughty?" called a little girl's voice, at last. "Yes," answered her mother, without a moment's hesitation. "Oh," said the little girl, but her look remained troubled.

"And *now*, boys and girls—" It was Sunny, cordial as ever, and the third scene was about to start. There was no doubt that the puppet was himself again; he bowed, he clapped his hands, he danced, he screeched, in his old dionysiac style. Bygones were bygones, all was forgiven, childhood was off on another spree.

Yet the children at first were wary and glanced toward their parents, seeking instruction, for they no longer knew what was expected of them. The parents nodded encouragement, and as the children still hesitated, the adults screwed their own faces into grimaces of pleasure, till everywhere the children looked, on the sides of the audience or, above them, on the stage, there was a large, energetic smile bidding them enjoy themselves. The more docile children began to laugh, rather mechanically; others joined in, and in a few moments the crisis was past and the mood of abandon tentatively re-established. The play proceeded, and before long the children were barking and howling like wolves, the timid little girl was whimpering with terror, and the parents were quietly rejoicing in the fact that another morning had been got through without serious damage to the children or emotional cost to themselves.

The last scruple died as Little Red Riding Hood was rescued and the play came safely to an end. The curtains closed, but the children were not quite disposed to go. They remained clapping and shouting in their seats, while their parents gathered up hats and coats.

At this moment, when all danger seemed past and former fears groundless and even morbid, the same little boy in the front row jumped up and asked his teacher a question. "Yes," she said, in a voice that penetrated the whole auditorium, "I think it will be all right for you to go backstage now."

Something in the teacher's tone arrested everyone; even those parents who had succeeded in getting their children halfway up the aisle now paused to watch as the party in the front row made a little procession up the stairs. The drama was not quite over; a reconciliation must follow between the puppet and the child; the child must handle the puppet, but ceremoniously, backstage, and with the puppet's permission.

Indulgently, the audience waited. The little procession reached the stage. Other children, emboldened, were starting down the aisle after it, when the curtains parted. There, her white hair disheveled, her well-bred features working with rage, stood the woman everyone had met in the lobby and who was now instantly identifiable as the apparition of anger, the face between the curtains. "Get out, get out of here, get out." She barred the way of the approaching group. "You dreadful, horrible children."

The voice, screaming, was familiar too; it was, of course, Sunny's. "You horrible, horrible children," she repeated, her r's trilling out in a kind of reflex of gentility. The children turned and ran, and she pursued them to the stairs, a trembling figure of terrible malevolence, in whom could be discerned, as in a triple exposure, traces of the gracious hostess and the frolicsome puppet.

From behind the curtains came someone to seize her. A man from the box office ran down the aisle to pacify the teacher, who, now seeing herself on firm ground, was repeating over and over again, "That is no way to talk to a child." The audience did not wait to see the outcome. In shame and silence, it fled out into the rain, pursued by the sound of weeping which intermingled with the word *child*, as pronounced by the teacher in a tone of peculiar piety and reverence, her voice genuflecting to it as though to the Host.

March 1946

---◆---

The Gentle, Perfect Knight

IT WAS THE INVARIABLE CUSTOM OF IRIS MUNRO'S FRIENDS TO SPEAK OF her among themselves, and occasionally among others, as "poor" Iris. This was to indicate, not that she was without charm or possessions, but that, at the age of twenty-seven, she was as yet unmarried. This disturbed her friends for a complexity of reasons, not the least of which was the suspicion that in her maidenhood Iris was somehow perfectly happy. The itch to do something about this had been ungovernable, so they had devised an endless series of dinner parties, rather in the spirit of a perpetual novena, hoping that at one of them Iris would meet The Man.

Iris always went to these parties. She was, of course, fully aware of their purpose, but she was a considerate girl, and she did not wish to appear ungrateful to her friends. Also, each time she went, in some deep corner of her mind there stirred the small, barely acknowledged thought that tonight she might fall in love. For her friends, in supposing Iris to be perfectly happy, were quite wrong. She was a fairly intelligent young woman, pretty in a quiet, unradiant way, and she was affectionate and often rather lonely. She had not known many men; she had been carefully, almost preciously reared by a widowed mother, whose mistrust of the pitfalls of life had not been diminished by the fact that she had married one of them. The few men who had filtered through the guarding periphery of Iris's youth had

EDWIN O'CONNOR

been pale, awkward, and incapable; in later years, those whom she met had acquired a jarring self-assurance and a frightening aggressiveness. She realized now, half humorously, half sadly, that she probably was in search of some gentle, perfect knight, and although she knew that there was small chance of discovering him in the dining rooms of her friends, nevertheless it was to them she went; and whenever she went, there quickened anew the unobtrusive hope.

It was on a Thursday morning that Camilla Chase telephoned, to remind her of the dinner the following Monday. "It's going to be cosy," she promised, her voice ringing like a good ship's bell. "Just you, myself and Douglas, and Avery Winton. I'm dying to have you meet him."

Iris murmured, politely and negligibly.

"He's not like the last one, darling!" said Camilla.

Iris remembered the evening at the Chases' during which she had been paired with "the last one." He had been an Arthur DiMaggio, a glossy, pneumatic little man with preposterously lustrous eyes. "No relation at *all* to the athletes, my dear!" Arthur DiMaggio had informed her, with a saucy toss of his head. It had not been a pleasant evening.

"Avery is my cousin, you know," continued Camilla. "He's an explorer, dear. In the Arctic. You'll be wild about him." She paused, reflecting perhaps on the unhappy episode of Arthur DiMaggio, and then added: "Avery's *all man!*"

"That's nice," said Iris. "Thank you again, Camilla. I'll be there at seven."

In the next four days, Iris thought often of Camilla's explorer cousin. She wondered if he resembled Camilla; in all charity to her friend, she rather hoped he did not. Explorer— Who could tell? It was a vocation suited to either romantic or misanthrope; and recalling Camilla's previous efforts in her behalf, Iris inclined toward the misanthrope. Avery Winton would be a bleak rock: wind-chipped, frosty, and silent as the polar night. She was almost convinced of this as she stood at the Chases' door on Monday evening, and yet, as always, there lurked the faint and curtained hope. It was a hope nurtured, in this instance, by the remembrance of the nobility of feature of Richard Evelyn Byrd.

Camilla opened the door. "Darling, he's here!" she hissed dramatically, her large eyes bulging and alive. She gave Iris a moist and rubbery kiss.

"He's in the library," she said, "talking with Douglas, poor soul!" It was Camilla's belief, widely expressed, that her husband was an odd sort of man for anyone to be alone with. "He just won't talk, you know," she had often complained. "He just sits there like a hick, smiling at nothing. Sometimes he whistles to himself. Honestly, I've thought of having the man committed."

56

Iris, for her part, liked Douglas Chase: he was a strange, prematurely wispy man, with a wry appreciation of his own position.

"Come along," urged Camilla. "I've got to rescue Avery before he goes mad. There's something about being alone with Douglas that makes everything seem so *meaningless.*" She rushed Iris along the hall and pushed open the library door. The two men, who, at least to Iris, seemed not to be finding each other uncongenial, arose, and Douglas vaguely raised his glass toward her and wiggled a greeting. Camilla, sliding into her dancing-school voice, pronounced the necessary introductions, and the explorer cousin and Iris smiled, spoke, and met.

IN THE INTERVAL PRECEDING DINNER, IRIS DECIDED THAT AVERY WINTON was an agreeable surprise. Her mental composite of the boreal explorer could not have been more inaccurate; Avery Winton, far from being gaunt and frozen, was a well-tailored man in his middle thirties, with rather dark, attractive features and a quick, pleasant smile. Beyond the few words of greeting, he said little; Iris thought this due both to a becoming reserve and to the real lack of opportunity. For tonight, as always, Camilla kept conversation shooting along her own carefully prepared, embarrassing channels. It was concerned with the virtues to be found in the active, outdoor man—"Well, take yourself, Avery dear!"—as against disappointments offered by a torpid, indoor type. She advanced no example of this latter class, although at one point Douglas coughed pleasantly. Once or twice, Avery smiled at Iris; it was a brief, mock-helpless smile, an invitation to join him in his grain of salt.

"I know what I want!" cried Camilla suddenly. "I want to hear Avery sing a song."

The request was an abrupt one, and Avery appeared startled. "No, no," he protested.

"Yes, yes!" Camilla insisted. "I'll tell you what, darling. Sing that wonderful one you learned in that Eskimo hut. The one about you and the violets."

"Not right now, Cam," said Avery. "Maybe after dinner."

"All right, then," said Camilla, assuming a monumental pout; and turning to Iris, "*You* ask him to sing, Iris dear. Tell him you'd love to hear that picturesque old thing about the violets."

Iris felt herself reddening; Camilla had a disastrous gift for badgering people into uncomfortable positions. She faced Avery Winton and stretched a smile. "I'd really like to hear you sing," she said. "That is, if you don't mind doing it."

Avery hesitated. "Well," he said, "I—"

Further urging came from an unexpected quarter. "Go ahead," said Douglas, hospitably. "Go ahead and sing."

"My God!" shouted Camilla, in a loud, mocking voice. "The music lover! Maybe you'd like to accompany him with that toothy whistle? Now you've simply *got* to sing, Avery."

"Well—" said Avery again, and gave in. He walked to the piano and, sitting, spoke apologetically to Iris. "I suppose this is an odd sort of song for a fellow like myself to sing," he said. "Actually, it's an old English love song. But I did learn it, as Cam says, up in the North country: this Englishman and I got caught by the winter and were isolated for quite a spell. He used to sing this all the time, and the words stuck with me. I hope you can stand it." Smiling again, self-effacingly, he turned to the keyboard and began his song. It was called "I'm Weaving Sweet Violets."

Iris, listening, thought that it was indeed an odd sort of song for him, and yet he did it very well. He had a warm, if unprofessional, baritone, and he sang the lovely lyric with much feeling. She was suddenly proud of him, for she realized that most men, accustomed to sturdier pursuits, would have dissolved in embarrassment if similarly called upon. Avery's voice faded huskily through the room, his fingers brushing the final declining chords.

"God!" breathed Camilla. "Every time I hear that song, I feel as if the whole English countryside had hit me right in the face." She popped her eyes, to suggest the experience. "That was lovely, Avery!" she cried. "Simply lovely!"

"It was beautiful," said Iris. She said it sincerely: she had enjoyed the song thoroughly.

"Nice little number," said Douglas, peering confusedly about for his tobacco. "Nice little number."

Avery wore his honors with modesty. "Nothing like having a few friends in the audience," he said.

"I'm starved!" announced Camilla, upon whom good music, apparently, wrought multiple effects. "Come on, everybody, let's go in to dinner." She sprang from her chair, a healthy woman going to table. "Come on!" she said, waving the others to their feet.

"May I?" inquired Avery, gallantly offering his arm to Iris. Pleased out of proportion by the simple gesture, she walked into the dining room with him, Camilla preceding them, Douglas trailing cheerfully behind.

FROM EXPERIENCE, IRIS KNEW THAT CAMILLA'S TABLE HAD ITS LIMITATIONS. It aimed at nourishment, little else: there was a steady, boiled-potato touch to all the food. Soup, meat, and great hunks of pastry or pudding formed the unvarying three-course menu, prepared by a puckered little woman in the Chase kitchen. Tonight there was a heavy soup; not, thought Iris, unlike oatmeal. It was not until she had nearly finished hers that she noticed that Avery had taken none; strangely enough, this had drawn no comment from Camilla. Next came the meat, each plate high with a pair of tan croquettes drowned in a sauce of chalk. These were distributed reverently by the puckered woman, who, in a proud whisper, reminded Camilla that there were plenty more where those came from.

"Thank you, Agatha," said Camilla grandly. "I think that will be all for now." Double-checking, her eyes leaped up and down the table in sharp survey. "Oh dear!" she moaned suddenly. "*Look* at my poor Avery!"

Everyone looked at Avery. Iris, astonished, saw that on his plate, instead of the nesting croquettes, there was a small tin-foiled square resembling a brick of packaged Liederkranz. The puckered woman sniffed in distaste and trotted haughtily from the room.

"Oh my God!" said Camilla, with a vast gesture of despair. "She's offended again. Avery darling, she just *won't* understand your stomach."

It was Avery's turn to redden. "It's not a question of understanding anyone's stomach, Cam," he said, a trifle stiffly. "This isn't a diet for freaks."

Camilla spun a huge piece of croquette about in the chalk sauce. "*I* know," she said, "but Agatha doesn't. I can't even begin to explain your ideas to her; she's not a very scientific person."

Avery shrugged; then, as if ashamed at having been nettled by so minor a cause, he smiled ruefully at Iris. "I guess this must seem strange at that," he said, pointing to the tin foil. "It's an old story to Cam and Doug, of course, but I have a difficult time convincing strangers that I'm perfectly serious. Can you guess what it is?"

Iris hesitated. For some reason that she could not explain, she hoped that Avery was not eating some kind of skin food. She took the plunge. "Yeast?" she hazarded.

Avery laughed. "No, no!" he said. "No, I should hope not! Actually, Miss Munro, I wouldn't have expected you to guess. No one ever does. You see," he explained, unwrapping the foil and revealing a compact brownish block, "this is the famous pemmican."

"Pemmican?" Searching hard, Iris was unable to place the famous pemmican; the word evoked echoes, imprecise and distant, of red men and early frontiers.

"Pemmican," he repeated. He pronounced the word with a strange respect: just so might a prospector have spoken of gold, or a whaler of ambergris.

"I know all about that," volunteered Camilla, chewing steadily. "They call it jerky."

"No," said Avery. "No, they don't, Cam. Jerky is a different food entirely. Jerky," he said, leaning instructively toward Iris, "is merely lean beef, dried in strips. You wouldn't like it, Miss Munro; it tastes a little like leather."

"I see," murmured Iris. Avery now seemed less withdrawn, more enthusiastic, than he had been in the library. It lent him a fuller personality, thought Iris, and for a moment she wished that the food, as a subject of table talk, interested her more.

"Pemmican," continued Avery, a friendly, didactic gleam in his eye, "is something else again. It's extremely palatable, something like roast beef. It's the finest concentrated food known to man. You see," he disclosed, lifting the brownish block from his plate, and twisting it in the light, like a goblet of fine wine, "it's a mixture of lean meat and *fat!*"

"I see," said Iris again. There was an expectant pause; unskilled in dietetic small talk, she groped for the pertinent question. "Then," she asked, "it's—just meat?"

"*All* meat!" he replied proudly. Iris was reminded of an odd parallel: Camilla, on the telephone, describing her cousin, in the same tone, as "All man!" All meat, all man, she thought.

Camilla spoke up. "Avery's a nut on meat," she said.

"That's one way of putting it, Cam," said Avery. Again, he seemed slightly annoyed by his cousin. He addressed himself to Iris. "The truth is, Miss Munro, that I prefer an all-meat diet. So do many people who have lived for any length of time in the North. The Eskimos, for example,— those who still live remote from the white man,—have never eaten anything but meat and fish."

"And that's all you eat?" asked Iris incredulously.

"That's all," he acknowledged. "And for the past few months, I've eaten nothing but pemmican. It really began as something of a test: I wanted to find out if pemmican alone was just an emergency food, or whether, here in the United States, it could really satisfy me, day after day. Well," he said, nodding his head in satisfaction, "it has. I haven't eaten any other meat for nearly three months."

It was truly a strange boast, Iris thought, and for the first time a faint, reluctant line of doubt flicked across her mind.

60

"*And,*" he announced, saving the best till last, "I haven't eaten a green vegetable in more than two years."

"But what that man *has* eaten!" cried Camilla, shuddering in delighted horror. "My dear, he's lived for months off the nose of a moose!"

"Well, hardly one moose, Cam," chuckled Avery. "I'm afraid that would have to be quite a moose. You remember what Churchill once said about the British Empire, I think it was? He said: 'Some chicken. Some neck!' The same thing goes here: Some moose. Some nose!" He led the laughter and then continued. "It's quite true, though," he assured Iris. "Boiled moose nose is considered a delicacy by the Eskimos and the Arctic Indians. Actually," he added, his face wreathed in reminiscence, "it's quite tasty."

"Ugh!" screamed Camilla. "Imagine that, darling! And that's not the worst. *Seal* flippers!" she said juicily. "They eat them, too."

"For the oil content," explained Avery.

"Isn't that the most disgusting thing you've ever heard?" asked Camilla, with a delicious shiver.

Iris nodded, in dumb agreement. It was disgusting; perfectly, appallingly disgusting. The fault, she thought, was not with Avery Winton. At least, not for the most part. It was Camilla, relentlessly sucking out those dreadful details. She prayed, hard, that she would stop.

"And what else?" asked Camilla. "What are some of those other awful things?"

Avery smiled indulgently. "Caribou paunch salad, polar bear paws," he supplied. "And, of course, marrow." Earnestly, he turned his attention to Iris once more. "You take the long bones of the caribou and crack them," he said, with an appropriate gesture to indicate the cracking of bones, "and then you extract the marrow. It comes out in sticks, and you eat it raw, like a candy bar."

Iris closed her eyes. She heard Douglas surprisingly introduce a more normal note among the esoterica. "Sometimes," he said, "they just eat rabbits."

"Well!" said Camilla, smothering this intruder with contempt. "Will you listen to that!"

"As a matter of fact, Cam," said Avery, "Doug isn't far wrong. They do eat rabbits a great deal, although of course not exclusively, the way they do other meats."

"Why?" asked Douglas, almost belligerently. "What's wrong with rabbits?"

"They're too lean," said Avery. "There's no fat on a rabbit. Let me tell you, Doug, that a man who ate nothing but rabbit for so much as a week would be letting himself in for trouble."

"For God's sake!" exclaimed Camilla. "What for?"

"Why," said Avery, in evident surprise, "he'd get diarrhea!"

Iris gasped; the gasp was blanketed by Camilla's hooting giggle.

"Avery!" she cried. "Naughty man!"

The naughty man looked puzzled. "But getting back to pemmican," he said, eagerly. And get back he did, the profligate carnivore joyfully returning to his first affection. "You can't find anything like it for convenience, for cost, and for taste," he stated. "I *know*. And as for health— Well, you take scurvy—"

BUT IRIS DID NOT TAKE SCURVY. SHE HAD SHUT HER EARS TO THIS MAN; disappointment had swept over her in a sudden flood. Dispiritedly poking at the cold, repellent food before her, she began to feel ill. It had happened too quickly, and with no preparation for the let-down. One moment, Avery Winton was a reserved attractive gentleman in a library (with a grimace, she remembered "I'm Weaving Sweet Violets"), the next a vulgar monomaniac.

"—and it lasts!" Avery chanted. "Actually, it's the most preservable food in the world. Why, this piece I have here"—and again the brownish block was elevated, and waved in display—"this piece I know to be at least ten years old." And, triumphantly, he popped a chunk into his mouth.

Dessert arrived. Avery took none: by this time it was quite clear that pemmican was his dessert, his meal, indeed his everything. "Three quarters of a pound a day," he announced. "That's all I need, and it keeps me in tip-top condition."

The pale mound of pudding quivered in invitation; Iris could not look at it. Her first feeling of disappointment had been superseded by a strong revulsion for this animal-man, who ran around the world, chewing meat and gloating about it so unashamedly. She half expected him to rip off his shirt, like that Macfadden man, so that she might swoon before the awful majesty of his meat-fed biceps. Dazed, she peered across the table. There was an indistinctness to the room: her eyes seemed to focus with clarity only on a pair of lean, accomplished jaws grinding in greedy demolition.

"Caries?" said Avery suddenly. "Caries, Cam? In these teeth?" His head thrust forward in a proud gape; Iris shrank in terror before the vulpine flash. "Stick to all meat," he advised generally, "and you won't be bothered by decay."

It was then that Iris pushed back her chair.

"Iris, darling!" exclaimed Camilla. "What's the matter? You look ghastly."

"I feel ghastly," said Iris, rising. "I don't really know how it happened. All of a sudden, I seem to have the most awful headache." She moved, wanly, towards Camilla. "Don't get up, dear," she said. "I'll be all right. It's just a matter of getting away and resting. I hate spoiling your party, though." She smiled, in brave apology.

"Don't think about it, darling," said Camilla, leaping to her feet. "You just come upstairs to my room and lie down awhile. Agatha will bring you some aspirin or something."

"No, no," said Iris, in some alarm. "I mean, thank you, Camilla, but I really think I'll have to go home. I've had this before; it's sure to be an all-night ache. I'd be miserable company for the rest of the evening."

"Migraine," said Avery, with knowing sympathy. "They're bad. I know. I used to have them." From the stress on the word "used," Iris knew without asking that he had been cured; she knew, also, what had cured him. Even her departure was serving the useful purpose of illustration.

"Well, you know best, I suppose," said Camilla, without enthusiasm. Her compassion was genuine, although hardly of the same intensity as her concern over her disrupted evening. "If you're sure you must go," she added, her voice trailing off.

"Quite sure. I'm terribly sorry." For a quick moment, viewing her hostess, Iris felt the beginnings of guilt; she chased such feelings away in panic. It was true that there was no headache, but that she was ill, irrecoverably so, as long as she remained in the direct presence of Avery Winton, was a greater truth. She had to go, and go immediately.

There was a brief, sympathetic huddle around the table, and then all went into the hallway together. Douglas took Iris's hand in farewell and looked at her wisely, wistfully. *He* knew, she thought, and the poor, dear man was envious. With outstretched hand, Avery Winton approached.

"It's a shame this had to happen, just as we were all having such a good time," he said. The hand that had cracked the long bones of the caribou now grabbed her hand firmly; perhaps appraisingly. "I wonder if I might see you home?" he asked.

"No!" said Iris. She almost shouted the word. "That is," she added hastily, "I live just around the corner. Thank you, though; it's been awfully nice meeting you."

He nodded. "I'm going to be around for another couple of days," he said. "Possibly we might see each other again?"

"That would be fine," she said, backing gently away. One bridge at a time, she thought; one more door, and she would be out into the night. She reached the door, opened it.

"Good night!" she cried, almost hysterically, she thought. The men chorused a reply, the door closed after her, and she was on the brick step, Camilla by her side. She breathed deeply, fiercely of the fresh, clear, palpably vegetative night: there was not so much as a hint of blood or bones or good red meat in the wonderful air. She breathed again.

"That'll clear away the cobwebs," observed Camilla. "You look better already, dear." Her voice switched key. "He *liked* you!" she throbbed.

"Ah?" said Iris, not quite comprehending, the night air still flowing through her brain.

"He liked you," Camilla repeated. "And I could see that you liked him. *Damn* that headache!" she muttered viciously. "You could have had *such* a perfect evening."

"Yes," said Iris, stepping down on the grass. "Well, good—"

"But he'll be here for a few more days," Camilla added hopefully. "You heard him say so. Call me up first thing tomorrow, darling, will you? We'll make arrangements!" she said archly.

"Yes, yes," said Iris hurriedly, closing her mind to the dread possibility. "Of course. Good night, Camilla. And thanks. Thanks so much for everything."

September 1947

The Man Below

IT BEGAN TO RAIN. HOLDING HER PURSE OVER HER HEAD, CARRIE RAN THE last few steps to the Lafayette Bar. Steve was waiting at the same table, the corner table next to the line of open doors at the sidewalk. He saw her, smiled, and half stood up.

She wondered how many times she'd come here in the two years she had known him. It had been almost every evening, when he'd finished with his work at the hospital. Every evening they hadn't had a regular date. Except for the past three, she thought, with a sudden twitch of pain.

She shook the water off her purse and went to meet him. He leaned over and gave her a peck on the cheek. Without having to be told, the waiter brought her a beer. He knew too, she thought.

The rain was falling in thick gray sheets, straight down, the color of fog. All along Bourbon Street, drain pipes began to rattle and sing as they dumped thick arcs of water out on the broken uneven sidewalks.

"And it never rains at night," Carrie said.

"Feel it turn to steam," Steve said.

Rain splashed through the line of open doors, ricocheting like bullets from the sidewalk. She could feel it on her legs, cool for a second, then a warm snaky line down to her ankles. She moved her foot from under the table and looked at it.

SHIRLEY ANN GRAU

"You getting wet?"

"Just looking."

"We can move back if you want."

On the sidewalk, not three feet away from them, a raincoated police-man walked by, sloshing through the puddles without looking. She leaned over and watched him. At the corner the shiny black coat merged into the shiny black street.

Out on the river a ship began blowing, urgent and mournful.

In the corner of the bar, there was a record player. The bartender changed the record, moving with slow deliberation. He turned up the volume.

"God," Steve said.

"What?"

"*Vesti la Giubba.*"

"Oh," she said, "I wasn't listening."

"You've got the darnedest habit these days."

"Like what?"

"Not listening. You just kind of disappear."

"I don't mean to."

"Oh, hell," he said, "everybody's got a right to be peculiar."

"I don't—" She stopped. Don't whine, she told herself firmly.

On the river the tug hooted again, insistently.

He cocked his head, listening. "Maybe some barges got loose."

"*Ridi, Pagliaccio. . . .*" There was a scratch in the record.

She asked quietly, "Your parents get off?" Her voice was more firm than she had intended.

"Sure. Why shouldn't they?"

She shook her head, smiling again. They had come down for a quick visit, his parents. And she hadn't seen him for the three days they'd been in town.

She wondered why she hadn't been asked at all. It bothered her. Sometimes.

They sat quietly, finishing one beer and beginning a second.

The same policeman sloshed wearily back along the walk. And on the other side a stray dog trotted along, hugging the wall, moving briskly.

"Where do you suppose he's going?"

"Who?"

"The dog."

Steve looked first at her and then out into the rain. "I don't know," he said. "Looks like he's heading for the docks."

"I can hear the ferries," she said suddenly. "I can hear their signals just before they pull off."

"I shouldn't wonder," he said. "It's not more than two blocks away."

"Let's go take the ferry over to Algiers."

"What for?"

"Might be fun."

"In the rain?"

She thought about that for a moment, and it was on the tip of her tongue to say yes. But finally, under the steady prompting of his eyes, she said softly, "No, I guess not."

"For a minute you had me worried."

"If we had a tree house we could go and sit in it," she said softly.

"What?"

His new bottle of beer had come, and she watched him pour it carefully.

"I've been looking for another place," she said. "I don't think I want to live in the Quarter any more."

"How come?"

"I don't know—seems kid stuff, in a way."

"You're not that old."

The record ended. The bartender walked over lazily and changed it. "Oh, God," Steve said, recognizing the first bars. It was the *Intermezzo* from *Cavalleria Rusticana*.

"I thought you liked that."

He made a face and did not answer.

The rain stopped, with the same suddenness with which it had begun. They listened to the small sucking sounds of bricks absorbing water.

"Okay," Steve said, "let's go."

They walked the few blocks down Bourbon Street to the high iron gate that led to her apartment. She fumbled for her key, then dropped it. He found it and wiped it on his handkerchief.

"I'm sorry," she said. "I was born clumsy."

She opened the gate, noticing for the first time that the rust came off in great smears on her hand. "I won't ask you up," she said. "I'm sort of beat today."

He hesitated, and she wondered if he were about to object. But he only said, "I'll call you tomorrow."

It was very dark in the courtyard. The small lantern over the gate didn't penetrate the thick heavy leaves and the vines. She stopped once and peered down, then shrugged. The walk must have been under water. She could feel the water slosh through the open toes of her shoes. Here under the wide leaves of the banana trees it was still raining, a light continuing sprinkle. She looked up and caught a quick glimpse of the sky through a tiny opening. There was a star stuck in it, like a piece of ice.

She climbed the stairs slowly. On one, halfway to the first landing, the sharp point of her heel jabbed through the wood, and she had to slip her foot free, bend down, and jerk the shoe loose. In the damp under the trees and between the thick moldy brick walls, boards lasted barely a year.

Her apartment was stuffy. She started the air conditioner, then methodically began to undress. Without thinking she hung her clothes away, brushed her hair, and gave her nails a quick buffing. The noise of the air conditioner bothered her, so she turned it off and opened the window. She took off the bedspread, folded it neatly, and put it away. Then she lay down, stretching herself carefully all over. She wanted to cry, but she told herself firmly that it was a silly thing to do, that it would only make her eyes achy and puffy and swollen in the morning. She said this quite a few times, and finally, just before she slept, she came to believe it.

SHE HAD BEEN ASLEEP FOR SOME TIME. AND FOR A WHILE SHE THOUGHT that the sounds were part of a dream. A rustling. And a scratching. For just a second behind the closed lids of her eyes she saw her father, sitting on the back porch on a Sunday morning, reading, the newspapers rustling under his hands. She could see the colors of the funny papers. She could even hear the flat-toned ringing of the Lutheran Mission bell down the block. And she could hear her mother complaining: "And he goes out in the yard in his pajamas. A big Tocko he is!"

Even at this distance Carrie smiled and whispered to herself, "And not for nothing is his name Francevich."

She didn't think of her parents very often, and when she did it was in terms of pyramids of fat, with a tiny head balanced on top like a rock. . . .

They had gone back, when she was still in high school, right after the war. The strange country had got to be too much for them, after nearly forty years. They had left her—to finish school—with a cousin, and they went back to Ragusa.

At first, in the unfamiliar smells of her cousin's house, she missed them. But when the year was done, and her cousin brought out the little savings book with her passage money marked in it in violet ink, she just shook her head. And she never went. Her parents wrote, once or twice, but then the letters stopped too.

She hardly saw her cousin any more, ever since the day years ago when she had got her first job and moved into her own apartment. She'd done well since then. She had a fine job, and a fine future. She was sharp and efficient, too, the sort of secretary nobody made passes at, though she was nice-looking, with a lush, full figure. It just didn't seem to occur to them.

Until Steve came. They had gone to bed on their second date. Cold sober, too. That was a couple of years ago, when he'd been a tall skinny medical student. He'd put on weight since then. You could begin to see the outline of a very heavy man in the making. Like his father, he said. His hair was thinning too, rapidly, though he was just her age, twenty-five. Sometimes when she stood above him, she could see the skull all pinkish under the thin blond hair. She always looked away quickly. As if she'd seen into a bedroom.

OUTSIDE HER WINDOW THE RUSTLING CONTINUED. THAT WOULD HAVE to be in the garden next door. Somebody must be walking about down there in the bamboo and banana bushes, a tangle so thick that even the cats circled around it.

She opened one eye and looked at the small green luminous hands of the clock: ten past one.

The rustling stopped. Far off, and muffled by the thick high brick walls of the houses, a siren wailed. It seemed to stop on the other side of the block.

She paid no particular attention. Sirens were so frequent, anyhow, you'd be up all night if you followed each one.

The voices came closer, and lights flickered on the ceiling.

Oh, hell, she told herself. And got up slowly and went to look out of the window. She propped both elbows on the sill and leaned her chin in them.

She looked directly down into five adjoining back yards, separated each from the other by the same thick brick wall that formed the houses. From her unusually high second floor, she looked over them, saw easily and clearly into the little squares. The two larger ones ran just under her window, met back to back with a wall edged by broken glass, just a little bit to the right. Across the length of these and running at right angles to them, she could see the three other yards, each of them behind an almost identical cottage.

On the roof of the farthest house several lights were flashing, the little jerky swings of flashlights. And even as she looked, two more figures stepped from the dormer window to the gentle slope. The lights joined in

69

a confused circle, she could hear some low voices, then the circle broke up and moved in single file across the roof. As they climbed the low wall that separated one roof from the other, she recognized the light-gray uniforms of the police.

She got a cigarette, lit it, and pulled a chair over to the window to watch.

The rustling in the growth almost directly beneath her had stopped. The lights were on the second roof now. The police had gathered again, three of them, and were waiting while two others clambered up the pitch of the roof and shone their lights down the other side. A woman's voice called from inside, "I saw him go that way there, for sure." And the police drifted slowly across the roof, looking like kids playing hide-and-seek in the dark.

Carrie thought: They're going over to the right, toward Royal Street, and they guess he's up on the roofs. But he isn't. He's in the yard directly below.

She bent forward until her head rested on the screen, and she stared down into the darkness. The top of the leaves reflected the flashlights dimly. Under them it was still and dark.

He must see me, she thought. He must see the cigarette.

The police walked slowly back and forth across the three roofs, searching.

"What about down in the patio?" somebody asked.

"Hell, man, don't jump."

"Hell of a drop."

"Go down around the doorway, man."

"He wouldn't jump down," the woman inside said, complainingly.

"Lady, I seen 'em go straight up brick walls from a running start, like a fly, and get hold of a second-floor porch."

He can hear them, Carrie thought, but maybe not too well down below the walls and smothered under the canes. But he can see me. He's got to have looked up and seen me.

She let her eyes move slowly around the five little squares of patios, let her eyes feel their outlines like tangible things.

And she saw something else. In the fifth yard, which backed into the cluttered, overgrown one, a screen door scraped open. No lights went on. But her eyes, accustomed to the dark, made out the shape of a policeman's cap. He stood leaning by the door, and the gray of his uniform blurred into the old wall. He seemed to be turning his head about slowly, but he did not appear to hear anything, though the rustle in the canes had begun again.

She pressed her forehead to the screen. The man down there seemed to be dragging something.

In the other yards doors slammed open and shut and heels scuffed the brick. A big police searchlight flashed on. She blinked and shook her head, dazzled. The roofs were outlined now, sharp, black and white; the uneven slates made big black shadows in the glare.

Then she saw the man below for the first time. She saw the back of his head and one hand. And all of a sudden she knew what it was he was trying to do.

He had dragged something over to the back wall; in that garden it wouldn't be hard to find a rusted chair and a couple of wooden crates—things you could stand on. And he was now climbing on them to get across the back wall.

On the other side the policeman still hadn't heard anything above the shouting. But he could not miss someone who crawled over the wall and tried to cut across that yard.

The hand was reaching higher and higher. She noticed it wasn't too steady or certain as it groped around for a hold on the bricks.

She thought, They'll catch him, and that'll be all. . . .

It wasn't anything to her. She pressed her forehead even harder against the screen, so that the dust fell tingling in her nose. And she lifted one finger and tapped on the screen so that a little rattling sound dropped out into the night.

The scratching stopped. The hand jerked back down into the dark shelter of the bamboo.

She said, in a whisper, not quite believing it was herself speaking: "Back of you, goddam it, back of you." There was no movement. "The gate. You didn't see it. And out the alley to Bourbon Street."

After a pause, a steady rustling. And a small rattle of the locked gate. "Goddam it," she whispered again, "get out!"

The banana trees grew almost right up to the gate, which was about six feet high, wrought iron with great squiggles of feathers and corn tassels. She saw a figure go over it like a cat, a large black cat, up one side and down the other, headlong. There was a single grunt when he hit the other side.

Like a fly, the policeman had said.

The cigarette burned her fingers. She dropped it on the sill and poked at it with her nail until it went out. Police now stood on the walls and turned their lights down into the overgrowth.

"Jeez," one said, "he could be down there."

71

"That house don't have a door on Dumaine," someone else said. "That's on Bourbon."

"You go around."

She turned away from the window. She went into the living room, still in the dark, and felt on the coffee table until she found the cigarettes.

SHE SMOKED QUIETLY, WATCHING THE TINY COAL IN THE DARK, LIGHTING one cigarette from the other. The phone rang. She let it ring for a while before she even thought about answering.

Steve said, "Where have you been?"

"Here."

"You sound funny."

"I don't mean to." She yawned slowly.

"Look," he said, "I'm coming over."

"I'm sort of sleepy."

"I've got to talk to you."

"Okay," she said listlessly.

She sat, half dozing, thinking of nothing at all, until he came. It took him only a very few minutes; he must have run all the way.

"What's going on out there?" he asked quickly. "There are four police cars over on Dumaine Street."

"Yes," she said, "I know."

"They're checking the alley that runs right under your window."

But he'd be gone, she thought, that dark figure who'd scrambled over the gate with such a hurt grunt. "He wasn't a very good burglar."

"What?"

"They were chasing him and he got away."

"Oh," he said. "Well listen to me."

"I helped him, but he wasn't very good, really."

"What in God's name are you talking about?"

She felt floating and pleasant. As if she had been drinking absinthe. "He made much too much noise."

Steve went over to the little bar and mixed two drinks.

Words drifted across the front of her mind. As they passed she read them aloud. "The way you do that, seems almost like you live here."

He brought back the two glasses.

She took hers, ducked her nose down into the tickling of the rising soda bubbles, played with the pieces of ice with her tongue.

"Quit," he said. "That's too damn suggestive when I'm talking to you."

She put the glass down on the coffee table and folded her hands and waited.

"I don't know how you guessed it," he said.

"Me?"

"You acted so strange. I should have caught on."

She said nothing, went on studying the small patch of yellow light over the spindly pink lamp in the corner. She did not remember turning it on. Steve must have done it when he came in.

"Look," he said, "there was something else all right."

"What else?"

"There was somebody else with my parents."

"Oh."

"A girl."

That was it, she thought. It was so simple. And still, she hadn't thought of it. She hadn't thought of it at all.

"I've known her ever since high school."

The way he said it made her think of football games in crisp clear Northern weather, and proms with all the dresses fluffy and pastel, like so many flowers. And everything cool and crisp like an air-conditioned office. . . . The only high school prom she had ever been to had been hot and crowded and steamy with perspiration. The dresses were streaked and wilted. The net of her dress sagged in the heat and drooped down and she caught her heel in it and tore it. And her skin stung and reddened in splotches from the perfume she had dabbed on it.

"My parents have been friends of her mother for years. Before she was born, even."

And do I have continuity like that? Carrie thought. Of friendships carried from generation to generation? Did my parents give me a single thing but my blood? . . .

"I guess they kind of decided that it would be a good thing if we made a couple. They had it all figured out. You know, the way parents do."

A crisp clear world where boy and girl infants held hands between their carriages. . . . She hadn't had a carriage at all. She had lain on a blanket on the floor of the front porch, fenced in by chairs turned on their sides.

"I didn't tell you before," he said, "because I didn't know if you'd understand."

"No," she said, "I probably wouldn't have."

"She'd been looking forward to coming down. It was a kind of holiday for her."

"Is she pretty?"

"I guess so."

"Like what?"

"Dark hair, dark eyes, sort of short."

"Oh," she said.

"I'd have told you before, only I thought it would just hurt your feelings."

"Oh," she said.

"I felt like a heel for not warning you before."

"But you feel better now."

"Well," he said, "yes."

"Are you going to marry her?"

"Now you are mad with me."

"I was asking."

"No," he said, "I'm not going to marry her."

"That's a shame, when she was counting on it."

She stared at the pink azalea on the table, thinking: If I had a wall I could climb over it, but I don't even have a wall. I don't have anything at all.

She reached out and patted his head, gently, absentmindedly, like a child. "Go home, little boy."

She did not hear the door. After a while she looked up and saw that he was gone. And the silence was no emptier than it had been with him there.

September 1960

In the Region of Ice

SISTER IRENE WAS A TALL, DEFT WOMAN IN HER EARLY THIRTIES. WHAT ONE
could see of her face made a striking impression—serious hard gray eyes, a
long slender nose, a face waxen with thought. Seen at the right time, from
the right angle, she was almost handsome; in her past teaching positions
she had drawn a little upon the fact of her being young and brilliant and
also a nun, but she was beginning to grow out of that.

This was a new university and an entirely new world. She had heard—
of course it was true—that the Jesuit administration of this school had hired
her at the last moment to save money and to head off the appointment of
a man of dubious religious commitment. She had prayed for the necessary
energy to get her through this first semester. She had no trouble with
teaching itself; once she stood before a classroom she felt herself capable of
anything. It was the world immediately outside the classroom that confused and alarmed her, though she let none of this show—the cynicism of
her colleagues, the indifference of many of the students, and above all, the
looks she got that told her nothing much would be expected of her because
she was a nun. This took energy, strength. At times she had the idea that
she was on trial and that the excuses she made to herself about her discomfort were only the common excuses
made by guilty people. But in front of
a class she had no time to worry
about herself or the conflicts in her

JOYCE CAROL OATES

mind. She became, once and for all, a figure existing only for the benefit of others, an instrument by which facts were communicated.

About two weeks after the semester began, Sister Irene noticed a new student in her class. He was slight and fair-haired, and his face was blank, but not blank by accident, blank on purpose, suppressed and restricted into a dumbness that looked hysterical. She was prepared for him before he raised his hand, and when she saw his arm jerk, as if he had at last lost control of it, she nodded to him without hesitation.

"Sister, how can this be reconciled with Shakespeare's vision in *Hamlet*? How can these opposing views be in the same mind?"

Students glanced at him, mildly surprised. He did not belong in the class, and this was mysterious, but his manner was urgent and blind.

"There is no need to reconcile opposing views," Sister Irene said, leaning forward against the podium. "In one play Shakespeare suggests one vision, in another play another; the plays are not simultaneous creations, and even if they were, we never demand a logical—"

"We must demand a logical consistency," the young man said. "The idea of education itself is predicated upon consistency, order, sanity—"

He had interrupted her, and she hardened her face against him—for his sake, not her own, since she did not really care. But he noticed nothing. "Please see me after class," she said.

After class the young man hurried up to her.

"Sister Irene, I hope you didn't mind my visiting today. I'd heard some things, interesting things," he said. He stared at her, and something in her face allowed him to smile. "I—could we talk in your office? Do you have time?"

They walked down to her office. Sister Irene sat at her desk, and the young man sat facing her; for a moment they were self-conscious and silent.

"Well, I suppose you know—I'm a Jew," he said.

Sister Irene stared at him. "Yes?" she said.

"What am I doing at a Catholic university, huh?" He grinned. "That's what you want to know."

She made a vague movement of her hand to show that she had no thoughts on this, nothing at all, but he seemed not to catch it. He was sitting on the edge of the straight-backed chair. She saw that he was young but did not really look young. There were harsh lines on either side of his mouth, as if he had misused that youthful mouth somehow. His skin was almost as pale as hers, his eyes were dark and somehow not quite in focus. He looked at her and through her and around her, as his voice surrounded them both. His voice was a little shrill at times.

"Listen, I did the right thing today—visiting your class! God, what a lucky accident it was; some jerk mentioned you, said you were a good teacher—I thought, what a laugh! These people know about good teachers, here? But yes, listen, yes, I'm not kidding—you are good. I mean that."

Sister Irene frowned. "I don't quite understand what all this means."

He smiled and waved aside her formality, as if he knew better. "Listen, I got my B.A. at Columbia, then I came back here to this crappy city. I mean, I did it on purpose, I wanted to come back. I wanted to. I have my reasons for doing things. I'm on a three-thousand-dollar fellowship," he said, and waited for that to impress her. "You know, I could have gone almost anywhere with that fellowship, and I came back home here—my home's in the city—and enrolled here. This was last year. This is my second year. I'm working on a thesis, I mean I was, my master's thesis—but the hell with that. What I want to ask you is this: Can I enroll in your class, is it too late? We have to get special permission if we're late."

Sister Irene felt something nudging her, some uneasiness in him that was pleading with her not to be offended by his abrupt, familiar manner. He seemed to be promising another self, a better self, as if his fair, childish, almost cherubic face were doing tricks to distract her from what his words said.

"Are you in English studies?" she asked.

"I was in history. Listen," he said, and his mouth did something odd, drawing itself down into a smile that made the lines about it deepen like knives, "listen, they kicked me out."

He sat back, watching her. He crossed his legs. He took out a package of cigarettes and offered her one. Sister Irene shook her head, staring at his hands. They were small and stubby and might have belonged to a ten-year-old, and the nails were a strange near-violet color. It took him a while to extract a cigarette.

"Yeah, kicked me out. What do you think of that?"

"I don't understand."

"My master's thesis was coming along beautifully, and then this bastard—I mean, excuse me, this professor, I won't pollute your office with his name—he started making criticisms, he said some things were unacceptable, he—" The boy leaned forward and hunched his narrow shoulders in a parody of secrecy. "We had an argument. I told him some frank things, things only a broad-minded person could hear about himself. That takes courage, right? He didn't have it! He kicked me out of the master's program, so now I'm coming into English. Literature is greater than history; European history is one big pile of garbage. Sky-high. Filth and rotting corpses, right? Aristotle says that poetry is higher than history; he's right; in your class today I suddenly realized that this is my field, Shakespeare, only Shakespeare is—"

Sister Irene guessed that he was going to say that only Shakespeare was equal to him, and she caught the moment of recognition and hesitation, the half-raised arm, the keen, frowning forehead, the narrowed eyes; then he thought better of it and did not end the sentence. "The students in your class are mainly negligible, I can tell you that. You're new here, and I've been here a year—I would have finished my studies last year but my father got sick, he was hospitalized, I couldn't take my exams and it was a mess— but I'll make it through English in one year or drop dead. I can do it, I can do anything. I'll take six courses at once—" He broke off, breathless. Sister Irene tried to smile. "All right then, it's settled? You'll let me in? Have I missed anything so far?"

He had no idea of the rudeness of his question. Sister Irene, feeling suddenly exhausted, said, "I'll give you a syllabus of the course."

"Fine! Wonderful!"

He got to his feet eagerly. He looked through the schedule, muttering to himself, making favorable noises. It struck Sister Irene that she was making a mistake to let him in. There were these moments when one had to make an intelligent decision. . . . But she was sympathetic with him, yes. She was sympathetic with something about him.

She found out his name the next day: Allen Weinstein.

AFTER THIS, SHE CAME TO HER SHAKESPEARE CLASS WITH A SENSE OF excitement. It became clear to her at once that Weinstein was the most intelligent student in the class. Until he had enrolled, she had not understood what was lacking, a mind that could appreciate her own. Within a week his jagged, protean mind had alienated the other students, and though he sat in the center of the class, he seemed totally alone, encased by a miniature world of his own. When he spoke of the "frenetic humanism of the High Renaissance," Sister Irene dreaded the raised eyebrows and mocking smiles of the other students, who no longer bothered to look at Weinstein. She wanted to defend him, but she never did, because there was something rude and dismal about his knowledge; he used it like a weapon, talking passionately of Nietzsche and Goethe and Freud until Sister Irene would be forced to close discussion.

In meditation, alone, she often thought of him. When she tried to talk about him to a young nun, Sister Carlotta, everything sounded gross. "But

78

no, he's an excellent student," she insisted. "I'm very grateful to have him in class. It's just that . . . he thinks ideas are real." Sister Carlotta, who loved literature also, had been forced to teach grade-school arithmetic for the last four years. That might have been why she said, a little sharply, "You don't think ideas are real?"

Sister Irene acquiesced with a smile, but of course she did not think so: only reality is real.

When Weinstein did not show up for class on the day the first paper was due, Sister Irene's heart sank, and the sensation was somehow a familiar one. She began her lecture and kept waiting for the door to open and for him to hurry noisily back to his seat, grinning an apology toward her—but nothing happened.

If she had been deceived by him, she made herself think angrily, it was as a teacher and not as a woman. He had promised her nothing.

Weinstein appeared the next day near the steps of the liberal arts building. She heard someone running behind her, a breathless exclamation: "Sister Irene!" She turned and saw him, panting and grinning in embarrassment. He wore a dark-blue suit with a necktie, and he looked, despite his childish face, like a little old man; there was something oddly precarious and fragile about him. "Sister Irene, I owe you an apology, right?" He raised his eyebrows and smiled a sad, forlorn, yet irritatingly conspiratorial smile. "The first paper—not in on time, and I know what your rules are . . . You won't accept late papers, I know—that's good discipline, I'll do that when I teach, too. But, unavoidably, I was unable to come to school yesterday. There are many—many—" He gulped for breath, and Sister Irene had the startling sense of seeing the real Weinstein stare out at her, a terrified prisoner behind the confident voice. "There are many complications in family life. Perhaps you are unaware—I mean—"

She did not like him, but she felt this sympathy, something tugging and nagging at her the way her parents had competed for her love, so many years ago. They had been whining, weak people, and out of their wet need for affection, the girl she had been (her name was Yvonne) had emerged stronger than either of them, contemptuous of tears because she had seen so many. But Weinstein was different; he was not simply weak, perhaps he was not weak at all, but his strength was confused and hysterical. She felt her customary rigidity as a teacher begin to falter. "You may turn your paper in today, if you have it," she said, frowning.

Weinstein's mouth jerked into an incredulous grin. "Wonderful! Marvelous!" he said. "You are very understanding, Sister Irene, I must say. I must say . . . I didn't expect, really. . . ." He was fumbling in a shabby old briefcase for the paper. Sister Irene waited. She was prepared for another of his excuses, certain that he did not have the paper, when he suddenly straightened up and handed her something. "Here! I took the liberty of writing thirty pages instead of just fifteen," he said. He was obviously quite excited; his cheeks were mottled pink and white. "You may disagree violently with my interpretation—I expect you to, in fact I'm counting on it— but let me warn you, I have the exact proof, precise, specific proof, right here in the play itself!" He was thumping at a book, his voice growing louder and shriller. Sister Irene, startled, wanted to put her hand over his mouth and soothe him.

"Look," he said breathlessly, "may I talk with you? I have a class now I hate, I loathe, I can't bear to sit through! Can I talk with you instead?"

Because she was nervous, she stared at the title page of the paper: "Erotic Melodies in *Romeo and Juliet*" by Allen Weinstein, Jr.

"All right?" he said. "Can we walk around here? Is it all right? I've been anxious to talk with you about some things you said in class."

She was reluctant, but he seemed not to notice. They walked slowly along the shaded campus paths. Weinstein did all the talking, of course, and Sister Irene recognized nothing in his cascade of words that she had mentioned in class. "The humanist must be committed to the totality of life," he said passionately. "This is the failing one finds everywhere in the academic world! I found it in New York and I found it here and I'm no ingénu, I don't go around with my mouth hanging open—I'm experienced, look, I've been to Europe, I've lived in Rome! I went everywhere in Europe except Germany, I don't talk about Germany . . . Sister Irene, think of the significant men in the last century, the men who've changed the world! Jews, right? Marx, Freud, Einstein! Not that I believe Marx, Marx is a madman . . . and Freud, no, my sympathies are with spiritual humanism. I believe that the Jewish race is the exclusive . . . the exclusive, what's the word, the exclusive means by which humanism will be extended . . . Humanism begins by excluding the Jew, and now," he said, with a high, surprised laugh, "the Jew will perfect it. After the Nazis, only the Jew is authorized to understand humanism, its limitations and its possibilities. So, I say that the humanist is committed to life in its totality and not just to his profession! The religious person is totally religious, he *is* his religion! What else? I recognize in you a humanist and a religious person—"

But he did not seem to be talking to her, or even looking at her. "Here, read this," he said. "I wrote it last night." It was a long free-verse poem, typed on a typewriter whose ribbon was worn out. "There's this trouble with my father, a wonderful man, a lovely man, but his health—his strength is fading, do you see? What must it be to him to see his son growing up? I mean, I'm a man now, he's getting old, weak, his health is bad—it's hell, right? I sympathize with him. I'd do anything for him, I'd cut open my veins, anything for a father—right? That's why I wasn't in school yesterday," he said, and his voice dropped for the last sentence, as if he had been dragged back to earth by a fact.

Sister Irene tried to read the poem, then pretended to read it. A jumble of words dealing with "life" and "death" and "darkness" and "love." What do you think?" Weinstein said nervously, trying to read it over her shoulder and crowding against her.

"It's very . . . passionate," Sister Irene said.

This was the right comment; he took the poem back from her in silence, his face flushed with excitement. "Here, at this school, I have few people to talk with. I haven't shown anyone else that poem." He looked at her with his dark, intense eyes, and Sister Irene felt them focus upon her. She was terrified at what he was trying to do—he was trying to force her into a human relationship.

"Thank you for your paper," she said, turning away.

WHEN HE CAME THE NEXT DAY, TEN MINUTES LATE, HE WAS HAUGHTY and disdainful. He had nothing to say and sat with his arms folded. Sister Irene took back with her to the convent a feeling of betrayal and confusion. She had been hurt. It was absurd, and yet— She spent too much time thinking about him, as if he were somehow a kind of crystallization of her own loneliness; but she had no right to think so much of him. She did not want to think of him or of her loneliness. But Weinstein did so much more than think of his predicament, he embodied it, he acted it out, and that was perhaps why he fascinated her. It was as if he were doing a dance for her, a dance of shame and agony and delight, and so long as he did it, she was safe. She felt embarrassment for him, but also anxiety; she wanted to protect him. When the dean of the graduate school questioned her about Weinstein's work, she insisted that he was an "excellent" student, though she knew the dean had not wanted to hear that.

She prayed for guidance, she spent hours on her devotions, she was closer to her vocation than she had been for some years. Life at the convent became tinged with unreality, a misty distortion that took its tone from the glowering skies of the city at night, identical smokestacks ranged against the clouds and giving to the sky the excrement of the populated and successful earth. The city was not her city, this world was not her world.

She felt no pride in knowing this, it was a fact. The little convent was not like an island in the center of this noisy world, but rather a kind of hole or crevice the world did not bother with, something of no interest. The convent's rhythm of life had nothing to do with the world's rhythm, it did not violate or alarm it in any way. Sister Irene tried to draw together the fragments of her life and synthesize them somehow in her vocation as a nun: she was a nun, she was recognized as a nun and had given herself happily to that life, she had a name, a place, she had dedicated her superior intelligence to the Church, she worked without pay and without expecting gratitude, she had given up pride, she did not think of herself but only of her work and her vocation, she did not think of anything external to these, she saturated herself daily in the knowledge that she was involved in the mystery of Christianity. A daily terror attended this knowledge, however, for she sensed herself being drawn by that student, that Jewish boy, into a relationship she was not ready for. She wanted to cry out in fear that she was being forced into the role of a Christian, and what did that mean? What could her studies tell her? What could the other nuns tell her? She was alone, no one could help, he was making her into a Christian, and to her that was a mystery, a thing of terror, something others slipped on the way they slipped on their clothes, casually and thoughtlessly, but to her a magnificent and terrifying wonder.

For days she carried Weinstein's paper, marked A, around with her; he did not come to class. One day she checked with the graduate office and was told that Weinstein had called in to say his father was ill and he would not be able to attend classes for a while. "He's strange, I remember him," the secretary said. "He missed all his exams last spring and made a lot of trouble. He was in and out of here every day."

So there was no more of Weinstein for a while, and Sister Irene stopped expecting him to hurry into class. Then, one morning, she found a letter from him in her mailbox.

He had printed it in black ink, very carefully, as if he had not trusted handwriting. The return address was in bold letters that, like his voice, tried to grab onto her: Birchcrest Manor. Somewhere north of the city. "Dear Sister Irene," the block letters said, "I am doing well here and have time for reading and relaxing. The Manor is delightful. My doctor here is an excellent, intelligent man who has time for me, unlike my former doctor. If you have time, you might drop in on my father, who worries about me too much, I think, and explain to him what my condition is. He doesn't seem to understand. I feel about this new life the way that boy, what's his name, in *Measure for Measure*, feels about the prospects of a different life; you remember what he says to his sister when she visits him in prison, how he is looking forward to an escape into another world. Perhaps you could *explain* this to my father and he would stop worrying." The letter ended with the father's name and address, in letters that were just a little too big. Sister Irene, walking slowly down the corridor as she read the letter, felt her eyes cloud over with tears. She was cold with fear, it was something she had never experienced before. She knew what Weinstein was trying to tell her, and the desperation of his attempt made it all the more pathetic; he did not deserve this, why did God allow him to suffer so?

She read through Claudio's speech to his sister, in *Measure for Measure*:

Ay, but to die, and go we know not where;
To lie in cold obstruction and to rot;
This sensible warm motion to become
A kneaded clod; and the delighted spirit
To bathe in fiery floods, or to reside
In thrilling region of thick-ribbèd ice,
To be imprison'd in the viewless winds
And blown with restless violence round about
The pendent world; or to be worse than worst
Of those that lawless and incertain thought
Imagines howling! 'Tis too horrible!
The weariest and most loathèd worldly life
That age, ache, penury, and imprisonment
Can lay on nature is a paradise
To what we fear of death.

Sister Irene called the father's number that day. "Allen Weinstein residence, who may I say is calling?" a woman said, bored. "May I speak to Mr. Weinstein? It's urgent—about his son," Sister Irene said. There was a pause at the other end. "You want to talk to his mother, maybe?" the woman said. "His mother? Yes, his mother, then. Please. It's very important."

She talked with this strange, unsuspected woman, a disembodied voice that suggested absolutely no face, and insisted upon going over that afternoon. The woman was nervous, but Sister Irene, who was a university professor after all, knew enough to hide her own nervousness. She kept waiting for the woman to say, "Yes, Allen has mentioned you . . ." but nothing happened.

She persuaded Sister Carlotta to ride over with her. This urgency of hers was something they were all amazed by. They hadn't suspected that the set of her gray eyes could change to this blurred, distracted alarm, this sense of mission that seemed to have come to her from nowhere. Sister Irene drove across the city in the late afternoon traffic, with the high whining noises from residential streets where trees were being sawed down in pieces. She understood now the secret, sweet wildness that Christ must have felt, giving himself for man, dying for the billions of men who would never know of him and never understand the sacrifice. For the first time she approached the realization of that great act. In her troubled mind the city traffic was jumbled and yet oddly coherent, an image of the world that was always out of joint with what was happening in it, its inner history struggling with its external spectacle. This sacrifice of Christ's, so mysterious and legendary now, almost lost in time—it was that by which Christ transcended both God and man at one moment, more than man because of his fate to do what no other man could do, and more than God because no god could suffer as he did. She felt a flicker of something close to madness.

She drove nervously, uncertainly, afraid of missing the street and afraid of finding it too, for while one part of her rushed forward to confront these people who had betrayed their son, another part of her would have liked nothing so much as to be waiting as usual for the summons to dinner, safe in her room . . . When she found the street and turned onto it, she was in a state of breathless excitement. Here, lawns were bright green and marred with only a few leaves, magically clean, and the houses were enormous and pompous, a mixture of styles: ranch houses, colonial houses, French country houses, white-bricked wonders with curving glass and clumps of birch trees somehow encircled by white concrete. Sister Irene stared as if she had blundered into another world. This was a kind of heaven, and she was too shabby for it.

The Weinsteins' house was the strangest one of all: it looked like a small Alpine lodge, with an inverted-V-shaped front entrance. Sister Irene drove up the black-topped driveway and let the car slow to a stop; she told Sister Carlotta she would not be long.

At the door she was met by Weinstein's mother, a small nervous woman with hands like her son's. "Come in, come in," the woman said. She had once been beautiful, that was clear, but now in missing beauty she was not handsome or even attractive but looked ruined and perplexed, the misshapen swelling of her white-blond professionally set hair like a cap lifting up from her surprised face. "He'll be right in. Allen?" she called, "Our visitor is here." They went into the living room. There was a grand piano at one end and an organ at the other. In between were scatterings of brilliant modern furniture, in conversational groups, and several puffed-up white rugs on the polished floor. Sister Irene could not stop shivering. "Professor, it's so strange, but let me say when the phone rang I had a feeling—I had a feeling," the woman said, with damp eyes. Sister Irene sat, and the woman hovered about her. "Should I call you Professor? We don't—you know—we don't understand the technicalities that go with— Allen, my son, wanted to go here to the Catholic school; I told my husband why not? Why fight? It's the thing these days, they do anything they want for knowledge. And he had to come home, you know. He couldn't take care of himself in New York, that was the beginning of the trouble— Should I call you Professor?"

"You can call me Sister Irene."

"Sister Irene?" the woman said, touching her throat in awe, as if something intimate and unexpected had happened.

Then Weinstein's father appeared, hurrying. He took long impatient strides. Sister Irene stared at him and in that instant doubted everything— he was in his fifties, a tall, sharply handsome man, heavy but not fat, holding his shoulders back with what looked like an effort, but holding them back just the same. He wore a dark suit, and his face was flushed, as if he had run a long distance.

"Now," he said, coming to Sister Irene and with a precise wave of his hand motioning his wife off, "now let's straighten this out. A lot of confusion over that kid, eh?" He pulled a chair over, scraping it across a rug and pulling one corner over, so that its brown underside was exposed. "I came home early just for this, Libby phoned me. Sister, you got a letter from him, right?"

The wife looked at Sister Irene over her husband's shoulder as if trying somehow to coach her, knowing that this man was so loud and impatient that no one could remember anything in his presence.

"A letter—yes—today—"

"He says what in it? You got the letter, eh? Can I see it?"

She gave it to him and wanted to explain, but he silenced her with a flick of his hand. He read through the letter so quickly that Sister Irene thought perhaps he was trying to impress her with his skill at reading. "So?" he said, raising his eyes, smiling, "so what is this? He's happy out there, he says. He doesn't communicate with us anymore, but he writes to you and says he's happy—what's that? I mean, what the hell is that?"

"But he isn't happy. He wants to come home," Sister Irene said. It was so important that she make him understand that she could not trust her voice; goaded by this man, it might suddenly turn shrill, as his son's did. "Someone must read the letters before they're mailed, so he tried to tell me something by making an allusion to—"

"What?"

85

"—an allusion to a play, so that I would know. He might be thinking of suicide, he must be very unhappy—"

She ran out of breath. Weinstein's mother had begun to cry, but the father was shaking his head jerkily back and forth. "Forgive me, Sister, but it's a lot of crap, he needs the hospital, he needs help—right? It costs me fifty a day out there, and they've got the best place in the state, I figure it's worth it. He needs help, that kid, what do I care if he's unhappy? He's unbalanced!" he said angrily. "You want us to get him out again? We argued with the judge for two hours to get him in, an acquaintance of mine. Look, he can't control himself—he was smashing things here, he was hysterical, his room is like an animal was in it. You ever seen anybody hysterical? They need help, lady, and you do something about it fast! You do something! We made up our minds to do something and we did it! This letter— what the hell is this letter? He never talked like that to us!"

"But he means the opposite of what he says—"

"Then he *is* crazy! I'm the first to admit it." He was perspiring, and his face had darkened. "I've got no pride left, this late. He's a little bastard, you want to know? He calls me names, he's filthy, got a filthy mouth—that's being smart, huh? They give him a big scholarship for his filthy mouth? I went to college too, and I got out and knew something, and I for Christ's sake did something with it; my wife is an intelligent woman, a learned woman, would you guess she does book reviews for the little newspaper out here? Intelligent isn't crazy—crazy isn't intelligent—maybe for you at the school he writes nice papers and gets an A, but out here, around the house, he can't control himself, and we got him committed!"

"But—"

"We're fixing him up, don't worry about it!" He turned to his wife. "Libby, get out of here, I mean it. I'm sorry, but get out of here, you're making a fool of yourself, go stand in the kitchen or something, you and the goddamn maid can cry on each other's shoulders. That one in the kitchen is nuts too, they're all nuts. Sister," he said, his voice lowering, "I thank you immensely for coming out here. This is wonderful, your interest in my son. And I see he admires you—that letter there. But what about that letter? If he did want to get out, which I don't admit—he was willing to be committed, in the end he said OK himself—if he wanted out I wouldn't do it. Why? So what if he wants to come back? The next day he wants something else, what then? He's a sick kid, and I'm the first to admit it."

Sister Irene felt that sickness spread to her. She stood. The room was so big that it seemed it must be a public place; there had been nothing personal or private about their conversation. Weinstein's mother was standing by the fireplace, sobbing. The father jumped to his feet and wiped his forehead in a gesture that was meant to help Sister Irene on her way out. "God, what a day," he said, his eyes snatching at hers for understanding, "you know—one of those days all day long? Sister, I thank you a lot. A professor interested in him—he's a smart kid, eh? Yes, I thank you a lot. There should be more people in the world that care about others, like you. I mean that."

On the way back to the convent, the man's words returned to her, and she could not get control of them; she could not even feel anger. She had been pressed down, forced back, what could she do? Weinstein might have been watching her somehow from a barred window, and he surely would have understood. The strange idea she had had on the way over, something about understanding Christ, came back to her now and sickened her. But the sickness was small. It could be contained.

ABOUT A MONTH AFTER HER VISIT TO HIS FATHER, WEINSTEIN HIMSELF showed up. He was dressed in a suit as before, even the necktie was the same. He came right into her office as if he had been pushed and could not stop.

"Sister," he said, and shook her hand. He must have seen fear in her because he smiled ironically. "Look, I'm released. I'm let out of the nut house. Can I sit down?"

He sat. Sister Irene was breathing quickly, as if in the presence of an enemy who does not know that he is an enemy.

"So, they finally let me out. I heard what you did. You talked with him, that was all I wanted. You're the only one who gave a damn. Because you're a humanist and a religious person, you respect . . . the individual. Listen," he said, whispering, "it was hell out there! Hell! Birchcrest Manor! All fixed up with fancy chairs and *Life* magazines lying around—and what do they do to you? They locked me up, they gave me shock treatments! Shock treatments, how do you like that, it's discredited by everybody now—they're crazy out there themselves, sadists—they locked me up, they gave me hypodermic shots, they didn't treat me like a human being! Do you know what that is," Weinstein demanded savagely, "not to be treated like a human being? They made me an animal—for fifty dollars a day! Dirty filthy swine! Now I'm an outpatient because I stopped swearing at them. I found somebody's bobby pin, and when I wanted to scream I pressed it under my fingernail, and it stopped me—the screaming went inside and not out—so they gave me good reports, those sick bastards, now I'm an outpatient and I can walk along the street and breathe in the same filthy exhaust from the buses like all you normal people! Christ," he said, and threw himself back against the chair.

Sister Irene stared at him. She wanted to take his hand, to make some gesture that would close the aching distance between them. "Mr. Weinstein—"

"Call me Allen!" he said sharply.

"I'm very sorry—I'm terribly sorry—"

"My own parents committed me, but of course they didn't know what it was like. It was hell," he said, thickly, "and there isn't any hell except what other people do to you. The psychiatrist out there, the main shrink, he hates Jews, too, some of us were positive of that, and he's got a bigger nose than I do, a real beak." He made a noise of disgust. "A dirty bastard, a sick, dirty, pathetic bastard—all of them— Anyway, I'm getting out of here, and I came to ask you a favor."

"What do you mean?"

"I'm getting out. I'm leaving. I'm going up to Canada and lose myself, I'll get a job, I'll forget everything, I'll kill myself maybe—what's the difference? Look, can you lend me some money?"

"Money?"

"Just a little! I have to get to the border, I'm going to take a bus."

"But I don't have any money—"

"No money?" He stared at her. "You mean—you don't have any? Sure you have some!"

She stared at him as if he had asked her to do something obscene. Everything was splotched and uncertain before her eyes. "You must . . . you must go back," she said, "you're making a—"

"I'll pay it back. Look, I'll pay it back, can you go to where you live or something and get it? I'm in a hurry. My friends are sons of bitches: one of them pretended he didn't see me yesterday—I stood right in the middle of the sidewalk and yelled at him, I called him some appropriate names! So he didn't see me, huh? You're the only one who understands me, you understand me like a poet, you—"

"I can't help you, I'm sorry—I—"

He looked to one side of her and then flashed his gaze back, as if he could not control it. He seemed to be trying to clear his vision. "You have the soul of a poet," he whispered, "you're the only one. Everybody else is rotten! Can't you lend me some money, ten dollars maybe? I have three thousand in the bank, and I can't touch it! They take everything away from me, they make me into an animal . . . You know I'm not an animal, don't you? Don't you?"

"Of course," Sister Irene whispered.

"You could get money. Help me. Give me your hand or something, touch me, help me—please—" He reached for her hand and she drew back. He stared at her and his face seemed about to crumble, like a child's. "I want something from you, but I don't know what—I want something!" he cried. "Something real! I want you to look at me like I was a human being, is that too much to ask? I have a brain, I'm alive, I'm suffering—what does that mean? Does that mean nothing? I want something real and not this phony Christian love garbage—it's all in the books, it isn't personal—I want something real—look—"

He tried to take her hand again, and this time she jerked away. She got to her feet. "Mr. Weinstein," she said, "please—"

"You! You—nun," he said scornfully, his mouth twisted into a mock grin. "You nun! There's nothing under that ugly outfit, right? And you're not particularly smart even though you think you are; my father has more brains in his foot than you—"

He got to his feet and kicked the chair.

"You bitch!" he cried.

She shrank back against her desk as if she thought he might hit her, but he only ran out of the office.

WEINSTEIN: THE NAME WAS TO BECOME DISEMBODIED FROM THE FIGURE, as time went on. The semester passed, the autumn drizzle turned into snow, Sister Irene rode to school in the morning and left in the afternoon, four days a week, anonymous in her black winter cloak, quiet and stunned. University teaching was an anonymous task, each day dissociated from the rest, with no necessary sense of unity among the teachers: they came and went separately and might for a year just miss a colleague who left his office five minutes before they arrived, and it did not matter.

She heard of Weinstein's death, his suicide by drowning, from the English department secretary, a handsome white-haired woman who kept a transistor radio on her desk. Sister Irene was not surprised; she had been thinking of him as dead for months. "They identified him by some special television way they have now," the secretary said. "They're shipping the body back. It was up in Quebec . . ."

Sister Irene could feel a part of herself drifting off, lured by the plains of white snow to the north, the quiet, the emptiness, the sweep of the Great Lakes up to the silence of Canada. But she called that part of herself back. She could only be one person in her lifetime. That was the ugly truth, she thought, that she could not really regret Weinstein's suffering and death; she had only one life and had already given it to someone else. He had come too late to her. Fifteen years ago, perhaps, but not now.

She was only one person, she thought, walking down the corridor in a dream. Was she safe in this single person, or was she trapped? She had only one identity. She could make only one choice. What she had done or hadn't done was the result of that choice, and how was she guilty? If she could have felt guilt, she thought, she might at least have been able to feel something.

August 1966

Lost in the Funhouse

FOR WHOM IS THE FUNHOUSE FUN? PERHAPS FOR LOVERS. FOR AMBROSE IT is *a place of fear and confusion.* He has come to the seashore with his family for the holiday, *the occasion of their visit is Independence Day, the most important secular holiday of the United States of America.* A single straight underline is the manuscript mark for italic type, *which in turn* is the printed equivalent to oral emphasis of words and phrases as well as the customary type for titles of complete works, not to mention. Italics are also employed, in fiction-stories especially, for "outside," intrusive, or artificial voices, such as radio announcements, the texts of telegrams and newspaper articles, *et cetera.* They should be used *sparingly.* If passages originally in roman type are italicized by someone repeating them, it's customary to acknowledge the fact. *Italics mine.*

Ambrose was "at that awkward age." His voice came out high-pitched as a child's if he let himself get carried away; to be on the safe side, therefore, he moved and spoke with *deliberate calm* and *adult gravity.* Talking soberly of unimportant or irrelevant matters and listening consciously to the sound of your own voice are useful habits for maintaining control in this difficult interval. *En route* to Ocean City he sat in the back seat of the family car with his brother, Peter, age fifteen, and Magda G____, age fourteen, a pretty girl an exquisite young lady, who lived not far from them on

JOHN BARTH

B____ Street in the town of D____, Maryland. Initials, blanks, or both were often substituted for proper names in nineteenth-century fiction to enhance the illusion of reality. It is as if the author felt it necessary to delete the names for reasons of tact or legal liability. Interestingly, as with other aspects of realism, it is an *illusion* that is being enhanced, by purely artificial means. Is it likely, does it violate the principle of verisimilitude, that a thirteen-year-old boy could make such a sophisticated observation? A girl of fourteen is *the psychological coeval* of a boy of fifteen or sixteen; a thirteen-year-old boy, therefore, even one precocious in some other respects, might be three years *her emotional junior.*

Thrice a year—on Memorial, Independence, and Labor Days—the family visits Ocean City for the afternoon and evening. When Ambrose and Peter's father was their age the excursion was made by train, as mentioned in the novel *The 42nd Parallel* by John Dos Passos. Many families from the same neighborhood used to travel together, with dependent relatives and often with Negro servants; schoolfuls of children swarmed through the railway cars; everyone shared everyone else's Maryland fried chicken, Virginia ham, deviled eggs, potato salad, beaten biscuits, iced tea. Nowadays (that is, in 19—, the year of our story) the journey is made by automobile— more comfortably and quickly though without the extra fun though without the *camaraderie* of a general excursion. It's all part of the deterioration of American life, their father declares; Uncle Karl supposes that when the boys take *their* families to Ocean City for the holidays, they'll fly in Autogiros. Their mother, sitting in the middle of the front seat like Magda in the second, only with her arms on the seat-back behind the men's shoulders, wouldn't want the good old days back again, the steaming trains and stuffy long dresses; on the other hand, she can do without Autogiros, too, if she has to become a grandmother to fly in them.

Description of physical appearance and mannerisms is one of several standard methods of characterization used by writers of fiction. It is also important to "keep the senses operating"; when a detail from one of the five senses, say visual, is "crossed" with a detail from another, say auditory, the reader's imagination is oriented to the scene, perhaps unconsciously. This procedure may be compared to the way surveyors and navigators determine their positions by two or more compass-bearings, a process known as triangulation. The brown hair on Ambrose's mother's forearms gleamed in the sun like. Though right-handed, she took her left arm from the seat-back to press the dashboard cigar-lighter for Uncle Karl. When the glass bead in its handle glowed red, the lighter was ready for use. The smell of Uncle Karl's cigar-smoke reminded one of. The fragrance of the ocean came strong to the picnic-ground where they always stopped for lunch, two miles inland from Ocean City. Having to pause for a full hour almost within sound of the breakers was difficult for Peter and Ambrose when they were younger; even at their present age it was not easy to keep their anticipation, *stimulated by the briny spume*, from turning into short temper. The Irish author James Joyce, in his unusual novel entitled *Ulysses*, now available in this country, uses the adjectives *snot-green* and *scrotum-tightening* to describe the sea. Visual, auditory, tactile, olfactory, gustatory. Peter and Ambrose's father, while steering their black 1936 LaSalle sedan with one hand, could with the other remove the first cigarette from a white pack of Lucky Strikes and, more remarkably, light it with a match forefingered from its book and thumbed against the flint-paper without being detached. The matchbook cover merely advertised U.S. War Bonds and Stamps. A fine metaphor, simile, or other figure of speech, in addition to its obvious "first-order" relevance to the thing it describes, will be seen upon reflection to have a second order of significance: it may be drawn from the *milieu* of the action, for example, or be particularly appropriate to the sensibility of the narrator, even hinting to the reader things of which the narrator is unaware; or it may cast further and subtler lights upon the thing it describes, sometimes ironically qualifying the more evident sense of comparison.

To say that Ambrose and Peter's mother was *pretty* is to accomplish nothing; the reader may acknowledge the proposition, but his imagination is not engaged. Besides, Magda was also pretty, yet in an altogether different way. Although she lived on B____ Street, she had very good manners and did better than average in school. Her figure was very well developed for her age. Her right hand lay casually on the plush upholstery of the seat, very near Ambrose's left leg, on which his own hand rested. The space between their legs, between her right and his left leg, was out of the line of sight of anyone sitting on the other side of Magda, as well as anyone glancing into the rear-view mirror. Uncle Karl's face resembled Peter's—rather, vice versa. Both had dark hair and eyes, short husky statures, deep voices. Magda's left hand was probably in a similar position on her left side. The boy's father is difficult to describe; no particular feature of his appearance or manner stood out. He wore glasses and taught English in the T____ County High School. Uncle Karl was a masonry contractor.

Although Peter must have known as well as Ambrose that the latter, because of his position in the car, would be the first to see the electrical towers of the power plant at V____, the halfway point of their trip, he leaned forward and slightly toward the center of the car and pretended to be looking for them through the flat pinewoods and tuckahoe creeks along the highway. For as long as the boys could remember, "looking for the Towers" had been a feature of the first half of their excursions to Ocean City, "looking for the standpipe" of the second. Though the game was childish, their mother preserved the tradition of rewarding the first to see the Towers with a candy-bar or piece of fruit. She insisted now that Magda play the game; the prize, she said, was "something hard to get nowadays." Ambrose decided not to join in; he sat far back in his seat. Magda, like Peter, leaned forward. Two sets of straps were discernible through the shoulders of her sun-dress; the inside right one, a brassiere-strap, was fastened or shortened with a small safety-pin. The right armpit of her dress, presumably the left as well, was damp with perspiration. The simple strategy for being first to espy the Towers, which Ambrose had understood by the age of four, was to sit on the right-hand side of the car. Whoever sat there, however, had also to put up with the worst of the sun, and so Ambrose, without mentioning the matter, chose sometimes the one and sometimes the other. Not impossibly, Peter had never caught on to the trick, or thought that his brother hadn't, simply because Ambrose on occasion preferred shade to a Baby Ruth or tangerine.

The shade-sun situation didn't apply to the front seat, owing to the windshield; if anything the driver got more sun, since the person on the passenger side not only was shaded below by the door and dashboard but might swing down his sun visor all the way too.

"Is that them?" Magda asked. Ambrose's mother teased the boys for letting Magda win, insinuating that "somebody [had] a girlfriend." Peter and Ambrose's father reached a long thin arm across their mother to butt his cigarette in the dashboard ashtray, under the lighter. The prize this time for seeing the Towers first was a banana. Their mother bestowed it after chiding their father for wasting a half-smoked cigarette when everything was so scarce. Magda, to take the prize, moved her hand from so near Ambrose's that he could have touched it as though accidentally. She offered to share the prize, things like that were so hard to find; but everyone insisted it was hers alone. Ambrose's mother sang an iambic trimeter couplet from a popular song, femininely rhymed:

> *What's good is in the Army;*
> *What's left will never harm me.* [1]

Uncle Karl tapped his cigar-ash out the ventilator window; some particles were sucked by the slipstream back into the car through the rear

[1] Copyright 1943 by M. Witmark & Sons. Used by permission.

window on the passenger side. Magda demonstrated her ability to hold a banana in one hand and peel it with her teeth. She still sat forward; Ambrose pushed his glasses back onto the bridge of his nose with his left hand, which he then negligently let fall to the seat-cushion immediately behind her. He even permitted the single hair, gold, on the second joint of his thumb to brush the fabric of her skirt. Should she have sat back at that instant, his hand would have been caught under her.

PLUSH UPHOLSTERY PRICKLES UNCOMFORTABLY THROUGH GABARDINE slacks in the July sun. The function of the *beginning* of a story is to introduce the principal characters, establish their initial relationships, set the scene for the main action, expose the background of the situation if necessary, plant motifs and foreshadowings where appropriate, and initiate the first complication or whatever of the "rising action." Actually, if one imagines a story called "The Funhouse," or "Lost in the Funhouse," the details of the drive to Ocean City don't seem especially relevant. The *beginning* should recount the events between Ambrose's first sight of the funhouse early in the afternoon and his entering it with Magda and Peter in the evening. The *middle* would narrate all relevant events from the time he goes in to the time he loses his way; middles have the double and contradictory function of delaying the climax while at the same time preparing the reader for it and fetching him to it. Then the *ending* would tell what Ambrose does while he's lost, how he finally finds his way out, and what everybody makes of the experience. So far there's been no real dialogue, very little sensory detail, and nothing in the way of a *theme*. And a long time has gone by already without anything happening; it makes a person wonder. We haven't even reached Ocean City yet: we will never get out of the funhouse.

The more closely an author identifies with the narrator, literally or metaphorically, the less advisable it is as a rule to use the first-person narrative viewpoint. Once five years previously the three young people *aforementioned* played Niggers and Masters in the backyard; when it was Ambrose's turn to be Master and theirs to be Niggers, Peter had to go serve his evening papers; Ambrose was afraid to punish Magda alone, but she led him to the whitewashed Torture Chamber between the woodshed and the privy in the Slaves Quarters; there she knelt sweating among the bamboo rakes and dusty mason jars, pleadingly embraced his knees, and while bumblebees droned in the lattice as if on an ordinary summer afternoon, purchased clemency at a surprising price set by herself. Doubtless she remembered nothing of this event; Ambrose on the other hand seemed unable to forget the least detail of his life. He even recalled how, standing beside himself with awed impersonality in the reeky heat, he'd stared the while at an empty cigar-box in which Uncle Karl kept stone-cutting chisels; beneath the words *El Producto*, a laureled, loose-toga'd lady regarded the sea from a marble bench; beside her, forgotten or not yet turned to, was a five-stringed lute. Her chin reposed on the back of her right hand; her left depended negligently from the bench-arm. The lower half of scene and lady was peeled away; the words EXAMINED BY ____ were inked there into the wood. Nowadays cigar-boxes are made of pasteboard. Ambrose wondered what Magda would have done. Ambrose wondered what Magda would do when she sat back on his hand as he resolved she should. Be angry. Make a teasing joke of it. Give no sign at all. For a long time she leaned forward, playing cow-poker with Peter against Uncle Karl and Mother and watching for the first sign of Ocean City. At nearly the same instant picnic-ground and Ocean-City-standpipe hove into view; an Amoco filling station on their side of the road cost Mother and Uncle Karl fifty cows and the game; Magda bounced back, clapping her right hand on Mother's right arm; Ambrose moved clear "in the nick of time."

At this rate our hero, at this rate our protagonist will remain in the funhouse forever. Narrative ordinarily consists of alternating dramatization and summarization. One symptom of nervous tension, paradoxically, is repeated and violent yawning; neither Peter nor Magda nor Uncle Karl nor Mother reacted in this manner. Although they were no longer small children, Peter and Ambrose were each given a dollar to spend on boardwalk amusements in addition to what money of their own they'd brought along. Magda too, though she protested she had ample spending money. The boys' mother made a little scene out of distributing the bills; she pretended that her sons and Magda were small children and cautioned them not to spend the sum too quickly or in one place. Magda promised with a merry laugh, and having both hands free, took the bill with her left. Peter laughed also and pledged in a falsetto to be a good boy. His imitation of a child was not clever. The boys' father was tall and thin, balding, fair-complexioned. Assertions of that sort are not effective; the reader may acknowledge the proposition, but. We should be much farther along than we are; something has gone wrong; not much of this preliminary rambling seems relevant. Yet everyone begins in the same place; how is it that most go along without difficulty but a few lose their way?

"Stay out from under the boardwalk," Uncle Karl growled from the side of his mouth. The boys' mother pushed his shoulder *in mock annoyance.* They were all standing before Fat May the Laughing Lady, who advertised the funhouse. Larger than life, Fat May mechanically shook, rocked on her heels, slapped her thighs while recorded laughter—uproarious, female—came amplified from a hidden loudspeaker. It chuckled, wheezed, wept; tried in vain to catch its breath; tittered, groaned, exploded raucous and anew. You couldn't hear it without laughing yourself, no matter how you felt. Father came back from talking to a Coast-Guardsman on duty and reported that the surf was spoiled with crude oil from tankers recently torpedoed offshore. Lumps of it, difficult to remove, made tarry tidelines on the beach and stuck on swimmers. Many bathed in the surf nevertheless and came out speckled; others paid to use a municipal pool and only sun-bathed on the beach. We would do the latter. We would do the latter. We would do the latter.

Under the boardwalk, cold sand littered with cigar-butts, treasured with cigarette-stubs, Coca-Cola caps, cardboard lollipop sticks, matchbook-covers warning that A Slip of the Lip Can Sink a Ship, grainy other things. What is the story's point? Ambrose is ill. He perspires in the dark passages; candied apples-on-a-stick, delicious-looking, disappointing to eat. Fun-houses need men's and ladies' rooms at intervals.

Magda's teeth. She *was* left-handed. Perspiration. They've gone all the way, through, Magda and Peter, they've been waiting for hours with Mother and Uncle Karl while Father searches for his lost son; they draw french-fried potatoes from a paper cup and shake their heads. They've named the children they'll one day have and bring to Ocean City on holidays. Can spermatozoa properly be thought of as male animalcules when there are no female spermatozoa? They grope through hot dark windings, past Love's Tunnel's fearsome obstacles. Some perhaps lose their way.

PETER SUGGESTED THEN AND THERE THAT THEY DO THE FUNHOUSE; HE had been through it before, so had Magda, Ambrose hadn't and suggested, his voice cracking on account of Fat May's laughter, that they swim first. All were chuckling, couldn't help it; Ambrose's father, Ambrose and Peter's father came up grinning like a lunatic with two boxes of syrup-coated popcorn, one for Mother, one for Magda; the men were to help themselves. Ambrose walked on Magda's right; being by nature left-handed, she carried the box in her left hand. Up front the situation was reversed.

"What are you limping for?" Magda inquired of Ambrose. He supposed in a husky tone that his foot had gone to sleep in the car. Her teeth flashed. "Pins and needles?" It was the honeysuckle on the lattice of the former privy that drew the bees. Imagine being stung there. How long is this going to take?

The adults decided to forgo the pool, but Uncle Karl insisted they change into swimsuits and do the beach. "He wants to watch the pretty girls," Peter teased, and ducked behind Magda from Uncle Karl's pretended wrath. "You've got all the pretty girls you need right here," Magda declared, and Mother said: "Now that's the gospel truth." Magda scolded Peter, who reached over her shoulder to sneak some popcorn. "Your brother and father aren't getting any." Uncle Karl wondered if they were going to have fireworks that night, with the shortages. It wasn't the shortages, Mr. M_____ replied; Ocean City had fireworks from pre-war. But it was too risky on account of the enemy submarines, some people thought.

"Don't seem like Fourth of July without fireworks," said Uncle Karl. The inverted tag in dialogue-writing is still considered permissible with proper names or epithets, but sounds old-fashioned with personal pronouns. "We'll have 'em again soon enough," predicted the boys' father. Their mother declared she could do without fireworks: they reminded her too much of the real thing. Their father said all the more reason to shoot off a few now and again. Uncle Karl asked *rhetorically* who needed reminding, just look at people's hair and skin.

"The oil, yes," said Mrs. M_____.

Ambrose had a pain in his stomach and so didn't swim but enjoyed watching the others. He and his father burned red easily. Magda's figure was exceedingly well developed for her age. She too declined to swim, and got mad, and became angry when Peter attempted to drag her into the pool. She always swam, he insisted; what did she mean not swim? Why did a person come to Ocean City?

"Maybe I want to lay here with Ambrose," Magda teased.

Nobody likes a pedant.

"Aha," said Mother. Peter grabbed Magda by one ankle and ordered Ambrose to grab the other. She squealed and rolled over on the beach blanket. Ambrose pretended to help hold her back. Her tan was darker than even Mother's and Peter's. "Help out, Uncle Karl!" Peter cried. Uncle Karl went to seize the other ankle. Inside the top of her swimsuit, however, you could see the line where the swimsuit ended and, when she hunched her shoulders and squealed again, one nipple's auburn edge. Mother made them behave themselves. "*You* should certainly know," she said to Uncle Karl. Archly. "that when a lady says she doesn't feel like swimming, a gentleman doesn't ask questions." Uncle Karl said excuse *him*; Mother winked at Magda; Ambrose blushed; stupid Peter kept saying "Phooey on *feel like!*" and tugging at Magda's ankle; then even he got the point, and cannonballed with a holler into the pool.

"I swear," Magda said, in mock *in feigned* exasperation.

The diving would make a suitable literary symbol. To go off the high board you had to wait in a line along the poolside and up the ladder. Fellows tickled girls and goosed one another and shouted to the ones at the top to hurry up, or razzed them for bellyfloppers. Once on the springboard some took a great while posing or clowning or deciding on a dive or getting up their nerve; others ran right off. Especially among the younger fellows the idea was to strike the funniest pose or do the craziest stunt as you fell, a thing that got harder to do as you kept on and kept on. But whether you hollered *Geronimo!* or *Sig heil!*, held your nose or "rode a bicycle," pretended to be shot or did a perfect jackknife or changed your mind halfway down and ended up with nothing, it was over in two seconds, after all that wait. Spring, pose, splash. Spring, neat-o, splash. Spring, aw shit, splash.

The grown-ups had gone on; Ambrose wanted to converse with Magda; she was remarkably well developed for her age; it was said that that came from rubbing with a Turkish towel, and there were other theories. Ambrose could think of nothing to say except how good a diver Peter was, who was showing off for her benefit. You could pretty well tell by looking at their bathing-suits and arm-muscles how far along the different fellows were. Ambrose was glad he hadn't gone in swimming, the cold water shrank you up so. Magda pretended not to be interested in the diving; she probably weighed as much as he did. If you knew your way around in the funhouse like your own bedroom you could wait until a girl came along and then slip away without ever getting caught, even if her boyfriend was right with her. She'd think *he* did it! It would be better to be the boyfriend, and act outraged, and tear the funhouse apart. Not act; *be*.

"He's a master diver," Ambrose said. In feigned admiration. "You really have to slave away at it to get that good." What would it matter anyhow if he asked her right out whether she remembered, even teased her with it as Peter would have?

THERE'S NO POINT IN GOING FARTHER; THIS ISN'T GETTING ANYBODY ANYwhere; they haven't even come to the funhouse yet. Ambrose is off the track, in some new or old part of the place that's not supposed to be used; he strayed into it by some one-in-a-million chance, like the time the rollercoaster-car left the tracks in the nineteen-teens against all the laws of physics and sailed over the boardwalk in the dark. And they can't locate him because they don't know where to look. Even the designer and operator has forgotten this other part, that winds around on itself like a whelk-shell. That winds around the right part like the snakes on Mercury's caduceus. Some people, perhaps, don't "hit their stride" until their twenties, when the growing-up business is over and women appreciate other things besides wisecracks and teasing and strutting. Peter didn't have one-tenth the imagination *he* had, not one-tenth. Peter did this naming-their-children thing as a joke, making up names like Aloysius and Murgatroyd, but Ambrose knew *exactly* how it would feel to be married and have children of your own, and be a loving husband and father, and go comfortably to work in the mornings and to bed with your wife at night, and wake up with her there. With a breeze coming through the sash and birds and mockingbirds singing in the chinese-cigar trees. His eyes watered, there aren't enough ways to say that. He would be quite famous in his line of work. Whether Magda was his wife or not, one evening when he was wise-lined and gray at the temples, he'd smile gravely, at a fashionable dinner-party, and remind her of his youthful passion. The time they went with his family to Ocean City; the *erotic fantasies* he used to have about her. How long ago it seemed, and childish! Yet tender, too, *n'est-ce pas?* Would she have imagined that the world-renowned whatever remembered how many strings were on the lute on the bench beside the girl on the label of the cigar-box he'd stared at in the toolshed at age eight while she, age nine. Even then he had felt *wise beyond his years;* he'd stroked her hair and said in his deepest voice and correctest English, as to a dear child: "I shall never forget this moment."

But though he had breathed heavily, groaned as if ecstatic, what he'd really felt throughout was an odd detachment, as though someone else were Master. Strive as he might to be transported, he heard his mind take notes upon the scene: *This is what they call* passion. *I am experiencing it.* Many of the digger-machines were out of order in the penny arcades and could not be repaired or replaced for the duration. Moreover, the prizes, made now in USA, were less interesting than formerly, paste-board items for the most part, and some of the machines wouldn't work on white pennies. The gypsy-fortuneteller machine might have provided foreshadowing of the climax of this story if Ambrose had operated it. It was even delapidateder than most: the silver coating was worn off the brown metal handles, the glass windows around the dummy were cracked and taped, her kerchiefs and silks long faded. If a man lived by himself he could take a department-store mannequin with flexible joints and modify her in certain ways. *However:* by the time he was that old he'd have a real woman. There was a machine that stamped your name around a white-metal coin with a star in the middle: A_____. His son would be the Third, and when the lad reached thirteen or so he would put a strong arm around his shoulder and tell him calmly: "It is perfectly normal. We have all been through it. It will not last forever." Nobody knew how to be what they were right. He'd smoke a pipe, teach his son how to fish and softcrab, assure him he needn't worry about himself. Magda would certainly give, Magda would certainly yield a great deal of milk, although guilty of occasional solecisms. It don't taste so bad. Suppose the lights came on now!

The day wore on. You think you're yourself, but there are other persons in you. Ambrose gets an erection when Ambrose doesn't want one, *and obversely.* Ambrose watches them disagreeing; Ambrose watches him watch. In the funhouse mirror-room you can't see yourself go on forever, because no matter how you stand your head gets in the way. Even if you had a glass periscope, the image of your eye would cover up the thing you really wanted to see. The police will come; there'll be a story in the papers. That must be where it happened. Unless he can find a surprise exit, an unofficial backdoor or escape-hatch opening on an alley, say, and then stroll up to the family in front of the funhouse and ask where everybody's been; *he's* been out of the place for ages. That's just where it happened, in that last lighted room: Peter and Magda found the right exit; he found one you weren't supposed to find and strayed off into the works somewhere. In a perfect funhouse you'd be able to go only one way, like the divers off the high board; getting lost would be impossible; the doors and halls would work like minnow-traps or the valves in veins.

On account of the German U-boats Ocean City was "browned out": streetlights were shaded on the seaward side; shopwindows and boardwalk amusement-places were kept dim, not to silhouette tankers and Liberty-ships for torpedoing. In a short-story about Ocean City, Maryland, during World War II the author could make use of the image of sailors on leave in the penny arcades and shooting-galleries, sighting through the cross hairs of toy machine-guns at swastika'd subs, while out in the black Atlantic a U-boat skipper squints through his periscope at real ships outlined by the glow of penny arcades. After dinner the family strolled back to the amusement end of the boardwalk. The boys' father had burnt red as always and was masked with Noxzema, a minstrel in reverse. The grown-ups stood at the end of the boardwalk where the Hurricane of '33 had cut an inlet from the ocean to Assawoman Bay.

"Pronounced with a long *o*," Uncle Karl reminded Magda with a wink. His shirt-sleeves were rolled up; Mother punched his brown biceps with the arrowed heart on it and said his mind was naughty. Fat May's laugh came suddenly from the funhouse, as if she'd just got the joke; the family laughed too at the coincidence. Ambrose went under the boardwalk to search for out-of-town matchbook-covers with the aid of his pocket flash-light; he looked out from the edge of the North American continent and wondered how far their laughter carried over the water. Spies in rubber rafts; survivors in life-boats. If the joke had been beyond his understanding, he could have said: *"The laughter was over his head."* And let the reader see the serious wordplay on second reading.

He turned the flashlight on and then off at once even before the woman whooped. He sprang away, heart athud, dropping the light. The man had snarled: "Cut da friggin' light!" Perspiration drenched and chilled him by the time he scrambled up to the family. "See anything?" his father asked. His voice wouldn't come; he shrugged and violently brushed sand from his pantlegs.

"Let's ride the old flying-horses!" Magda cried. I'll never be an author. It's been forever already, everybody's gone home, Ocean City's deserted, the ghost-crabs are tickling across the beach and down the littered cold streets. And the empty halls of clapboard hotels and abandoned funhouses. A tidal wave; an enemy air raid; a monster-crab swelling like an island from the sea. *The inhabitants fled in terror.* Magda clung to his trouserleg; he alone knew the maze's secret. "He gave his life that we might live," said Uncle Karl with a scowl of pain, as he. The woman's legs had been twined behind the man's neck; he'd spread her fat cheeks with tattooed hands and pumped like a whippet. *An astonishing coincidence.* He yearned to tell Peter. He wanted to throw up for excitement. They hadn't even chased him. He wished he were dead.

One possible ending would be to have Ambrose come across another lost person in the dark. They'd match their wits together against the fun-house, struggle like Ulysses past obstacle after obstacle, help and encourage each other. Or a girl. By the time they found the exit they'd be closest friends, sweethearts if it were a girl; they'd know each other's inmost souls, be bound together *by the cement of shared adventure;* then they'd emerge into the light, and it would turn out that his friend was a Negro. A blind girl. President Roosevelt's son. Ambrose's former arch-enemy.

Shortly after the mirror-room he'd groped along a musty corridor, his heart already misgiving him at the absence of phosphorescent arrows and other signs. He'd found a crack of light—not a door, it turned out, but a seam between the plyboard wall-panels—and squinting up to it, espied a small old man nodding upon a stool beneath a bare speckled bulb. A crude panel of toggle- and knife-switches hung beside the open fuse-box near his head; elsewhere in the little room were wooden levers and ropes belayed to boat-cleats. At the time, Ambrose wasn't lost enough to rap or call; later he couldn't find that crack. Now it seemed to him that he'd possibly dozed off for a few minutes somewhere along the way; certainly he was exhausted from the afternoon's sunshine and the evening's problems; he couldn't be sure he hadn't dreamed part or all of the sight. Had an old black wall fan droned like bumblebees and shimmied two flypaper streamers? Had the funhouse operator—gentle, somewhat sad and tired-appearing—murmured in his sleep? Is there really such a person as Ambrose, or is he a figment of the author's imagination? Was it Assawoman Bay or Sinepuxent? Are there other errors of fact in this fiction? Was there another sound besides the little slap slap of thigh on ham, like water sucking at the chine-boards of a skiff?

When you're lost, the smartest thing to do is stay put till you're found, hollering if necessary. But to holler guarantees humiliation as well as rescue; keeping silent permits some saving of face—you can act surprised at the fuss when your rescuers find you and swear you weren't lost, if they do. What's more you might find your own way yet, *however belatedly*.

"Don't tell me your foot's still asleep!" Magda exclaimed as the three young people walked from the inlet to the area set aside for ferris-wheels, carrousels, and other carnival rides, they having decided in favor of the vast and ancient merry-go-round instead of the funhouse. What a sentence, everything was wrong from the outset. People don't know what to make of him, he doesn't know what to make of himself, he's only thirteen, *athletically and socially inept*, not astonishingly bright, but there are antennae; he has . . . some sort of receivers in his head; things speak to him, he understands more than he should, the world winks at him through its objects, grabs grinning at his coat. Everybody else is in on some secret he doesn't know; they've forgotten to tell him. Through simple *procrastination* his mother put off his baptism until this year. Everyone else had it done as a baby; he'd assumed the same of himself, as had his mother so she claimed, until it was time for him to join Grace Methodist-Protestant and the oversight came out. He was mortified, but pitched sleepless through his private catechizing, intimidated by the ancient mysteries, a thirteen-year-old would never say that, resolved to experience conversion like St. Augustine. When the water touched his brow and Adam's sin left him, he contrived by a strain like defecation to bring tears into his eyes—but felt nothing. There was some simple, radical difference about him; he hoped it was genius, feared it was madness, devoted himself to amiability and inconspicuousness. Alone on the seawall near his house he was seized by the terrifying transports he'd thought to find in summershed, in Communion-cup. The grass was alive! The town, the river, himself, were not imaginary; time roared in his ears like wind; the world was *going on!* This part ought to be dramatized. The Irish author James Joyce once wrote. Ambrose M_____ is going to scream.

There is no *texture of rendered sensory detail,* for one thing. The faded distorting mirrors beside Fat May; the impossibility of choosing a mount when one had but a single ride on the great carrousel; the *vertigo attendant on his recognition* that Ocean City was worn out, the place of fathers and grandfathers, straw-boatered men and parasoled ladies survived by their amusements. Money spent, the three paused at Peter's insistence beside Fat May to watch the girls get their skirts blown up. The object was to tease Magda, who said: "I swear, Peter M_____, you've got a one-track mind! Amby and me aren't *interested* in such things." In the tumbling barrel, too, just inside the Devil's-mouth entrance to the funhouse, the girls were upended, and their boyfriends and others could see up their dresses if they cared to. Which was the whole point, Ambrose realized. Of the entire funhouse! If you looked around, you noticed that almost all the people on the boardwalk were paired off into couples except the small children; in a way, that was the whole point of Ocean City! If you had X-ray eyes and could see everything going on at that instant under the boardwalk and in all the hotel-rooms and cars and alleyways, you'd realize that all that normally *showed,* like restaurants and dance-halls and clothing and test-your-strength machines, was merely preparation and intermission. Fat May screamed.

BECAUSE HE WATCHED THE GOINGS-ON FROM THE CORNER OF HIS EYE, IT was Ambrose who spied the half-dollar on the boardwalk near the tumbling-barrel. Losers weepers. The first time he'd heard some people moving through a corridor not far away, just after he'd lost sight of the crack of light, he'd decided not to call to them, for fear they'd guess he was scared and poke fun; it sounded like roughnecks; he'd hoped they'd come by and he could follow in the dark without their knowing. Another time he'd heard just one person, unless he imagined it, bumping along as if on the other side of the plywood; perhaps Peter coming back for him, or Father, or Magda lost too. Or the owner and operator of the funhouse. He'd called out once, as though merrily: "Anybody know where the heck we are?" But the query was too stiff, his voice cracked, when the sounds stopped he was terrified: maybe it was a queer who waited for fellows to get lost, or a longhaired filthy monster that lived in some cranny of the funhouse. He stood rigid for hours it seemed like, scarcely respiring. His future was shockingly clear, in outline. He tried holding his breath to the point of unconsciousness. There ought to be a button you could push to end your life absolutely without pain; disappear in a flick, like turning out a light. He would push it instantly! He despised Uncle Karl. But he despised his father too, for not being what he was supposed to be. Perhaps his father hated *his* father, and so on, and his son would hate him, and so on. Instantly!

Naturally he didn't have nerve enough to ask Magda to go through the funhouse with him. With incredible nerve and to everyone's surprise he invited Magda, quietly and politely, to go through the funhouse with him. "I warn you, I've never been through it before," he added, *laughing easily;* "but I reckon we can manage somehow. The important thing to remember, after all, is that it's meant to be a *fun*house; that is, a place of amusement. If people really got lost or injured or too badly frightened in it, the owner'd go out of business. There'd even be lawsuits. No character in a work of fiction can make a speech this long without interruption or acknowledgement from the other characters."

Mother teased Uncle Karl: "Three's a crowd, I always heard." But actually Ambrose was relieved that Peter now had a quarter too. Nothing was what it looked like. Every instant, under the surface of the Atlantic Ocean, millions of living animals devoured one another. Pilots were falling in flames over Europe; women were being forcibly raped in the South Pacific. His father should have taken him aside and said: "There is a simple secret to getting through the funhouse, as simple as being first to see the Towers. Here it is. Peter does not know it; neither does your Uncle Karl. You and I are different. Not surprisingly, you've often wished you weren't. Don't think I haven't noticed how unhappy your childhood has been! But you'll understand, when I tell you, why it had to be kept secret until now. And you won't regret not being like your brother and your uncle. *On the contrary.*" If you knew all the stories behind all the people on the boardwalk you'd see that *nothing* was what it looked like. Husbands and wives often hated each other; parents didn't necessarily love their children; et cetera. A child took things for granted because he had nothing to compare his life to, and everybody acted as if things were as they should be. Therefore each saw himself as the hero of the story, when the truth might turn out to be that he's the villain, or the coward. And there wasn't one thing you could do about it!

Hunchbacks, fat ladies, fools—that no one chose what they were was unbearable. In the movies he'd meet a beautiful young girl in the funhouse; they'd have hairsbreadth escapes from real dangers; he'd do and say the right things; she also; in the end they'd be lovers; their dialogue-lines would match up; he'd be perfectly at ease; she'd not only like him well enough, she'd think he was *marvelous*; she'd lie awake thinking of *him*, instead of vice versa—the way *his* face looked in different lights and how he stood and exactly what he'd said—and yet that would be only one small episode in his wonderful life, among many many others. Not a *turning-point* at all. What had happened in the toolshed was nothing. He hated, he loathed his parents! One reason for not writing a lost-in-the-funhouse story is that either everybody's felt what Ambrose feels, in which case it goes without saying, or else no normal person feels such things, in which case Ambrose is a freak. "Is anything more tiresome, in fiction, than the problems of sensitive adolescents?" And it's all too long and rambling, as if the author. For all a person knows the first time through, the end could be just around any corner; perhaps, *not impossibly* it's been within reach any number of times. On the other hand he may be scarcely past the start, with everything yet to get through, an intolerable idea.

Fill in: His father's raised eyebrows when he announced his decision to do the funhouse with Magda. Ambrose understands now, but didn't then, that his father was wondering whether he knew what the funhouse was *for*—especially since he didn't object, as he should have, when Peter decided to come along too. The ticket-woman, witchlike, mortifying him when inadvertently he gave her his name-coin instead of the half-dollar, then unkindly calling Magda's attention to the birthmark on his temple: "Watch out for him, girlie, he's a marked man!" She wasn't even cruel, he understood, only vulgar and insensitive. Somewhere in the world there was a young woman with such splendid understanding that she'd see him entire, like a poem or story, and find his words so valuable after all that when he confessed his apprehensions she would explain why they were in fact the very things that made him precious to her . . . and to Western Civilization! There was no such girl, the simple truth being. Violent yawns as they approached the mouth. Whispered advice from an old-timer on a bench near the barrel: "Go crabwise and ye'll get an eyeful without upsetting!" Composure vanished at the first pitch: Peter hollered joyously, Magda tumbled, shrieked, clutched her skirt; Ambrose scrambled crabwise, tight-lipped with terror, was soon out, watched his dropped name-coin slide among the couples. Shamefaced he saw that to get through expeditiously was not the point; Peter feigned assistance in order to trip Magda up, shouted "I see Christmas!" when her legs went flying. The old man, his latest betrayer, cacked approval. A dim hall then of blackthread cobwebs and recorded gibber: he took Magda's elbow to steady her against revolving discs set in the slanted floor to throw your feet out from under, and explained to her in a calm deep voice his theory that each phase of the funhouse was triggered either automatically, by a series of photoelectric devices, or else manually by operators stationed at peepholes. But he lost his voice thrice as the discs unbalanced him; Magda was anyhow squealing; but at one point she clutched him about the waist to keep from falling, and her right cheek pressed for a moment against his belt-buckle. Heroically he drew her up, it was his chance to clutch her close as if for support and say: "I love you." He even put an arm lightly about the small of her back before a sailor-and-girl pitched into them from behind, sorely treading his left big toe and knocking Magda asprawl with them. The sailor's girl was a string-haired hussy with a loud laugh and light-blue drawers; Ambrose realized that he wouldn't have said "I love you" anyhow, and was smitten with self-contempt. How much better it would be to be that common sailor! A wiry little Seaman 3rd, the fellow squeezed a girl to each side and stumbled hilarious into the mirror-room, closer to Magda in thirty seconds than Ambrose had got in thirteen years. She giggled at something the fellow said to Peter; she drew her hair from her eyes with a movement so womanly it struck Ambrose's heart; Peter's smacking her backside then seemed particularly coarse. But Magda made a pleased indignant face and cried, "All right for *you*, mister!" and pursued Peter into the maze without a backward glance. The sailor followed after, leisurelily, drawing his girl against his hip; Ambrose understood not only that they were all so relieved to be rid of his burdensome company that they didn't even notice his absence, but that he himself shared their relief. Stepping from the treacherous passage at last into the mirror-maze, he saw once again, more clearly than ever, how readily he deceived himself into supposing he was a person. He even foresaw, wincing at his dreadful self-knowledge, that he would repeat the deception, at ever-rarer intervals, all his wretched life, so fearful were the alternatives. Fame, madness, suicide; perhaps all three. It's not believable that so young a boy could articulate that reflection, and in fiction the merely true must always yield to the plausible. Yet Ambrose M____ understood, as few adults do, that the famous loneliness of the great was no popular myth but a general truth—and moreover, that it was as much cause as effect.

ALL THE PRECEDING EXCEPT THE LAST FEW SENTENCES IS EXPOSITION that should've been done earlier or interspersed with the present action instead of lumped together. No reader would put up with so much with such *prolixity*. It's interesting that Ambrose's father, though presumably an intelligent man (as indicated by his role as high-school teacher), neither encouraged nor discouraged his children at all in any way—as if he either didn't care about them or cared all right but didn't know how to act. If this fact should contribute to one of his children's becoming a celebrated but wretchedly unhappy scientist, was it a good thing or not? He too might someday face that question; it would be useful to know whether it had tortured his father for years, for example, or never once crossed his mind.

In the mirror-maze two important things happened. First, our hero found a name-coin someone else had lost or discarded: *AMBROSE*, suggestive of the famous lightship and of his father's favorite dessert, which his mother prepared on special occasions out of coconut, oranges, grapes, and what else. Second, as he wondered at the endless replication of his image in the mirrors—second, as he *lost himself in the reflection* that the necessity for an observer makes perfect observation impossible, better make him eighteen at least, yet that would render other things unlikely, he heard Peter and Magda chuckling somewhere in the maze. "Here!" "No, here!" they shouted to each other; Peter said, "Where's Amby?" Magda murmured. "Amb?" Peter called. In a pleased, friendly voice. He didn't reply. The truth was, his brother was a *happy-go-lucky youngster* who'd've been better off with a regular brother of his own, but who seldom complained of his lot and was generally cordial. Ambrose's throat ached; there aren't enough different ways to say that. He stood quietly while the two young people giggled and thumped through the glittering maze, hurrah'd their discovery of its exit, cried out in joyful alarm at what next beset them. Then he set his mouth and followed after, as he supposed, took a wrong turn, strayed into the pass *wherein he lingers yet.*

The action of conventional dramatic narrative may be represented by a diagram called Freitag's Triangle— $\underline{A}\diagup^{B}\diagdown\underline{C}$ —or more accurately by a variant of that diagram— $\underline{A}\ \underline{B}\diagup^{C}\diagdown\underline{D}$ —in which *AB* represents the exposition, *B* the introduction of conflict, *BC* the "rising action," complication, or development of the conflict, *C* the climax or turn of the action, *CD* the *dénouement* or resolution of the conflict.

While there is no reason to regard this pattern as an absolute necessity, like many other conventions it became conventional because great numbers of people over great numbers of years learned by trial and error that it was effective; one ought not to forsake it, therefore, unless one wishes to forsake as well the effect of drama or has clear cause to feel that deliberate violation of the "normal" pattern can better can better effect that effect. This can't go on much longer; it can go on forever. He died telling stories to himself in the dark; years later, when that vast unsuspected area of the funhouse came to light, the first expedition found his skeleton in one of its labyrinthine corridors and mistook it for part of the entertainment. He died of starvation telling himself stories in the dark; but unbeknownst unbeknownst to him, an assistant operator of the funhouse, happening to overhear him, crouched just behind the plyboard partition and wrote down his every word. The operator's daughter, an exquisite young woman with a figure unusually well developed for her age, crouched just behind the partition and transcribed his every word. Though she had never laid eyes on him, she recognized that here was one of Western Culture's truly great imaginations, the eloquence of whose suffering would be an inspiration to unnumbered. And her heart was torn between her love for the misfortunate young man (yes, she loved him, though she had never laid though she knew him only—but how well!—through his words, and the deep, calm voice in which he spoke them) between her love et cetera and her woman's intuition that only in suffering and isolation could he give voice et cetera. Lone dark dying. Quietly she kissed the rough plyboard, and a tear fell upon the page. Where she had written in shorthand *Where she had written in shorthand* Where she had written in shorthand *Where she* et cetera. A long time ago we should have passed the apex of Freitag's Triangle and made brief work of the *dénouement;* the plot doesn't rise by meaningful steps but winds upon itself, digresses, retreats, hesitates, sighs, collapses, expires. The climax of the story must be its protagonist's discovery of a way to get through the funhouse. But he has found none, may have ceased to search.

What relevance does the war have to the story? Should there be fireworks outside or not?

Ambrose wandered, languished, dozed. Now and then he fell into his habit of rehearsing to himself the unadventurous story of his life, narrated from the third-person point of view, from his earliest memory parenthesis of maple-leaves stirring in the summer breath of tidewater Maryland end of parenthesis to the present moment. Its principal events, on this telling, would appear to have been *A, B, C,* and *D.*

He imagined himself years hence, successful, married, at ease in the world, the trials of his adolescence far behind him. He has come to the seashore with his family for the holiday: how Ocean City has changed! But at one seldom at one ill-frequented end of the boardwalk a few derelict amusements survive from times gone by: the great carrousel from the turn of the century, with its monstrous griffins and mechanical concert-band;

the roller-coaster rumored since 1916 to have been condemned; the mechanical shooting-gallery in which only the image of our enemies changed. His own son laughs with Fat May and wants to know what a funhouse is; Ambrose hugs the sturdy lad close and smiles around his pipestem at his wife.

The family's going home. Mother sits between Father and Uncle Karl, who teases him good-naturedly who chuckles over the fact that the comrade with whom he'd fought his way shoulder to shoulder through the funhouse had turned out to be a colored boy—to their mutual discomfort, as they'd opened their souls. But such are the walls of custom, which even. Whose arm is where? How must it feel. He dreams of a funhouse vaster by far than any yet constructed; but by then they may be out of fashion, like steamboats and excursion-trains. Already quaint and seedy: the draperied ladies on the frieze of the carrousel are his father's father's mooncheeked dreams; if he thinks of it more he will vomit his apple-on-a-stick.

He wonders: will he become a regular person? Something has gone wrong; his vaccination didn't take; at the Boy-Scout initiation campfire he only pretended to be deeply moved, as he pretends to this hour that it is not so bad after all in the funhouse, and that he has a little limp. How long will it last? He envisions a truly astonishing funhouse, incredibly complex yet utterly controlled from a great central switchboard like the console of a pipe-organ. Nobody had enough imagination. He could design such a place himself, wiring and all, and he's only thirteen years old. He would be its operator: panel-lights would show what was up in every cranny of its cunning of its multifarious vastness; a switch-flick would ease this fellow's way, complicate that's, to balance things out; if anyone seemed lost or frightened, all the operator had to do was.

He wished he had never entered the funhouse. No: he wishes he had never been born. But he was. Then he wishes he were dead. But he's not. Therefore he will construct funhouses for others and be their secret operator—though he would rather be among the lovers for whom funhouses are designed.

November 1967

Distance

YOU WOULD CERTAINLY BE GLAD TO MEET ME. I WAS THE LADY WHO appreciated youth. Yes, all that happy time, I was not like some. It did not go by me like a flitting dream. Tuesdays and Wednesdays was as gay as Saturday nights.

Have I suffered since? No, sir, we've had as good times as this country gives; cars, renting in Jersey summers, TV the minute it first came out, everything grand for the kitchen. I have no complaints worth troubling the manager about.

Still it is like a long hopeless homesickness my missing those young days. To me, they're like my own place that I have gone away from forever, and I have lived all the time since among great pleasures but in a foreign town. Well, OK. Farewell, certain years.

But that's why I have an understanding of that girl Ginny downstairs and her kids. They're runty, underdeveloped. No sun, no beef. Noodles, beans, cabbage. Well, my mother off the boat knew better than that.

Once upon a time, as they say, her house was the spit of mine. You could hear it up and down the air shaft, the singing from her kitchen, banjo playing in the parlor, she would admit it first, there was a tambourine in the bedroom. Her husband wasn't American. He had black hair—like Gypsies do. And everything then was spotless, the kitchen was all inlay like broken-

GRACE PALEY

up bathroom tiles, pale lavender. Formica on all surfaces, everything bright. The shine of the pots and pans was turned to stun the eyes of company . . . you could see it, the mischievousness of that family home.

Of course, on account of misery now, she's always dirty. Crying crying crying. She would not let tap water touch her.

Five ladies on the block, old friends, nosy, me not included, got up a meeting and wrote a petition to Child Welfare. I already knew it was useless as the requirement is more than dirt, drunkenness, and a little once in a while whoring. That is probably something why the children in our city are in such a state. I've noticed it for years, though it's not my business. Mothers and fathers get up when they wish, half being snuggled in relief, go to bed in the afternoon with their rumpy bumpy sweethearts pumping away before three P.M. (So help me.) Child Welfare does not show its concern. No matter who writes them. People of influence, known in the district, even the district leader, my cousin Leonie, who put her all into electing the mayor, she doesn't get a reply if she sends in a note. So why should I as I'm nothing but a Primary Day poll watcher?

Anyhow there are different kinds coming into this neighborhood, and I do not mean the colored people alone. I mean people like you and me, religious, clean, many of these have gone rotten. I go along with live and let live, but what of the children?

Ginny's husband ran off with a Puerto Rican girl who shaved between the legs. This is common knowledge and well known or I'd never say it. When Ginny heard that he was going around with this girl, she did it too, hoping to entice him back, but he got nauseated by her and that tipped the scales.

Men fall for terrible weirdos in a dumb way more and more as they get older; my old man, fond of me as he constantly was, often did. I never give it the courtesy of my attention. My advice to mothers and wives: Do not imitate the dimwit's girlfriends. You will be damnfool-looking, what with your age and all. Have you heard the saying "Old dough won't rise in a new oven?"

Well, you know it, I know it, even the punks and the queers that have wiggled their way into this building are in on the inside dope. John, my son, is a constant attendant now at that Ginny's poor grubby flat. Tired, who can blame him, of his Margaret's shiny face all pitted and potted by Jersey smog. My grandchildren, of which I have close to six, are pale, as the sun can't have a chance through the oil in Jersey. Even the leaves of the trees there won't turn a greenish green.

John! Look me in the eye once in a while! What a good little twig you were always, we did try to get you out with the boys and you did go when we asked you. After school when he was eight or so, we got him into a bunch of Cub Scouts, a very raw bunch with a jawful of curse words. All of them tough and wild, but at attention when the master came among them. Right turn! You would've thought the United States Marines was in charge they was that accurate in marching, and my husband on Tuesday nights taught them what he recalled from being a sergeant. Hup! two, three, four! I guess is what he knew. But John, good as his posture was, when he come home I give him a hug and a kiss and "what'd you do today at Scouts, son? Have a parade, darling?"

"Oh, no, Mother," says he. "Mrs. McClennon was collecting money the whole time for the district-wide picnic, so I just got the crayons and I drew this here picture of Our Blessed Mother," he says.

That's my John. And if you come with a Polaroid Land Camera you couldn't snap much clearer.

People have asked and it's none of their business. Why didn't the two of you (meaning Jack and me—both working) send the one boy you had left to college?

Well now to be honest, he would have had only grief in college. Truth: He was not bright. His father was not bright, and he inherited his father's brains. Our Michael was clever. But Michael is dead. We had it all talked over, his father and me, the conclusion we come to: A trade. My husband Jack was well established in the union from its early struggle, he was strong and loyal. John just floated in on the ease of recommendation and being related. We were wise. It's proved.

For now (this very minute) he's a successful man with a wonderful name in the building trade, and he has a small side business in cement plaques, his own beautiful home, and every kid of his dressed like the priest's nephew.

But don't think I'm the only one that seen Ginny and John when they were the pearls of this pitchy pigsty block. Oh, there were many, and they are still around holding the picture in the muck under their skulls, like crabs. And I am never surprised when they speak of it, when they try to make something of it, that nice-looking time, as though *I* was in charge of its passing.

"Ha," Jack said about twenty times that year, "She's a wild little bird. Our Johnny's dying . . . Watch her."

OK. Wild enough. I guess. But no wilder than me when *I* was seventeen, as I never told him, that whole year, long ago, mashing the grass of Central Park with Anthony Aldo. Why I'd put my wildness up against any wildness of present day, though I didn't want Jack to know. For he was a simple man . . . Put in the hours of a wop, thank God pulled the overtime of a decent American. I didn't like to worry worry worry him. He was kindness itself, as they say.

He come home 6:00 P.M. I come home 6:15 P.M. from where I was afternoon cashier. Put supper up. Seven o'clock, we ate it up and washed the dishes; 7:45 P.M. sharp, if there was no company present and the boy out visiting, he liked his pussy. Quick and very neat. By 8:15 he had showered every bit of it away. I gave him his little whiskey. He tried that blabbermouth *Journal American* for news of the world. It was too much. Good night, Mr. Raftery, my pal.

Leaving me, thank goodness, the cream of the TV and a cup of sweet wine till midnight. Though I liked the attentions as a man he daily give me as a woman, it hardly seemed to tire me as it exhausted him. I could stay with the late show not fluttering an eyelid till the very end of the last commercial. My wildness as a girl is my own life's business, no one else's.

NOW: AS A TOKEN FOR FRIENDSHIP UNDER GOD, JOHN'D GIVEN GINNY HIS high school G O pin, though he was already a working man. He couldn't of given her his union card (that never got customary), though he did take her to a famous dinner in honor of Klaus Schnauer: thirty-five years at Camillo, the only heinie they ever let into that American local; he was a disgusting fat-bottomed Nazi so help me, he could've turned you into a pink Commie, his ass, excuse me, was that fat. Well, as usual for that younghearted gang, Saturday night went on and on, it give a terrible jolt to Sunday morning, and John staggered into breakfast, not shaved or anything. (A man, husband, son, or lodger should be shaved at breakfast.) "Mother," he said, "I am going to ask Virginia to marry me."

"I told you so," said my husband and dropped the funnies on his bacon.

"You are?" I said.

"I am, and if God is good, she'll have me."

"No blasphemy intended," I said, "but He'll have to be off in the old country fishing if she says yes."

"Oh, Mother!" said John. He is a nice boy, loyal to friends and good.

"She'll go out with anyone at all," I said.

"Mother!" said John, meaning they weren't engaged, and she could do what she wanted.

"Go out is nothing," I said. "I seen her only last Friday night with Pete, his arm around her, going into Phelan's."

"Pete's like that, Mother," meaning it was no fault of hers.

"Then what of last Saturday night, you had to go to the show yourself as if there wasn't no one else in the Borough of Manhattan to take to a movie, and when you was gone I seen her buy two Cokes at Carlo's and head straight to the third floor to John Kameron's . . .

"So? So?"

". . . and come out at 11 P.M. and *his* arm was around her."

"So?"

" . . . and his hand was well under her sweater . . ."

"That's not so, Mother."

"It *is* so, and tell me, young man, how you'll feel married to a girl that every wild boy on the block has been leanin' his thumbs on her titties like she was a Carvel dairy counter, tell me that?"

"Dolly!" says Jack. "You went too far . . ."

John just looked at me as red and dumb as a baby's knees.

"I haven't gone far enough into the facts, and I'm not ready to come out yet, and you listen to me, Johnny Raftery, you're somebody's jackass, I'll tell you, you look out that front window and I bet you if you got yourself your dad's spyglass you would see some track of your little lady. I think there are evenings she don't get out of the back of the trailer truck parked over there and it's no trouble at all for Pete or Kameron's half-witted kid to get his way of her. Listen Johnny, there isn't a grown-up woman who was sitting on the stoop last Sunday when it was so damn windy that doesn't know that Ginny don't wear underpants."

"Oh, Dolly," says my husband, and plops his head into his hands.

"I'm going, Mother, that's libel, I'll have her sue you for libel," dopey John starts to holler out of his tomato red face. "I'm going and I'll ask her and I love her and I don't care what you say. Truth or lies, I don't care."

"And if you go, Johnny," I said, calm as a dead fish, my eyes rolling up to pray and be heeded, "this is what I must do," and I took a kitchen knife, a bit blunt, and plunged it at least an eighth of an inch in the fat of my heart. I guess that the heart of a middle-aged lady is jammed in deeper than an eighth of an inch, for I am here to tell the tale. But some blood did come soon, to my son's staring, it touched my nightie and spread out on my bathrobe, and it was as red on my apron as a picture in an Italian church. John fell down on his knees, and hid his head in my lap. He cried, "Mother, Mother, you've hurt yourself." My husband didn't say a word to me. He kept his madness in his teeth but he told me later, Face it: the feelings in his heart was cracked.

I met Ginny the next morning in Carlo's store. She didn't look at me. Then she did. Then she said, "It's a nice day, Mrs. Raftery."

"Mm," I said. (It was.) "How can you tell the kind of day it is?" (I don't know what I meant by that.)

"What's wrong, Mrs. Raftery?" she said.

"Hah! wrong?" I asked.

"Well, you know, I mean, you act mad at me, you don't seem to like me this morning." She made a little laugh.

"I do. I like you a great deal," I said, outwitting her. "It's you, you know, you don't like Johnny, you don't."

"What?" she said, her head popping up to catch sight of that reply.

"Don't, don't don't," I said. "Don't, don't!" I hollered, giving Ginny's arm a tug. "Let's get out of here. Ginny, you don't like John. You'd let him court you, squeeze you, and he's very good, he wouldn't press you further."

"You ought to mind your business," says Ginny very soft, me being the elder (but with tears).

"My son is my business."

"No," she says, "he's his own."

"My son is my business. I have one son left, and he's my business."

"No," she says. "He's his own."

MY SON IS MY BUSINESS. BY LOVE AND DUTY.

"Oh, no," she says. Soft because I am the older one, but very strong. (I've noticed it. All of a sudden they look at you, and then, it comes to them, young people, they are bound to outlast you, so they temper up their icy steel and stare into about an inch away from you a lot. Have you noticed it?)

At home, I said, "Jack now, the boy needs guidance. Do you want him to spend the rest of his life in bed with an orphan on welfare?"

"Oh," said Jack. "She's an orphan, is she? It's just her mother that's dead. What has one thing to do with another? You're a pushy damn woman, Dolly. I don't know what use you are . . . "

What came next often happens in a family causing sorrow at the time. Looking back, it's a speck compared to life.

For: Following this conversation, Jack didn't deal with me at all, and he broke his many years after-supper habits and took long walks. That's what killed him, I think, for he was a habitual person.

And: Alongside him on one of these walks was seen a skinny crosstown lady, known to many people over by Tompkins Square—wears a giant Ukrainian cross in and out of the tub, to keep from going down the drain, I guess.

"In that case, the hell with you," is what I said. "I don't care. Get yourself a cold-water flat on Avenue D."

"Why not? I'll go. OK," said Jack. I think he figured a couple of weeks vacation with his little cuntski and her color television would cool his requirements.

"Stay off the block," I said, "you slippery relic. I'll send your shirts by the diaper-service man."

"Mother," said poor John, when he noticed his dad's absence, "what's happening to you? The way you talk. To Dad. It's the wine, mother. I know it."

"You're a bloated beer guzzler!" I said quietly. (People that drink beer are envious against the ones in favor of wine. Though my dad was a mick in cotton socks, in his house, we had a choice.)

"No, Mother, I mean you're not clear sometimes."

"Crazy, you mean, son. Huh? Split personality?"

"Something's wrong!" he said. "Don't you want Dad back?" He was nervous to his fingernails.

"Mind your business, he'll be back, it's happened before, Mr. Two-Weeks Old."

"What?" he said, horrified.

"You're blind as a bat, Mr. Just Born. Where was you three Christmases ago?"

"What! But Mother! Didn't you feel terrible? Terrible! How'd you stand for him acting that way? Dad!"

"Now quit it, John, you're a damnfool kid. Sure I don't want to look at his dumb face being pleased. That'd kill."

"Mother, it's not right."

"Phoo, go to work and mind your business, sonny boy."

"It is my business," he said, "and don't call me sonny."

About two months later, John came home with Margaret, both of them blistered from Lake Hopatcong at ninety-four degrees. I will be fair. She was not yet ruined by Jersey air, and she was not too terrible-looking, at least to the eye of a clean-minded boy.

"This is Margaret," he says. "She's from Monmouth, Jersey."

"Just come over on the *Queen Mary*, dear?" I asked for the joke in it.

"I have to get her home for supper. Her father's strict."

"Sure," I said, "have a Coke first."

"Oh, thank you so much," says Margaret. "Thank you, thank you, thank you, Mrs. Raftery."

"Has she blood in her?" hollered Jack after his shower. He had come home by then, skinny and dissatisfied. Is there satisfaction anywhere in getting old?

John didn't inquire an OK of his dad or me, nor answer to nobody Yes or No. He was that age that couldn't live without a wife. He had to use this Margaret.

It was his time to go forward like we all did once. And he has. Number 1: She is kept plugged up with babies. Number 2: As people nowadays need a house, he has bought one and tangled it around in Latin bushes. Nobody but the principal at Holy Redeemer High knows what the little tags on the twigs say. Every evening after hard work you can find him with a hose scrubbing down his lawn. His oldest kid is now fourteen and useless. The littlest one is four, and she reminds me of me with the flashiest eyes and a little tongue sharpened to a scrappy point.

"How come you never named one for *me*, Margaret?" I asked her straight in her face.

"Oh," she said, "There's only the two girls, Teresa, for my mother, and Cathleen, for my best sister. The very next'll be for you."

"What, next! Are you trying to kill my son?" I asked her. "Why he has to be working nights as it is. You don't look well, you know. You ought to see a smart Jewish doctor and get your tubes tied up."

"Oh," she said, "Never!"

I have to tease a little to grapple any sort of a reply out of her. But mostly it doesn't work. It is something like I am a crazy construction worker in conversation with fresh cement. Can there be more in the world like her? Don't answer. Time will pass in spite of her slow wits.

In fact it has, for here we are in the present, which is happening now, and I am a famous widow baby-sitter for whoever thinks I am unbalanced but within reason. I am a grand storybook reader to the little ones. I read like an actress, Joan Crawford or Maureen O'Sullivan, my voice is deeper than it was. So I do make a little extra for needs, though my Johnny sees to the luxuries I must have. I won't move away to strangers. This is my family street, and I don't need to.

And of course as friendship never ends, Johnny comes twice a week for his entertainment to Ginny. Ginny and I do not talk a word though we often pass. She knows I am right as well as victorious. She's had it unusually lovely (most people don't)—a chance to be some years with a young fellow like Blackie that gave her great rattling shivers, top to bottom, though it was all cut off before youth ended. And as for my Johnny, he now absolutely has her as originally planned and desired, and she depends on him in all things. She requires him. Her children lean on him. They climb up his knees to his shoulder. They cry out the window for him, *John, John,* if his dumb Margaret keeps him home.

It's a pity to have become so right and Jack's off stalking the innocent angels.

I wait on the stoop steps to see John on summer nights as he hasn't enough time to visit me and Ginny both, and I need the sight of him, though I don't know why. I like the street anyway, and the hot night when the ice-cream truck brings all the dirty kids and the big nifty boys with their hunting-around eyes. I put a touch of burgundy on my strawberry ice-cream cone as my father said we could on Sunday, which drives these sozzle-headed ladies up the brown brick wall, so help me Mary.

Now, some serious questions, so far unasked:

What the devil is it all about, the noisiness and the speediness, when it's no distance at all? How come John had to put all of them courtesy calls into Margaret on his lifelong trip to Ginny? Also, Jack, what was his real nature? Was he for or against? And that Anthony, what *did* he have in mind as I knuckled under again and again (and I know I was the starter)? He did not get me pregnant as in books it happens at once. How come the French priest said to me, crying tears and against his order, "Oh, no, Dolly, if you are enceinte (meaning pregnant), he will certainly marry you, poor child, now smile, poor child, for that is the church's promise to infants born." To which, how come, tough and cheery as I used to be, all I could say before going off to live and die was: "No, Father, he doesn't love me."

December 1967

Alternatives

IT IS THE SUMMER OF 1935, AND THERE ARE TWO PEOPLE SITTING AT THE end of a porch. The house is in Maine, at the edge of a high bluff that over-looks a large and for the moment peaceful lake. Tom Todd and Barbara Rutherford. They have recently met (she and her husband are houseguests of the Todds). They laugh a lot, they are terribly excited about each other, and they have no idea what to do with what they feel. She is a very blond, bright-eyed girl in her twenties, wearing very short white shorts, swinging long thin legs below the high hammock on which she is perched, looking down at Tom. He is a fair, slender man with sad lines beside his mouth, but (not now!) now he is laughing with Babs. Some ten years older than she, he is a professor, writing a book on Shelley (Oh wild West Wind!) but the Depression has had unhappy effects on his university (Hilton, in the Mid-dle South): 10 percent salary cuts, cancellation of sabbaticals. He is unable to finish his book (no promotion); they rely more and more on his wife's small income from her bookstore. And he himself has been depressed—but not now. What a girl, this Babs!

The house itself is old, with weathered shingles that once were green, and its shape is peculiar; it used to be the central lodge for a girls' camp for underprivileged girls that Jessica Todd owned and ran before her marriage to Tom. The large, high living room is still full of souvenirs from that era:

ALICE ADAMS

group pictures of girls in bloomers and middies, who danced or rather posed in discreet Greek tunics, and wore headbands; and over the fireplace, just below a moldering deer's head, there is a mouse-nibbled triangular felt banner, once dark green, that announced the name of the camp: Wabuwana. Why does Jessica keep all those things around, as though those were her happiest days? No one ever asked. Since there were no bedrooms Tom and Jessica sleep in a curtained-off alcove, with not much privacy; two very small rooms that once were storage closets are bedrooms for their children, Avery and Devlin. Babs and her husband, Wilfred Rutherford, have been put in a tent down the path, on one of a row of gray plank tent floors where all the camper girls used to sleep. Babs said, "How absolutely divine—I've never slept in a tent." "You haven't?" Jessica asked. "I think I sleep best in tents."

A narrow screened-in porch runs the length of the house, and there is a long table out there—too long for just the four Todds, better (less lonely) with even two guests. The porch widens at its end, making a sort of round room, where Tom and Babs now are, not looking at the view.

Around the house there are clumps of hemlocks, tall Norway pines, white pines, and birches that bend out from the high bank. Across the smooth bright lake are the White Mountains, the Presidential Range—sharp blue Mount Adams and farther back, in the exceptionally clear days of early fall, such as this day is, you can see Mount Washington silhouetted. Lesser, gentler slopes take up the foreground: Mount Pleasant, Douglas Hill.

Beside Babs in the hammock lies a ukelele—hers, which Tom wants her to play.

"Oh, but I'm no good at *all*," she protests. "Wilfred can't stand it when I play!"

"I'll be able to stand it, I can promise you that, my dear."

Her accent is very Bostonian, his Southern; both tendencies seem to intensify as they talk together.

She picks up the instrument, plucks the four strings as she sings, "My dog has fleas."

"So does Louise," he sings mockingly, an echo. Tom is fond of simple ridiculous jokes but he feels it necessary always to deliver them as though someone else were talking. In fact, he says almost everything indirectly.

They both laugh, looking at each other.

They are still laughing when Jessica comes out from the living room where she has been reading (every summer she rereads Jane Austen) and walks down the length of the porch to where they are, and says, "Oh, a ukelele, how nice, Barbara. Some of our girls used to play."

Chivalrous Tom gets up to offer his chair—"Here you are, old dear." She did not want to sit so close to the hammock but does anyway, a small shapeless woman on the edge of her chair.

Jessica is only a few years older than Tom but she looks considerably more so, with graying hair and sad brown eyes, a tightly compressed mouth. She has strong and definite Anglo-Saxon notions about good behavior (they all do, this helpless group of American Protestants, Tom and Jessica, Barbara and Wilfred) which they try and almost succeed in passing on to their children. Jessica wears no makeup and is dressed in what she calls "camp clothes," meaning things that are old and shabby (what she thinks she deserves). "Won't you play something for us?" she asks Babs.

"Perhaps you will succeed in persuasion where I have failed," says Tom. As he sees it, his chief duty toward his wife is to be unfailingly polite, and he always is, although sometimes it comes across a little heavily.

Of course Jessica feels the currents between Babs and Tom but she accepts what she senses with melancholy resignation. There is a woman at home whom Tom likes too, small, blond Irene McGinnis, and Irene is crazy about Tom—that's clear—but nothing happens. Sometimes they kiss; Jessica has noticed that Verlie, the maid, always hides Tom's handkerchiefs. Verlie also likes Tom. Nothing more will happen with Babs. (But she is wrong.) It is only mildly depressing for Jessica, a further reminder that she is an aging, not physically attractive woman, and that her excellent mind is not compelling to Tom. But she is used to all that. She sighs, and says, "I think there's going to be a very beautiful sunset," and she looks across the lake to the mountains. "There's Mount Washington," she says.

Then the porch door bangs open and Wilfred walks toward them, a heavy, dark young man with sleeves rolled up over big hairy arms; he has been washing and polishing his new Ford. He is a distant cousin of Jessica's. "Babs, you're not going to play that thing, are you?"

"No, darling, I absolutely promise."

"Well," Tom says, "surely it's time for a drink?"

"It surely is," says Babs, giggling, mocking him.

He gestures as though to slap at the calf of her long leg, but of course he does not; his hand stops some inches away.

Down a wide pine-needled path, some distance from the lodge, there is a decaying birchbark canoe, inside which white Indian pipes grow. They were planted years back by the camper girls. Around the canoe stands a grove of pines with knotted roots, risen up from the ground, in which chipmunks live. Feeding the chipmunks is what Jessica and Tom's children do when they aren't swimming or playing on the beach. Skinny, dark Avery and smaller, fairer Devlin—in their skimpy shorts they sit cross-legged on the pine needles, making clucking noises to bring out the chipmunks.

A small chipmunk comes out, bright-eyed, switching his tail back and forth, looking at the children, but then he scurries off.

Devlin asks, "Do you like Babs?" He underlines the name, meaning that he thinks it's silly.

"She's OK." Avery's voice is tight; she is confused by Babs. She doesn't know whether to think, as her mother probably does, that Babs's white shorts are too short, that she is too dressed up in her pink silk shirt for camp, or to be pleased at the novel sort of attention she gets from Babs, who said last night at dinner, "You know, Avery, when you're a little older you should have an evening dress this color," and pointed to the flame-gold gladioli on the table, in a gray stone crock.

"Her shorts are too short," says Devlin.

"What do you know about clothes? They're supposed to be short—*shorts*." Saying this, for a moment Avery feels that she *is* Babs, who wears lipstick and anything she wants to, whom everyone looks at.

"Mother doesn't wear shorts, ever."

"So what? You think she's well dressed?"

Devlin is appalled; he has no idea what to make of what she has said. "I'll tell!" He is desperate. "I'll tell her what you said."

"Just try, you silly little sissy. Come on, I'll race you to the lodge."

Both children scramble up, Avery first, of course, and run across the slippery pines, their skinny brown legs flashing between the trees, and arrive at the house together and slam open the screen door and tear down the length of the porch to the cluster of grown-ups.

"Mother, do you know what Avery said?"

"No, darling, but please don't tell me unless it was something very amusing." This is out of character for Jessica, and Devlin stares at his mother, who strokes his light hair, and says, "Now, let's all be quiet. Barbara is going to play a song."

Babs picks up her ukelele and looks down at it as she begins her song, which turns out to be a long ballad about a lonely cowboy and a pretty city girl. She has an attractive, controlled alto voice. She becomes more and more sure of herself as she goes along, and sometimes looks up and smiles around the group—at Tom—as she sings.

Tom has an exceptional ear, as well as a memory for words; somewhere, sometime, he has heard that ballad before, so that by the time she reaches the end he is singing with her, and they reach the last line together, looking into each other's eyes with a great stagy show of exaggeration; they sing together, "And they loved forever more."

But they are not, that night, lying hotly together on the cold beach, furiously kissing, wildly touching everywhere. That happens only in Tom's mind, as he lies next to Jessica and hears her soft sad snores. In her cot, in the tent, Babs sleeps very soundly, as she always does, and she dreams of the first boy she ever kissed, whose name was not Tom.

IN THE LATE FORTIES, ALMOST THE SAME GROUP GATHERS FOR DINNER around a large white restaurant table, the Buon Gusto, in San Francisco. There are Tom and Jessica, and Babs, but she is without Wilfred, whom she has just divorced in Reno. Devlin is there, Devlin grown plump and sleek, smug with his new job of supervising window display at the City of Paris. Avery is there, with her second husband, fat, intellectual Stanley. (Her first marriage, to Paul Blue, the black trumpet player, was annulled; Paul was already married, and his first wife had lied about the divorce.)

Tom and Barbara have spent the afternoon in bed together, in her hotel room—that old love finally consummated. They are both violently aware of the afternoon behind them; they are partly still there, together in the tangled sea-smelling sheets. Barbara presses her legs close. Tom wonders if there is any smell of her on him that anyone could notice.

No one notices anything; they all have problems of their own.

In the more than ten years since they were all in Maine Jessica has sunk further into her own painful and very private despair. She is not fatter, but her body has lost all definition, and her clothes are deliberately middle-aged, as though she were eager to be done with being a sexual woman. Her melancholy eyes are large, terribly dark; below them her cheeks sag, and the corners of her mouth have a small sad downward turn. Tom is always carrying on—the phrase she uses to herself—with someone or other; she has little energy left with which to care. But sometimes, still, a lively rebellious voice within her cries out that it is all cruelly unfair; she has done everything that she was taught a wife is expected to do; she has kept house and cared for children and listened to Tom, laughed at his jokes and never said no when he felt like making love—done all those things, been a faithful and quiet wife when often she didn't want to at all, and there he is, unable to keep his eyes off Babs, laughing at all *her* jokes.

Tom has promised Barbara that he will leave Jessica; this winter they will get a divorce, and he will apply for a teaching job at Stanford or

U.C., and he and Babs will live in San Francisco; they are both in love with the city.

Avery has recently begun psychoanalysis with a very orthodox Freudian; he says nothing, and she becomes more and more hysterical—she is lost! And now this untimely visit from her parents; agonized, she questions them about events of her early childhood, as though to get her bearings. "Was I nine or ten when I had whooping cough?"

"What?" says Jessica, who had daringly been embarked on an alternate version of her own life, in which she did not marry Tom but instead went on to graduate school herself, and took a doctorate in Classics. (But who would have hired a woman professor in the twenties?) "Tom, I'd love another drink," she says. "Barbara? you too?" Late in her life Jessica has discovered the numbing effects of drink—you can sleep!

"Oh, yes, divine."

Sipping what is still his first vermouth, Devlin repeats to himself that most women are disgusting. He excepts his mother. He is sitting next to Babs, and he cannot stand her perfume, which is Joy.

Looking at Jessica, whom, curiously, she has always liked, Barbara feels a chill in her heart. Are they doing the right thing, she and Tom? He says they are; he says Jessica has her bookstore and her student poet friends ("Fairies, most of them, from the look of them," Tom says), and that living with him does not make her happy at all; he has never made her happy. Is he only talking to himself, rationalizing? Barbara doesn't know.

All these people, so many of them Southern, make Avery's husband, Stanley, feel quite lost; in fact, he finds it hard to understand anything they say. Tom is especially opaque: the heavy Southern accent and heavier irony combine to create confusion, which is perhaps what Tom intends. Stanley thinks Tom is a little crazy, and feels great sympathy for Jessica, whom he admires. And he thinks: poor Avery, growing up in all that—no wonder Devlin's queer and Avery has to go to a shrink. Stanley feels an awful guilt toward Avery, for not supplying all that Tom and Jessica failed to give her, and for his persistent "premature ejaculations"—and putting the phrase in quotes is not much help.

"I remember your whooping cough very well indeed," says Tom, pulling in his chin so that the back of his head jerks up; it is a characteristic gesture, an odd combination of self-mockery and self-congratulation. "It was the same summer you pushed Harry McGinnis into the swimming pool." He turns to Stanley, who is as incomprehensible to him as he is to Stanley, but he tries. "Odd gesture, that. Her mother and I thought she had a sort of 'crush' on young Harry, and then she went and pushed him into the pool." He chuckles. "Don't try to tell me that ladies aren't creatures of whim, even twelve-year-old girls."

"I was nine," says Avery, and does not add: you had a crush on Harry's mother, you were crazy about Irene that summer.

Jessica thinks the same thing, and she and Avery are both looking at Tom, so that he feels the thought.

"I remember teasing Irene about the bathing suit she wore that day," he says recklessly, staring about with his clear blues eyes at the unfamiliar room.

"What was it like?" asks Barbara, very interested.

"Oh, some sort of ruffled thing. You know how those Southern gals are," he says, clearly not meaning either his wife or his daughter.

"I must have thought the whooping cough was a sort of punishment," Avery says. "For having a crush on Harry, as you put it."

"Yes, probably," Jessica agrees, being herself familiar with many varieties of guilt. "You were awful sick—it was terrible. There was nothing we could do."

"When was the first summer you came to Maine?" Devlin asks Babs, coldly curious, nearly rude. It is clear that he wishes she never had.

"1935. In September. In fact September ninth," she says, and then blushes for the accuracy of her recall, and looks at Tom.

"Verlie took care of me," says Avery, still involved with her whooping cough.

Jessica sighs deeply. "Yes, I suppose she did."

ALMOST TEN YEARS LATER, IN THE MIDDLE FIFTIES, TOM AND BARBARA ARE married. In the chapel of the little church, the Swedenborgian, in San Francisco, both their faces stream with tears as the minister says those words.

In her forties, Barbara is a striking woman still, with her small disdainful nose, her sleekly knotted pale hair, and her beautiful way of walking, holding herself forward like a present. She has aged softly, as very fineskinned very blond women sometimes do. And Tom is handsome still; they make a handsome couple (they always have).

Avery is there; she reflects that she is now older than Barbara was in 1935, that summer in Maine. She is almost thirty, divorced from Stanley, and disturbingly in love with two men at once. Has Barbara never loved anyone but Tom? (Has she?) Avery sees their tears as highly romantic.

She herself is a nervy, attractive girl with emphatic dark eyebrows, large dark eyes, and a friendly soft mouth, heavy breasts on an otherwise slender body. She wishes she had not worn her black silk suit, despite its chic; two friends have assured her that no one thought about wearing black to weddings anymore, but now it seems a thing not to have done. "I wore black to my father's wedding"—thank God she is not still seeing Dr. Gunderscheim, and will use that sentence only as a joke. Mainly, Avery is wondering which of the two men to marry, Charles or Christopher. (The slight similarity of the names seems ominous—what does it mean?) This wondering is a heavy obsessive worry for her; it drags at her mind, pulling it down. Now for the first time, in the small dim chapel, candlelit, it wildly occurs to her that perhaps she should marry neither of them, perhaps she should not marry at all, and she stares about the chapel, terrified.

"I pronounce you man and wife," says the minister, who is kindly, thin, white-haired. He is very old; in fact he quietly dies the following year.

And then, almost as though nothing had happened, they have all left the chapel: Tom and Barbara, Avery and Devlin, who was Tom's best man. ("I gave my father away," is another of Avery's new postwedding jokes.) But something has happened: Tom and Barbara are married. They don't believe it either. He gives her a deep and prolonged kiss (why does it look so awkward?) which embarrasses Devlin terribly, so that he stares up and down the pretty, tree-lined street. He is thinking of Jessica, who is dead.

And he passionately wishes that she had not died, savagely blames Tom and Barbara for that death. Trivial, entirely selfish people—so he sees them; he compares the frivolity of their connection with Jessica's heavy suffering. Since Jessica's death Devlin has been in a sort of voluntary retreat. He left his window-display job and most of his friends; he stays at home on the wrong side of Telegraph Hill, without a view. He reads a lot and listens to music and does an occasional watercolor. He rarely sees Avery, and disapproves of what he understands to be her life. ("You don't think it's dykey, the way you sleep around?" was the terrible sentence he spoke to her, on the eve of Jessica's funeral, and it has never been retracted.) Sometimes in his fantasies it is ten years back, and Tom and Jessica get a divorce and she comes out to live in San Francisco. He finds her a pretty apartment on Telegraph Hill and her hair grows beautifully white and she wears nice tweeds and entertains at tea. And Tom and Barbara move to hell—Los Angeles or Mexico or somewhere. Most people who know him assume Devlin to be homosexual; asexual is actually the more accurate description.

They stand there, that quite striking group, all blinking in a brilliant October sun that instantly dries all tears; for several moments they are all transfixed there, unable to walk, all together, to their separate cars, to continue to the friend's house where there is to be a wedding reception. (Why this hesitation? do none of them believe in the wedding? what is a marriage?)

FIVE YEARS LATER, IN THE EARLY SIXTIES, AVERY DRIVES UP TO MAINE FROM Hilton, for various reasons which do not include a strong desire to see Tom and Barbara. She has been married to Christopher for four years, and she came out from San Francisco to Hilton to see how it was away from him. Away from him she fell wildly in love with a man in Hilton named Jason Valentine, and now (for various reasons) she has decided that she needs some time away from Jason.

She drives smoothly, quietly, along the pine-needled road in her Corvair to find no one there. No car.

But the screen door is unlatched, and she goes in, stepping up from the old stone step onto the long narrow porch, from which the long table has been removed, replaced with a new one that is small and round. (But where did they put the old one?) And there are some bright yellow canvas chairs, new and somehow shocking against the weathered shingled wall.

Inside the house are more violent changes, more bright new fabrics: curtains, bandanna-red, and a bandanna bedspread on the conspicuous wide bed. Beside the fireplace is a white wicker sofa (new) with chintz cushions—more red. So much red and so much newness make Avery dizzy; almost angrily she wonders where the old things are, the decaying banners and sepia photographs of girls in Greek costumes. She goes into the kitchen and it is all painted yellow, into what was the large closet where she used to sleep—but a wall has been knocked out between her room and Devlin's; it is all one room now, a new room, entirely strange, with a new iron bed, a crocheted bedspread, which is white. Is that where they will expect her to sleep? She wishes there were a phone. Tomorrow she will have to drive into town to call Jason at his studio.

Needing a drink, Avery goes back into the kitchen, and finds a bottle of an unfamiliar brand of bourbon. She gets ice from the refrigerator (terrifyingly new—so white!), water from the tap—thank God, the same old sink. With her clutched drink she walks quickly through the living room to the porch, down to the end. She looks out across the lake with sentimentally teared eyes, noting that it is clear but not quite clear enough to see Mount Washington.

Being in love with Jason, who is a nonpracticing architect (he would rather paint), who worries about his work (his nonwork), who loves her but is elusive (she has no idea when they will see each other again), has tightened all Avery's nerves: she is taut, cries easily, and is all concentrated on being in love with Jason.

A car drives up, a Mustang—Barbara is faithful to Fords. And there they are saying, "Avery, but we didn't *expect* you, we went into *Portland*, for *lobsters*. Oh dear, how awful, we only bought *two!*" Embracing, laughing. Tears (why?) in everyone's eyes.

They settle down, after packages are put away, Avery's bags in the new guest room, and they watch the sunset: a disappointing pale pastel. And they drink a lot.

Barbara is nervous, both because of this shift in schedule and because of Avery, whom she regards as an intellectual, like Tom. She is always afraid of what Avery will say—a not-unfounded fear. Also, she is upset about the prospect of two lobsters for three people.

What he considers her untimely arrival permits Tom's usual ambivalence about Avery to yield to a single emotion: extreme irritation. How inconsiderate she is—always has been! Besides, he was looking forward to his lobster.

Avery chooses this unpropitious moment to announce that she is leaving Christopher. "We've been making each other miserable," she says. "We have been, for a long time." She trails off.

Tom brightens. "Well, old dear, I always think incompatibility is a good reason not to live together." He has no notion of his own prurience in regard to his daughter.

She does. She says, "Oh, Christ."

Barbara goes into the kitchen to divide up the lobster; a skilled hostess, she does quite well, and she makes a good mayonnaise, as she listens to the jagged sounds of the quarrel on the porch. Avery and Tom. She sighs.

Now darkness surrounds the house, and silence, except for a faint soft lapping of small waves on the shore, and tiny noises from the woods: small animals shifting weight on the leaves, a bird moving on a branch.

"Although I have what I suppose is an old-fashioned prejudice against divorce," Tom unfortunately says.

"Christ, is that why you stayed married to mother and made her as miserable as you could? Christ, I have a prejudice against misery!" Avery feels her voice (and herself) getting out of control.

Barbara announces dinner, and they go to the pretty new table, where places are set, candles lit. Barbara distributes the lobster, giving Tom the major share, but he scowls down at his plate.

As Avery does at hers—in Hilton, with Jason, she was generally too overstimulated, too "in love" to eat; now she is exhausted and very hungry. She turns to Barbara, as though for help. "Don't you ever wish you'd got married before you did? What a waste those years were. That time in San Francisco, why not then?"

Startled, Barbara has no idea what to answer. She has never allowed herself to think in these terms, imaginatively to revise her life. "I feel lucky we've had these years we have had," she says—which, for her, is the truth. She loves Tom; she feels that she is lucky to be his wife.

"But those last years were horrible for mother," Avery says. "You might have spared her that time."

"I think I might be in a better position than you to be the judge of that." Enraged, Tom takes a characteristic stance: his chin thrust out, he is everyone's superior—he is especially superior to women and children, particularly his own.

"Oh, yeah?" In her childhood, this was considered the rudest remark one could make; then Avery would never have said it to Tom. "You think she just plain died of a heart attack, don't you? Well, her room was full of empty sherry bottles. All over. Everywhere those drab brown empty bottles, smelling sweet. Julia told me, when she cleaned it out."

This information (which is new) is so shocking (and so absolutely credible) to Tom that he must dismiss it at once. His desperate and hopeless guilts toward Jessica have forced him to take a sanctimonious tone in speaking of her. He must dismiss this charge at once. "As a matter of fact, Julia is quite unreliable, as Verlie was," he says.

Avery explodes. "Julia is unreliable! Verlie was! Christ—why? because they're black? because they're women?"

Barbara has begun to cry. "You've got to stop this," she says. "Why quarrel about the past? It's over—"

Tom and Avery stare at each other, in terrible pain; they would like to weep, to embrace, but they are unable to do either.

Tom draws himself up stiffly—stiffly he turns to Barbara. "You're quite right, old dear," he says.

Several things attack Avery's mind at once: one, that she would like to say, goddam you both, or something obscene, and take off down the turnpike, back to Boston; two, she is too drunk for the turnpike; and three, she has just noticed that Tom speaks to Barbara exactly as though she were Jessica, as though neither of them were people but something generic named Wife.

And so the moment goes, the awful emotions subside, and they all retreat to trivia. Although Avery's hands still shake, she comments on the mayonnaise (she is not excruciatingly Southern Jessica's daughter for nothing), which Barbara gratefully takes up.

"I'm never sure it will come out right," she says. "I've had the most embarrassing failures, but of course tonight, just for family—" She is unable to finish the sentence, or to remember what she meant.

Later, during the next few years before Tom's death, Avery looks back and thinks that yes, she should have left then, drunk or not. She could have found a motel. That would have been a strong gesture, a refusal to put up with any more of what she saw as Tom's male imperialism, his vast selfishness. (But poor Avery was constantly plagued with alternatives; she constantly rewrote her life into new versions in which she did not marry Stanley. Or Christopher. Sometimes she thought she should have stayed with Paul Blue; in that version, of course, he was not married.) After Tom died she thought that perhaps it was just as well she hadn't left, but she was never quite sure.

AGAINST EVERYONE'S ADVICE, EARLY IN THE SUMMER AFTER TOM DIED, Barbara drove alone to Maine. Even Devlin had called to dissuade her (in fact ever since Tom's funeral, to which Avery did not even come—Tom had died while she was in Mount Zion Hospital being treated for depression—a new and warm connection had been established between Barbara and Devlin; they wrote back and forth; she phoned him for various pieces of advice—she had begun to rely on him as she was used to relying on Tom).

Devlin said, "Darling Barbara, do you see it as an exercise in masochism? I wouldn't have thought it of you."

"Angel, you don't understand. I love that house. I've been extremely happy there."

"Barbara, let me be blunt: don't you think you'll be fantastically lonely?"

"No, I don't."

And so, after visits with friends and relatives in Boston, Barbara drives on to Maine in her newest Ford, and arrives in a twilight of early July. She parks near the house, gets out, pausing only briefly to observe the weather, which is clear, and to smile at the warm familiar smell of pines. Then she walks briskly over to the porch and opens the padlock on the screen door.

Her first reaction, stepping up onto the porch, could be considered odd: she decides that those yellow chairs are wrong for the porch. This pleases her: changing them for something else will give her something to do. She enters the living room, sniffs at the musty, airless space, and goes into the kitchen, where last summer she hid a bottle of bourbon in the flour bin. (Sometimes stray hunters or fishermen break into the house and take things.) No one has taken it, and she makes herself a good stiff drink, and goes to the rounded end of the porch, to sit and rest.

And much more clearly than she can remember anything that happened last month, last winter or fall, she sees that scene of over thirty years ago, sees Tom (how young he was, how handsome), as he urged her to play her ukelele (play what? did he name a song?), and she sees Jessica come out to where they are (making some reference to the girls who used to come to camp—poor Jessica), and Wilfred, as always angrily serious, puffing although not yet fat, and then wild, skinny Avery (why did she and Jason Valentine not marry?) and frightened Devlin, holding his mother's arm. She sees all those people, and herself among them, and for an instant she has a sense that she *is* all of them—that she is Jessica as well as Barbara, is Wilfred, Avery, Devlin, and Tom.

But this is an unfamiliar mood, or sense, for her, and she shakes it off, literally shaking her head and lifting her chin. She remembers then that she put the old chairs and the table in the shed next to the kitchen.

Three days later Barbara has restored the lodge to what (to herself) she calls its "old look." The old chairs and old long table are back. She has even put up some of Jessica's old pictures in the living room.

She has no idea why she made such an effort, except that she firmly believes (always has) in the efficacy of physical work; she was driven by a strong, controlling instinct, and she also believes in her instincts. She even laughs to herself at what could seem a whim, and in writing a note to Devlin she says, "You'd have thought I was restoring Williamsburg, and you should see my blisters!"

And so at the end of the day she is seated there at the end of the porch, and everything but herself looks just as it did when she first saw it. She drinks the two stiff highballs that she allows herself before dinner, and she remembers all the best times with Tom, San Francisco hotels and Paris honeymoon, the big parties in Hilton, and she sheds a few tears, but she does not try to change anything that happened. She does not imagine an altered, better life that she might have had.

April 1973

Shiny Objects

MRS. GILLNETTER WAS A DARK, SERIOUS-LOOKING PERSON. HER HANDS, folded in her lap, were blunt and rough. Small, hard muscles showed in her arms from years of work. A heavy grayness hung under her eyes and around her mouth, as if she lived on food without any taste to it and was deaf to all musical sound. She had hardly moved in more than an hour, and then only to secure in her coarse black hair the two small tortoise-shell combs, sharp as cats' teeth, that fastened her braids.

She sat on her porch in a wicker rocker, looking down the long dirt track that led from her house to the road. Before yesterday, when Mr. Cunningham had spent the entire afternoon in her parlor, nobody but herself had traveled up that track in over a year.

On a wire directly in front of her sat a quivering blue-and-rust-colored swallow. Clean, dark fire showed in its eyes. It glanced back and forth between Mrs. Gillnetter and a river-mud nest with four eggs in it under the eaves.

Over Mrs. Gillnetter's head, an old, wide-spreading locust, dense with bees, rubbed its flowering branches mournfully across the roof, and nearby, where the yard ended and the cactus began, a band of sheep with two new lambs ranged along the wire fence. One of these sheep, though it stayed close with the others and gave no evidence of suffering any particular problem, had been bleating monotonously all morning.

DIANNE BENEDICT

Though the springtime was in full progress all around her, Mrs. Gillnetter gave no thought to it. She was awaiting the arrival of a child, a boy of twelve. She had been informed, by means of a fat letter stuffed with medical records, that this child was in need of special care and that the county would pay her handsomely for taking him in. She had never seen him, and she disliked everything Mr. Cunningham had told her about him in her parlor yesterday afternoon.

"I am not exaggerating," Mr. Cunningham had said, "when I tell you that we're speaking here of an individual who spends every waking hour rewriting the Bible."

Mrs. Gillnetter didn't hold with the Bible. She found all the turbulence in it upsetting, and she doubted whether any amount of attention given to it by a twelve-year-old boy, who was himself in need of special care, was going to lighten it up any.

Mr. Cunningham had shown her a photograph in which all she could make out clearly was a wide, dead-white face set directly onto a pair of frail shoulders, the eyes in shadow under a shelf of dark hair. Later, along with her copy of the child-care papers, Mrs. Gillnetter had thrown this photograph into the oil drum out back and burned it. She had indicated on the form they had given her to fill out in the beginning that she wanted a teenage girl. Now this sickly looking boy with an overlarge head was due to arrive at any moment. Mrs. Gillnetter felt as if the county people had her by the wrists and around the waist, and were rushing her against her will into an ugly situation.

"You got nobody but yourself to blame," she said aloud to herself, by which she meant that when Mr. Cunningham had squatted spread-legged on a stool yesterday afternoon, carrying on about the boy and showing off his photograph, she, for her part, had only sat staring at the oval rug with pansies on it lying on the floor between them and had said nothing. It was always that way. While she was casting about for the right words to express her feelings, the other person always ran off with the decision.

She recalled that Mr. Cunningham had smelled like a lemon meringue pie that had been left out too long in the room. He was a stout man, dressed in a white summer suit and a string tie secured by a knob of turquoise as big as a turkey egg. He had stood over her, mopping his neck with a red kerchief, while she worked on the papers.

"The boy's full name is Ulysses Montgomery Dade," he had said, leaning so close that she nearly stopped breathing. "But take your time, Miss Lucy. We got all the time in the world."

She always got so angry she could hardly control herself whenever anybody called her Lucy, but instead of strangling Mr. Cunningham by hauling backward with sudden and unexpected force on his string tie, like she wanted to, she had excused herself and gone and stood for a long time in the pantry with her arms rolled up in her apron.

Now she looked down the dirt track once more and caught sight of a man in a fedora hat standing at the gate. This man was so short that he was obliged to peer over the top board, holding on to it with both hands. Mrs. Gillnetter perceived some sort of footgear on this person, shaped like two black-leather buckets, that was unfamiliar to her. She thought to herself that it never failed that if you already had one thing to deal with on a particular afternoon, another was always bound to come along.

She went to the edge of the porch steps and called out, "You'd best go on now. This here isn't any place to be waiting around." The man continued to peer at her, making no move to leave. She looked intently at him and made out a pair of thick, rimless glasses under the fedora hat and a mustard-colored heavy woolen suit. Resting under the gate, in the dust of the track, was an old black satchel and a cardboard box tied shut with hemp rope. "Looks like some kind of dwarf salesman has run out of gas," Mrs. Gillnetter said.

"Mr. Gillnetter and I don't have any gas right now," she called out, "but down the next house is a telephone."

"I know you ain't married," the person at the gate called out to her, and this immediately made her so angry that she had to turn and go inside the house.

For the next half-hour, she kept watch through the front windows. On about the seventeenth time she went to do this, she was relieved to see that the dwarf was gone. "It always pays to just go on about your life," Mrs. Gillnetter said, and then the telephone rang.

"Miss Lucy, I'm afraid there is going to be maybe a short delay," Mr. Cunningham said to her on the phone. "There is no sense making up a story to you about it, the boy has received the bad news this morning that his condition is terminal, and it was temporarily upsetting to him, and now he has run off."

While she was having this conversation with Mr. Cunningham in her kitchen, she was able to see, through the window over the sink-pump, a short person with an overlarge head climbing into the back of the blue-and-green Plymouth truck that had rested unused beside the tractor shed for fourteen years. He hauled the black satchel and the cardboard box with him up into the bed of the truck and went and sat down with his back against the cab. Mrs. Gillnetter watched him take off his heavy glasses and wipe them carefully on a fold in his shirtfront and put them back on, adjusting the delicate wires over his ears one at a time. Then he sat with his arms around the satchel, fanning off bluebottle flies with his battered fedora.

Mrs. Gillnetter laid the phone down gently on the counter while Mr. Cunningham was still talking and went out onto the screened porch and stood there watching. The person in the truck, she could see now, was a boy. Before long, he appeared to come to a decision. He took off his jacket, climbed down out of the truck, and disappeared into the shed. He emerged a few moments later dragging a small bedspring. As he hauled this bedspring through the dust of the yard, Mrs. Gillnetter was able to see for the first time that his legs were severely bowed and that his feet were tilted to the sides, which action had caused the black leather buckets with their heavy laces to run down over the soles.

Mrs. Gillnetter felt safe on the screened porch. She sat on a stack of newspapers and began to cast about for the right words to express her feelings to the county people. "I am not equipped," she said to them in a whisper.

The boy struggled for a long time getting the bedspring up into the truckbed, then returned to the shed and dragged out the mattress. This narrow bed was the very one Mrs. Gillnetter had slept on as a child, and she wondered if he was going to set up the wooden-spool bedstead in the back of the truck too. She remembered that she had been waked up out of that bed every morning of the world by a black-and-white terrier named Gabriel, who used to stand on her chest licking her face until she threw him off.

"That dog is long dead," she said. She began to search for the words to tell the boy that he would not be staying.

While she was doing this, he went several times back into the shed. He brought out a lacquered-paper Chinese screen, a table-top with bluebirds stenciled on it, a coatrack, a stack of horse blankets, and an old leaded green-glass window. He arranged these belongings carefully, with many pauses and considerations, in the back of the truck.

The sun was getting down low over the fields, making long shadows, when Mrs. Gillnetter opened the screen door and went outside. She crossed the yard slowly, with her arms wrapped up in her apron, and stopped under a persimmon tree a few feet away from the boy. He sat on the mattress, writing on an Indian Head tablet that he had in his lap. There were maybe two-dozen wadded-up balls of yellow paper lying around him, and his hair showed clearly that he's been running his fingers every which way through it. He wore a troubled look, as if he were possessed by thoughts not meant to be conjured up together. He glanced at her with his eyes full of dark feeling and reached for the fedora, pulling it on very low to the front. From the shadow of the brim, he studied her with a strong, direct gaze.

"You a Mexican?" he asked.

She didn't answer him.

"You colored?"

"You have got to go back," she said. "I am very sorry for the inconvenience."

"There wouldn't be no problem with that," the boy said, "except that I have moved in here."

"No, you have not," she said.

"Yes. I saw it in a dream."

Mrs. Gillnetter unrolled her arms from her apron and moved out of the shadow of the persimmon tree. The orange color from the late sun slanted over her, filling her with a sense of beauty and power that came seldom to her. "You think you are big enough that you can work it so you get your way, only you are not," she said. "You are only a puny child."

The boy swung his strange leather boots over the edge of the mattress and stood up, bracing himself with a hand on the coatrack, and Mrs. Gillnetter saw that he was about as tall as an eight-year-old child.

"I am a new voice," he said.

"You are a dwarf child without so much as a penny nor any place to live, and you had better take heed that you are at the mercy of strangers," Mrs. Gillnetter said.

"You are at the mercy of the stranger, too," the boy said.

He took off the fedora and came a step forward, emerging out of the shadows, and when Mrs. Gillnetter looked at his face turned full toward her, she felt as if a deep, sad, far-off note had rung from a bell.

"The stranger," the boy said. "The thief. He has come into your household even now for gold."

Mrs. Gillnetter rolled her arms back up in her apron. She went a step nearer. They remained that way for a while, like two solitary people thrown together suddenly on a journey, the dwarf child in the truck and the woman on the ground, looking at each other in genuine alarm.

THAT EVENING ULYSSES MONTGOMERY CARRIED ALL HIS FURNITURE INTO the house and up the stairs and locked himself away in a room on the second floor. In the days following, the total silence, combined with Mrs.

Gillnetter's unwillingness to knock on the door, caused her many vexations of the spirit. She abandoned as hopeless several schemes to evict the child from her house, progressing from these to the possibility of going to live in a hotel she had once stayed at in Sweet Water, which had a small room over the back stairwell that was shut off altogether from the traffic. At meal-times, she left the boy food on a tray with a cross-stitch napkin over it out-side the door, but he never touched it.

On the afternoon of the third day, she heard him singing about pomegranates. She was in the kitchen, scalding a chicken. She heard the song through a grate in the ceiling over her head. After the song about pomegranates, he began a song about cinnamon and grapes. While he was singing this song, Mrs. Gillnetter became aware of energetic flapping, and a full-grown crow appeared at the window over the sink-pump, causing her to drop the pullet off the fork in the scalding water, which splashed up over the edge and half drenched the fire. She stood with the fork in one hand and the lid to the scalding pot in the other, watching the crow, which seemed as if it were appearing to her in a dream. It strode back and forth along the windowsill, putting its head first to one side and then to the other. In the tip of its beak it held a small tin star. It dropped the star through a hole in the screen, looked in keenly after it, then flew away.

"Give a crow a shiny object," Mrs. Gillnetter said.

She went to the window and looked inside the sill. She saw a tarnished tin star lying there. She lifted the edge of it with a prong of the fork, but it was as homely and black on one side as it was on the other. She looked out the window at the persimmon tree, which had dark leaves pointing upward crisply and a multitude of small, purple-throated flowers. This tree seemed to her, like the crow, as if it were about to speak to her out of a dream. A pale-blue fire stirred the air around it. Mrs. Gillnetter studied this for a while, then turned back into the kitchen to relight the stove.

Late that evening, she put away everything in the kitchen and scrubbed the table with a coarse brush and a sprinkling of salt. She took the bucket of ashes outdoors and spread them evenly among her onions. Then she went upstairs to where the boy was locked away in his room and spoke to him for the first time.

"I'm not bringing no more food up here to this door," she said.

She heard his heavy dragging step approach and stop close by.

"Food?" he said.

"That's right. And I am not equipped for no more conjuring, neither."

"What food?" the boy said.

"Why, the food I have brought up here three times a day."

"There's food there?"

"Not no more, there ain't."

"Where'd it go?"

"Where'd it go? Why, I took it back down again."

"Well, say what it was. Was it yams? And parsnips? And nutmeats? And the whole business melted over with brown sugar?"

"Pshaw, boy! It was *food*. Regular *food*. "

"Was it barley cakes? Stuffed with raisins, maybe, and pork and pineapple?"

Mrs. Gillnetter, finding it tedious to go on with this conversation, fell silent. The boy opened the door and stood before her, barefoot and barechested in his heavy woolen suit.

"Are you playing tricks on me about the food?" he said. His eyes were bright with pain.

"You have got grit to say that," Mrs. Gillnetter said. "You with your devil crows. You with your fiery trees."

The boy lowered his head and moved, with a dragging step, out into the hall toward the stairs.

"I have to go find food now," he said.

"Not in my kitchen, you don't," Mrs. Gillnetter said.

She hurried past him on the stairs and went into the kitchen and bolted the door. After a moment, she heard him go out the front, and she stood in the middle of the darkening kitchen, thinking maybe he had left, maybe he was headed out to the road, intent on returning to the county home; but then she heard a scratch on the window screen and, turning, saw him looking in at her, his large head dark against the red of the late-evening sky. The sight of him made her suddenly very angry. She took off her apron and flapped it at him and rushed toward the window, calling, "Shush, now! Shush!" She beat on the screen, seeking to drive him away, but he was intent on getting in. He forced his fingers around the edges of the screen and rattled it in its frame. The sound of his labored breathing, coming from so close in the darkness, was alarming.

She went around the unlit kitchen swiftly, closing all the windows, after which she sat down at the table, trembling. She took up from the center of the table the small red rooster that held the pepper, and set to polishing his head with her apron.

The boy had disappeared into the night. Suddenly Mrs. Gillnetter heard a pounding like thunder along the bottom of the sill.

"He has got hold of a fair-sized stone," she said. She set the rooster down again beside the white hen and folded her hands in her lap.

The pounding progressed from window to window, and after a while Mrs. Gillnetter could take no more of it. She got a plate off the shelf and went to the cooler and took out chicken and butter. She brought out greens and black-eyed peas and mixed these with vinegar and a little pork fat in the skillet. She blew a fire up under a handful of faggots, and warmed the boy's food over the direct flame.

He was taking the screen door off its hinges when she got to the back porch. She opened the inside door the space of its chain and called through.

"You listen here to me," she said. "It's only the lowest kind of animal behaves thataway outside the house."

"How come you to shut me out?" he said. "I can't abide it. I can't abide it, hear?"

"Now, quit!" Mrs. Gillnetter said. "And sit right there on that stair."

But the boy went down the steps and disappeared in the dark yard. Soon she heard him come in the front and go up the stairs to his room. He shut the door with a crash, throwing the bolt loudly, and drew something heavy against it.

"No telling what will happen now," Mrs. Gillnetter said.

She went out onto the porch and stood looking into the darkness, the plate of food growing cold in her hand.

"How quick it all comes up, without no warning," she said. "Land, it's like when we was little, and it would be a sunshiny day, with nothing untoward at all, and then one of the hands would holler out, 'Better head home, chirren, they's wolves sighted on the far hill.'"

She set the plate of food down at the top of the steps and peered into the night.

"Black as pitch," she said.

TOWARD MIDNIGHT MRS. GILLNETTER LAY AWAKE IN THE MOONLIGHT FOR a long while, troubled with sleeplessness and indecision. Finally she got up out of bed and went to the door of the boy's room and knocked on it sharply.

"Tomorrow morning early I am going to take a screwdriver to the hinges on this door," she called out.

After a moment she heard the sound of the bedsprings and the laboring commotion the boy made when he got to his feet. Soon the latch was lifted and the door opened. Ulysses Montgomery stood before her, squinting in the harsh light from the hallway, barely awake. He was clad only in his undershorts, and his naked legs were startling in their deformity. His head, which he carried laid back slightly, appeared to burden him with its weight, and his chest was like an old peach basket with the ribs sprung. The frailty of the whole of him gave Mrs. Gillnetter suddenly an entirely new feeling about him. She reached out and pulled the door closed gently and waited there in the hall, listening. She heard no sound whatever. She pictured him leaning with his forehead against the door frame, fast asleep. After a moment, she turned out the light and went back to bed.

She had slipped away into a dream in which she was crossing over a wide bridge together with a multitude of people, when she woke to find Ulysses Montgomery standing beside her in the moonlight.

"You scared?" he asked her.

She raised herself up on her elbow and peered at him. He looked at her as if they had been in conversation most of the night and had only just that moment reached a mutual conclusion.

"Well, I am," he said. He turned and disappeared into the dark. She heard him dragging his feet over the floorboards, through the hall, down the stairs.

Mrs. Gillnetter lay back on her pillows. For the second time that night, she was overcome by the hugeness of her misfortune. Memory pictures of all that had happened since she had first caught sight of the boy at her gate assaulted her out of the darkness. She thought back to the way her life had been before he had come. The long days of the locust limbs creaking, and the wash on the line billowing in the sun. The great banks of clouds appearing out of one quarter of the sky and disappearing soundlessly into another. The gentle changes in the light. The stars at night so dense in their mantle.

A memory came over her suddenly of the blissful feeling she had had all those years ago after Mr. Gillnetter left, the peace and gladness that no words could circumscribe. That feeling had stayed with her, true and unchanging through all the years of solitude.

In the midst of these thoughts, she heard the screen door on the back porch open and clatter shut.

"Now he has gone out of the house in the middle of the night," she said.

She got up and looked out the window, and there was Ulysses Montgomery crossing the yard in the moonlight. He moved haltingly without his shoes. She watched him cross, with his dragging step, between the trough and the windmill.

"He is headed out into the pasturage," she said.

She went down the stairs with her nightgown in a billow around her and sat on the stack of newspapers on the porch and laced on her boots.

"He is going to get caught in the cactus," she said.

She took the lantern from the nail. After lighting it, she put the matches in her pocket. She let the screen door slam and crossed the yard swiftly. The circle of light from the lantern swung violently around her as she went under the barbed wire. Beyond the fence began the vast expanse of prickly-pear cactus and mesquite.

Soon she saw Ulysses Montgomery ahead of her, dragging his feet laboriously over the rough ground. He kept on at the same pace, looking straight ahead, even when the light from the lantern slipped over him. When she caught up with him, she could think of nothing whatever to say and was forced to walk slowly alongside him, stumbling over the stony ground, getting her nightgown caught repeatedly in the pricklebush and thistles.

Finally, he stopped.

"This here's the top of the rise," he said.

Mrs. Gillnetter looked around her. She couldn't see that they were at the top of anything. The land was flat as a griddle.

"Put that thing out," he said, and he took hold of the lantern before she could do anything about it and blew out the flame. When he did this, the night sky with its stars became a bowl over them.

"Over yonder in that direction is the river they call the Jordan, which flows into the Sea of Galilee," he said. "All acrost the Holy Land is olive trees and fields of wheat growing and poppy flowers. I saw it in a picture."

He swung the unlit lamp slowly forward. "And thataway lies the polar ice cap, which is all over miles deep with ice as blue as any diamond. They's whole mountains of ice moving by slow degree toward the sea."

He set the lantern on the ground between them.

"And over there. Know what's over there?" Ulysses Montgomery said.

Mrs. Gillnetter knew what lay in that direction. It was a road that led to the home of a friend who had long ago deserted her. Looking across the moonlit trees toward that road, Mrs. Gillnetter saw this woman clearly as she had been when they were both young, the abundant chestnut hair held back in a ribbon, the narrow lace collar closed with an abalone pin.

"It's a no-account place without even a church," she said, thinking of the town where the other woman still lived.

"China," Ulysses Montgomery said. "Thataway lies China. It's all the wonders you can imagine. Gold and silver ships, and lakes with swans, and streets paved with ivory and jasper. Only no man has ever seen it. Not ever. It all lies beyond a wall no man has ever climbed."

Mrs. Gillnetter was picturing the abalone pin, which her friend had given her. She had placed it on velvet in a small drawer of her dresser. Abruptly, she picked up the lantern.

"It's too far out there for us to be standing about dreaming on such things," she said. She took the matches from her pocket and lit the lantern and held it up between them. They looked at each other in silence. "There's cattle out here," she said.

"And snakes, too, probably," Ulysses Montgomery said.

"Yes, snakes, too," she said.

"I wisht I was a snake."

Mrs. Gillnetter was forced against her will to laugh. "That's some kind of low life," she said.

"Yes, a snake has been consigned low," he said. "He has been consigned so low he can't never lift up any part of himself off the ground, only his head. He don't have any power to laugh nor anything to laugh at. So how can Jesus love him? Why, he loves him *because* he can't fly. He loves him *because* he can't sing. He loves him because he has intimate knowledge of everything from having to crawl *over* it."

Mrs. Gillnetter studied Ulysses Montgomery in the lantern light. His limbs were sunken over the long bones and swollen at the joints. There were hollows under his eyes. He looked frail and spongy as a tumbleweed. She couldn't imagine where he had got the strength to come this far out into the pasturage.

"No chance you'll make it back," she said.

The boy's face, which had been bright until that moment, went dull and tired. He looked at the ground. "You're right, there," he said. "I have ruint my feet for this night. I can't walk no more tonight."

Mrs. Gillnetter looked back toward the house, wishing she'd left a light on. She could just make out the windmill fluttering, small and far away.

"How are we going to get you back?" she said.

"You are going to carry me," he said.

She felt a wave of sickness come over her at the suggestion of this. She looked away from him.

"Give me that thing," he said, taking the lantern. He stood sideways to her. "Ain't nothing for it only to just go ahead with it," he said. "Nobody ever minds it too much after the first time."

She bent and caught him under the knees and around the ribs. She had never carried anybody before, not even an infant. When she felt him fold against her, like a bird drawing its wings in, she caught sight, suddenly, of something very like the whole of his life. It was as if he had pulled his life in with him so small and compact and vivid that it could almost be put into her pocket.

She carried him carefully over the stony ground. The lantern, swinging in front of them, cast great shadows dancing from the trees. She was amazed at the feel of him, the smallness of his bones.

He held very still and didn't look up, but after a while he said to her, "What would you be for an animal?"

"I don't hold with all that," she said.

"A fish," he said. The hand holding the lantern sank lower, and she felt his head lean heavily against her. "You are a fish. In the waters. In amongst the bread." He spoke in a whisper.

She was able to take the lantern from him before it slipped down. He was very still as they crossed under the low trees, and she thought he was asleep, but after a moment he began to meddle with the long braid that had come forward over her shoulder. He unwound the strands of it.

"I wouldn't keep on with that," she said.

But he pulled the braid loose into the heavy waves that she never liked to live with except for the time it took to brush them, and he drew the mass of her hair forward and lifted his head onto it and wound his hand in it.

"Feeding on the bread," he said, his voice so low that she could barely hear.

Soon his breathing was steady, warm on her neck, and she knew by the subtle change in the weight of him that he was asleep.

February 1982

Visitors

MILDRED HAD JUST COME INTO THE KITCHEN AND WAS LOOKING AT THE clock, which said five to two. She had thought it might be at least half-past. Wilfred came in from the back, through the utility room, and said, "Hadn't you ought to be out there keeping them company?"

His brother Albert's wife, Grace, and her sister, Vera, were sitting out in the shade of the carport making lace tablecloths. Albert was out at the back of the house, sitting beside the patch of garden where Wilfred grew beans, tomatoes, and cucumbers. Every half-hour Wilfred checked to see which tomatoes were ripe enough to pick. He picked them half-ripe and spread them out on the kitchen windowsill, so the bugs wouldn't get them.

"I was," said Mildred. She ran a glass of water. "I maybe might take them for a drive," she said when she had finished drinking it.

"That's a good idea."

"How is Albert?"

Albert had spent most of the day before, the first full day of the visit, lying down.

"I can't figure out."

"Well, surely if he felt sick he'd say so."

ALICE MUNRO

"That's just it," said Wilfred. "That's just what he wouldn't."

This was the first time Wilfred had seen his brother in more than thirty years.

Wilfred and Mildred were retired. Their house was small and they weren't, but they got along fine in the space. They had a kitchen not much wider than a hallway, a bathroom about the usual size, two bedrooms that were pretty well filled up when you got a double bed and a dresser into them, a living room where a large sofa sat five feet in front of a large television set, with a low table about the size of a coffin in between, and a small glassed-in porch.

Mildred had set up a table on the porch to serve meals on. Ordinarily, she and Wilfred ate at the table under the kitchen window. If one of them was up and moving around, the other always stayed sitting down. There was no way five people could have managed there, even when three of them were as skinny as these visitors were.

Fortunately there was a daybed on the porch, and Vera, the sister-in-law, slept on that. The sister-in-law had been a surprise to Mildred and Wilfred. Wilfred had done the talking on the phone (nobody in his family, he said, had ever written a letter); according to him, no sister-in-law had been mentioned, just Albert and his wife. Mildred thought Wilfred might not have heard, because he was so excited. Talking to Albert on the phone, from Logan, Ontario, to Elder, Saskatchewan, taking in the news that his brother proposed to visit him, Wilfred had been in a dither of hospitality, reassurances, amazement.

"You come right ahead," he yelled over the phone to Saskatchewan. "We can put you up as long as you want to stay. We got plenty of room. We'll be glad to. Never mind your return tickets. You get on down here and enjoy the summer." It might have been while he was going on like this that Albert was explaining about the sister-in-law.

"How do you tell them apart?" said Wilfred on first meeting Grace and Vera. "Or do you always bother?" He meant it for a joke.

"They're not twins," said Albert, without a glance at either of them. Albert was a short, thin man in dark clothes, who looked as if he might weigh heavy, like dense wood. He wore a string tie and a westerner's hat, but these did not give him a jaunty appearance. His pale cheeks hung down on either side of his chin.

"You look like sisters, though," said Mildred genially to the two dried-out, brown-spotted, gray-haired women. Look what the prairie did to a woman's skin, she was thinking. Mildred was vain of her own skin; it was her compensation for being fat. Also, she put an ash-gold rinse on her hair and wore coordinated pastel pants and tops. Grace and Vera wore dresses with loose pleats over their flat chests, and cardigans in summer. "You look a lot more like sisters than those two look like brothers."

It was true. Wilfred had a big head as well as a big stomach, and an anxious, eager, changeable face. He looked like a man who put a high value on joking and chatting, and so he did.

"It's lucky there's none of you too fleshy," Wilfred said. "You can all fit into the one bed. Naturally Albert gets the middle."

"Don't pay attention to him," said Mildred. "There's a good daybed if you don't mind sleeping on the porch," she said to Vera. "It's got blinds on the windows and it gets the best breeze of anywhere."

God knows if the women even caught on to what Wilfred was joking about.

"That'll be fine," said Albert.

With Albert and Grace sleeping in the spare room, which was where Mildred usually slept, Mildred and Wilfred had to share a double bed. They weren't used to it. In the night, Wilfred had one of his wild dreams, which were the reason Mildred had moved to the spare room in the first place.

"Grab ahold!" yelled Wilfred, in terror. Was he on a lake boat, trying to pull somebody out of the water?

"Wilfred, wake up! Stop hollering and scaring everybody to death."

"I am awake," said Wilfred. "I wasn't hollering."

"Then I'm Her Majesty the Queen."

They were lying on their backs. They both heaved and turned to face the outside. Each kept a courteous but firm hold on the blankets.

"Is it whales that can't turn over when they get up on the beach?" Mildred said.

"I can turn over," said Wilfred. They aligned backsides. "Maybe you think that's the only thing I can do."

"Keep still, now, you've got them all listening."

In the morning she said, "Did Wilfred wake you up? He's a terrible hollerer in his sleep."

"I hadn't got to sleep anyway," Albert said.

SHE WENT OUT AND GOT THE TWO LADIES INTO THE CAR. "WE'LL TAKE A little drive and raise a breeze to cool us off," she said. They sat in the back, because there wasn't really room left over in the front, even for two such skinnies.

"I'm the chauffeur!" said Mildred merrily. "Where to, your ladyships?"

"Just anyplace you'd like," said one of them. When she wasn't looking at them Mildred couldn't be sure which was talking.

147

She drove them around Winter Court and Chelsea Drive to look at the new houses with their landscaping and swimming pools. Then she took them to the Fish and Game Club, where they saw the ornamental fowl, the family of deer, the raccoons, and the caged bobcat. She felt as tired as if she had driven to Toronto, and in need of refreshment, so she headed out to the place on the highway to buy ice-cream cones. They both asked for a small vanilla. Mildred had a mixed double: rum-raisin and praline cream. They sat at a picnic table licking their ice-cream cones and looking at a field of corn.

"They grow a lot of corn around here," Mildred said. Albert had been the manager of a grain elevator before he retired, so she supposed they might be interested in crops. "Do they grow a lot of corn out west?"

They thought about it. Grace said, "Well. Some."

Vera said, "I was wondering."

"Wondering what?" said Mildred cheerfully.

"You wouldn't have a Pentecostal Church here in Logan?"

They set out in the car again, and after some blundering, Mildred found the Pentecostal Church. It was not one of the handsomer churches in town. It was a plain building, of cement blocks, with the doors and the window-trim painted orange. A sign told the minister's name and the times of service. There was no shade tree near it and no bushes or flowers, just a dry yard. Maybe that would remind them of Saskatchewan.

"Pentecostal Church," said Mildred, reading the sign. "Is that the church you people go to?"

"Yes."

"Wilfred and I are not regular churchgoers. If we went, I guess we would go to the United. Do you want to get out and see if it's unlocked?"

"Oh, no."

"If it was locked, we could try and locate the minister. I don't know him, but there's a lot of Logan people I don't know yet. I know the ones that bowl and the ones that play euchre at the Legion. Otherwise, I don't know many. Would you like to call on him?

They said no. Mildred was thinking about the Pentecostal Church, and it seemed to her that it was the one where people spoke in tongues. She thought she might as well get something out of the afternoon, so she went ahead and asked them: was that true?

"Yes, it's true."

"But what are tongues?"

A pause. One said, with difficulty, "It's the voice of God."

"Heavens," said Mildred. She wanted to ask more—did they speak in tongues themselves?—but they made her nervous. It was clear that she made them nervous, too. She let them look a few minutes more, then asked if they had seen enough. They said they had, and thanked her.

IF SHE HAD MARRIED WILFRED YOUNG, MILDRED THOUGHT, SHE WOULD have known something about his family and what to expect of them. Mildred and Wilfred had married in late middle age, after a courtship of only six weeks. Neither of them had been married before. Wilfred had moved around too much, or so he said. He had worked on the lake boats and in lumber camps, he had helped build houses and had pumped gas and had pruned trees; he had worked from California to the Yukon and from the east coast to the west. Mildred had spent most of her life in the town of McGaw, twenty miles from Logan, where she now lived. She had been an only child, and had been given tap-dancing lessons and then sent to business school. From business school she went into the office of the Toll Shoe Factory, in McGaw, and shortly became the sweetheart of Mr. Toll, who owned it. There she stayed.

It was during the last days of Mr. Toll's life that she met Wilfred. Mr. Toll was in the psychiatric hospital overlooking Lake Huron. Wilfred was working there as a groundsman and guard. Mr. Toll was eighty-two years old and didn't know who Mildred was, but she visited him anyway. He called her Sadie, that being the name of his wife. His wife was dead now but she had been alive all the time Mr. Toll and Mildred were taking their little trips together, staying at hotels together, staying in the cottage Mr. Toll had bought for Mildred at Amberley Beach. In all the time she had known him, Mildred had never heard him speak of his wife except in a dry, impatient way. Now she had to listen to him tell Sadie he loved her, ask Sadie's forgiveness. Pretending she was Sadie, Mildred said she forgave him. She dreaded some confession regarding a brassy-headed floozy named Mildred. Nevertheless, she kept on visiting. She hadn't the heart to deprive him. That had been her trouble all along. But when the sons or daughters or Sadie's sisters showed up, she had to make herself scarce. Once, taken by surprise, she had to get Wilfred to let her out a back way. She sat down on a cement wall by the back door and had a cigarette, and Wilfred asked her if anything was the matter. Being upset, and having nobody in McGaw to talk to, she told him what was going on, even about the letter she had received from a lawyer telling her she had to get out of the Amberley cottage. She had thought all along it was in her name, but it wasn't.

Wilfred took her side. He went in and spied on the visiting family, and reported that they were sitting staring at the poor old man like crows on a fence. He didn't point out to Mildred what she already knew: that she should have seen the writing on the wall. She herself said it.

"I should've gotten out while I still had something going for me."

"You must've been fond of him," said Wilfred reasonably.

"It was never love," said Mildred sadly. Wilfred scowled with deep embarrassment. Mildred had the sense not to go on, and couldn't have explained, anyway, how she had been transfixed by Mr. Toll in his more vigorous days, when his need for her was so desperate she thought he would turn himself inside out.

Mr. Toll died in the middle of the night. Wilfred phoned Mildred at seven in the morning.

"I didn't want to wake you up," he said. "But I wanted to make sure you knew before you heard it out in public."

Then he asked her to have supper with him in a restaurant. Being used to Mr. Toll, she was surprised at Wilfred's table manners. He was nervous, she decided. He got upset because the waitress hadn't brought their glasses of water. Mildred told him that she was going to quit her job, she wanted to get clear of McGaw, and she might end up out west.

"Why not end up in Logan?" Wilfred said. "I've got a house there. It's not so big a house, but it'll take two."

So it dawned on her. His nervousness, his bad temper with the waitress, his sloppiness, must all relate to her. She asked if he had ever been married before, and if not, why not?

He said he had always been on the go, and besides, it wasn't often you met a goodhearted woman. She was about to make sure he had things straight, by pointing out that she expected nothing from Mr. Toll's will (nothing was what she got), but she saw in the nick of time that Wilfred was the kind of man who would be insulted.

Instead, she said, "You know I'm secondhand goods?"

"None of that," he said. "We won't have any of that kind of talk around the house. Is it settled?"

Mildred said yes. She was glad to see an immediate improvement in his behavior to the waitress. In fact, he went overboard, apologizing for his impatience earlier, telling her he had worked in a restaurant himself. He told her where the restaurant was, up on the Alaska Highway. The girl had trouble getting away to serve coffee at the other tables.

No such improvement took place in Wilfred's table manners. She guessed that was one of his bachelor ways she would just have to learn to live with.

"You better tell me a bit about where you were born, and so on," Mildred said.

He told her he had been born on a farm in Hullett Township, but left there when he was three days old.

"Itchy feet," he said, and laughed. Then he sobered, and told her that his mother had died within a few hours of his birth, and his aunt had taken him. His aunt was married to a man who worked on the railway. They moved around, and when he was twelve his aunt died. Then the man she was married to looked at Wilfred and said, "You're a big boy. What size shoe do you wear?"

"Number nine," said Wilfred.

"Then you're big enough to earn your own living."

"Him and my aunt had eight kids of their own," said Wilfred. "So I don't blame him."

"Did you have any brothers and sisters in your real family?" Mildred thought cozily of her own life long ago: her mother fixing her curls in the morning, the kitten, named Pansy, that she used to dress up in doll's clothes and wheel round the block in the doll buggy.

"I had two older sisters, married. Both dead now. And one brother. He went out to Saskatchewan. He has a job managing a grain elevator. I don't know what he gets paid but I imagine it's pretty good. He went to business college, like yourself. He's a different person than me, way different."

THE DAY THAT ALBERT HAD STAYED IN BED, HE WANTED THE CURTAINS shut. He didn't want a doctor. Wilfred couldn't get out of him what was wrong. Albert said he was just tired.

"Then maybe he is tired," said Mildred. "Let him rest."

But Wilfred was in and out of the spare room all day. He was talking, smoking, asking Albert how he felt. He told Albert he had cured himself of migraine headaches by eating fresh leeks from the garden in the spring. Albert said he didn't have a migraine headache, even if he did want the curtains closed. He said he had never had a bad headache in his life. Wilfred explained that you could have migraine headaches without knowing it— that is, without having the actual ache—so that could be what Albert had. Albert said he didn't see how that was possible.

Early that afternoon Mildred heard Wilfred crashing around in the clothes closet. He emerged calling her name.

"Mildred! Mildred! Where is the Texas mickey?"

"In the buffet," said Mildred, and she got it out for him so he wouldn't be rummaging around in there in her mother's china. It was in a tall box, gold-embossed, with the Legion crest on it. Wilfred bore it into the bedroom and set it on the dresser for Albert to see.

"What do you think that is and how do you think I come by it?"

It was a bottle of whiskey, a gallon bottle of whiskey, 110-proof, that Wilfred had won playing darts at the tournament in Owen Sound. The tournament had taken place in February three years before. Wilfred described the terrible drive from Logan to Owen Sound, himself driving, the other members of the dart team urging him to stop in every town they reached, and not to try to get farther. A blizzard blew off Lake Huron, they were enveloped in whiteouts, trucks and buses loomed up in front of their eyes out of the wall of snow, there was no room to maneuver because the road was walled with drifts ten feet high. Wilfred kept driving; driving blind, driving through skids and drifts across the road. At last, on Highway No. 6, a blue light appeared ahead of him, a twirling blue light, a beacon, a rescue-light. It was the snowplow, traveling ahead of them. The road was filling in almost as fast as the snowplow cleared it, but by keeping close behind the plow they were guided safely into Owen Sound. There they played in the tournament, and were victorious.

"Do you ever play darts yourself?" Mildred heard Wilfred ask his brother.

"As a rule they play darts in places that serve liquor," Albert said. "As a rule I don't go into those places."

"Well, this here is liquor I would never consider drinking. I keep it for the honor of it."

THEIR SITTING TOOK ON A REGULAR PATTERN. IN THE AFTERNOON GRACE and Vera sat in the driveway crocheting their tablecloths. Mildred sat with them off and on. Albert and Wilfred sat at the back of the house, by the vegetables. After supper they all sat together, moving their chairs to the lawn in front of the flower beds, which was then in the shade. Grace and Vera went on crocheting as long as they could see.

Wilfred admired the crocheting.

"How much would you get for one of those things?"

"Hundreds of dollars," Albert said.

"It's sold for the church," said Grace.

"Blanche Black," said Wilfred, "was the greatest crocheter, knitter, sewer, what-all, and cook of any girl I ever knew."

"What a name," said Mildred.

"She lived in the state of Michigan. It was when I got fed up with working on the boats and I had a job over there working on a farm. She could make quilts or anything. And bake bread, fancy cake, anything. But not very good-looking. In fact, she was about as good-looking as a turnip, and about the shape."

Now came a story that Mildred had heard before. It was told when the subject of pretty girls and homely girls came up, or baking, or box socials, or pride. Wilfred told how he and a friend went to a box social, where at intermission in the dancing you bid on a box, and the box contained a lunch, and you ate lunch with the girl whose box you had bought. Blanche Black brought a box lunch and so did a pretty girl, Miss Buchanan, and Wilfred and his friends got into the back room and switched all the wrappings around on these two boxes. So when it came time to bid, a fellow named Jack Fleck, who had a very good opinion of himself and a case on Miss Buchanan, bid for the box he thought was hers, and Wilfred and his friend bid for the box that everybody thought was Blanche Black's. The boxes were given out, and to his consternation Jack Fleck was compelled to sit down with Blanche Black. Wilfred and his friend were set up with Miss Buchanan. Then Wilfred looked in the box and saw there was nothing but sandwiches with a kind of pink paste on them.

"So over I go to Jack Fleck and I say, 'Trade you the lunch and the girl.' I didn't do it entirely on account of the food but because I saw how he was going to treat that poor creature. He agreed like a shot and we sat down. We ate fried chicken. Home-cured ham and biscuits. Date pie. Never fed better in my life. And tucked down at the bottom of the box she had a mickey of whiskey. So I sat eating and drinking and looking at him over there with his paste sandwiches."

Wilfred must have started that story as a tribute to ladies whose crocheting or baking or whatever put them away ahead of ladies who had better looks to offer, but Mildred didn't think even Grace and Vera would be pleased to be put in the category of Blanche Black, who looked like a turnip. And mentioning the mickey of whiskey was a mistake. It was a mistake as far as she was concerned, too. She thought of how much she would like a drink at this moment. She thought of Old Fashioneds, Brown Cows, Pink Ladies, every fancy drink you could imagine.

"I better go and see if I can fix that air-conditioner," Wilfred said. "We'll roast tonight if I don't."

Mildred sat on. Over in the next block there was a blue light that sizzled loudly, catching bugs.

"I guess those things make a difference with the flies," she said.

"Fries them," said Albert.

"I don't like the noise, though."

She thought he wasn't going to answer but he finally said, "If it doesn't make a noise it can't destroy the bugs."

When she went into the house to put on some coffee (a good thing Pentecostals had no ban on that), Mildred could hear the air-conditioner humming away. She looked into the bedroom and saw Wilfred stretched out asleep. Worn out.

"Wilfred?"

He jumped. "I wasn't asleep."

"They're still sitting out front. I thought I'd make us some coffee." Then she couldn't resist adding, sweetly, "I'm glad it isn't anything too serious the matter with the air-conditioner."

ON THE NEXT-TO-LAST DAY OF THE VISIT, THEY DECIDED TO DRIVE FORTY-five miles over to Hullet Township to see the place where Wilfred and Albert were born. This was Mildred's idea. She had thought Albert might suggest it, and she was waiting for that, because she didn't want to push Albert into doing anything he was too tired to do. But at last she mentioned it. She said she had been trying for a long time to get Wilfred to take her, but he said he wouldn't know where to go, since he had never been back after being taken away as a baby. The buildings were all gone, the farms were gone; that whole part of the township had become a conservation area.

Grace and Vera brought along their tablecloths. Mildred wondered why they didn't get sick, working with their heads down in a moving car. She sat between them in the back seat, feeling squashed, although she knew that she was the one doing the squashing. Wilfred drove and Albert sat beside him.

Wilfred always got into an argumentative mood when driving.

"Now what is so wrong with taking a bet?" he said. "I don't mean gambling. I don't mean you go down to Las Vegas and you throw all your money away on those games and machines. With betting you can sometimes be lucky. I once had a free winter in Port Arthur on a bet."

"Thunder Bay, it is now," Albert said.

"Port Arthur is what it was then. Or half of it was. I was off the *Lethbridge*, I was in for the winter. The old *Lethbridge*, that was a terrible boat. One night in the bar they were listening to the hockey game on the radio. Before television. Playing Ottawa. Ottawa four, Port Arthur nothing."

"We're getting to where we turn off the highway," Albert said.

Mildred said, "Watch for the turn, Wilfred."

"I am watching."

Albert said, "Not this one but the next one."

"I was helping them out in there, I was slinging beer for tips because I didn't have a union card, and a grouchy fellow was cursing at Port Arthur. They might come out of it yet, I said. Port Arthur might beat them yet."

"Right here," said Albert.

Wilfred made a sharp turn. "Put your money where your mouth is! Put your money where your mouth is! That's what he said to me. Ten to one. I didn't have the money, but the fellow that owned the hotel was a good fellow, and I was helping him out, so he says, take the bet, Wilfred! He says, you go ahead and take the bet!"

"The Hullet Conservation Area," Mildred read from a sign. They drove along the edge of a dark swamp.

"Heavens, it's gloomy in there!" she said. "And water standing, at this time of the year."

"The Hullet Swamp," said Albert. "It goes for miles."

They came out of the swamp and on either side was wasteland, churned-up black earth, ditches, uprooted trees. The road was very rough.

"I'll back you, he says. So I went ahead and took the bet."

Mildred read the crossroad signs: "Dead end. No winter maintenance beyond this point."

Albert said, "Now we'll want to turn south."

"South?" said Wilfred. "South. I took it and you know what happened? Port Arthur came through and beat Ottawa seven to four!"

There was a large pond and a lookout stand, and a sign saying "Wildfowl Observation Point."

"Wildfowl," said Mildred. "I wonder what there is to see?"

Wilfred was not in the mood to stop. "You wouldn't know a crow from a hawk, Mildred! Port Arthur beat Ottawa seven to four and I had my bet. That fellow sneaked out when I was busy but the manager knew where he lived and next day I had a hundred dollars. When I got called to go back on the *Lethbridge* I had exactly to the penny the amount of money I had when I got off before Christmas. I had the winter free in Port Arthur."

"This looks like it," Albert said.

"Where?" asked Wilfred.

"Here."

"Here? I had the winter free, all from one little bet."

They turned off the road into a rough sort of lane, where there were wooden arrows on a post. "Hawthorn Trail. Sugar Bush Trail. Tamarack

Trail. No motor vehicles beyond this point." Wilfred stopped the car and he and Albert got out. Grace got out to let Mildred out and then got back in. The arrows were all pointing in the same direction. Mildred thought some children had probably tampered with them. She didn't see any trails at all. They had climbed out of the low swampland and were among rough little hills.

"This where your farm was?" she asked Albert.

"The house was up there," said Albert, pointing uphill. "The lane ran up there. The barn was behind."

There was a brown wooden box on the post under the arrows. She opened it up and took out a handful of brightly colored pamphlets. She looked through them.

"These tell about the different trails."

"Maybe they'd like something to read if they aren't going to get out," said Wilfred, nodding toward the women in the car. "Maybe you should go and ask them."

"They're busy," Mildred said. She thought she should go and tell Grace and Vera to roll down the windows so they wouldn't suffocate, but she decided to let them figure that out for themselves. Albert was setting off up the hill and she and Wilfred followed him, plowing through goldenrod, which, to her surprise, was easier than grass to walk in. It didn't tangle you so, and felt silky. Goldenrod she knew, and wild carrot, but what were these little white flowers on a low bush, and this blue one with coarse petals, and this feathery purple? You always heard about the spring flowers, buttercups and trilliums and marsh marigolds, but here were just as many, names unknown, at the end of summer. There were also little frogs leaping from underfoot, and small white butterflies, and hundreds of bugs she couldn't see that nibbled at and stung her bare arms.

Albert walked up and down in the grass. He made a turn, he stopped and looked around and started again. He was trying to get the outline of the house. Wilfred frowned at the grass, and said, "They don't leave you much."

"Who?" said Mildred faintly. She fanned herself with goldenrod.

"Conservation people. They don't leave one stone of the foundation, or the cellar hole, or one brick or beam. They dig it all out and fill it all in and haul it all away."

"Well, they couldn't leave a pile of rubble, I guess, for people to fall over."

"You sure this is where it would have been?" Wilfred said.

"Right about here," Albert said, "facing south. Here would've been the front door."

"You could be standing on the step, Albert," said Mildred, with as much interest as she had energy for.

But Albert said, "We never had a step at the front door. We only opened it once that I can remember, and that for Mother's coffin. We put some chunks of wood down then, to make a temporary step."

"That's a lilac," said Mildred, noticing a bush near where he was standing. "Was that there then? It must have been there then."

"I think it was."

"Is it a white one or a purple?"

"I can't say."

That was the difference between him and Wilfred, she thought. Wilfred would have said. Whether he remembered or not, he would have said, and then believed himself. Brothers and sisters were a mystery to her. There were Grace and Vera, speaking like two mouths out of the same head, and Wilfred and Albert without a thread of connection between them.

THEY ATE LUNCH IN A CAFÉ DOWN THE ROAD. IT WASN'T LICENSED, OR Mildred would have ordered beer, never mind how she shocked Grace and Vera or how Wilfred glared at her. She was hot enough. Albert's face was a bright pink and his eyes had a fierce, concentrating look. Wilfred looked cantankerous.

"It used to be a lot bigger swamp," Albert said. "They've drained it."

"That's so people can get in and walk and see different things," said Mildred. She still had the red and green and yellow pamphlets in her hand, and she smoothed them out and looked at them.

"Squawks, calls, screeches, and cries echo throughout this bush," she read. "Do you recognize any of them? Most are made by birds." What else would they be made by? she wondered.

"A man went into the Hullett Swamp and remained there," Albert said.

Wilfred made a mess of his ketchup and gravy, then dipped his french fries into it with his fingers.

"For how long?" he said.

"Forever."

"You going to eat them?" said Wilfred, indicating Mildred's french fries.

"Forever?" said Mildred, dividing them and sliding half onto Wilfred's plate. "Did you know him, Albert?"

"No. It was too long ago."

"Did you know his name?"

"Lloyd Sallows."

"Who?" said Wilfred.

"Lloyd Sallows," said Albert. "He worked on a farm."

"I never heard of him," Wilfred said.

"How do you mean, he went into the swamp?" said Mildred.

"They found his clothes on the railway tracks and that's what they said, he went into the swamp."

"Why would he go in there without his clothes on?"

Albert thought for a few minutes and said, "He could have wanted to go wild."

"Did he leave his shoes, too?"

"I would think so."

"He might have committed suicide," Mildred said briskly. "Did they look for a body?"

"They did look."

"Or might have been murdered. Did he have any enemies? Was he in trouble? Maybe he was in debt or in trouble about a girl."

"No," said Albert.

"So they never found a trace of him?"

"No."

"Was there any suspicious sort of person around at the time?"

"No."

"Well, there must be some explanation," said Mildred. "A person, if they're not dead, they go on living somewhere."

Albert forked the hamburger patty out of his bun onto his plate, where he proceeded to cut it up into little pieces. He had not yet eaten anything.

"He was thought to be living in the swamp."

"They should've looked in the swamp, then," Wilfred said.

"They went in at both ends and said they'd meet in the middle but they didn't."

"Why not?" said Mildred.

"You can't just walk your way through that swamp. You couldn't then."

"So they thought he was in there?" Wilfred persisted. "Is that what they thought?"

"Most did," said Albert, rather grudgingly. Wilfred snorted.

"What was he living on?"

Albert put down his knife and fork and said somberly, "Flesh."

All of a sudden, after being so hot, Mildred's arms came out in goose bumps.

"Did anybody ever see him?" she asked, in a more subdued and thoughtful voice than before.

"Two said so."

"Who were they?"

"One was a lady that when I knew her, she was in her fifties. She had been a little girl at the time. She saw him when she was sent back to get the cows. She saw a long white person running behind the trees."

"Near enough that she could tell if it was a boy or a girl?" said Wilfred.

Albert took the question seriously.

"I don't know how near."

"That was one person," Mildred said. "Who was the other?"

"It was a boy fishing. This was years later. He looked up and saw a white fellow watching him from the other bank. He thought he'd seen a ghost."

"Is that all?" said Wilfred. "They never found out what happened?"

"No."

"I guess he'd be dead by now anyway," Mildred said.

"Dead long ago," said Albert.

If Wilfred had been telling that story, Mildred thought, it would have gone someplace, there would have been some kind of ending to it. Lloyd Sallows might reappear stark naked to collect on a bet, or he would come back dressed as a millionaire, maybe having tricked some gangsters who had robbed him. In Wilfred's stories you could always be sure that the gloomy parts would give way to something better, and if somebody behaved in a peculiar way there was an explanation for it. If Wilfred figured in his own stories, as he usually did, there was always a stroke of luck for him somewhere, a good meal or a bottle of whiskey or some money. Neither luck nor money played a part in this story. She wondered why Albert had told it, what it meant to him.

"How did you happen to remember that story, Albert?"

As soon as she said that, she knew she shouldn't have spoken. It was none of her business.

"I see they have apple or raisin pie," she said.

"No apple or raisin pie in the Hullet Swamp!" said Wilfred raucously. "I'm having apple."

Albert picked up a cold piece of hamburger and put it down and said, "It's not a story. It's something that happened."

159

MILDRED HAD STRIPPED THE BED THE VISITORS HAD SLEPT IN, AND HADN'T got it made up again, so she lay down beside Wilfred, on their first night by themselves.

Before she went to sleep she said to Wilfred, "Nobody in their right mind would go and live in a swamp."

"If you did want to live someplace like that," said Wilfred, "the place to live would be the bush, where you wouldn't have so much trouble making a fire if you wanted one."

He seemed restored to good humor. But in the night she was wakened by his crying. She was not badly startled, because she had known him to cry before, usually at night. It was hard to tell how she knew. He wasn't making any noise and he wasn't moving. Maybe that in itself was the unusual thing. She knew that he was lying beside her on his back with tears welling up in his eyes and wetting his face.

"Wilfred?"

Any time before, when he had consented to tell her why he was crying, the reason had seemed to her very queer, something thought up on the spur of the moment, or only distantly connected with the real reason. But maybe it was as close as he could get.

"Wilfred."

"Albert and I will probably never see each other again," said Wilfred in a loud voice with no trace of tears, or any clear indication of either satisfaction or regret.

"Unless we did go to Saskatchewan," said Mildred. An invitation had been extended, and she had thought at the time she would be as likely to visit Siberia.

"Eventually," she added.

"Eventually, maybe," Wilfred said. He gave a prolonged, noisy sniff that seemed to signal content. "Not next week."

April 1982

The Retreat

GEORGEANN HAS PUT OFF PACKING FOR THE ANNUAL CHURCH RETREAT. "There's plenty of time," she tells Shelby when he bugs her about it. "I can't do things that far ahead."

"Don't you want to go?" he asks her one evening. "You used to love to go."

"I wish they'd do something different, just once. Something besides pray and yack at each other." Georgeann is basting facings on a child's choir robe, and she looks at him testily as she bites off a thread.

Shelby says, "You've been looking peaked lately. I believe you've got low blood."

"There's nothing wrong with me."

"I think you better get a checkup before we go. Call Dr. Armstrong in the morning."

When Georgeann married Shelby Pickett, her mother warned her about the disadvantages of marrying a preacher. Delinquents who suddenly get saved always make the worst kind of preachers, her mother said—just like former drug addicts in their zealousness. Shelby was never that bad, though. In high school, when Georgeann first knew him, he was on probation for stealing four cases of Sundrop cola and a ham from Kroger's. There was something charismatic about him even then, although

BOBBIE ANN MASON

he frightened her at first with his gloomy countenance—a sort of James Dean brooding—and his tendency to contradict whatever the teachers said. But she admired the way he argued so smoothly and professionally in debate class. He always had a smart answer that left his opponent speechless. He was the type of person who could get away with anything. Georgeann thought he seemed a little dangerous—he was always staring people down, as though he held a deep grudge—but when she started going out with him, at the end of her senior year, she was surprised to discover how serious he was. He had spent a month studying the life of Winston Churchill. It wasn't even a class assignment. No one she knew would have thought of doing that. When the date of the senior prom approached, Shelby said he couldn't take her because he didn't believe in dancing. Georgeann suspected that he was just embarrassed and shy. On a Friday night, when her parents were away at the movies, she put on a Kinks album and tried to get him to loosen up, to get in shape for the prom. It was then that he told her his ambition to be a preacher. Georgeann was so moved by his sense of atonement and his commitment to the calling—he had received the call while hauling hay for an uncle—that she knew she would marry him. On the night of the prom, they went instead to the Burger King, and he showed her the literature on the seminary while she ate a Double Whopper and french fries.

The ministry is not necessarily a full-time calling, Georgeann discovered. The pay is too low. While Shelby attended seminary, he also went to night school to learn a trade, and Georgeann supported him by working at Kroger's—the same one her husband had robbed. Georgeann had wanted to go to college, but they were never able to afford for her to go.

Now they have two children, Tamara and Jason. During the week, Shelby is an electrician, working out of his van. In ten years of marriage, they have served in three different churches. Shelby dislikes the rotation system and longs for a church he can call his own. He says he wants to grow with a church, so that he knows the people and doesn't have to preach only the funerals of strangers. He wants to perform the marriages of people he knew as children. Shelby lives by many little rules, some of which come out of nowhere. For instance, for years he has rubbed baking soda onto his gums after brushing his teeth, but he cannot remember who taught him to do this, or exactly why. Shelby comes from a broken home, so he wants things to last. But the small country churches in western Kentucky are dying, as people move to town or simply lose interest in the church. The membership at the Grace United Methodist Church is seventy-five, but attendance varies between thirty and seventy. The day it snowed this past winter, only three people came. Shelby was so depressed afterward that he couldn't eat Sunday dinner. He was particularly upset because he had prepared a special sermon aimed at Hoyt Jenkins, who somebody said had begun drinking, but Hoyt did not appear. Shelby had to deliver the sermon anyway, on the evils of alcohol, to old Mr. and Mrs. Elbert Flood and Miss Addie Stone, the president of the WCTU chapter.

"Even the best people need a little reinforcement," Shelby said half-heartedly to Georgeann.

She said, "Why didn't you just save that sermon? You work yourself half to death. With only three people there, you could have just talked to them, like a conversation. You didn't have to waste a big sermon like that."

"The church isn't for just a conversation," said Shelby.

The music was interesting that snowy day. Georgeann plays the piano at church. As she played, she listened to the voices singing—Shelby booming out like Bert Parks; the weak, shaky voices of the Floods; and Miss Stone, with a surprisingly clear and pretty little voice. She sounded like a folk singer. Georgeann wanted to hear more, so she abruptly switched hymns and played "Joy to the World," which she knew the Floods would have trouble with. Miss Stone sang out, high above Shelby's voice. Later, Shelby was annoyed that Georgeann had changed the program because he liked for the church bulletins that she typed and mimeographed each week before the Sunday service to be an accurate record of what went on that day. Georgeann made corrections on the bulletin and filed it in Shelby's study. She penciled in a note, "Three people showed up." She even listed their names. Writing this, Georgeann felt peculiar, as though a gear had shifted inside her.

Even then, back in the winter, Shelby had been looking forward to the retreat, talking about it like a little boy anticipating summer camp.

GEORGEANN HAS BEEN FEELING DISORIENTED. SHE CAN'T THINK ABOUT the packing for the retreat. She's not finished with the choir robes for Jason and Tamara, who sing in the youth choir. On the Sunday before the retreat, Georgeann realizes that it is Communion Sunday and she has forgotten to buy grape juice. She has to race into town at the last minute to buy it. It is overpriced at the Kwik-Pik, but that is the only place open on Sunday. Waiting in line, she discovers that she still has hair clips in her hair. As she stands there, she watches two teenage boys in everyday clothes playing an electronic video game. One boy is pressing buttons, his fingers working rapidly and a look of rapture on his face. The other boy is watching and murmuring "Gah!" Georgeann holds her hand out automatically for the change when the salesgirl rings up the grape juice. She stands by the door for a few minutes, watching the boys. The machine makes tom-tom sounds, and blips fly across the screen. When she gets to the church, she is so nervous that she sloshes the grape juice while pouring it into the tray of tiny Communion glasses. Two of the glasses are missing because she broke them last month while washing them after Communion service. She has forgotten to order replacements. Shelby will notice, but she will say that it doesn't matter, because there won't be that many people at church anyway.

"You spilled some," says Tamara.

"You forgot to let us have some," Jason says, taking one of the little glasses and holding it out. Tamara takes one of the glasses too. This is something they do every Communion Sunday.

"I'm in a hurry," says Georgeann. "This isn't a tea party."

They are still holding the glasses out to her.

"Do you want one too?" Jason asks.

"No, I don't have time."

Both children look disappointed, but they drink the sip of grape juice, and Tamara takes the glasses to wash them.

"Hurry," says Georgeann.

Shelby doesn't mention the missing glasses. But over Sunday dinner, they quarrel about her going to a funeral he has to preach that afternoon.

"Why should I go? I didn't even know the man."

"Who is he?" Tamara wants to know.

Shelby says, "No one you know. Hush."

Jason says, "I'll go with you. I like to go to funerals."

"I'm not going," says Georgeann. "They give me nightmares, and I didn't even know the guy."

Shelby glares at her icily for talking like this in front of the children. He agrees to go alone, and promises Jason he can go to the next one. Today the children are going to Georgeann's sister's to play with their cousins. "You don't want to disappoint Jeff and Lisa, do you?" Shelby asks Jason.

As he is getting ready to leave, Shelby asks Georgeann, "Is there something about the way I preach funerals that bothers you?"

"No, your preaching's fine. I like the weddings. And the piano and everything. But just count me out when it comes to funerals." Georgeann suddenly bangs a skillet in the sink. "Why do I have to tell you that ten times a year?"

They quarrel infrequently, but after they do, Georgeann always does something spiteful. Today, while Shelby and the kids are away, she cleans out the hen-house. It gives her pleasure to put on her jeans and shovel manure into a cart. She wheels it to the garden, not caring who sees. People drive by and she waves. There's the preacher's wife, cleaning out her hen-house on Sunday, they are probably saying. Georgeann puts down new straw in the hen-house and gathers the eggs. She sees a hen looking droopy in a corner. "Perk up," she says. "You look like you've got low blood." After she finishes with the chore, she sits down to read the Sunday papers, feeling relieved that she is alone and can relax. She gets very sleepy, but in a few minutes she has to get up and change clothes. She is getting itchy under the waistband, probably from chicken mites.

She turns the radio on and finds a country-music station.

When Shelby comes in, with the children, she is asleep on the couch. They tiptoe around her and she pretends to sleep on. "Sunday is a day of rest," Shelby is saying to the children. "For everybody but preachers, that is." Shelby turns off the radio.

"Not for me," says Jason. "That's my day to play catch with Jeff."

When Georgeann gets up, Shelby gives her a hug, one of his proper Sunday embraces. She apologizes for not going with him. "How was the funeral?"

"The usual. You don't really want to know, do you?"

"No."

GEORGEANN PLANS FOR THE RETREAT. SHE MAKES A DOCTOR'S APPOINT-ment for Wednesday. She takes Shelby's suits to the cleaners. She visits some shut-ins she neglected to see on Sunday. She arranges with her mother to keep Tamara and Jason. Although her mother still believes Georgeann married unwisely, she now promotes the sanctity of the union. "Marriage is forever, but a preacher's marriage is longer than that," she says.

Today, Georgeann's mother sounds as though she is making excuses for Shelby. She knows that Georgeann is unhappy, but she says, "I never gave him much credit at first, but Lord knows he's ambitious. I'll say that for him. And practical. He knew he had to learn a trade so he could support himself in his dedication to the church."

"You make him sound like a junkie supporting a habit."

Georgeann's mother laughs uproariously. "It's the same thing! The same thing." She is a stout, good-looking woman who loves to drink at parties. She and Shelby have never had much to say to each other, and Georgeann gets very sad whenever she realizes that her mother treats her marriage like a joke. It isn't fair.

When Georgeann feeds the chickens, she notices the sick hen unable to get up on its feet. Its comb is turning black. She picks it up and sets it in the hen-house. She puts some mash in a Crisco can and sets it in front of the chicken. It pecks indifferently at the mash. Georgeann goes to the house and finds a margarine tub and fills it with water. There is nothing to do for a sick chicken, except to let it die. Or kill it, to keep disease from spreading to the others. She won't tell Shelby the chicken is sick, because Shelby will get the ax and chop its head off. Shelby isn't being cruel. He believes in the necessities of things.

Shelby will have a substitute in church next Sunday, while he is at the retreat, but he has his sermon ready for the following Sunday. On Tuesday evening, Georgeann types it for him. He writes in longhand on yellow legal pads, the way Nixon wrote his memoirs, and after ten years Georgeann has finally mastered his corkscrew handwriting. The sermon is on sex education in the schools. When Georgeann comes to a word she doesn't know, she goes downstairs.

"There's no such word as 'pucelage,'" she says to Shelby, who is at the kitchen table, trying to fix a gun-shaped hair-dryer. Parts are scattered all over the table.

"Sure there is," he says, " 'Pucelage' means virginity."

"Why didn't you say so! Nobody will know what it means."

"But it's just the word I want."

"And what about this word in the next paragraph? 'Maturescent'? Are you kidding?"

"Now don't start in on how I'm making fun of you because you haven't been to college," Shelby says.

Georgeann doesn't answer. She goes back to the study and continues typing. Something pinches her on the stomach. She raises her blouse and scratches a bite. She sees a tiny brown speck scurrying across her flesh. Fascinated, she catches it by moistening a fingertip. It drowns in her saliva. She puts in on a scrap of yellow legal paper and folds it up. Something to show the doctor. Maybe the doctor will let her look at it under the microscope.

The next day, Georgeann goes to the doctor, taking the speck with her. "I started getting these bites after I cleaned out the hen-house," she tells the nurse. "And I've been handling a sick chicken."

The nurse scrapes the speck onto a slide and instructs Georgeann to get undressed and put on a paper robe so that it opens in the back. Georgeann piles her clothes in a corner behind a curtain and pulls on the paper robe. As she waits, she twists and stretches a corner of the robe, but the paper is tough, like the "quicker picker-upper" paper towel she has seen in TV ads. When the doctor bursts in, Georgeann gets a whiff of strong cologne.

The doctor says, "I'm afraid we can't continue with the examination until we treat you for that critter you brought in." He looks alarmed.

"I was cleaning out the hen-house," Georgeann explains. "I figured it was a chicken mite."

"What you have is a body louse. I don't know how you got it, but we'll have to treat it completely before we can look at you further."

"Do they carry diseases?"

"This *is* a disease," the doctor says. "What I want you to do is take off that paper gown and wad it up very tightly into a ball and put it in the wastebasket. Whatever you do, don't shake it! When you get dressed, I'll tell you what to do next."

Later, after prescribing a treatment, the doctor lets her look at the louse through the microscope. It looks like a bloated tick from a dog; it is lying on its back and its legs are flung around crazily.

"I just brought it in for fun," Georgeann says. "I had no idea."

At the library, she looks up "louse" in a medical book. There are three kinds, and to her relief she has the kind that won't get in the hair. The book says that body lice are common only in alcoholics and indigent elderly persons who rarely change their clothes. Georgeann cannot imagine how she got lice. When she goes to the drugstore to get her prescription filled, a woman brushes close to her, and Georgeann sends out a silent message: I have lice. She is enjoying this.

"I've got lice," she announces when Shelby gets home. "I have to take a fifteen-minute hot shower and put this cream on all over, and then I have to wash all the clothes and curtains and everything—and what's more, the same goes for you and Tamara and Jason. You're incubating them, the doctor said. They're in the bedcovers and the mattresses and the rugs. Everywhere." Georgeann make creepy-crawling motions with her fingers.

The pain on Shelby's face registers with her after a moment. "What about the retreat?" he asks.

"I don't know if I'll have time to get all this done first."

"This sounds fishy to me. Where would you get lice?"

Georgeann shrugs. "He asked me if I'd been to a motel room lately. I probably got them from one of those shut-ins. Old Mrs. Speed, maybe. That filthy old horsehair chair of hers."

Shelby looks really depressed, but Georgeann continues brightly, "I thought sure it was chicken mites because I'd been cleaning out the hen-house? But he let me look at it in the microscope and he said it was a body louse."

"Those doctors don't know everything," Shelby says. "Why don't you call a vet? I bet that doctor you went to wouldn't know a chicken mite if it crawled up his leg."

"He said it was lice."

"I've been itching ever since you brought this up."

"Don't worry. Why don't we just get you ready for the retreat—clean clothes and hot shower—and then I'll stay here and get the rest of us fumigated?"

"You don't really want to go to the retreat, do you?"

Georgeann doesn't answer. She gets busy in the kitchen. She makes a pork roast for supper, with fried apples and mashed potatoes. For dessert she makes Jell-O and peaches with Dream Whip. She is really hungry. While she peels potatoes, she sings a song to herself. She doesn't know the name of it, but it has a haunting melody. It is either a song her mother used to sing to her or a jingle from a TV ad.

They decide not to tell Tamara and Jason that the family has lice. Tamara was inspected for head lice once at school, but there is no reason to make a show of this, Shelby tells Georgeann. He gets the children to take long baths by telling them it's a ritual cleansing, something like baptism. That night in bed, after long showers, Georgeann and Shelby don't touch each other. Shelby lies flat with his hands behind his head, looking at the ceiling. He talks about the value of spiritual renewal. He wants Georgeann to finish washing all the clothes so that she can go to the retreat. He says, "Every person needs to stop once in a while and take a look at what's around him. Even preaching wears thin."

"Your preaching's up-to-date," Georgeann says. "You're more up-to-date than a lot of those old-timey preachers who haven't even been to seminary." Georgeann is aware that she sounds too perky.

"You know what's going to happen, don't you? This little church is falling off so bad they're probably going to close it down and re-assign me to Deep Springs."

"Well, you've been expecting that for a long time, haven't you?"

"It's awful," Shelby says. "These people depend on this church. They don't want to travel all the way to Deep Springs. Besides, everybody wants their own home church." He reaches across Georgeann and turns out the light.

The next day, after Shelby finishes wiring a house, he consults with a veterinarian about chicken mites. When he comes home, he tells Georgeann that in the veterinarian's opinion, the brown speck was a chicken mite. "The vet just laughed at that doctor," Shelby says. "He said the mites would leave of their own accord. They're looking for chickens, not people."

"Should I wash all these clothes or not? I'm half finished."

"I don't itch anymore, do you?"

Shelby has brought home a can of roost paint, a chemical to kill chicken mites. Georgeann takes the roost paint to the hen-house and applies it to the roosts. It smells like fumes from a paper mill, and almost makes her gag. When she finishes, she gathers eggs, and then sees that the sick hen has flopped outside again and can't get up on her feet. Georgeann carries the chicken into the hen-house and sets her down by the food. She examines the chicken's feathers. Suddenly she notices that the chicken is covered with moving specks. Georgeann backs out of the hen-house and looks at her hands in the sunlight. The specks are swarming all over her hands. She watches them head up her arms, spinning crazily, disappearing on her.

THE RETREAT IS AT A LODGE AT KENTUCKY LAKE. IN THE MORNINGS, A hundred people eat a country-ham breakfast on picnic tables, out of doors by the lake. The dew is still on the grass. Now and then a speedboat races by, drowning out conversation. Georgeann wears a badge with her name on it and "BACK TO BASICS," the theme of the gathering, in Gothic lettering. After the first day, Shelby's spirit seems renewed. He talks and laughs with old acquaintances, and during social hour, he seems cheerful and relaxed. At the workshops and lectures, he takes notes like mad on his yellow legal paper, which he carries on a clipboard. He already has fifty ideas for new sermons, he tells Georgeann happily. He looks handsome in his clean suit. She has begun to see him as someone remote, like a meter-reader. Georgeann thinks: He is not the same person who once stole a ham.

On the second day, she skips silent prayers after breakfast and stays in the room watching Phil Donahue. Donahue is interviewing parents of murdered children; the parents have organized to support each other in their grief. There is an organization for everything, Georgeann realizes. When Shelby comes in, before the noon meal, she is asleep and the farm-market report is blaring from the TV. As she wakes up, he turns off the TV. Shelby is a kind and good man, she says to herself. He still thinks she has low blood. He wants to bring her food on a tray, but Georgeann refuses.

"I'm alive," she says. "There's a workshop this afternoon I want to go to. On marriage. Do you want to go to that one?"

"No, I can't make that one," says Shelby, consulting his schedule. "I have to attend The Changing Role of the Country Pastor."

"It will probably be just women," says Georgeann. "You wouldn't enjoy it." When he looks at her oddly, she says, "I mean the one on marriage." Shelby winks at her. "Take notes for me."

The workshop concerns Christian marriage. A woman leading the workshop describes seven kinds of intimacy, and eleven women volunteer their opinions. Seven of the women present are ministers' wives. Georgeann isn't counting herself. The women talk about marriage enhancement, a term that is used five times.

A fat woman in a pink dress says, "God made man so that he can't resist a woman's adoration. She should treat him as a priceless treasure, for man is the highest form of creation. A man is born of God—and, just think, *you* get to live with him."

"That's so exciting I can hardly stand it," says a young woman, giggling, then looking around innocently with an expansive smile.

"Christians are such beautiful people," says the fat woman. "And we have such nice-looking young people. We're not dowdy at all."

"People just get that idea," someone says.

A tall woman with curly hair stands up and says, "The world has become so filled with the false, the artificial—we have gotten so phony that we think the First Lady doesn't have smelly feet. Or the Pope doesn't go to the bathroom."

"Leave the Pope out of this," says the fat woman in pink. "He can't get married." Everyone laughs.

Georgeann stands up and asks a question. "What do you do if the man you're married to—this is just a hypothetical question—say, he's the cream of creation and all, and he's sweet as can be, but he turns out to be the wrong one for you? What do you do if you're just simply mismatched?"

Everyone looks at her.

SHELBY STAYS BUSY WITH THE WORKSHOPS AND LECTURES, AND Georgeann wanders in and out of them, as though she is visiting someone else's dreams. She and Shelby pass each other casually on the path, hurrying along between the lodge and the conference building. They wave hello like friendly acquaintances. In bed she tells him, "Christella Simmons told me I looked like Mindy on *Mork & Mindy.* Do you think I do?"

Shelby laughs. She expects him to lecture her on false women and all their finery. "Don't be silly," he says. When he reaches for her, she turns away.

The next day, Georgeann walks by the lake. She watches sea gulls flying over the water. It amazes her that sea gulls have flown this far inland, as though they were looking for something, the source of all that water. They arc above the water, flying away from her. She expects them to return, like hurled boomerangs. The sky changes as she watches, puffy clouds thinning out into threads, a jet contrail intersecting them and spreading, like something melting: an icicle. The sun pops out. Georgeann walks past a family of picnickers. The family is having an argument over who gets to use an inner tube first. The father says threateningly, "I'm going to get me a switch!" Georgeann feels a stiffening inside her. Instead of letting go, loosening up, relaxing, she is tightening up. But this means she is growing stronger.

Georgeann goes to the basement of the lodge to buy a Coke from a machine, but she finds herself drawn to the electronic games along the wall. She puts a quarter in one of the machines, the Galaxians. She is a Galaxian, with a rocket ship something like the *Enterprise* on *Star Trek*, firing at a convoy of fleeing, multi-colored aliens. When her missiles hit them, they make satisfying little bursts of color. Suddenly, as she is firing away, three of them—two red ships and one yellow ship—zoom down the screen and blow up her ship. She loses her three ships one right after the other and the game is over. Georgeann runs upstairs to the desk and gets change for a dollar. She puts another quarter in the machine and begins firing. She likes the sound of the firing and the siren-wail of the diving formation. She is beginning to get the hang of it. The hardest thing is controlling the left and right movements of her ship with her left hand as she tries to aim or to dodge the formation. The aliens keep returning and she keeps on firing and firing until she goes through all her quarters.

After supper, Georgeann removes her name badge and escapes to the basement again. Shelby has gone to the evening service, but she told him she had a headache. She has five dollars' worth of quarters, and she loses two of them before she can regain her control. Her game improves and she scores 3,660. The high score of the day, according to the machine, is 28,480. The situation is dangerous and thrilling, but Georgeann feels in control. She isn't running away; she is chasing the aliens. The basement is dim, and some men are playing at the other machines. One of them begins watching her game, making her nervous. When the game ends, he says, "You get 800 points when you get those three zonkers, but you have to get the yellow one last or it ain't worth as much."

"You must be an expert," says Georgeann, looking at him skeptically.

"You catch on after a while."

The man says he is a trucker. He wears a yellow billed cap and a denim jacket lined with fleece. He says, "You're good. Get a load of them fingers."

"I play the piano."

"Are you with them church people?"

"Uh-huh."

"You don't look like a church lady."

Georgeann plugs in another quarter. "This could be an expensive habit," she says idly. It has just occurred to her how good-looking the man is. He has curly sideburns that seem to match the fleece inside his jacket.

"I'm into Space Invaders myself," the trucker says. "See, in Galaxians, you're attacking from behind. It's a kind of cowardly way to go at things."

"Well, they turn around and get you," says Georgeann. "And they never stop coming. There's always more of them."

The man takes off his cap and tugs at his hair, then puts his cap back on. "I'd ask you out for a beer, but I don't want to get in trouble with the church." He laughs. "Do you want a Coke? I'll buy you a Co'-Cola."

Georgeann shakes her head no. She starts the new game. The aliens are flying in formation. She begins the chase. When the game ends—her best yet—she turns to look for the man, but he has left.

Georgeann spends most of the rest of the retreat in the basement, playing Galaxians. She doesn't see the trucker again. Eventually, Shelby finds her in the basement. She has lost track of time, and she has spent all their reserve cash. Shelby is treating her like a mental case. When she tries to explain to him how it feels to play the game, he looks at her indulgently, the way he looks at shut-ins when he takes them baskets of fruit. "You forget everything but who you are," Georgeann tells him. "Your mind leaves your body." Shelby looks depressed.

As they drive home, he says, "What can I do to make you happy?"

Georgeann doesn't answer at first. She's still blasting aliens off a screen in her mind. "I'll tell you when I can get it figured out," she says slowly. "Just let me work on it."

Shelby lets her alone. They drive home in silence. As they turn off the main highway toward the house, she says suddenly, "I was happy when I was playing that game."

"We're not children," says Shelby. "What do you want—toys?"

At home, the grass needs cutting. The brick house looks small and shabby, like something abandoned. In the mailbox, Shelby finds his reassignment letter. He has been switched to the Deep Springs church, sixty miles away. They will probably have to move. Shelby folds up the letter and puts it back in the envelope, then goes into his study. The children are not home yet, and Georgeann wanders around the house, pulling up the shades, looking for things that have changed in her absence. A short while later, she goes to Shelby's study, and knocks on the door. One of his little rules. She says, "I can't go to Deep Springs. I'm not going with you."

Shelby stands up, blocking the light from the windows. "I don't want to move either," he says. "But it's too awful far to commute."

"You don't understand. I don't want to go at all. I want to stay here by myself so I can think straight."

"What's got into you lately, girl? Have you gone crazy?" Shelby draws the blind on the window so the sun doesn't glare in. He says, "You've got me so confused. Here I am in this big crisis and you're not standing by me."

"I don't know how."

Shelby snaps his fingers. "We can go to a counselor."

"I went to that marriage workshop and it was a lot of hooey."

Shelby's face has a pallor, Georgeann notices. He is distractedly thumbing through some papers, his notes from the conference. Georgeann realizes that Shelby is going to compose a sermon directed at her. "We're going to have to pray over this," he says quietly.

"Later," says Georgeann. "I have to go pick up the kids."

Before leaving, she goes to check on the chickens. A neighbor has been feeding them. The sick chicken is still alive, but it doesn't move from a corner under the roost. Its eyelids are half shut, and its comb is dark and crusty. The hen-house still smells of roost paint. Georgeann gathers eggs and takes them to the kitchen. Then, without stopping to reflect, she gets the ax from the shed and returns to the hen-house. She picks up the sick chicken and takes it outside to a stump behind the hen-house. She sets the chicken on the stump and examines its feathers. She doesn't see any mites on it now. Taking the hen by the feet, she lays it on its side, its head pointing away from her. She holds its body down, pressing its wings. The chicken doesn't struggle. When the ax crashes down blindly on its neck, Georgeann feels nothing, but knows she has done her duty.

July 1982

Emperor of the Air

LET ME TELL YOU WHO I AM. I'M SIXTY-NINE YEARS OLD, LIVE IN THE SAME house I was raised in, and have been the high school biology and astronomy teacher in this town so long that I have taught the grandson of one of my former students. I wear my father's wristwatch, which tells me it is past four-thirty in the morning, and though I have thought otherwise, I now think hope is the essence of all good men.

My wife, Vera, and I have no children, and this has enabled us to do a great many things in our lives: we have stood on the Great Wall of China, toured the Pyramid of Cheops, sunned in Lapland at midnight. Vera, who is near my age, is off on the Appalachian Trail. She has been gone two weeks and expects to be gone one more, on a trip on which a group of men and women, some of them half her age, are walking all the way through three states. Age, it seems, has left my wife alone. She ice-skates and hikes and will swim nude in a mountain lake. She does these things without me, however, for now my life has slowed. Last fall, as I pushed a lawnmower around our yard, I felt a squeezing in my chest and a burst of pain in my shoulder, and I spent a week in a semi-private hospital room. A heart attack. Myocardial infarction, minor. I will no longer run for a train, and in my shirt pocket I keep a small vial of nitroglycerine pills. In slow supermarket lines or traffic snarls I tell myself that impatience is not worth dying

ETHAN CANIN

over, and last week, as I stood at the window and watched my neighbor, Mr. Pike, cross the yard toward our front door carrying a chain saw, I told myself that he was nothing but a doomed and hopeless man.

I had found the insects in my elm a couple of days before, the slim red line running from the ground up the long trunk and vanishing into the lower boughs. I brought out a magnifying glass to examine them—their shiny arthroderms, torsos elongated like drops of red liquid; their tiny legs, jointed and wiry, climbing the fissured bark. The morning I found them, Mr. Pike came over from next door and stood on our porch. "There's vermin in your elm," he said.

"I know," I said. "Come in."

"It's a shame, but I'll be frank: there's other trees on this block. I've got my own three elms to think of."

Mr. Pike is a builder, a thick and unpleasant man with whom I have rarely spoken. Though I had seen him at high school athletic events, the judgmental tilt to his jaw always suggested to me that he was merely watching for the players' mistakes. He is short, with thick arms and a thick neck and a son, Kurt, in whose bellicose shouts I can already begin to hear the thickness of his father. Mr. Pike owns or partly owns a construction company that erected a line of low prefabricated houses on the outskirts of town, on a plot I remember from my youth as having been razed by fire. Once, a plumber who was working on our basement pipes told me that Mr. Pike was a poor craftsman, a man who valued money over quality. The plumber, a man my age who kept his tools in a wooden chest, shook his head when he told me that Mr. Pike used plastic pipes in the houses he had built. "They'll last ten years," the plumber told me. "Then the seams will go and the walls and ceilings will start to fill with water." I myself had had little to do with Mr. Pike until he told me he wanted my elm cut down to protect the three saplings in his yard. Our houses are separated by a tall stand of rhododendron and ivy, so we don't see each other's private lives as most neighbors do. When we talked on the street, we spoke only about a football score or the incessant rain, and I had not been on his property since shortly after he moved in, when I had gone over to introduce myself and he had shown me the spot where, underneath his rolling back lawn, he planned to build a bomb shelter.

Last week he stood on my porch with the chain saw in his hands. "I've got young elms," he said. "I can't let them be infested."

"My tree is over two hundred years old."

"It's a shame," he said, showing me the saw, "but I'll be frank. I just wanted you to know I could have it cut down as soon as you gave the word."

175

All week I had a hard time sleeping. I read Dickens in bed, heated cups of milk, but nothing worked. The elm was dying. Vera was gone, and I lay in bed thinking of the insects, of their miniature jaws carrying away heartwood. It was late summer, the nights were still warm, and sometimes I went outside in my nightclothes and looked up at the sky. I teach astronomy, as I have said, and though sometimes I try to see the stars as milky dots or pearls, they are forever arranged in my eye according to the astronomic charts. I stood by the elm and looked up at Ursa Minor and Lyra, at Cygnus and Corona Borealis. I went back inside, read, peeled an orange. I sat at the window and thought about the insects, and every morning at five a boy who had once taken my astronomy class rode by on his bicycle, whistling the national anthem, and threw the newspaper onto our porch.

Sometimes I heard them, chewing the heart of my splendid elm.

The day after I first found the insects I called a man at the tree nursery. He described them for me, the bodies like red droplets, the wiry legs; he told me their genus and species.

"Will they kill the tree?"

"They could."

"We can poison them, can't we?"

"Probably not," he said. He told me that once they were visible outside the bark they had already invaded the tree too thoroughly for pesticide. "To kill them," he said, "we would end up killing the tree."

"Does that mean the tree is dead?"

"No," he said. "It depends on the colony of insects. Sometimes they invade a tree but don't kill it, don't even weaken it. They eat the wood, but sometimes they eat it so slowly that the tree can replace it."

When Mr. Pike came over the next day, I told him this. "You're asking me to kill a two-hundred-and-fifty-year-old tree that otherwise wouldn't die for a long time."

"The tree's over eighty feet tall," he said.

"So?"

"It stands fifty-two feet from my house."

"Mr. Pike, it's older than the Liberty Bell."

"I don't want to be unpleasant," he said, "but a storm could blow twenty-eight feet of that tree through the wall of my house."

"How long have you lived in that house?"

He looked at me, picked his tooth. "You know."

"Four years," I said. "I was living here when a czar ruled Russia. An elm grows one quarter inch in width each year, when it's still growing. That tree is four feet thick, and it has yet to chip the paint on either your house or mine."

"It's sick," he said. "It's a sick tree. It could fall."

"Could," I said. "It *could* fall."

"It very well *might* fall."

We looked at each other for a moment. Then he averted his eyes, and with his right hand adjusted something on his watch. I looked at his wrist. The watch had a shiny metal band, with the hours, minutes, seconds, blinking in the display.

The next day he was back on my porch.

"We can plant another one," he said.

"What?"

"We can plant another tree. After we cut the elm, we can plant a new one."

"Do you have any idea how long it would take to grow a tree like that one?"

"You can buy trees half-grown. They bring them in on a truck and replant them."

"Even a half-grown tree would take a century to reach the size of the elm. A century."

He looked at me. Then he shrugged, turned around, and went back down the steps. I sat down in the open doorway. A century. What would be left of the earth in a century? I didn't think I was a sentimental man, and I don't weep at plays or movies, but certain moments have always been peculiarly moving to me, and the mention of a century was one. There have been others. Standing out of the way on a fall evening, as couples and families converge on the concert hall from the radiating footpaths, has always filled me with a longing, though I don't know for what. I have taught the life of the simple hydra that is drawn, for no reasons it could ever understand, toward the bright surface of the water, and the spectacle of a thousand human beings organizing themselves into a single room to hear the quartets of Beethoven is as moving to me as birth or death. I feel the same way during the passage in an automobile across a cantilever span above the Mississippi, mother of rivers. These moments overwhelm me, and sitting on the porch that day as Mr. Pike retreated up the footpath, paused at the elm, and then went back into his house. I felt my life open up and present itself to me.

When he had gone back into his house I went out to the elm and studied the insects, which emerged from a spot in the grass and disappeared above my sight, in the lowest branches. Their line was dense and unbroken. I went inside and found yesterday's newspaper, which I rolled up and brought back out. With it I slapped up and down the trunk until the line

177

was in chaos. I slapped until the newspaper was wet and tearing; with my fingernails I squashed stragglers between the narrow crags of bark. I stamped the sod where they emerged, dug my shoe tip into their underground tunnels. When my breathing became painful, I stopped and sat on the ground. I closed my eyes until the pulse in my neck was calm, and I sat there, mildly triumphant, master at last. After a while I looked up again at the tree and found the line perfectly restored.

THAT AFTERNOON I MIXED A STRONG INSECT POISON, WHICH I BROUGHT outside and painted around the bottom of the trunk. Mr. Pike came out onto his steps to watch. He walked down, stood on the sidewalk behind me, made little chuckling noises. "There's no poison that'll work," he whispered.

But that evening, when I came outside, the insects were gone. The trunk was bare. I ran my fingers around the circumference. I rang Mr. Pike's doorbell and we went out and stood by the tree together. He felt the notches of the bark, scratched bits of earth from the base. "I'll be damned," he said.

WHEN I WAS A BOY IN THIS TOWN, THE SUMMERS WERE HOT AND THE forest to the north and east often dried to the point where the undergrowth, not fit to compete with the deciduous trees for groundwater, turned crackling brown. The shrubbery became as fragile as straw, and the summer I was sixteen the forest ignited. A sheet of flame raced and bellowed day and night as loud as a fleet of propeller planes. Whole families gathered in the street and evacuation plans were made, street routes drawn out beneath the night sky, which, despite the ten miles' distance to the fire, shone with orange light. My father had a wireless with which he communicated to the fire lines. He stayed up all night and promised that he would wake the neighbors if the wind changed or the fire otherwise turned toward town. That night the wind held, and by morning a firebreak the width of a street had been cut. My father took me down to see it the next day, a ribbon of cleared land as bare as if it had been drawn with a razor. Trees had been felled, the underbrush sickled down and removed. We stood at the edge of the cleared land, the town behind us, and watched the fire. Then we got into my father's Plymouth and drove as close as we were allowed. A fireman near the flames had been asphyxiated, someone said, when the cone of fire had turned abruptly and sucked up all the oxygen in the air. My father explained to me how a flame breathed oxygen like a man. We got out of the car. The heat curled the hair on our arms and turned the ends of our eyelashes white.

My father was a pharmacist and had taken me to the fire out of curiosity. Anything scientific interested him. He kept tide tables, and collected the details of nature—butterflies and moths, seeds, wildflowers—and stored them in glass-fronted cases, which he leaned against the stone wall of our cellar. One summer he taught me the constellations of the Northern Hemisphere. We went outside at night, and as the summer progressed he showed me how to find Perseus and Arcturus and Andromeda, how some of the brightest stars illuminated Lyra and Aquila, how, though the constellations proceed with the seasons, Polaris remains most fixed and is thus the set point of a mariner's navigation. He taught me the night sky, and I find now that this is rare knowledge. Later, when I taught astronomy, my students rarely cared about the silicon or iron on the sun, but when I spoke of Cepheus or Lacerta, they were silent and attended my words. At a party now I can always find a drinking husband who will come outside with me and sip cognac while I point out the stars and say their names.

That day, as I stood and watched the fire, I thought the flames were as loud and powerful as the sea, and that evening, when we were home, I went out to the front yard and climbed the elm to watch the forest burn. Climbing the elm was forbidden me, because the lower limbs even then were well above my reach and because my father believed that anybody lucky enough to make it up into the lower boughs would almost certainly fall on the way down. But I knew how to climb it anyway. I had done it before, when my parents were gone. I had never made it as far as the first limbs, but I had learned the knobs and handholds on which, with balance and strength, I could climb to within a single jump of the boughs. The jump frightened me, however, and I had never attempted it. To reach the boughs one had to gather strength and leap upward into the air, propelled only by the purchase of feet and hands on the small juttings of bark. It was a terrible risk. I could no more imagine myself making this leap than I could imagine diving headlong from a coastal cliff into the sea. I was an adventurous youth, as I was later an adventurous man, but all my adventures had a quality about them of safety and planned success. This is still true. In Ethiopia I have photographed a lioness with her cubs; along the Barrier Reef I have dived among barracuda and scorpion fish—but these things have never frightened me. In my life I have done few things that have frightened me.

That night, though, I made the leap into the lower boughs of the elm. My parents were inside the house, and I made my way upward until I crawled out of the leaves onto a narrow top branch and looked around me at a world that on two sides was entirely red and orange with flame. After a time I came back down and went inside to sleep, but that night the wind changed. My father woke us, and we gathered outside on the street with all the other families on our block. People carried blankets filled with the treasures of their lives. One woman wore a fur coat, though the air was suffused with ash and was as warm as an afternoon. My father stood on the hood of a car and spoke. He had heard through the radio that the fire had leaped the break, that a house on the eastern edge of town was in full flame, and, as we all could feel, that the wind was strong and blowing straight west. He told the families to finish loading their cars and leave as soon as possible. Though the fire was still across town, he said, the air was filling with smoke so rapidly that breathing would soon be difficult. He got down off the car and went inside to gather things together. We had an RCA radio in our living room and a set of Swiss china in my mother's cupboard, but my father instead loaded a box with the *Encyclopaedia Britannica* and carried up from the basement the heavy glass cases that contained his species chart of the North American butterflies. We carried these things outside to the Plymouth. When we returned, my mother was standing in the doorway.

"This is my home," she said.

"We're in a hurry," my father said.

"This is my home, this is my children's home. I'm not leaving."

My father stood on the porch looking at her. "Stay here," he said to me. Then he took my mother's arm and they went into the house. I stood on the steps outside, and when my father came out again in a few minutes, he was alone, just as when we drove west that night and slept with the rest of the neighborhood on Army cots in the high school gym in the next town, we were alone. My mother had stayed behind.

Nothing important came of this. That night the wind calmed and the burning house was extinguished; the next day a heavy rain wet the fire and it was put out. Everybody came home, and the settled ash was swept from the houses and walkways into black piles in the street. I mention the incident now only because it points out, I think, what I have always lacked: I inherited none of my mother's moral stubbornness. In spite of my age, still, arriving on foot at a crosswalk where the light is red but no cars are in sight, I'm thrown into confusion. My decisions never seem to engage the certainty that I had hoped to enjoy late in my life. But I was adamant and angry when Mr. Pike came to my door. The elm was ancient and exquisite: we could not let it die.

Now, though, the tree was safe. I examined it in the morning, in the afternoon, in the evening, and with a lantern at night. The bark was clear. I slept.

THE NEXT MORNING MR. PIKE WAS AT MY DOOR.

"Good morning, neighbor," I said.

"They're back."

"They can't be."

"They are. Look," he said, and walked out to the tree. He pointed up to the first bough.

"You probably can't see them," he said, "but I can. They're up there, a whole line of them."

"They couldn't be."

"They sure are. Listen," he said, " I don't want to be unpleasant, but I'll be frank."

That evening he left a note in our mail slot. It said that he had contacted the authorities, who had agreed to enforce the cutting of the tree if I didn't do it myself. I read the note in the kitchen. Vera had been cooking some Indian chicken before she left for the Appalachian Trail, and on the counter was a big jar filled with flour and spices that she shook pieces of chicken in. I read Mr. Pike's note again. Then I got a fishing knife and a flashlight from the closet, emptied Vera's jar, and went outside with these things to the elm. The street was quiet. I made a few calculations, and then with the knife cut the bark. Nothing. I had to do it only a couple more times, however, before I hit the mark and, sure enough, the tree sprouted insects. Tiny red bugs shot crazily from the slit in the bark. I touched my finger there and they spread in an instant all over my hand and up my arm. I had to shake them off. Then I opened the jar, laid the fishing knife out from the opening like a bridge, and touched the blade to the slit in the tree. They scrambled up the knife and began to fill the jar as fast as a trickling spring. After a few minutes I pulled out the knife, closed the lid, and went back into the house.

Mr. Pike is my neighbor, and so I felt a certain remorse. What I contemplated, however, was not going to kill the elms. It was going to save them. If Mr. Pike's trees were infested, they would still more than likely live, and he would no longer want mine chopped down. This is the nature of the world. In the dark house, feeling half like a criminal and half like a man of mercy, my heart arrhythmic in anticipation, I went upstairs to prepare. I put on black pants and a black shirt. I dabbed shoe polish on my cheeks, my neck, my wrists, the backs of my hands. Over my white hair I stretched a tight black cap. Then I walked downstairs. I picked up the jar and the flashlight and went outside into the night.

I have always enjoyed gestures—never failing to bow, for example, when I finished dancing with a woman—but one attribute I have acquired with age is the ability to predict when I am about to act foolishly. As I slid calmly into the shadowy cavern behind our side-yard rhododendron and paused to catch my breath, I thought that perhaps I had better go back inside and get into my bed. But then I decided to go through with it. As I stood there in the shadow of the swaying rhododendron, waiting to pass into the back yard of my neighbor, I thought of Hannibal and Napoleon and MacArthur. I tested my flashlight and shook the jar, which made a soft colliding sound as if it were filled with rice. A light was on in the Pikes' living room, but the alley between our houses was dark. I passed through.

The Pikes' yard is large, larger than ours, and slopes twice within its length, so that the lawn that night seemed like a dark, furrowed flag stretching back to the three elms. I paused at the border of the driveway, where the grass began, and looked out at the young trees outlined by the lighted houses behind them. In what strange ways, I thought, do our lives turn. Then I got down on my hands and knees. Staying along the fence that separates our yards, I crawled toward the back of the Pikes' lawn. In my life I have not crawled a lot. With Vera I have gone spelunking in the limestone caves of southern Minnesota, but there the crawling was obligate, and as we made our way along the narrow, wet channel into the heart of the rock, I felt a strange grace in my knees and elbows. The channel was hideously narrow, and my life depended on the sureness of my limbs. Now, in the Pikes' yard, my knees felt arthritic and torn. I made my way along the driveway toward the young elms against the back fence. The grass was wet and the water dampened my trousers. I was hurrying as best I could across the open lawn, the insect-filled jar in my hand, the flashlight in my pocket, when I put my palm on something cement. I stopped and looked down. In the dim light I saw what looked like the hatch door on a submarine. Round, the size of a manhole, marked with a fluorescent cross—oh, Mr. Pike, I didn't think you'd do it. I put down the jar and felt for the handle in the dark, and when I found it I braced myself and turned. I certainly didn't expect it to give, but it did, circling once, twice, around in my grasp and loosening like the lid of a bottle. I pulled the hatch and up it came. Then I picked up the insects, felt with my feet for the ladder inside, and went down, closing the hatch behind me.

I still planned to deposit the insects on his trees, but something about crime is contagious. I knew that what I was doing was foolish and that it increased the risk of being caught, but as I descended the ladder into Mr. Pike's bomb shelter, I could barely distinguish fear from elation. At the bottom of the ladder I switched on the flashlight. The room was round, the ceiling and floor were concrete, and against the wall stood a cabinet of metal shelves filled with canned foods. On one shelf were a dictionary and some magazines. Oh, Mr. Pike. I thought of his sapling elms, of the roots making their steady, blind way through the earth; I thought of his houses ten years from now, when the pipes cracked and the ceilings began to pool with water. What a hopeless man he seemed to me then, how small and afraid.

I stood thinking about him, and after a moment I heard a door close in the house. I climbed the ladder and peeked out under the hatch. There on the porch stood Kurt and Mr. Pike. As I watched, they came down off the steps and walked over and stood on the grass near me. I could see the watch blinking on Mr. Pike's wrist. I lowered my head. They were silent, and I wondered what Mr. Pike would do if he found me in his bomb shelter. He was thickly built, as I have said, but I didn't think he was a violent man. One afternoon I had watched as Kurt slammed the front door of their house and ran down the steps onto the lawn, where he stopped and threw an object—an ashtray, I think it was—right through the front window of the house. When the glass shattered, he ran, and Mr. Pike soon appeared on the front steps. The reason I say that he is not a violent man is that I saw something beyond anger, perhaps a certain doom, in his posture as he went back inside that afternoon and began cleaning up the glass with a broom. I watched him through the broken front window of their house.

How would I explain to him, though, the bottle of mad insects I now held? I could have run then, I suppose, made a break up and out of the shelter while their backs were turned. I could have been out the driveway and across the street without their recognizing me. But there was, of course, my heart. I moved back down the ladder. As I descended and began to think about a place to hide my insects, I heard Mr. Pike speak. I climbed back up the ladder. When I looked out under the hatch, I saw the two of them, backs toward me, pointing at the sky. Mr. Pike was sighting something with his finger, and Kurt followed. Then I realized that he was pointing out the constellations, but that he didn't know what they were and was making up their names as he spoke. His voice was not fanciful. It was direct and scientific, and he was lying to his son about what he knew. "These," he said, "these are the Mermaid's Tail, and south you can see the three peaks of Mount Olympus, and then the sword that belongs to the Emperor of the Air." I looked where he was pointing. It was late summer, near midnight, and what he had described was actually Cygnus's bright tail and the outstretched neck of Pegasus.

Presently he ceased speaking, and after a time they walked back across the lawn and went into the house. The light in the kitchen went on, then off. I stepped from my hiding place. I suppose I could have continued with my mission, but the air was calm, it was a perfect and still night, and my plan, I felt, had been interrupted. In my hand the jar felt large and dangerous. I crept back across the lawn, staying in the shadows of the ivy and rhododendron along the fence, until I was in the driveway between our two houses. In the side window of the Pikes' house a light was on. I paused at a point where the angle allowed me a view through the glass, down the hallway, and through an open door into the living room. Mr. Pike and Kurt were sitting together on a brown couch against the far wall of the room, watching television. I came up close to the window and peered through. Though I knew this was foolish, that any neighbor, any man walking his dog at night, would have thought me a burglar in my black clothing, I stayed and watched. The light was on inside, it was dark around me, and I knew I could look in without being seen. Mr. Pike had his hand on Kurt's shoulder. Every so often when they laughed at something on the screen, he moved his hand up and tousled Kurt's hair. The sight of this suddenly made me feel the way I do on the bridge across the Mississippi River. When he put his hand on Kurt's hair again, I moved out of the shadows and went back to my own house.

I wanted to run, or kick a ball, or shout a soliloquy into the night. I could have stepped up on a car hood then and lured the Pikes, the paper boy, all the neighbors, out into the night. I could have spoken about the laboratory of a biology teacher, about the rows of specimen jars. How could one not hope here? At three weeks the human embryo has gill arches on its neck, like a fish; at six weeks, amphibians' webs still connect its blunt fingers. Miracles. This is true everywhere in nature. The evolution of 500 million years is mimicked in each gestation: birds that in the egg look like fish; fish that emerge like their spineless, leaflike ancestors. What it is to study life! Anybody who had seen a cell divide could have invented religion.

I sat down on the porch steps and looked at the elm. After a while I stood up and went inside. With turpentine I cleaned the shoe polish from my face, and then I went upstairs. I got into bed. For an hour or two I lay there, sleepless, hot, my thoughts racing, before I gave up and went to the bedroom window. The jar, which I had brought up with me, stood on the sill, and I saw that the insects were either asleep or dead. I opened the window then and emptied them down onto the lawn, and at that moment, as they rained away into the night, glinting and cascading, I thought of asking Vera for a child. I knew it was not possible, but I considered it anyway. Standing there at the window, I thought of Vera, ageless, in forest boots and shorts, perspiring through a flannel blouse as she dipped drinking water from an Appalachian stream. What had we, she and I? The night was calm, dark. Above me Polaris blinked.

I tried going to sleep again. I lay in bed for a time, and then gave up and went downstairs. I ate some crackers. I drank two glasses of bourbon. I sat at the window and looked out at the front yard. Then I got up and went outside and looked up at the stars, and I tried to see them for their beauty and mystery. I thought of billions of tons of exploding gases, hydrogen and helium, red giants, supernovas. In places they were as dense as clouds. I thought of magnesium and silicon and iron. I tried to see them out of their constellatory order, but it was like trying to look at a word without reading it, and I stood there in the night unable to scramble the patterns. Some clouds had blown in and begun to cover Auriga and Taurus. I was watching them begin to spread and refract moonlight when I heard the paper boy whistling the national anthem. When he reached me, I was standing by the elm, still in my nightclothes, unshaven, a little drunk.

"I want you to do something for me," I said.

"Sir?"

"I'm an old man and I want you to do something for me. Put down your bicycle," I said. "Put down your bicycle and look up at the stars."

December 1984

Men under Water

THE PETER PAN DINER, 10:30 A.M. BREAKFAST WITH GUNTHER.

"You're depressed again," Gunther says to me. "I can tell." He has the catsup bottle in one fist like a chisel or a caulking gun, and with the heel of his other hand he's hammering catsup over his hashbrowns and scrambled eggs. He's getting some on the bacon and toast, too.

"I'm not depressed," I say.

"You're not eating."

"Gunther, I eat at home, remember? At breakfast time. I never eat here."

He slips into his pouting voice. "You used to," he says.

This is a bad sign. It means that Gunther is especially needy and delusional today. I haven't ordered anything but coffee in the Peter Pan since the first week I worked for him, more than six months ago.

I look at him, busying himself with breakfast on the other side of the booth. Lately I've spent more time with Gunther than I've spent with my wife, and still there are times—this moment is one of them—when I see him as I saw him the day we met, times when I cannot get beyond the amazing epidermal surface of the man. Gunther is one of the largest people I've ever known, but it's more than that, more than his general enormousness, the smooth expanse of his completely bald head, the perfect beardlessness

RALPH LOMBREGLIA

of his broad face. Gunther has no eyebrows, no body hair whatsoever as far as I know; even the large nostrils of his great, wide nose are pink, hairless tunnels running up into his skull. His velour pullover is open to his sternum and the exposed chest is precisely the complexion of all the rest of him—the shrimplike color of new Play-Doh, the substance from which Gunther sometimes seems to be made. Under the movie lights he likes to muck around with, his skin goes translucent and you can watch the blood vessels keeping him alive.

"If you're not depressed," he says around a mouthful of catsup and eggs, "what are you?"

"Subdued," I say.

"Oh," he says. "Well, would you mind knocking off being subdued? You're not putting out any energy. I can't do it all by myself."

"Do what?"

"Write this goddamn screenplay," he says.

"Oh. Which screenplay is this?"

"You know perfectly well which screenplay. The sci-fi one with the giant radioactive crayfish and the girl scientist who understands them, and who's also the love interest for the guy scientist. The one we've been working on all week."

"Oh, that one," I say. "I forgot. I thought maybe you meant the Kung Fu screenplay. I guess that was last week."

"You want to work on that one? Hey, we could even do a hybrid of the two. Say these huge, radioactive crayfish attack mankind with a sort of lobster version of Kung Fu, bopping people with their big claws. The guy scientist also happens to be a martial-arts master. In the end he conquers the lobsters by building robots programmed to hit them in their pressure points. But before that there's a scene where the lobsters grab the girl and he has to take a couple of them down with his bare hands."

"No, Gunther." I sip my coffee and stare out the window above the personal jukebox mounted on the wall of our booth. The jukebox is playing Roy Orbison's "Pretty Woman," Gunther's favorite song. He put it on to cheer me up.

Outside, a light gray ash is falling from the sky like rain. Cleveland has a lot of smokestack industry, and the Peter Pan is one of the venerable old smokestack-area diners. That's why we come here to eat. Not because we work in the plants ourselves—our work, like God, is everywhere and nowhere—but because this is where reality is, the life and labor of the folk, the source of all art. Someday, after he's made the two or three commercial pictures that will establish him as one of the major film forces of our time,

Gunther wants to celebrate his native city in a cinematic tone-poem about the ballet of heavy manufacture, the romance of rubber and steel.

I show him my wristwatch. "What about the Puerto Rican couple on Liberty Place? With the gas leak in their stove? Or the nursing students on Meadow with no hot water. You told them today for sure. And your answering service. I'll bet you didn't call your answering service. You'll call it at three this afternoon, and then we'll have to work until nine tonight."

Gunther throws his fork onto his plate. People at the counter turn on their stools to look at us. "This is your whole problem," he says. He clangs his coffee cup with his spoon to get the attention of our waitress. It's Alice today, a good woman. If Gunther gets too abusive, she'll pour coffee in his lap. She's done it before. She comes over now and fills our cups.

"I try to foster a creative spirit," Gunther says to me. Alice flashes him a look, the coffee pot poised in the air. He stops talking and stares at the table until she's gone on her way. "I try to pay you for your imagination," he says, "not just for dumb monkey work I could get anybody to do. I try to treat you like an artist. And all you want to do is fix toilets." He picks up the cream and sugar and pours a long stream of each into his cup. Then he starts the singsongy voice. "Yes, for a certain number of hours each week we have to do some essentially non-creative work, things that are not really what artists like us should be doing—painting apartments, replacing water heaters, fixing toilets. But it keeps us humble, I say. I try to be philosophical about it. I don't go into a mood just because I can't work on my movies every minute of every day."

"I left my house three hours ago, Gunther."

"Here we go again," he says.

He doesn't start paying my hourly wages until we leave the diner. But if I don't go over to Gunther's house each morning and wake him up and, while he takes a shower, watch parts of movies he's videotaped, and then listen to him rant about screenplays over breakfast at the Peter Pan, he won't go to work at all, and I won't be paid anything.

He turns to the jukebox and speaks to Roy Orbison. "Roy," he says, "what am I going to do with this guy? Sensitive and gifted, yes, but he has real limitations. He actually wants to work for wages." He turns back to me. "You're not being flexible," he says. "That's a major character flaw, you should watch that. How many times have I explained this to you? You're working for—and will soon be the partner of—an important motion-picture producer who happens at the moment to be trapped inside a land-lord's body."

"That's not how it was advertised," I say. "It was advertised: 'Handyman and general helper, no experience necessary.' That's the ad I responded to. You changed it to scriptwriter after I was hired."

"After I discovered the talent I can't let you throw away, even if you want to. A good part of each week is ours to be talented together, you and me. We toss some ideas back and forth"—he slaps my shoulder—"and in a couple of weeks we have a screenplay. I round up some investors, we start shooting the movie, we're on our way. We could have made some progress on this movie right here at breakfast, but no, you're subdued. You think that just because we have to go fix a toilet today, that's all we are, two guys who have to fix a toilet, and you let it get you down."

"What toilet?" I say. "You're keeping something from me."

"Weren't you the one who wanted me to call my answering service?"

He stands up and tosses his wadded napkin onto his plate, smiling and bobbing his head from side to side like Hardy to Laurel. He leans toward me over the table as if to confide a great truth, a truth that will be true long after everything else is dust. "Rock band," he says, and strides away from the booth. Then he comes back, doing his wicked leer. "The horror, the horror," he adds.

We pay our bill and stroll out of the Peter Pan into the sunlight and ashes, me in my paint-spattered carpenter's pants and sweatshirt, Gunther swaggering in his red-and-yellow-striped velour pullover and racing shades. It's 11:30 A.M., almost time for lunch. The rest of the world has already accomplished much since waking, and laid down foundations for the accomplishment of much more. We have accomplished nothing. But neither have we yet lost everything, I remind myself. We still have much of what we had when the day began. I have my job with Gunther—twenty dollars an hour under the table, starting now—and Gunther has his small real-estate empire, his Ford Bronco, the ability to pay me twenty dollars for each hour I ride around in it with him, and an unflagging, magical belief in the rightness of his life and methods despite all evidence to the contrary.

And he has me. We have each other.

TINA, MY WIFE, CANNOT BELIEVE THAT I CONTINUE TO HOLD THIS JOB. We need the money, but Tina has had enough. She can't take any more stories about Gunther. She can't take what working for Gunther is doing to me. I'm no longer the man she married, Tina says. My inability to leave Gunther has raised serious questions about the deep structure of my personality, and now Tina wants us both to go in for counseling. She says she's become a kind of co-alcoholic, living through my experiences with this man. She's had to go through it all with me, even though it's not her life, and now in some perverse way she feels that she works for Gunther too.

Every night when I get home I must drink for one full hour and rail to Tina about Gunther. I tell her what Gunther has done to me that day, what he's done to his tenants, the lies he's made me tell the tenants about those things, the movie-script ideas he's forced me to invent. After an hour or so I'm able to take a shower and have dinner. But it's growing longer now, up to two hours sometimes. At first it was exotic and Tina enjoyed it. Every night I would bring home amazing new stories. Tina would listen and shake her head in wonder, marveling over the character of Gunther, the shamelessness of the business world, the length and breadth of the illusions men can entertain about themselves.

But then, late last winter, I came home one night with the Pakistani-baby story. Tina teaches in a day-care center, and the Pakistani-baby story pushed her over the edge. I'd been shoveling snow at Gunther's garden-apartment buildings when a Pakistani woman came out into the parking lot in her flowing ocher robes, weeping and screaming because she had no heat and her baby was freezing. I went inside to have a look, something I'm not supposed to do on my own. I'm supposed to refer tenants to Gunther's answering service, nothing more. In the apartment I could see my breath more clearly than I could outside. The woman's baby was swaddled in many blankets; only its nose and lips were sticking out, and they were blue. Sitting at a dinette table in his overcoat was the woman's husband, a little brown man with mournful eyes, eating a bowl of curry and shivering. Something big snapped inside me when I saw their lives. I showed them how to call the tenants'-rights division of Legal Aid, and then I gave them Gunther's unlisted home number, the most forbidden thing there is. Gunther and I had our biggest fight over the Pakistani family. When I got home, Tina spent the whole evening trying to calm me down. I quit for two entire weeks that time, finally going back for three dollars more an hour.

But now I must quit this job forever, Tina says—really quit, not just quit the way I do every week.

Every Friday, when Gunther pays me what I'm owed, I put the cash in my pocket and say Sayonara. After a full week of Gunther I can't envision one more day. He shakes his head, looks at the ground, asks me what he's done wrong. Nothing, Gunther, I always say, not a thing, you're a prince. I just can't take the real-estate life anymore.

You lack vision, he always says. You're turning your back on a brilliant future. The real estate is only a stop along the way, Reggie. Next stop, Hollywood!

No can do, Gunther, I say. We shake hands and go our separate ways forever. Sunday morning I buy the paper and read the ads. Again each week, in return for two thirds of a person's waking life, the free market offers enough money to rent a shed and eat a can of beans every day. "I'm currently holding the best job in Cleveland," I tell Tina. She puts her hands over her ears. Then Sunday afternoon Gunther calls to offer me an hourly increase of fifty cents over what I made the previous week. I accept his new offer. I started at four dollars an hour. I'm up to twenty now. In his big house on a hill above town, Gunther has shown me where he hides his gun. When I reach fifty dollars an hour, he wants me to kill him.

GUNTHER'S REAL-ESTATE HOLDINGS CONSIST OF TWO THREE-STORY BRICK garden-apartment buildings down near the projects, eight or nine rambling wooden Victorians scattered all over the rest of town, and miscellaneous. Miscellaneous includes some garages Gunther rents to people for their cars, and a couple of apartments he has the nerve to rent over the garages. Of the enormous Victorians, three are divided vertically into two-families, and another five or six—the ones in the better areas—have been partitioned into warrens of small studios and one-bedrooms for which Gunther charges outrageous rents. A massage parlor is in one of those; when Gunther's feeling uninspired, we go there and pretend we have to check on things. Only one of the Victorians—the biggest one, in the worst neighborhood—has its original structure and gets rented as one place, to one party.

Acid Rain, the rock band, lives there.

Now Gunther hits the gravel of Acid Rain's horseshoe drive going fast, and then jumps on the brake so that we slide sideways the last thirty feet to the house. Three old Chevy vans are parked around the drive, all painted with the band's name and logo—a thundercloud with a skull and crossbones in it—along with seven huge Harley-Davidsons. In the back yard is a big Doberman and an even bigger shepherd, both on frail-looking chains. They start howling at us. The washing machine and dryer are still out there, their doors torn off, birds and squirrels living in them, and enough old hibachi grills to make a rusty bridge to Barbecueland. Here and there stray concrete blocks and bricks are making dead rectangular voids in the two-foot-high crabgrass.

Gunther loads my arms with equipment from the back of the Bronco —coils of pipe, rolls of solder, garnet paper, a plumber's snake, a portable light, extension cords, a large toolbox. He leads the way with the propane torch, me following him to the house like a pack mule. Luke, the leader of Acid Rain, greets us.

"Why the fuck don't you call your answering service?" Luke says.

"Now, Luke," Gunther says, "I don't think you should be the one to start casting stones. I could say hurtful things to you too. I could say, for instance, Why don't you stop trying to flush each other down the toilets? It clogs them up."

"Ha, ha," Luke says. Then he doesn't say anything else, because he doesn't know where Gunther's breaking point is. Luke is not dumb, but you can see in his face that he can't figure Gunther out. He understands that Gunther didn't go from being a poor, snot-nosed son of a drunked-up electrician to owning a small real-estate empire by taking unlimited abuse from people like him. But then sometimes Gunther seems a jolly fellow who doesn't always act in his own best interest. It's confusing for Luke. I sympathize.

And then there's the way Gunther looks, the massive pink presence of him.

Luke reports that all three of the toilets in the house are broken. I look at Gunther and narrow my eyes. He looks away, sheepish. On the ride over here, Gunther let slip that Acid Rain first called about their toilet a week ago. It was just the first-floor toilet then.

We make our way through the house. Acid Rain's place was an opulent Cleveland mansion once, and great cut-glass chandeliers still hang in the downstairs rooms above the drums and amplifiers and dismantled motorcycles. The glass pendants are gray blobs now, coated with greasy dust. The residents have decorated the chandeliers with pantyhose, pictures from motorcycle magazines, tennis balls, guitar strings. We head upstairs to begin with the topmost toilet. The law of gravity. Various tattooed men are wandering around with women in black leather. Catastrophic metal music is playing in all the rooms on the second floor.

I'd like to mention here that I'm a great lover of music, and so is Tina. We believe that music transcends all the differences between people, and we like to get out when we can to hear a band and dance and have fun. Even after all the things I had witnessed here, we still had perfectly open minds the night we went to see Acid Rain play at The Glo-Worm, over on the other side of the beltway. That's all I can say. When Tina finds out I was here again today, she'll go crazy. Maybe I won't even go home tonight.

Otis, the keyboard player, appears in a doorway. Otis is completely blind, and two of Acid Rain's roadies—all the roadies and many other people live in the house with the band—are blind in one eye apiece. People can be blind for many reasons, and you don't ordinarily think of blindness as caused by the blind person, the result of something he did to himself. But with Acid Rain the thought leaps to mind. Over the months I've watched to see if other ones become blind too—from drinking rubbing alcohol, say, or fighting among themselves over food or females, the way squirrels do. So far, it's only the same three.

"Is that my landlord?" Otis says. "Do I hear my landlord's voice?"

"My man Otis," Gunther says. "How you doing, Otis?"

"How am I doing? I'm going to the bathroom in the back yard, motherfucker. That's how I'm doing."

"It's under control now, Otis," Gunther says, stepping quietly around him and motioning for me to follow. But I'm draped with coils of pipe, the extension cords, the plumber's snake, and I clank when I move.

Otis grabs me. "The dude who mows the lawn, right?" he says. "The landlord's sidekick?"

"I just work for the guy, Otis," I say. "You think it's a picnic? You think he doesn't do the same to me? Every day's a nightmare with this bozo, Otis."

Otis smiles and holds out his palm. "Hey," he says.

I slap his hand. "Renters of the world unite. Death to the landlords."

"Right on!" Otis says, slapping me back. "Let's do it now!"

"No, Otis," I say. "Let him fix the toilets first."

"Good point," Otis says. "Okay. I'll be waiting right here."

We head up the last flight of stairs. "You overdid it a little," Gunther says, "but I was still impressed. You were convincing, and I liked the way you improvised under pressure. I thought you were just a writer. Now I find out you have natural acting ability. I'm giving you a screen test when we get back home."

On the third floor Gunther sees the toilet from the hallway. His face becomes an image of the human capacity for sadness. "I think I just got a blown mind-gasket," he says. He lights up the propane torch and shoots little bursts of blue flame into the bathroom. "Firing retro rockets," he says. "Leaving doomed planet."

"Two words, Gunther," I say. "Just two little words."

"I know," he says. "You quit."

"No," I say. "Roto-Rooter."

"That's one word," he says. We back away from the bathroom. Gunther grips the banister and looks down into the spacious stairwell as though he might plunge himself into it. Then his head snaps up and he slaps me in the belly. "I just had an incredible idea," he says.

"No, Gunther," I say. "Whatever it is. Please, no."

193

"Everything just fell together for me," he says. "Oh man, this is good."

Back down on the landing Otis is waiting. "Otis," Gunther says. "It's bigger than we thought. We have to call Roto-Rooter."

"You lie," Otis says, producing a length of chain from his leather vest.

"No, Otis," I say. "He's telling the truth this one time. It was my idea to call Roto-Rooter. There's no way this clown can fix these toilets."

"Okay," Otis says. "I believe you, brother. But if you lie, I kill you too."

"Don't worry, Otis," I say.

We head downstairs. In the kitchen we find Luke and some of the women swigging on bottles of Colt 45.

"Luke," Gunther says. "My man. I want to ask you a question. You like movies, Luke?"

"I like going to the bathroom," Luke says, slamming his bottle on the table.

"We're calling Roto-Rooter on that, Luke. Okay? Roto-Rooter, like on TV? The guys in the big yellow truck with the little sissy uniforms? You'll be able to make poo-poo right here tonight. Now sit down. I want you to answer my question. You like movies?"

"Yeah, sure."

"Okay. When was the last time you saw a really great movie about an American rock-and-roll band? I mean a movie that had it all—bar scenes, motorcycle scenes, dressing-room scenes, rehearsal scenes, groupie love scenes, and the monster victory-concert scene at the end when the band comes back to its home town after making it big. A movie that captured all the suffering and the glory, the whole incredible life of a great, semi-famous cult rock band in a medium-sized American city. Luke, when was the last time you saw a movie like that?"

"I never saw no such movie," Luke says.

"That's right!" Gunther says.

THE PETER PAN DINER, 2:00 P.M. ALICE COMES OVER WITH THE MENUS. "You guys really making a big day of it, huh?" she says.

"We're celebrating, Alice," Gunther says. "Two meat-loaf specials, one for me and one for my lucky charm here. Gravy on everything. That's the password today, Alice. Gravy."

Alice flashes me a look—can I handle him by myself? I nod and she takes the menus away.

Gunther is on an inspirational roll. "This is it!" he says, gripping my shoulder. "My movie! Plot, characters, myth, fantasy! Commercial potential!

It was right under my nose! But that's the way it always is in the art game, eh, Roscoe?" He pulls a legal pad out of his briefcase. "So what do you think? I say we start with the Luke character—let's call him Luke—we start with him as an inner-city kid, you know, getting his first guitar, getting beat up on by his alcoholic father because he practices guitar instead of getting a job. Plays good pool and B-ball, but he's better on guitar. Everybody's against him. His fellow gang members think guitar is for queers. And we need the bad father, right? We've got to give Luke something big to rebel against. I mean, he can't *like* his father."

"Cliché, Gunther. Cliché, cliché, cliché."

"You always say that. Well I say life's a cliché! I'm not letting that stop me!"

"Scratch the childhood," I say. "It begins with music, the band rehearsing in this tenement while the titles roll up the screen. Helicopter shot of the building, close in on the window of their apartment, music getting louder and louder until we're right in there with them. Then the landlord bursts in, demanding the rent. They don't have any money, so they beat the landlord to death with their guitars."

"Sounds like a cliché to me!" Gunther says, chortling and writing it all down. "But it's not bad! We might be able to use that! Okay, no childhood. Maybe we can put it back later. Or maybe—how about this?—Luke can go back and see his old dad in the hospital after he's famous. The old dad has the big C in his liver now, but together they watch Luke in concert on the tube in his hospital room. Just before he dies, he recognizes how wrong he always was."

"And he apologizes for the way things were. And it straightens Luke's head out about his life."

"Right!"

"Perfect."

"And the record biz, hey? We need a big scene with these parasitic record-producer types who want to tell Luke how to play, what kinds of clothes to wear. They want to make Luke like everybody else so they can use him to get all this money to put up their own noses. But Luke has a dream. He tells everybody to screw themselves. In the end they all want to kiss his ass."

"That's good," I say. "That's original." The meat-loaf specials arrive. We dive into gravy. "Gunther," I say after a few bites, "it takes millions of dollars to make a real movie. You realize that, right? Millions."

"I have a little surprise for you," he says in the nursery-rhyme voice.

"No, Gunther, please, whatever it is, no."

"We're going to my place after lunch," he says. "Hollywood's paying your salary for the rest of the day. Before, I was going to leave you with the toilets and do the heavy business on my own. And I was worried, I admit it, because I didn't have the killer idea to show the big boys. But it came to me when I needed it. We're partners now, Ricardo. I always said you wouldn't be sorry if you stuck with me."

"Big boys?" I say. "What big boys?"

AT GUNTHER'S HOUSE A SILVER MERCEDES WITH VANITY PLATES IS PARKED at the top of the drive. Gunther downshifts the Bronco and creeps toward the silver car as though he can't believe it's actually there. "This is really happening," he says.

For a year now he's been running an ad in the paper to attract investors to his film-production company. Every month a few cranks respond; that's all, nobody with money. But yesterday when he called his answering service he found a message from these guys. They've invested in movies before. He told me about it on the way over here.

He parks the Bronco and gets out. The two men getting out of the Mercedes look like they want to get back in when they see him. The driver is a thin young guy with a spiky haircut, blue-green iridescent jacket, Hawaiian shirt, black jeans, red shoes. The passenger is a small man in his early sixties, salt-and-pepper hair brushed back, business suit. Gunther introduces himself and shakes hands. He motions for me to come over. "Gentlemen," he says," this is my associate, Flip. Flip is the co-author of my new screenplay."

I shake hands too. The driver's name is Willie. He's into the whole sullen James Dean thing. The passenger is Joseph, kindly and softspoken, with an Eastern European accent. His voice makes me see scenes for a movie version of our horrible century—bombings and occupations, pogroms, refugee camps, a boy in shabby knickers calling out the prices of fruit on the streets of the New World.

Both men are looking at my clothes. I brush the front of myself, but none of the paint splatters come off. "We like to be comfortable," I say.

Willie licks his lips, dubious, but Joseph smiles and nods. We go inside. Willie and Joseph look around. Gunther's place looks good. It's a big old house that didn't look so good when I first saw it, but often, while his tenants suffer, Gunther has me work around here. I've painted every room, sanded and finished the floors. One week in the winter we tore out the whole kitchen and put in a new one. Sometimes Gunther even has me clean the bathrooms for MaryLou, his wife, while he sits on a hassock in the hall telling me about screenplay ideas.

"You're prospering, Gunther," Joseph says.

"I guess I'm doing all right," Gunther says. He's more nervous than I thought. He tries to wink at me but botches it and looks like he's just been poked in the eye. "Flip, would you show Joseph and Willie into the living room? Gin and tonics, gentlemen?"

"Very good," Joseph says.

"Flip? Or would you prefer one of those good English ales?"

"Gin and tonic is fine, Gunther," I say. I take the men into the living room. The furnishings are trim and tasteful, vaguely Scandinavian. They were chosen by MaryLou. Gunther would have chosen a lot of chrome bars and Naugahyde. The living room makes me realize in a sudden, sweet way just how completely MaryLou holds Gunther's life together for him, what an impossible piece of luck or inspiration it was that he married her. If she ever left him he'd have to die, but she never will. She's a loving soul, from people even poorer than his, her head not easily turned from grateful devotion. Gunther put her through college while he worked, and never made it to college himself. She teaches grammar school now and thinks his carryings-on are what you put up with when you're married to a genius.

We sit down. French doors open from the living room into the dining room, now the office of the production company, where the big, useless 16mm Movieola is poised like an old burro grazing among the bundles of screenplay drafts stacked everywhere. I've written whole scenes of them while Gunther's tenants acted out their martyrdom. Joseph and Willie are peering in there from the sofa. They don't know what to make of it all. I hear Gunther clinking glassware in the distant kitchen.

In a voice as soft as Joseph's I say, "Gunther is an unusual person." It's hardly an outlandish statement. They nod, meaning that they've noticed, and wait for me to go on. "He's actually rather amazing. Four, five years ago he had nothing. Now he owns properties all over town. Everything he has he built up for himself, with no help from anyone. His drive to succeed is unstoppable. All his life he's dreamed of making movies. He works on screenplays in his sleep." I lean forward and lower my voice even further. "His father was an electrician who drank himself to death, beat the kids, and smashed up the house all the time when Gunther was growing up. Now Gunther supports his old mother, bought a nice little house for her to live in across town. He put his wife through college. You'll see him come in here with a Coke for himself. He never touches a drink, straight as an arrow. You understand what I'm saying. I'm talking about character, what motivates a man."

Everything I'm telling Willie and Joseph is true. Yes, I'm casting it in a certain light, even perceiving it as I say it, but I'm not telling a single lie.

"A lot of people have had it tough," Willie says.

But Joseph waves his hand. "I appreciate what you say," he says.

Gunther comes in with the drinks on a tray, three gin and tonics, and a Coke for himself. He sits down in a big chair. "Well," he says. Then he's about to say something else, but nothing comes out. We sip our drinks, waiting.

"So, Gunther," Joseph says, "you want to make a movie."

Gunther nods without expression. To the untrained eye he looks as enigmatic as Buddha, full of secret knowledge. But I've learned to read the fantastic face. He wants to speak, but his body has locked up on him. He never really believed that a man like Joseph would come to his house some-day. His stage fright is as immense and immovable as he is.

"Joseph," I say. "Willie. Have you ever noticed that beyond the basic animal requirements there are very few things that all human beings must have, and that these few things are not physical but rather metaphysical, things of the spirit? Faith of some kind is the obvious example. Can you think of another?"

Willie looks at Joseph. "This is kind of a weird thing to be talking about," Willie says. But Joseph thinks it over and says, "Love, of course."

"Oh good," I say. "Right. The big one. And how about learning, some systematic acquisition of knowledge?"

"Yes," Joseph says, nodding his head.

"Now I'm thinking of one more," I say. "One more non-physical thing that all people must have, a thing that is always present whenever human beings gather in grief or in joy."

Willie looks at his watch. Part of his job is to protect Joseph's precious time. "This is kind of like Twenty Questions," he says. "This might be fun at at party."

"Party is a clue," I say.

Joseph straightens up on the sofa. "Music!" he says.

I nod my head and smile. "Yes, Joseph, music."

"The non-physical part fooled me," Willie says.

"Now, friends," I say, "the movie we're going to make is about music. Joseph, I'll bet there's a tape machine in your car out there. I'm going to guess what's on it at this very moment. Mozart."

"Wrong!" Joseph says, clapping his hands. "Mozart is in the glove compart-ment, I'll grant you that! But on the machine is Prokofiev. We listened to it on the way over here." He wags a finger at me. "You were wrong, smart boy!"

"Ha, ha!" I say. "But still I've made my point. You take your favorite music with you wherever you go. *And*," I say, "the second part of my point—it's music that Willie doesn't like."

"Right!" Joseph says. "He complains every day. But that part was easy, smart boy. Look at Willie's clothes, look at his hair."

"Sure," I say. "But look further, Joseph. Look at Willie and see the American moviegoer. We practically have Mister Entertainment, sitting right here. And that, Joseph, is why—for the crucial question—we must now defer to Willie."

I sip my drink. "Willie," I say. "I have a question for you. When was the last time you saw a really great movie about an American rock-and-roll band? I mean a movie that had it all—bar scenes, motorcycle scenes, dressing-room scenes, rehearsal scenes, groupie love scenes, and the monster victory-concert scene at the end when the band comes back to its home town after making it big. A movie that captured all the suffering and the glory, the whole incredible life of a great, semi-famous cult rock band in a medium-sized American city. Willie, when was the last time you saw a movie like that?"

"I never saw any such movie," Willie says.

"That's right," I say.

GUNTHER'S KITCHEN, 5:00 P.M. GUNTHER ON THE FLOOR ON HIS HANDS and knees.

"Gunther, get up," I say, looking in the refrigerator for those good English ales he was talking about. "Stop doing that. Show some self-respect. Where are those ales, you charlatan, you complete fraud? What if I'd decided to have one?"

"There wouldn't have been any left," he says, continuing to do what he's been doing—crawling on all fours, nudging MaryLou's silver serving tray around the floor with his nose the way a dog nudges its bowl. Periodically he howls like a dog too, and when he does, tears spring from his eyes which he takes care not to let drip up on the small slip of blue paper resting on the silver tray.

"I'm making a movie!" he keeps bawling between howls.

The slip of blue paper is the check Joseph wrote to Gunther before driving away in the silver Mercedes ten minutes ago. It's for an amount so large I can't bring myself to say it. When he wrote it, Joseph called it good-faith money. He has more, and he knows other investors.

I finish making another gin and tonic. "Gunther," I say. "I have to tell

199

you something, and I want you to brace yourself. I'm not doing this movie with you."

He clambers up from the floor, Joseph's check in his hand. "Flip," he says. "Don't even joke about things like that, Flip."

"I'm not joking. Where did you get 'Flip,' by the way?"

"It just came to me. But I like it. That's you from now on. Flip, my man Flip."

"It's not bad," I say. "But you'll have to find somebody else."

"There is nobody else! Nobody like you! Nobody with your talent! Hey! A third of this money's yours! Half of it's yours! It's all yours, Flip!"

"I already have to go to a marriage counselor on account of you," I say. "If I throw in on this movie, Tina divorces me."

"She won't!" Gunther says. "Not when she hears about the money! I'll talk to her. Call her right now, I'll talk to her. No! We'll bring her in! Can she write? Can she act? Can she sing?"

"No, Gunther. She can't do anything. She's a vegetable now. The only thing she can do is say the word *quit*, over and over. If you ask me again, I'm leaving, and I still have most of a drink here." I raised my glass. "Congratulations, pal."

"Thanks, Flip. Flip! We have to celebrate somehow! We have to do something fun together!"

"I can't think of anything, Gunther."

"It's hot out. It's muggy. Flip! You've never been in my pool!"

"I didn't bring my suit today."

"You can use one of my suits."

"Really, Gunther."

He pounds upstairs. When he comes back down, he's in his trunks, a total embodiment of what it is to be flesh. He tosses me an extra pair. They're like a hot-air balloon or a parachute. I put them on in the bathroom and come out holding a yard of excess suit behind me. Gunther has the stapler from his desk. He staples the trunks until they stay up by themselves.

We go out the back door and into the yard. Gunther's pool is a big one, with all the fixtures—three ladders, two diving boards, ropes with colorful floats. The blue water sparkles with points of early-evening light. "Just a quick dip in the low end here, Gunther," I say. "I have to get home for dinner."

"Flip," he says. "Did I tell you I started taking real scuba-diving lessons? From a registered diving teacher at the Y? He's been showing the class all this neat stuff, special things you have to do in case of emergencies. I have to show you a couple of these things. I can teach you the basics of diving in about two minutes."

"Gunther, no, really. I've always had a slight fear of the water, to tell you the truth. I was swept out into the ocean once when I was a kid, and lifeguards had to save me with a motorboat."

"You never told me that," he says. "That would make a great scene. You should be a little more forthcoming with your experiences. It would help you rise above them." He starts getting the scuba stuff out of the equipment shed. "Now, look, these are what we call weight belts. They keep you from floating to the top." He hands me one and starts putting one on himself.

I drop it on the grass. "See you, Gunther. It's been, you know, nice."

He grabs my shoulder. "MaryLou goes diving with me, Flip, and she can't even drive a stick shift. Are you telling me you're afraid to do this? I know, you have to go home. Hey, it's been a special day. I'm asking you to take a little dive with me to celebrate. Ten lousy minutes for a little fun, and then you can go home."

I pick up the weight belt and put it on. Gunther is tying a heavy rope around his waist. About twenty feet of rope is left when he's finished, and he proceeds to tie the other end around me. "Like mountain climbers," he says.

"Divers don't do that, Gunther. No diver ties himself to another diver."

"Yes, they do, Flip. In certain kinds of salvage operations they do. It's a special knot that comes undone when you pull on it." He pulls on the knot and the rope drops off my waist onto the grass. "Okay?" He reties the rope for me. "I have this neat maneuver I want to show you—what divers do when one diver for some reason loses his tank or runs out of air. We have to do this particular maneuver if we want to have some fun here today, because I have only one tank with air in it."

"Oh, Christ."

"Put on your flippers, Flip," he says, putting on the only tank with air in it.

I put on the flippers and we slap across the lawn to the concrete apron along the edge of the pool. Gunther explains that we're going to fall into the deep end on our backs, get ourselves oriented under water, and then start sharing the one mouthpiece. I'm going to love it, he says. It'll be much more interesting than simply having my own tank. He shows me how to put the mouthpiece in and take it out without swallowing water. "Granted, it's a little different up here on land," he says. "Ready? Lower your mask."

I lower my mask. Then, without even giving me a signal, Gunther topples backward like a bomb leaving a plane. The splash he makes comes right over my head, and then the rope runs out and snaps me into the vortex behind him.

Under water it's white and opaque, with millions of tiny bubbles, and I can't see anything. Then I make out Gunther, his legs and arms wafting gently like seaweed fronds. I watch him swim for a few seconds, fascinated by how graceful he is under water, the way whales are said to be. I can see him smiling around the mouthpiece. He waves good-bye to me as I sink. The weight belt is doing much more to me than to Gunther; soon I'm directly beneath him and panicking. I try to swim upward, but I don't know how to use the flippers and can't kick with them on. I pull on the special knot, but it doesn't work now that it's wet. I try to undo the weight belt, but it's jammed by the rope. I'm about to start crying, despite the unexpected thought that crying under water would be absurd.

Then I feel myself rising toward the surface. Arm over arm, Gunther is hauling me up by the umbilical rope. When he gets me to his level, he pushes the mouthpiece into my face. I'm afraid to breathe through it. *Breathe!* he says with his hands. I breathe. The air from the tank is the most wonderful thing I've ever known, physical ecstasy and my life to do over again. After a few breaths I'm all calmed down.

Gunther points to me and moves his arms and legs. *You're supposed to hold yourself up,* he's saying. I point to myself and make some gestures: *I can't.* He gestures, *Try,* takes the mouthpiece away and lets go of the rope. I try again and sink stupidly, all the way down. He hauls me back up, collects the excess rope, and ties it all into one big bow between us, so that I can't sink too far away.

We fall into a rhythm with the tank, two breaths each time, passing the hose back and forth peace-pipe fashion. Peace is what it is, an amazing, liquid peace. Each sharing of the air is the deepest cooperation between comrades, something solid and good that would never be withheld. We hear nothing but the gurgling of the tank and somewhere, very distant, the persistent OM of the pool filter. Random thoughts and memories bubble through me like Aqualung air, one notion after another in bubbly succession, each considered for a globular instant and then allowed to bubble away forever. I've never envied anything Gunther has, but maybe I've misunderstood it all, because I envy this. If I had a lot of money, a swimming pool and a scuba tank would be the first things I'd buy, so that I could leave the earth this way for an hour or two every evening.

A small kick or motion of the arm sends us orbiting slowly around each other in the water like space walkers. Behind Gunther's face mask his eyes are closed. He might almost be sleeping. I see that this is the essential

Gunther—who he really is and who he'd be on land, too, if he didn't have to do what he does up there because of what his father did to him.

He opens his eyes and sees me staring at him. He smiles and gestures at the blueness around him as if to say, *Aren't you glad you stayed to check this out?* I nod and give him the okay sign. He points to the surface of the water, shrugs his shoulders, and flops his arms. He actually laughs, and a bubble floats out of his mouth with the message, *You really saved me up there.*

I tap my chest, meaning, *I know I did, you huge oaf.*

But the rock-and-roll movie was my idea! he says, slapping his own chest defiantly. *And I'm not a bad man!* he says, kicking his feet. *Not as bad as you make out, that's for sure. You're such a judgmental person. My tenants don't need to talk to me about every goddamn leaky faucet.*

What about the Pakistani baby? I signal, imitating the mother's flowing robes and jutting out my chin self-righteously.

Okay, he nods, *that was wrong. I admit it.*

I make a signal to my heart, meaning, *That really upset my wife. You almost destroyed my marriage.*

He shakes his head with great irritation. He lashes his pink fists through the blue water. *Me destroy your marriage! Did you ever think that maybe you shouldn't complain to your wife so much? I'll bet she doesn't bring home every single stupid thing that happens to her every day and inflict it on you. You're such a baby!*

I nod sadly. *Okay, you have a point.*

He rolls onto his back and starts paddling both of us around the depths of the pool. I let myself be towed along, staring up at the silvery surface of the water, taking my turns on the scuba tank. The water's surface reminds me of the silver screen of a movie theater, and as a game I try to see a movie in it. At first I don't see anything, and then after a while I begin to see the rock-and-roll movie. I see precisely how it ought to go, what scenes it ought to have, all the things about life that you could make people understand while you had their attention with the music. I see that the world really needs this great, honest, full-of-heart movie about an American band, and that if I don't do it with Gunther he'll screw it up and it won't be the movie I'm seeing. Or Joseph will bring in somebody else to take my place. Somebody else will get to give the world all the pleasure and instruction of the great rock-and-roll movie, and then the world will give that person the swimming pool and scuba tank in return. Why shouldn't it be me?

January 1986

203

The Man
Who Knew Belle Starr

ON HIS WAY WEST McRAE PICKED UP A HITCHER, A YOUNG WOMAN CARRY-ing a paper bag and a leather purse, wearing jeans and a shawl—which she didn't take off, though it was more than ninety degrees out and McRae had no air-conditioning. He was driving an old Dodge Charger with a bad exhaust system and one long crack in the wraparound windshield. He pulled over for her, and she got right in, put the leather purse on the seat between them, and settled herself with the paper bag on her lap between her hands. He had just crossed into Texas from Oklahoma. This was the third day of the trip.

"Where you headed?" he asked.

She said, "What about you?"

"Nevada, maybe."

"Why maybe?"

And that fast he was answering *her* questions. "I just got out of the Air Force," he told her, though this wasn't exactly true. The Air Force had given him a dishonorable discharge, after four years at Leavenworth for assaulting a staff sergeant. He was a bad character. He had a bad temper that had got him into a load of trouble already, and he just wanted to get out west, out to the wide open spaces. Just to see it, really. He had the feeling that people didn't require as much from a person way out where there was that kind of

RICHARD BAUSCH

room. He didn't have any family now. He had five thousand dollars from his father's insurance policy, and he was going to make the money last a while. He said, "I'm sort of undecided about a lot of things."

"Not me," she said.

"You figured out where you're going?"

"You could say that."

"So where might that be?"

She made a fist and then extended her thumb, and turned it over. "Under," she said. "Down."

"Excuse me?"

"Does the radio work?" she asked, reaching for it.

"It's on the blink," he said.

She turned the knob anyway. Then she sat back and folded her arms over the paper bag.

He took a glance at her. She was skinny and long-necked, and her hair was the color of water in a metal pail. She looked just old enough for high school.

"What's in the bag?" he said.

She sat up a little. "Nothing. Another blouse."

"Well, so what did you mean back there?"

"Back where?"

"Look," he said, "we don't have to do any talking if you don't want to."

"Then what will we do?"

"Anything you want," he said.

"What if I just want to sit here and let you drive me all the way to Nevada?"

"That's fine," he said. "That's just fine."

"Well, I won't do that. We can talk."

"Are you going to Nevada?" he asked.

She gave a little shrug of her shoulders. "Why not?"

"All right," he said, and for some reason he offered her his hand. She looked at it and then smiled at him, and he put his hand back on the wheel.

IT GOT A LITTLE AWKWARD ALMOST RIGHT AWAY. THE HEAT WAS AWFUL, and she sat there sweating, not saying much. He never thought he was very smooth or anything, and he had been in prison; it had been a long time since he had found himself in the company of a woman. Finally she fell asleep, and for a few miles he could look at her without worrying about anything but staying on the road. He decided that she was kind of good-looking around the eyes and mouth. If she ever filled out, she might be something. He caught himself wondering what might happen, thinking of sex. A girl who traveled alone like this was probably pretty loose. Without quite realizing it, he began to daydream about her, and when he got aroused by the daydream he tried to concentrate on figuring his chances, playing his cards right, not messing up any opportunities—but being gentlemanly, too. He was not the sort of man who forced himself on young women. She slept very quietly, not breathing loudly or sighing or moving much; and then she simply sat up and folded her arms over the bag again and stared out at the road.

"God," she said. "I went out."

"You hungry?" he asked.

"No."

"What's your name? I never got your name."

"Belle Starr," she said, and, winking at him, she made a clicking sound out of the side of her mouth.

"Belle Starr," he said.

"Don't you know who Belle Starr was?"

All he knew was that it was a familiar-sounding name. "Belle Starr."

She put her index finger to the side of his head and said, "Bang."

"Belle Starr," he said.

"Come on," she said. "Annie Oakley. Wild Bill Hickok."

"Oh," McRae said. "Okay."

"That's me," she said, sliding down in the seat. "Belle Starr."

"That's not your real name."

"It's the only one I go by these days."

They rode on in silence for a time.

"What's *your* name?" she asked.

He told her.

"Irish?"

"I never thought about it."

"Where you from, McRae?"

"Washington, D.C."

"Long way from home."

"I haven't been there in years."

"Where *have* you been?"

"Prison," he said. He hadn't known he would say it, and now that he had, he kept his eyes on the road. He might as well have been posing for her; he had an image of himself as he must look from the side, and he shifted his weight a little, sucked in his belly. When he stole a glance at her, he saw that she was simply gazing out at the Panhandle, one hand up like a visor to shade her eyes.

"What about you?" he asked, and felt like somebody in a movie—two people with a past come together on the open road. He wondered how he could get the talk around to the subject of love.

"What *about* me?"

"Where you from?"

"I don't want to bore you with all the facts," she said.

"I don't mind," McRae said. "I got nothing else to do."

"I'm from way up north."

"Okay," he said, "you want me to guess?"

"Maine," she said. "Land of moose and lobster."

He said, "Maine. Well, now."

"See?" she said. "The facts are just a lot of things that don't change."

"Unless you change them," McRae said.

She reached down and, with elaborate care, as if it were fragile, put the paper bag on the floor. Then she leaned back and put her feet up on the dash. She was wearing low-cut tennis shoes.

"You going to sleep?" he asked.

"Just relaxing," she said. But a moment later, when he asked if she wanted to stop and eat, she didn't answer. He looked over and saw that she was sound asleep.

HIS FATHER HAD DIED WHILE HE WAS AT LEAVENWORTH. THE LAST TIME McRae saw him, he was lying on a gurney in one of the bays of D.C. General's emergency ward, a plastic tube in his mouth, an IV set into an ugly yellow-blue bruise on his wrist. McRae had come home on leave from the Air Force—which he had joined on the suggestion of a juvenile judge—to find his father on the floor in the living room, in a pile of old newspapers and bottles, wearing his good suit, with no socks or shoes and no shirt. He looked like he was dead. But the ambulance drivers found a pulse and rushed him off to the hospital. McRae cleaned the house up a little and then followed in the Charger. The old man had been going steadily downhill from the time McRae was a boy, so this latest trouble wasn't new. In the hospital they got the tube in his mouth and hooked him to the IV, and then left him there on the gurney. McRae stood at his side, still in uniform, and when the old man opened his eyes and looked at him, it was clear that he didn't know who it was. The old man blinked, stared, and then sat up, took the tube out of his mouth, and spit something terrible-looking into a small metal dish that was suspended from the complicated apparatus of the room, which made a continual water-dropping sound, like a leaking sink. He looked at McRae again, and then he looked at the tube. "Jesus Christ," he said.

"Hey," McRae said.

"What."

"It's me."

The old man put the tube back in his mouth and looked away.

"Pops," McRae said. He didn't feel anything.

The tube came out. "Don't look at me, boy. You got yourself into it. Getting into trouble, stealing and running around. You got yourself into it."

"I don't mind it, Pops. It's three meals a day and a place to sleep."

"Yeah," the old man said, and then seemed to gargle something. He spit into the little metal dish again.

"I got thirty days of leave, Pops."

"Eh?"

"I don't have to go back for a month."

"Where are you going?"

"Around," McRae said.

The truth was that he hated the Air Force, and he was thinking of taking the Charger and driving to Canada or someplace like that, and hiding out for the rest of his life. The Air Force felt like punishment—it *was* punishment—and he had already been in trouble for his quick temper and his attitude. That afternoon he left his father to whatever would happen, got in the Charger, and started north. But he didn't make it. He lost heart a few miles south of New York City, and he turned around and came back. The old man had been moved to a room in the alcoholic ward, but McRae didn't go to see him. He stayed in the house, watching television and drinking beer, and when old high school buddies came by he went around with them a little. Mostly he stayed home, though, and at the end of his leave he locked the place and drove back to Chanute, in Illinois, where he was stationed. He hadn't been there two months before he got into the scrape that landed him in prison. A staff sergeant caught him drinking beer in the dayroom of one of the training barracks and asked for his name. McRae walked over to him, said, "My name is trouble," and, at the word *trouble*, struck the other man in the face. He'd had a lot of beer, and he had been sitting there in the dark, going over everything in his mind, and the staff sergeant, a baby-faced man with a spare tire of flesh around his waist and an attitude about the stripes on his sleeves, had just walked into it. McRae didn't even know him. Yet he stood over the sergeant where he had fallen and started kicking him. The poor man wound up in the hospital with a broken jaw (the first punch had done it), a few cracked ribs, and multiple lacerations and bruises. The court-martial was swift. The sentence was four years at hard labor, along with a dishonorable discharge. He'd had less than a month on the sentence when he got the news about his father. He felt no surprise, nor, really, any grief, yet there was a little thrill of something like fear; he was in his cell, and for an instant some part of him actually wanted to remain there, inside walls, where things were certain and no decisions had to be made. A week later he learned of the money from the insurance, which would have been more than the five thousand except that his father had been a few months behind on the rent and on other payments. McRae settled what he had to of those things, and kept the rest. He had started to feel like a happy man, out of Leavenworth and the Air Force. And now he was on his way to Nevada, or someplace like that—and he had picked up a girl.

HE DROVE ON UNTIL DUSK, STOPPING ONLY FOR GAS, AND THE GIRL SLEPT right through. Just past the line into New Mexico he pulled off the interstate and went north for a mile or so, looking for some place other than a chain restaurant to eat. She sat up straight and pushed the hair back from her face. "Where are we?"

"New Mexico," he said. "I'm looking for a place to eat."

"I'm not hungry."

"Well," he said, "you might be able to go all day without eating, but I got a three-meal-a-day habit to support."

She brought the paper bag up from the floor and held it in her lap. "You got food in there?"

"No."

"You're very pretty—childlike, sort of, when you sleep."

"I didn't snore?"

"You were quiet as a mouse."

"And you think I'm pretty."

"I guess you know a thing like that. I hope I didn't offend you."

"I don't like dirty remarks," she said. "But I guess you don't mean to be dirty."

"Dirty."

"Sometimes people can say a thing like that and mean it very dirty, but I could tell you didn't."

He pulled in at a roadside diner and turned the ignition off. "Well?" he said.

She sat there with the bag on her lap. "I don't think I'll go in with you."

"You can have a cold drink or something," he said.

"You go in. I'll wait out here."

"Come on in there with me and have a cold drink," McRae said. "I'll buy it for you. I'll buy you dinner, if you want."

"I don't want to," she said.

He got out and started for the entrance, and before he reached it, he heard her door open and close, and turned to watch her come toward him, thin and waiflike in the shawl, which hid her arms and hands.

The diner was empty. A long, low counter ran along one side, with soda fountains and glass cases in which pies and cakes were set. There were booths along one wall. Everything seemed in order, except that no one was around. McRae and the girl stood in the doorway for a moment and waited, and finally she stepped in and took a seat in the first booth. "I guess we're supposed to seat ourselves," she said.

"This is weird," McRae said.

"Hey," she said, rising. "A jukebox." She strode over to it and leaned on it, crossing one leg behind the other at the ankle, her hair falling down to hide her face.

"Hello?" McRae said. "Anybody here?"

"Got any change?" the girl asked.

He gave her a quarter and then sat at the counter. A door at the far end of the diner swung in and a big, red-faced man entered, wearing a white cook's apron over a sweat-stained baby-blue shirt, the sleeves of which he had rolled up past the meaty curve of his elbows. "Yeah?" he said.

"You open?" McRae said.

"That jukebox don't work, honey," the man said.

"You open?" McRae said, as the girl came and sat down beside him.

"I guess maybe I am."

"Place is kind of empty."

"What do you want to eat?"

"You got a menu?"

"You want a menu?"

"Sure," McRae said. "Why not."

"Truth is," the big man said, "I'm selling this place. I don't have menus anymore. I make hamburgers and breakfast stuff. Some french fries and cold drinks. A hot dog, maybe. I'm not keeping track."

"Let's go somewhere else," the girl said.

"Yeah," the big man said, "why don't you do that."

"Look," McRae said, "what's the story here?"

210

The other man shrugged. "You came in at the end of the run, you know what I mean? I'm going out of business. Sit down and I'll make you a hamburger, on the house."

McRae looked at the girl.

"Okay," she said, in a tone that made it clear that she would've been happier to leave.

The big man put his hands on the bar and leaned toward her. "Miss, if I were you, I wouldn't look a gift horse in the mouth."

"I don't like hamburgers," she said.

"You want a hot dog?" the man asked. "I got a hot dog for you. Guaranteed to please."

"I'll have some french fries," she said.

The big man turned to the grill and opened the metal drawer under it. He was very wide at the hips, and his legs were like tree trunks. "I get out of the Army after twenty years," he said, "and I got a little money put aside. The wife and I decide we want to get into the restaurant business. The government's going to be paying me a nice pension, and we got the savings, so we sink it all in this Goddamn diner. Six and a half miles from the interstate. You get the picture? The guy's selling us this diner at a great price, you know? A terrific price. For a song, I'm in the restaurant business. The wife will cook the food and I'll wait tables, you know, until we start to make a little extra, and then we'll hire somebody—a high school kid, or somebody like that. We might even open another restaurant, if the going gets good enough. But, of course, this is New Mexico. This is six and a half miles from the interstate. You know what's up the road? Nothing." He had put the hamburger on, and a basket of frozen french fries. "Now the wife decides she's had enough of life on the border, and off she goes to Seattle to sit in the rain with her mother, and here I am trying to sell a place nobody else is dumb enough to buy. You know what I mean?"

"That's rough," McRae said.

"You're the second customer I've had all *week*, bub."

The girl said, "I guess that cash register's empty, then, huh."

"It ain't full, honey."

She got up and wandered across the room. For a while she stood gazing out the windows over the booths, her hands invisible under the woolen shawl. When she came back to sit next to McRae, the hamburger and french fries were ready.

"On the house," the big man said.

And the girl brought a gun out from under the shawl—a pistol that looked like a toy. "Suppose you open up that register, Mr. Poor Mouth," she said.

211

The big man looked at her, then at McRae, who had taken a large bite of his hamburger and had it bulging in his cheeks.

"This thing is loaded, and I'll use it."

"Well, for Christ's sake," the big man said.

McRae started to get off the stool. "Hold on a minute," he said to them both, his words garbled by the mouthful of food, and then everything started happening at once. The girl aimed the pistol. There was a popping sound—a single small pop, not much louder than the sound of a cap gun—and the big man took a step back, into the dishes and pans. He stared at the girl, wide-eyed, for what seemed like a long time, and then went down, pulling dishes with him in a tremendous shattering.

"Jesus Christ," McRae said, swallowing, standing back far from her, raising his hands.

She put the pistol back in her jeans, under the shawl, and then went around the counter and opened the cash register. "Damn," she said.

McRae said, low, "Jesus Christ."

And now she looked at him; it was as if she had forgotten he was there. "What're you standing there with your hands up like that?"

"God," he said, "oh, God."

"Stop it," she said. "Put your hands down."

He did so.

"Cash register's empty." She sat down on one of the stools and gazed over at the body of the man where it had fallen. "Damn."

"Look," McRae said, "take my car. You can have my car."

She seemed puzzled. "I don't want your car. What do I want your car for?"

"You—" he said. He couldn't talk, couldn't focus clearly, or think. He looked at the man, who lay very still, and then he began to cry.

"Will you stop it?" she said, coming off the stool, reaching under the shawl and bringing out the pistol again.

"Jesus," he said. "Good Jesus."

She pointed the pistol at his forehead. "Bang," she said. "What's my name?"

"Your—name?"

"My name."

"Belle—" he managed.

"Come on," she said. "The whole thing. You remember."

"Belle—Belle Starr."

"Right." She let the gun hand drop to her side, into one of the folds of the shawl. "I like that so much better than Annie Oakley."

212

"Please," McRae said.

She took a few steps away from him and then whirled and aimed the gun. "I think we better get out of here. What do you think?"

"Take the car," he said, almost with exasperation; he was frightened to hear it in his voice.

"I can't drive," she said simply. "Never learned."

"Jesus," he said. It went out of him like a sigh.

"Lordy," she said, gesturing with the pistol for him to move to the door, "it's hard to believe you were ever in *prison.*"

THE INTERSTATE WENT ON INTO THE DARK, BEYOND THE GLOW OF THE headlights. He lost track of miles, road signs, other traffic, time; trucks came by and surprised him, and other cars seemed to materialize as they started the lane change that would bring them over in front of him. He saw their taillights grow small in the distance, and all the while the girl sat watching him, her hands somewhere under the shawl. For a long time he heard only the sound of the rushing night air at the windows, and then she moved a little, shifted her weight, bringing one leg up on the seat.

"What were you in prison for, anyway?"

Her voice startled him, and for a moment he couldn't think of an answer.

"Come on," she said. "I'm getting bored with all this quiet. What were you in prison for?"

"I—beat up a guy."

"That's all?"

"Yes, that's all." He couldn't keep the irritation out of his voice.

"Tell me about it."

"It was just—I just beat up a guy. It wasn't anything."

"I didn't shoot that man for money, you know."

McRae said nothing.

"I shot him because he made a nasty remark to me about the hot dog."

"I didn't hear any nasty remark."

"If he hadn't said it, he'd still be alive."

McRae held tight to the wheel.

"Don't you wish it was the Wild West?" she said.

"Wild West," he said. "Yeah." He could barely speak for the dryness in his mouth and the deep ache of his own breathing.

"You know," she said, "I'm not really from Maine."

He nodded.

213

"I'm from Florida."

"Florida," he managed.

"Yes, only I don't have a southern accent, so people think I'm not from there. Do you hear any trace of a southern accent at all when I talk?"

"No," he said.

"Now you—you've got an accent. A definite southern accent."

He was silent.

"Talk to me," she said.

"What do you want me to say?" he said. "Jesus."

"You could ask me things."

"Ask you things—"

"Ask me what my name is."

Without hesitating, McRae said, "What's your name?"

"You know."

"No, really," he said, trying to play along.

"It's Belle Starr."

"Belle Starr," he said.

"Nobody *but*," she said.

"Good," he said.

"And I don't care about money, either," she said. "That's not what I'm after."

"No," McRae said.

"What I'm after is adventure."

"Right," McRae said.

"Fast living."

"Fast living, right."

"A good time."

"Good," he said.

"I'm going to live a ton before I die."

"A ton, yes."

"What about you?"

"Yes," he said. "Me too."

"Want to join up with me?"

"Join up," he said. "Right." He was watching the road.

She leaned toward him a little. "Do you think I'm lying about my name?"

"No."

"Good," she said.

He had begun to feel as though he might start throwing up what he'd had of the hamburger. His stomach was cramping on him, and he was dizzy. He might even be having a heart attack.

"Your eyes are as big as saucers," she said.

He tried to narrow them a little. His whole body was shaking now.

"You know how old I am, McRae? I'm nineteen."

He nodded, glanced at her and then at the road again.

"How old are you?"

"Twenty-three."

"Do you believe people go to heaven when they die?"

"Oh, God," he said.

"Look, I'm not going to shoot you while you're driving the car. We'd crash if I did that."

"Oh," he said. "Oh, Jesus, please—look, I never saw anybody shot before—"

"Will you *stop it?*"

He put one hand to his mouth. He was soaked: he felt the sweat on his upper lip, and then he felt the dampness all through his clothes.

She said, "I don't kill everybody I meet, you know."

"No," he said. "Of course not." The absurdity of this exchange almost brought a laugh up out of him. How astonishing, that a laugh could be anywhere in him at such a time, but here it was, rising up in his throat like some loosened part of his anatomy. He held on with his whole mind, and a moment passed before he realized that *she* was laughing.

"Actually," she said, "I haven't killed all that many people."

"How—" he began. Then he had to stop to breathe. "How many?"

"Take a guess."

"I don't have any idea," he said.

"Well," she said, "you'll just have to guess. And you'll notice that I haven't spent any time in prison."

He was quiet.

"*Guess*," she said.

McRae said, "Ten?"

"No."

He waited.

"Come on, keep guessing."

"More than ten?"

"Maybe."

"More than ten," he said.

"Well, all right. Less than ten."

"Less than ten," he said.

"Guess," she said

"Nine."

215

"No."

"Eight."

"No, not eight."

"Six?"

"Not six."

"Five?"

"Five and a half people," she said. "You almost hit it right on the button."

"Five and a half people," McRae said.

"Right. A kid who was hitchhiking, like me; a guy at a gas station; a dog that must've got lost—I count him as the half; another guy at a gas station; a guy that took me to a motel and made an obscene gesture to me; and the guy at the diner. That makes five and a half."

"Five and a half," McRae said.

"You keep repeating everything I say. I wish you'd quit that."

He wiped his hand across his mouth and then feigned a cough to keep from having to speak.

"Five and a half people," she said, turning a little in the seat, putting her knees up on the dash. "Have you ever met anybody like me? Tell the truth."

"No," McRae said, "nobody."

"Just think about it, McRae. You can say you rode with Belle Starr. You can tell your grandchildren."

He was afraid to say anything to this, for fear of changing the delicate balance of the thought. Yet he knew the worst mistake would be to say nothing at all. He was beginning to sense something of the cunning that he would need to survive, even as he knew that the slightest miscalculation might mean the end of him. He said, with fake wonder, "I knew Belle Starr."

She said, "Think of it."

"Something," he said.

And she sat farther down in the seat. "Amazing."

HE KEPT TO FIFTY-FIVE MILES AN HOUR, AND EVERYONE ELSE WAS SPEEDING. The girl sat straight up now, nearly facing him on the seat. For long periods she had been quiet, simply watching him drive. Soon they were going to need gas; they had less than half a tank.

"Look at those people speeding," she said. "We're the only ones obeying the speed limit. Look at them."

"Do you want me to speed up?"

"I think they ought to get tickets for speeding, that's what I think. Sometimes I wish I were a policeman."

"Look," McRae said, "we're going to need gas pretty soon."

"No, let's just run it until it quits. We can always hitch a ride with somebody."

"This car's got a great engine," McRae said. "We might have to outrun the police, and I wouldn't want to do that in any other car."

"This old thing? It's got a crack in the windshield. The radio doesn't work."

"Right. But it's a fast car. It'll outrun a police car."

She put one arm over the seat back and looked out the rear window. "You really think the police are chasing us?"

"They might be," he said.

She stared at him a moment. "No. There's no reason. Nobody saw us."

"But if somebody did—this car, I mean, it'll go like crazy."

"I'm afraid of speeding, though," she said. "Besides, you know what I found out? If you run slow enough, the cops go right past you. Right on past you, looking for somebody who's in a hurry. No, I think it's best if we just let it run until it quits and then get out and hitch."

McRae thought he knew what might happen when the gas ran out: she would make him push the car to the side of the road, and then she would walk him back into the cactus and brush there, and when they were far enough from the road, she would shoot him. He knew this as if she had spelled it all out, and he began again to try for the cunning he would need. "Belle," he said. "Why don't we lay low for a few days in Albuquerque?"

"Is that an obscene gesture?" she asked.

"No!" he said, almost shouted. "No! That's—it's outlaw talk. You know. Hide out from the cops—lay low. It's—it's prison talk."

"Well, I've never been in prison."

"That's all I meant."

"You want to hide out."

"Right," he said.

"You and me?"

"You—you asked if I wanted to join up with you."

"Did I?" She seemed puzzled by this.

"Yes," he said, feeling himself press it a little. "Don't you remember?"

"I guess I do."

"You did," he said.

"I don't know."

"Belle Starr had a gang," he said.

"She did?"

"I could be the first member of your gang."

217

She sat there thinking this over. McRae's blood moved at the thought that she was deciding whether or not he would live. "Well," she said, "maybe."

"You've got to have a gang, Belle."

"We'll see," she said.

A moment later she said, "How much money do you have?"

"I have enough to start a gang."

"It takes money to start a gang?"

"Well—" He was at a loss.

"How much do you have?"

He said, "A few hundred."

"Really?" she said. "That much?"

"Just enough to—just enough to get to Nevada."

"Can I have it?"

He said, "Sure." He was holding the wheel and looking out into the night.

"And we'll be a gang?"

"Right," he said.

"I like the idea. Belle Starr and her gang."

McRae started talking about what the gang could do, making it up as he went along, trying to sound like all the gangster movies he'd seen. He heard himself talking about things like robbery and getaway cars and not getting nabbed and staying out of prison, and then, as she sat there staring at him, he started talking about being at Leavenworth, what it was like. He went on about it, the hours of forced work and the time alone, the harsh day-to-day routines, the bad food. Before he was through, feeling the necessity of deepening her sense of him as her new accomplice—and feeling strangely as though in some way he had indeed become exactly that—he was telling her everything, all the bad times he'd had: his father's alcoholism, and growing up wanting to hit something for the anger that was in him; the years of getting into trouble; the fighting and the kicking and what it had got him. He embellished it all, made it sound worse than it really was, because she seemed to be going for it and because, telling it to her, he felt oddly sorry for himself; a version of this story of pain and neglect and lonely rage was true. He had been through a lot. And as he finished describing for her the scene at the hospital the last time he saw his father, he was almost certain he had struck a chord in her. He thought he saw it in the rapt expression on her face.

"Anyway," he said, and smiled at her.

"McRae?" she said.

"Yeah?"

"Can you pull over?"

"Well," he said, his voice shaking, "why don't we wait until it runs out of gas?"

She was silent.

"We'll be that much farther down the road," he said.

"I don't really want a gang," she said. "I don't like dealing with other people that much. I mean, I don't think I'm a leader."

"Oh, yes," McRae said. "No—you're a leader. You're definitely a leader. I was in the Air Force and I know leaders, and you are definitely what I'd call a leader."

"Really?"

"Absolutely. You are leadership material all the way."

"I wouldn't have thought so."

"Definitely," he said. "Definitely a leader."

"But I don't really like people around, you know."

"That's a leadership quality. Not wanting people around. It is definitely a leadership quality."

"Boy," she said, "the things you learn."

He waited. If he could only think himself through to the way out. If he could get her to trust him, get the car stopped—be there when she turned her back.

"You want to be in my gang, huh?"

"I sure do," he said.

"Well, I guess I'll have to think about it."

"I'm surprised nobody's mentioned it to you before."

"You're just saying that."

"No, really."

"Were you ever married?" she asked.

"Married?" he said, and then stammered over the answer. "Ah—uh, no."

"You ever been in a gang before?"

"A couple of times, but—they never had good leadership."

"You're giving me a line, huh."

"No," he said, "it's true. No good leadership. It was always a problem."

"I'm tired," she said, shifting toward him a little. "I'm tired of talking."

The steering wheel was hurting the insides of his hands. He held tight, looking at the coming-on of the white stripes in the road. There were no other cars now, and not a glimmer of light anywhere beyond the head-lights.

"Don't you ever get tired of talking?"

"I never was much of a talker," he said.

"I guess I don't mind talking as much as I mind listening," she said.

He made a sound in his throat which he hoped she took for agreement.

"That's just when I'm tired, though."

"Why don't you take a nap?" he said.

She leaned back against the door and regarded him. "There's plenty of time for that later."

"SO," HE WANTED TO SAY, "YOU'RE NOT GOING TO KILL ME—WE'RE A GANG?"

They had gone for a long time without speaking, an excruciating hour of minutes, during which the gas gauge had sunk to just above empty, and finally she had begun talking about herself, mostly in the third person. It was hard to make sense of most of it, yet he listened as if to instructions concerning how to extricate himself. She talked about growing up in Florida, in the country, and owning a horse; she remembered when she was taught to swim by somebody she called Bill, as if McRae would know who that was; and then she told him how when her father ran away with her mother's sister, her mother started having men friends over all the time. "There was a lot of obscene things going on," she said, and her voice tightened a little.

"Some people don't care what happens to their kids," McRae said.

"Isn't it the truth?" she said. Then she took the pistol out of the shawl. "Take this exit."

He pulled onto the ramp and up an incline to a two-lane road that went off through the desert, toward a glow that burned on the horizon. For perhaps five miles the road was straight as a plumb line, and then it curved into long, low undulations of sand and mesquite and cactus.

"My mother's men friends used to do whatever they wanted to me," she said. "It went on all the time. All sorts of obscene goings-on."

McRae said, "I'm sorry that happened to you, Belle." And for an instant he was surprised by the sincerity of his feeling: it was as if he couldn't feel sorry enough. Yet it was genuine: it had to do with his own unhappy story. The whole world seemed very, very sad to him. "I'm really very sorry," he said.

She was quiet a moment, as if thinking about this. Then she said, "Let's pull over now. I'm tired of riding."

"It's almost out of gas," he said.

220

"I know, but pull it over anyway."

"You sure you want to do that?"

"See?" she said. "That's what I mean—I wouldn't like being told what I should do all the time, or asked if I was sure of what I wanted or not."

He pulled the car over and slowed to a stop. "You're right," he said. "See? Leadership. I'm just not used to somebody with leadership qualities."

She held the gun a little toward him. He was looking at the small, dark, perfect circle at the end of the barrel. "I guess we should get out," she said.

"I guess so," he said.

"Do you have any relatives left anywhere?"

"No."

"Your folks are both dead?"

"Right, yes."

"Which one died first?"

"I told you," he said. "Didn't I? My mother, my mother died first."

"Do you feel like an orphan?"

He sighed. "Sometimes." The whole thing was slipping away from him.

"I guess I do too." She reached back and opened her door. "Let's get out now."

And when he reached for the door handle, she aimed the gun at his head. "Get out slow."

"Aw, Jesus," he said. "Look, you're not going to do this, are you? I mean, I thought we were friends and all."

"Just get out real slow, like I said to."

"Okay," he said. "I'm getting out." He opened his door, and the ceiling light surprised and frightened him. Some wordless part of him understood that this was it, and all his talk had come to nothing: all the questions she had asked him, and everything he had told her—it was all completely useless. This was going to happen to him, and it wouldn't mean anything; it would just be what happened.

"Real slow," she said. "Come on."

"Why are you doing this?" he asked. "You've got to tell me that before you do it."

"Will you please get out of the car now?"

He just stared at her.

"All right, I'll shoot you where you sit."

"Okay," he said. "Don't shoot."

She said in an irritable voice, as though she were talking to a recalcitrant child, "You're just putting it off."

He was backing himself out, keeping his eyes on the little barrel of the gun, and he could hear something coming, seemed to notice it in the same instant that she said, "Wait." He stood half in and half out of the car, doing as she said, and a truck came over the hill ahead of them, a tractor trailer, all white light and roaring.

"Stay still," she said, crouching, aiming the gun at him.

The truck came fast, was only fifty yards away, and without having to decide about it, without even knowing that he would do it, McRae bolted into the road. He was running; he heard the exhausted sound of his own breath, the truck horn blaring, coming on, louder, the thing bearing down on him, something buzzing past his head. Time slowed. His legs faltered under him, were heavy, all the nerves gone out of them. In the light of the oncoming truck he saw his own white hands outstretched as if to grasp something in the air before him, and then the truck was past him, the blast of air from it propelling him over the side of the road and down the embankment, in high, dry grass, which pricked his skin and crackled like hay.

He was alive. He lay very still. Above him was the long shape of the road, curving off in the distance, the light of the truck going on. The noise faded and was nothing. A little wind stirred. He heard the car door close. Carefully he got to all fours and crawled a few yards away from where he had fallen. He couldn't be sure of which direction—he only knew he couldn't stay where he was. Then he heard what he thought were her footsteps in the road, and he froze. He lay on his side, facing the embankment. When she appeared there he almost cried out.

"McRae?" she said. "Did I get you?" She was looking right at where he was in the dark, and he stopped breathing. "McRae?"

He watched her move along the edge of the embankment.

"McRae?" She put one hand over her eyes and stared at a place a few feet over from him, and then she turned and went back out of sight. He heard the car door again, and again he began to crawl farther away. The ground was cold and rough, sandy.

He heard her put the key in the trunk. He stood up, tried to run, but something went wrong in his leg, something sent him sprawling, and a sound came out of him that seemed to echo, to stay on the air, as if to call her to him. He tried to be perfectly still, tried not to breathe, hearing now the small pop of the gun. He counted the reports: one, two, three. She was standing there at the edge of the road, firing into the dark, toward where she must have thought she heard the sound. Then she was rattling the paper bag. She was reloading—he could hear the click of the gun. He tried to get up and couldn't. He had sprained his ankle, had done something very bad to it. Now he was crawling wildly, blindly, through the tall grass, hearing again the small report of the pistol. At last he rolled into a shallow gully. He lay there with his face down, breathing the dust, his own voice leaving him in a whimpering, animal-like sound that he couldn't stop, even as he held both shaking hands over his mouth.

"McRae?" She sounded so close. "Hey," she said. "McRae?"

He didn't move. He lay there perfectly still, trying to stop himself from crying. He was sorry for everything he had ever done. He didn't care about the money, or the car, or going out west, or anything. When he lifted his head to peer over the lip of the gully and saw that she had started down the embankment with his flashlight, moving like someone with time and the patience to use it, he lost his sense of himself as McRae; he was just something crippled and breathing in the dark, lying flat in a little winding gully of weeds and sand. McRae was gone, was someone far, far away, from ages ago—a man fresh out of prison, with the whole country to wander in and insurance money in his pocket, who had headed west with the idea that maybe his luck, at long last, had changed.

April 1987

The Halfway Diner

SOME OF THE OTHER GIRLS CAN READ ON THE WAY BUT I GET SICK. I NEED somebody to talk to, it don't matter who so much, just someone to shoot the breeze with, pass time. *Si no puedes platicar, no puedes vivir*, says my mother and though I don't agree that the silence would kill me, twelve hours is a long stretch. So when Goldilocks climbs on all big-eyed and pale and almost sits herself in Renee's seat by the window I take pity and put her wise.

"You can't sit in that seat," I say.

Her face falls like she's a kid on the playground about to get whupped. "Pardon?" she says. *Pardon.*

"That's Renee's seat," I tell her. "She's got a thing about it. Something about the light."

"Oh. Sorry." She looks at the other empty seats like they're all booby-trapped. Lucky for her I got a soft heart and a mouth that needs exercise.

"You can sit here if you want."

She just about pees with relief and sits by me. She's not packing any magazines or books which is good cause like I said, I get sick. If the person next to me reads I get nosy and then I get sick plus a stiff neck.

"My name's Pam," she says.

"It would be. I'm Lourdes." We shake hands. I remember the first time I made the ride, four years ago, I was sure somebody was gonna cut me with

JOHN SAYLES

a razor or something. I figured they'd all of them be women who'd done time themselves, a bunch of big tough mamas with tattoos on their arms who'd snarl out stuff like "Whatsit to you, sister?" Well, we're not exactly the Girl Scout Jamboree, but mostly people are pretty nice to each other, unless something happens like with Lee and Delphine.

"New meat?" I ask her.

"Pardon?"

"Is your guy new meat up there?" I ask. "Is this his first time inside?"

She nods and hangs her head like it's the disgrace of the century. Like we're not all on this bus for the same reason.

"You hear from him yet?"

"I got a letter. He says he doesn't know how he can stand it."

Now this is good. It's when they start to get comfortable up there you got to worry. We had this girl on the bus, her guy made parole first time up, only the minute he gets home he starts to mope. Can't sleep nights, can't concentrate, mutters to himself all the time, won't take an interest in anything on the outside. She lives with this a while, then one night they have a fight and really get down and he confesses how he had this kid in his cell, this little *mariquita*, and they got to doing it, you know, like some of the guys up there will do, only this guy fell in *love*. These things happen. And now he's *jealous*, see, cause his kid is still inside with all these *men*, right, and damn if a week later he doesn't go break his parole about a dozen different ways so he gets sent back up. She had to give up on him. To her it's a big tragedy, which is understandable, but I suppose from another point of view it's kind of romantic, like *Love Story*, only instead of Ali McGraw you got a sweetboy doing a nickel for armed robbery.

"What's your guy in for?" I ask.

Pam looks at her feet. "Auto theft."

"Not *that*. I mean how much *time*."

"The lawyer says he'll have to do at least a year and a half."

"You don't go around asking what a guy's rap is in here," I tell her. "That's like *personal*, you know? But the length of sentence—hey, everybody counts the days."

"Oh."

"A year and a half is small change," I tell her. "He'll do that with his eyes closed."

The other girls start coming in then. Renee comes to her seat and sets up her equipment. She sells makeup, Renee, and her main hobby is wearing it. She's got this stand that hooks onto the back of the seat in front of her, with all these drawers and compartments and mirrors and stuff and an empty shopping bag for all the tissues she goes through during the trip. I made the mistake of sitting next to her once and she bent my ear about lip gloss for three hours straight, all the way to the Halfway Diner. You wouldn't think there'd be that much to say about it. Then after lunch she went into her sales pitch and I surrendered and bought some eye goop just so I wouldn't have to hear her say "our darker-complected customers" one more time. I mean it's all relative, right, and I'd rather be my shade than all pasty-faced like Renee, look like she's never been touched by the sun. She's seen forty in the rearview mirror though she does her best to hide it, and the big secret that everybody knows is that it's not her husband she goes to visit but her *son*, doing adult time. She just calls him "my Bobby."

Mrs. Tucker settles in front with her knitting, looking a little tired. Her guy is like the Birdman of Alcatraz or something, he's been in since back when they wore stripes like in the Jimmy Cagney movies, and she's been coming up faithfully every weekend for thirty, forty years, something incredible like that. He killed a cop way back when is what Yayo says the word on the yard is. She always sits by Gus, the driver, and they have these long lazy Mr. and Mrs. conversations while she knits and he drives. Not that there's anything going on between them off the bus, but you figure over the years she's spent more time with Gus than with her husband. He spaces out sometimes, Gus, the road is so straight and long, and she'll bring him back with a poke from one of her needles.

The ones we call the sisters go and sit in the back, talking nonstop. Actually they're married to brothers who are up for the same deal but they look alike and are stuck together like glue so we call them the sisters. They speak one of those Indio dialects from up in the mountains down south, so I can't pick out much of what they say. What my mother would call *mojadas*. Like she come over on the *Mayflower*.

Dolores comes in, who is a sad case.

"I'm gonna tell him this trip," she says. "I'm really gonna do it."

"Attagirl."

"No, I really am. It'll break his heart but I got to."

"It's the only thing to do, Dolores."

She has this boyfriend inside, Dolores, only last year she met some nice square Joe and got married. She didn't tell him about her guy inside and so far hasn't told her guy inside about the Joe. She figures he waits all week breathless for her visit, which maybe is true and maybe is flattering herself, and if she gives him the heave-ho he'll fall apart and kidnap the warden or something. Personally I think she likes to collect guilt, like some people collect stamps or coins or dead butterflies or whatever.

226

"I just feel so *guilty*," she says and moves on down across from the sisters.

We got pretty much all kinds on the bus, black girls, white girls, Chicanas like me who were born here and new fish from just across the border, a couple of Indian women from some tribe down the coast, even one Chinese girl, whose old man is supposed to be a very big cheese in gambling. She wears clothes I would kill for, this girl, only of course they wouldn't look good on me. Most of your best clothes are designed for the flat-chested type, which is why the fashion pages are full of Orientals and anorexics like Renee.

This Pam is another one, the kind that looks good in a man's T-shirt, looks good in almost anything she throws on. I decide to be nice to her anyway.

"You gonna eat all that?"

She's got this big plastic sack of food under her feet, wrapped sandwiches and fruit and what looks like a pie.

"Me? Oh—no, I figure, you know—the food inside—"

"They don't let you bring food in."

Her face drops again. "No?"

"Only cigarettes. One carton a month."

"He doesn't smoke."

"That's not the point. Cigarettes are like money inside. Your guy wants anything, wants anything done, he'll have to pay in smokes."

"What would he want to have done?"

I figure I should spare her most of the possibilities, so I just shrug. "Whatever. We get to the Halfway you get some change, load up on Camels from the machine. He'll thank you for it."

She looks down at the sack of goodies. She sure isn't going to eat it herself, not if she worked at it for a month. I can picture her dinner plate alone at home, full of the kind of stuff my Chuy feeds his gerbil. A celery cruncher.

"You want some of this?" she says, staring into the sack.

"No thanks, honey," I tell her. "I'm saving myself for the Halfway Diner."

LATER ON I WAS STRUCK BY HOW IT HAD ALREADY HAPPENED, THE DICE had already been thrown, only they didn't know it. So they took the whole trip up sitting together and talking and palling around unaware that they weren't friends anymore.

Lee and Delphine are as close as the sisters only nobody would ever mistake them for relatives, Lee being blonde and Delphine being one of our darker-complected customers. Lee is a natural blonde, unlike certain cosmetics saleswomen I could mention, with light blue eyes and a build that borders on the chunky although she would die to hear me say it. Del is thin and sort of elegant and black like you don't see too much outside of those documentaries on TV where people stick wooden spears in lions. *Negro como el fondo de la noche* my mother would say and on Del it looks great. The only feature they share is a similar nose, Del because she was born that way and Lee because of a field-hockey accident.

Maybe it was because they're both nurses or maybe just because they have complementary personalities, but somehow they found each other on the bus and since before I started riding they've been tight as ticks. You get the feeling they look forward to the long drive to catch up on each other's lives. They don't socialize off the bus, almost nobody does, but how many friends spend twelve hours a week together? Some of the black girls are friendly with some of the white girls, and us Chicanas can either spread around or sit together and talk home-talk, but black and white as tight as Lee and Del is pretty rare. Inside, well, inside you stay with your own, that's the beginning and the end of it. But inside is a world I don't even like to think about.

They plunk down across from us, Del lugging all these magazines—*Cosmo, People, Vogue, Essence*—that they sort of read and sort of make fun of, and Lee right away starts in on the food. Lee is obsessed with food the way a lot of borderline-chunky girls are, she can talk forever about what she didn't eat that day. She sits and gets a load of the sack at Pam's feet.

"That isn't food, is it?" she asks.

"Yeah," Pam apologizes. "I didn't know."

"Let's see it."

Obediently Pam starts shuffling through her sack, holding things up for a little show-and-tell. "I got this, and this," she says, "and this, I thought, maybe, they wouldn't have—I didn't know."

It's all stuff you buy at the bus station—sandwiches that taste like the cellophane they're wrapped in filled with that already-been-chewed kind of egg and chicken and tuna salad, stale pies stuffed with mealy applesauce, spotted fruit out of a machine. From all reports the food is better in the joint.

"How old are you, honey?" I ask.

"Nineteen."

"You ever cook at home?" Lee asks.

Pam shrugs. "Not much. Mostly I eat—you know, like salads. Maybe some fish sticks."

Del laughs. "I tried that fish-stick routine once when Richard was home," she says. "He ask me, 'What is this?' That's their code for 'I don't like the look of it.' It could be something *basic*, right, like a fried egg starin up at em, they still say, 'What's this?' So I say, 'It's fish, baby.' He says, 'If it's fish, which end is the *head* and which is the *tail?*' When I tell him it taste the same either way he says he doesn't eat nothin with square edges like that, on account of inside they always be cookin everything in these big cake pans and serve it up in squares—square egg, square potato, square macaroni. That and things served out in ice-cream scoops. Unless it really *is* ice cream Richard don't want no *scoops* on his plate."

"Lonnie's got this thing about chicken bones," Lee says, "bones of any kind, but especially chicken ones. Can't stand to look at em while he's eating."

"Kind of rules out the Colonel, doesn't it?"

"Naw," she says. "He *loves* fried chicken. We come back with one of them buckets, you know, with the biscuits and all, and I got to go perform surgery in the kitchen before we can eat. He keeps callin in—'It ready yet, hon? It ready yet? I'm starvin here.' I'll tell you, they'd of had those little McNugget things back before he went up our marriage woulda been in a lot better shape."

They're off to the races then, Lee and Del, yakking away, and they sort of close up into a society of two. Blondie is sitting there with her tuna-mash sandwiches in her lap, waiting for orders, so I stow everything in the sack and kick it deep under the seat.

"We get to the Halfway," I tell her, "we can dump it."

SOMETIMES I WONDER ABOUT GUS. THE HIGHWAY IS SO STRAIGHT, CUT-ting up through the Valley with the ground so flat and mostly dried up, like all its effort goes into those little square patches of artichokes or whatever you come past and after that it just got no more green in it. What can he be thinking about, all these miles, all these trips, up and down, year after year? He don't need to think to do his *yups* and *uh-huhs* at Mrs. Tucker, for that you can go on automatic pilot like I do with my Blanca when she goes into one of her stories about the tangled who-likes-who in her class. It's a real soap opera, *Dallas* for fifth-graders, but not what you need to concentrate on over breakfast. I wonder if Gus counts the days like we do, if there's a retirement date in his head, a release from the bus. Except to Mrs. Tucker he doesn't say but three things. When we first leave he says, "Headin out, ladies, take your seats." When we walk into the Halfway he always says, "Make it simple, ladies, we got a clock to watch." And when we're about to start the last leg, after dinner, he says, "Sweet dreams, ladies, we're bringin it home." Those same three things, every single trip. Like Mrs. Tucker with her blue sweater, always blue. Sometimes when I can't sleep and things are hard and awful and I can't see how they'll ever get better I'll lie awake and invent all these morbid thoughts, sort of torture myself with ideas, and I always start thinking that it's really the same exact sweater, that she goes home and pulls it apart stitch by stitch and starts from scratch again next trip. Not cause she wants to but cause she has to, it's her part of the punishment for what her husband done.

Other times I figure she just likes the color blue.

For the first hour or so Renee does her face. Even with good road and a fairly new bus this takes a steady hand, but she is an artist. Then she discovers Pam behind her, a new victim for her line of cosmetics, and starts into her pitch, opening with something tactful like, "You always let your hair go like that?" I'm dying for Pam to say, "Yeah, whatsit to you, sister?" but she is who she is and pretty soon Renee's got her believing it's at least a misdemeanor to leave the house without eye-liner on. I've heard all this too many times so I put my head back and close my eyes and aim my radar past it over to Lee and Del.

They talk about their patients like they were family. They talk about their family like they were patients. Both are RNs, they work at different hospitals but both on the ward. Lee has got kids and she talks about them, Del doesn't but wants some and she talks about that. They talk about how Del can eat twice as much as Lee but Del stays thin and Lee gets chunky. They talk about their guys, too, but usually not till we get pretty close to the facility.

"My Jimmy," Lee says, "is now convinced he's the man of the house. This is a five-year-old squirt, he acts like he's the Papa Bear."

"He remembers his father?"

"He likes to think he does, but he doesn't. His favorite saying these days is 'Why should I?'"

"Uh-oh."

"At least he doesn't go around saying he's an orphan like his sister. I introduce her, 'This is my daughter, Julie,' right, she says, 'Hi, I'm a orphan.' Cute."

"I used to do that," says Delphine. "Evertime my daddy spanked me that's what I'd spread round the neighborhood."

230

"So Julie says she's an orphan and Jimmy says his father works for the state."

Del laughs. "That's true enough."

"And he picks up all this stuff in the neighborhood. God I want to get out of there. Lonnie makes parole this rotation I'm gonna get him home and get his head straight and get us moved outa there."

"Like to the country or something?"

"Just anywheres it isn't so mean and he's not near his asshole so-called buddies."

"Yeah—"

"And I want—oh, I don't know, it sounds kinda stupid, really—"

"What?" Del says.

"I want a *dish*washer."

Del laughs again. Lee is embarrassed.

"You know what I mean—"

"Yeah, I know—"

"I want something in my life I just get it started and then it takes care of itself."

"I hear you *talkin*—"

"The other night Jimmy—now I know some of this is from those damn He-Man cartoons and all, but some of it is not having a father, I swear—he's in their room doing his prayers. He does this thing, the nuns told him praying is just talking to God, that's the new breed of nuns, right, so you'll go by their room and you'll hear Jimmy still up, having like these one-sided telephone conversations. 'Uh-huh, yeah, sure, I will, no problem, I'll try, uh-huh, uh-huh,' and he thinks he's talking with *God*, see, like a kid does with an imaginary friend. Or maybe he really *is* talking to God, how would I know? Anyhow, the other night I peek in and he's doing one of these numbers only now he's got that tough-guy look I hate so much pasted on his face like all the other little punks in the neighborhood and he's quiet for a long time, listening, and then he kind of sneers and says—'Why should I?'"

WE ALL SORT OF PRETEND THE FOOD IS BETTER AT THE HALFWAY THAN IT really is. Not that it's bad—it's okay, but nothing to write home about. Elvira, who runs the place, won't use a microwave, which makes me happy. I'm convinced there's vibes in those things that get into the food and ten years from now there'll be a national scandal. Whenever I have something from a microwave I get bad dreams, I swear it, so if something comes out a little lukewarm from her kitchen I don't complain.

The thing is, Elvira really seems to look forward to seeing us, looks forward to all the noise and hustle a busload of hungry women carry into the place, no matter what it is that brung them together. I imagine pulling into someplace different, with the name of the facility rolled up into the little destination window at the front of the bus, us flocking in and the waitresses panicking, the cooks ready to mutiny, the other customers sure we're pickpockets, prostitutes, baby-snatchers—no way José. So maybe the food here tastes better cause it comes through Elvira, all the square edges rounded off.

She's a big woman, Elvira, and if the country about here had a face it would look like hers. Kind of dry and cracked and worn, but friendly. She says she called the Halfway the Halfway because everyplace on earth is halfway between somewhere and somewhere else. I don't think being halfway between the city and the facility was what she had in mind, though.

When we bust in and spill out around the room there's only one other customer, a skinny old lizard in a Tecate cap and a T-shirt, never once looking up from his grilled-cheese sandwich.

"Make it simple, ladies," Gus says. "We got a clock to watch."

At the Halfway it's pretty hard to make it anything but simple. When they gave out the kits at Diner Central, Elvira went for bare essentials. She's got the fly-strip hanging by the door with a dozen little boogers stuck to it, got the cornflakes pyramided on a shelf, the specials handprinted on paper plates stuck on the wall behind the counter, the morning's Danishes crusting over under their plastic hood, the lemon and chocolate cream pies with huge bouffants of meringue behind sliding glass, a cigarette machine, a phone booth, and a machine that tells your exact weight for a quarter which Lee feeds both coming in and going out.

"Have your orders ready, girls!" Elvira calls as we settle at the counter and in the booths, pretty much filling the place. "I want to hear numbers."

Elvira starts at one end of the counter and her girl Cheryl does the booths. Cheryl always seems like she's about to come apart, sighing a lot, scratching things out, breaking her pencil points. A nervous kid. What there is to be nervous about way out there in the middle of nowhere I couldn't tell you, but she manages. I'm sitting at the counter with Mrs. Tucker on one side, Pam on the other, then Lee and Del. Lee and Del get talking about their honeymoons while Pam goes off to pump the cigarette machine.

"So anyhow," says Lee, "he figures we'll go down to Mexico, that old bit about how your money travels further down there? I don't know how *far* it goes, but after that honeymoon I know how *fast*. He was just trying to be sweet, really, he figured he was gonna show me this wonderful time, cause he's been there and I haven't and he knows what to order and I don't and he knows where to go and all that, only he *doesn't*, you know, he just *thinks* he does. Which is the whole thing with Lonnie—he dreams things up and pretty soon he believes they're *true*, right, so he's more surprised than anybody when the shit hits the fan."

"Sounds familiar," says Del.

"So he's heard of this place—jeez, it's so long ago—Santa Maria de la Playa, something like that—" Lee looks to me for help. "You must know it, Lourdes. It's on the coast—"

"Lots of coast down there."

"There's like these mountains, and the ocean—"

"Sorry," I tell her. "I've never been to Mexico."

Delphine can't feature this. "You're shittin me," she says. "*You?*"

"You ever been to Africa?"

Del cracks up, which is one of the things I like about her. She's not oversensitive about that stuff. Usually.

"Anyway," says Lee, "he says to me, 'Baby, we're talkin Paradise here, we're talkin Honeymoon *Heaven*. I got this deal—' "

"They *always* got a deal," says Del.

Elvira comes by then with her pad, working fast but friendly all the time. "Hey girls," she says, "how's it going? Mrs. Tucker?"

"Just the water," Mrs. Tucker says. "I'm not really hungry."

She doesn't look too good, Mrs. Tucker, kind of drawn around the eyes. Elvira shakes her head.

"Not good to skip lunch, Mrs. Tucker. You got a long ride ahead."

"Just the water, thank you."

Lee and Del get the same thing every week. "Let's see, we got a Number Three and a Number Five, mayo on the side," Elvira says. "Ice tea or lemonade?"

They both go for the lemonade and then Pam comes back dropping packs of Camels all over.

"How bout you, hon?"

"Um could I see a menu?" More cigarettes tumble from her arms. I see that Pam is one of those people who is accident-prone for life, and that her marrying a car thief is no coincidence. A catastrophe waiting to happen, this girl. Elvira jerks a thumb to the wall. Pam sees the paper plates. "Oh um—what are you having?"

"Number Three," says Lee.

"Number Five," says Delphine.

"Oh. I'll have a Number Four, please. And a club soda?"

"You know what a Number Four *is*, hon?"

"No, but I'll eat it."

Elvira thinks this is a scream but writes it down without laughing. "Four and a club," she says and moves on.

"So he's got this deal," says Del, getting back to the story.

"Right. He's got this deal where he brings these tapes down to San Miguel de los Nachos, whatever it was, and this guy who runs a brand-new resort down there is gonna give us the royal-carpet treatment in exchange—"

"Like cassette tapes?"

"Fresh from the K mart. Why they can't go to their own stores and buy these things I don't know—what's the story down there, Lourdes?"

"It's a mystery to me," I say.

"Anyhow, we got thousands of the things we're bringing through without paying a duty, a junior version of the scam he finally went up for, only I don't know because they're under the back seat and he keeps laying this Honeymoon Heaven jazz on me."

"With Richard his deals always have to do with clothes," says Del. "Man come in and say, 'Sugar, what size dress you wear?' and my stomach just hits the *floor*."

"And he brings the wrong size, right?"

"Ever damn time." Del shakes her head. "We took our honeymoon in Jamaica, back when we was livin high. Girl, you never saw nobody with more fluff in her head than me back then."

"You were young."

"Young ain't no excuse for *stupid*. I had one of those posters in my head—soft sand, violins playing, rum and Coke on ice and I was the girl in the white bikini. I thought it was gonna be like that *always*." Del gets kind of distant then, thinking back. She smiles. "Richard gets outa there, gets his health back, we gonna *party*, girl. That's one thing the man knows how to do is party."

"Yeah, Lonnie too. They both get clear we should all get together sometime, do the town."

As soon as it's out Lee knows different. There's a silence then, both of them just smiling, uncomfortable. Guys inside, black and white, aren't likely to even know who each other is, much less get together outside and make friendly. It does that to you, inside. Yayo is the same, always on about *los gavachos* this and *los pinches negros* that, it's a sickness you pick up there. Or maybe you already got it when you go in and the joint makes it worse. Lee finally breaks the silence.

"I bet you look great in a white bikini," she says.

Del laughs. "That's the *last* time I been to any *beach*, girl."

Cheryl shows with the food and Mrs. Tucker excuses herself to go to the ladies'. Lee has the diet plate, a scoop of cottage cheese with a cherry on top, Del has a BLT with mayo on the side, and Pam has the Number Four, which at the Halfway is a Monte Cristo—ham and cheese battered in egg, deep fried, and then rolled in confectioner's sugar. She turns it around and around on her plate, studying it like it fell from Mars.

"I think maybe I'll ask him this visit," says Del. "About the kids."

"You'd be a good mother," says Lee.

"You think so?"

"Sure."

"Richard with a baby in his lap . . . " Del grimaces at the thought. "Sometimes I think it's just what he needs—responsibility, family roots, that whole bit, settle him down. Then I think how maybe he'll just feel more pressure, you know? And when he starts feelin pressure is when he starts messin up." Del lets the thought sit for a minute and then gives herself a little slap on the cheek as if to clear it away. "Just got to get him healthy first. Plenty of time for the rest." She turns to Pam. "So how's that Number Four?"

"It's different," says Pam. She's still working on her first bite, scared to swallow.

"You can't finish it," says Lee, "I might take a bite."

Del digs her in the ribs. "Girl, don't you even *look* at that Number Four. Thing is just *evil* with carbohydrates. I don't wanta be hearing you bellyache about how you got no willpower all the way home."

"I got willpower," Lee says. "I'm a goddamn tower of strength. It's just my *ap*petite is stronger—"

"Naw—"

"My appetite is like Godzilla, Del, you seen it at work, layin waste to everything in its path—"

"Hah-*baaah!*"

"But I'm gonna whup it—"

"That's what I like to hear."

"Kick its butt—"

"Tell it, baby—"

"I'm losin twenty pounds—"

"Go for it!"

"An I'm quittin smoking too—"

"You can do it, Lee—"

"And when that man makes parole he's gonna buy me a dishwasher!"

"Get *down!*"

They're both of them giggling then, but Lee is mostly serious. "You know," she says, "as much as I want him out, sometimes it feels weird that it might really happen. You get used to being on your own, get your own way of doing things—"

"I hear you talkin—"

"The trouble is, it ain't so bad that I'm gonna leave him but it ain't so good I'm dying to stay."

There's hardly a one of us on the bus hasn't said the exact same thing at one time or another. Del looks around the room.

"So here we all are," she says, "at the Halfway Diner."

BACK ON THE ROAD PAM GETS QUIET SO I COUNT DEAD RABBITS FOR A while, and then occupy the time imagining disasters that could be happening with the kids at Graciela's. You'd be surprised at how entertaining this can be. By the time we pass the fruit stand Chuy has left the burners going on the gas stove and Luz, my baby, is being chewed by a rabid Doberman. It's only twenty minutes to the facility after the fruit stand and you can hear the bus get quieter, everybody but Dolores. She's still muttering her good-bye speech like a rosary. The visits do remind me of confession—you go into a little booth, you face each other through a window, you feel weird afterward. I think about the things I don't want to forget to tell Yayo. Then I see myself in Renee's mirror and hit on her for some blush.

THE FIRST WE KNOW OF IT IS WHEN THE GUARD AT SECURITY CALLS LEE and Del's names and they're taken off in opposite directions. That sets everybody buzzing. Pam is real nervous, this being her first visit, and I think she is a little afraid of who her guy is going to be all of a sudden. I tell her not to ask too much of it, one visit. I can't remember me and Yayo just sitting and talking a whole hour that many times *before* he went up. Add to that the glass and the little speaker boxes and people around with rifles, and you have definitely entered Weird City. We always talk home-talk cause all the guards are Anglos and it's fun for Yayo to badmouth them under their noses.

"Big blowout last night in the mess," he says to me. "*Anglos contra los negros.* One guy got cut pretty bad."

I get a sick feeling in the pit of my stomach. The night Yayo got busted I had the same feeling but couldn't think of anything to keep him in the house. "Black or white?" I ask.

"A black dude got stabbed," he says. "This guy Richard. He was a musician outside."

"And the guy who cut him?" I say, although I already know without asking.

"This guy Lonnie, was real close to parole. Got him up in solitary now. *Totalmente jodido.*"

It was just something that kind of blew up and got out of control. Somebody needs to feel like he's big dick by ranking somebody else in front of the others and when you got black and white inside that's a fight, maybe a riot, and this time when the dust clears there's Lee's guy with his shank stuck in Del's guy. You don't ask it to make a lot of sense. I tell Yayo how the kids are doing and how they miss him a lot but I feel this weight pulling down on me, knowing about Lee and Del, I feel like nothing's any use and we're wasting our time squawking at each other over these microphones. We're out of rhythm, it's a long hour.

"I think about you all the time," he says as the guard steps in and I step out.

"Me too," I say.

It isn't true. Whole days go by when I hardly even give him a thought, and when I do it's more an idea of him than really him in the flesh. Sometimes I feel guilty about this, but what the hell. Things weren't always so great when we were together. So maybe it's like the food at the Halfway, better to look forward to than to have.

Then I see how small he looks going back inside between the guards and I love him so much that I start to shake.

THE BUS IS ONE BIG WHISPER WHEN I GET BACK ON. THE ONES WHO HAVE heard about Lee and Del are filling in the ones who haven't. Lee gets in first, pale and stiff, and sits by me. If I touched her with my finger she'd explode. Pam steps in then, looking shaky, and I can tell she's disappointed to see I'm already by someone. When Del gets on everybody clams up. She walks in with her head up, trying not to cry. If it had been somebody else cut her guy, somebody not connected with any of us on the bus, we'd all be around bucking her up and Lee would be first in line. As it is a couple of the black girls say something but she just zombies past them and sits in the very back next to Pam.

It's always quieter on the way home. We got things that were said to chew over, mistakes to regret, the prospect of another week alone to face. But after Del comes in it's like a morgue. Mrs. Tucker doesn't even knit, just stares out at the Valley going by kind of blank-eyed and sleepy. Only Pam, still in the dark about what went down inside, starts to talk. It's so quiet I can hear her all the way from the rear.

"I never thought about how they'd have those guns," she says, just opening up out of the blue to Del. "I never saw one up close, only in the movies or TV. They're *real*, you know? They look so heavy and like if they shot it would just take you *apart*—"

"White girl," says Del, interrupting, "I don't want to be hearin bout none of your problems."

After that all you hear is the gears shifting now and then. I feel sick, worse than when I try to read. Lee hardly blinks beside me, the muscles in her jaw working as she grinds something out in her head. It's hard to breathe.

I look around and see that the white girls are almost all up front but for Pam who doesn't know and the black girls are all in the back, with us Chicanas on the borderline between as usual. Everybody is just stewing in her own thoughts. Even the sisters have nothing to say to each other. A busload of losers slogging down the highway. If there's life in hell this is what the field trips are like. It starts to get dark. In front of me, while there is still a tiny bit of daylight, Renee stares at her naked face in her mirror and sighs.

ELVIRA AND CHERYL LOOK TIRED WHEN WE GET TO THE HALFWAY. Ketchup bottles are turned on their heads on the counter but nothing is sliding down. Gus picks up on the mood and doesn't tell us how we got a clock to watch when he comes in.

Pam sits by me with Dolores and Mrs. Tucker on the other side. Dolores sits shaking her head. "Next time," she keeps saying. "I'll tell him next time." Lee shuts herself in the phone booth and Del sits at the far end of the counter.

Pam whispers to me, "What's up?"

"Big fight in the mess last night," I tell her. "Lee's guy cut Delphine's."

"My God. Is he okay?"

"He's alive if that's what you mean. I've heard Delphine say how he's got this blood problem, some old drug thing, so this ain't gonna help any."

Pam looks at the booth. "Lee must feel awful."

"Her guy just wrecked his parole but good," I say. "She's gettin it with both barrels."

Elvira comes by taking orders. "Rough trip, from the look of you all. Get your appetite back, Mrs. Tucker?"

"Yes, I have," she says. Her voice sounds like it's coming from the next room. "I'm very, very hungry."

"I didn't tell him," Dolores confesses to no one in particular. "I didn't have the heart."

We order and Elvira goes back in the kitchen. We know there is a cook named Phil but we have never seen him.

I ask Pam how her guy is making out. She makes a face, thinking. I can see her in high school, Pam, blonde and popular, and her guy, a good-looking charmer up to monkey business. An Anglo version of Yayo, full of promises that turn into excuses.

"He's okay, I guess. He says he's going to do his own time, whatever that means."

I got to laugh. "They all say that, honey, but not many manage. It means like mind your own business, stay out of complications."

"Oh."

Delphine is looking bullets over at Lee in the phone booth, who must be calling either her kids or her lawyer.

"Maybe that's how you got to be to survive in there," I say. "Hell, maybe out here, too. Personally I think it bites." Mrs. Tucker puts her head down into her arms and closes her eyes. It's been a long day. "The thing is," I say to Pam, "we're all of us doing time."

Lee comes out of the booth and goes to the opposite end of the counter from Del. It makes me think of me and Graciela. We used to be real jealous, her and me, sniff each other like dogs whenever we met, on account of her being Yayo's first wife. Not that I stole him or anything, they were bust long before I made the scene, but still you got to wonder what's he see in this bitch that I don't have? A natural human reaction. Anyhow, she's in the neighborhood and she's got a daughter by him who's ahead of my Chuy at the same school and I see her around but it's very icy. Then Yayo gets sent up and one day I'm stuck for a babysitter on visiting day. I don't know what possesses me, but desperation being the mother of a whole lot of stuff I ask Graciela. She says why not. When I get back it's late and I'm wasted and we get talking and I don't know why but we really hit it off. She's got a different perspective on Yayo of course, talks about him like he's her little boy gone astray which maybe in some ways he is, and we never get into sex stuff about him. But he isn't the only thing we got in common. Yayo, of course, thinks that's all we do, sit and gang up on him verbally, and he's not too crazy about the idea. We started shopping together and sometimes her girl comes over to play or we'll dump the kids with my mother and go out and it's fun, sort of like high school where you hung around not necessarily looking for boys. We go to the mall, whatever. There's times I would've gone right under without her, I mean I'd be *gonzo* today. I look at Lee and Del, sitting tight and mean inside themselves, and I think that's me and Graciela in reverse. And I wonder what happens to us when Yayo gets out.

"Mrs. Tucker, can you hear me? Mrs. Tucker?"

It's Gus who notices that Mrs. Tucker doesn't look right. He's shaking her and calling her name, and her eyes are still open but all fuzzy, the life gone out of them. The sisters are chattering something about cold water and Cheryl drops a plate of something and Pam keeps yelling, "Where's the poster? Find the poster!" Later she tells me she meant the anti-choking poster they're supposed to have up in restaurants, which Elvira kind of hides behind the weight-telling machine cause she says it puts people off their feed. Mrs. Tucker isn't choking, of course, but Pam doesn't know this at the time and is sure we got to look at this poster before we do anything wrong. Me, even with all the disasters I've imagined for the kids and all the rescues I've dreamed about performing, I've never dealt with this particular glassy-eyed-older-lady type of thing so I'm no help. Gus is holding Mrs. Tucker's face in his hands, her body gone limp, when Lee and Del step in.

"Move back!" says Lee. "Give her room to breathe."

"You got a pulse?" says Del.

"Not much. It's fluttering around."

"Get an ambulance here," says Del to Elvira and Elvira sends Cheryl running to the back.

"Any tags on her?"

They look around Mrs. Tucker's neck but don't find anything.

"Anybody ever hear her talk about a medical problem?" asks Del to the rest of us, while she holds Mrs. Tucker's lids up and looks deep into her eyes.

We rack our brains but come up empty, except for Gus. Gus looks a worse color than Mrs. Tucker does, sweat running down his face from the excitement. "She said the doctor told her to watch her intake," he says. "Whatever that means."

"She didn't eat lunch," says Elvira. "You should never skip lunch."

Lee and Del look at each other. "She got sugar, maybe?"

"Or something like it."

240

"Some orange juice," says Lee to Elvira and she runs off. Mrs. Tucker is kind of gray now, and her head keeps flopping if they don't hold it up.

"Usually she talks my ear off," says Gus. "Today she was like depressed or something."

Elvira comes back out. "I brung the fresh-squoze from the fridge," she says. "More vitamins."

Del takes it and feeds a little to Mrs. Tucker, tipping her head back to get it in. We're all of us circled around watching, opening our mouths in sympathy like when you're trying to get the baby to spoon-feed. Some dribbles out and some stays down.

"Just a little," says Lee. "It could be the opposite."

Mrs. Tucker takes another sip and smiles dreamily. "I like juice," she says.

"Here, take a little more."

"That's good," she says in this tiny, little-girl voice. "Juice is good."

By the time the ambulance comes we have her lying down in one of the booths covered by the lap blanket the sisters bring, her head pillowed on a couple of bags full of hamburger rolls. Her eyes have come clear and eventually she rejoins the living, looking up at all of us staring down around her and giving a little smile.

"Everybody's here," she says in that strange, far-off voice. "Everybody's here at the Halfway Diner."

THE AMBULANCE GUYS TAKE SOME ADVICE FROM LEE AND DEL AND THEN drive her away. Just keep her overnight for observation is all. "See?" Elvira keeps saying. "You don't never want to skip your lunch." Then she bags up dinners for those who want them cause we have to get back on the road.

Nobody says anything, but when we get aboard nobody will take a seat. Everybody just stands around in the aisle talking about Mrs. Tucker and waiting for Lee and Del to come in and make their move. Waiting and hoping, I guess.

Lee comes in and sits in the middle. Pam moves like she's gonna sit next to her but I grab her arm. Delphine comes in, looks around kind of casual, and then like it's just a coincidence she sits by Lee. The rest of us settle in real quick, then, pretending it's business as usual but listening real hard.

We're right behind them, me and Pam. They're not talking, not looking at each other, just sitting there side by side. Being nurses together might've cracked the ice but it didn't break it all the way through. We're parked right beneath the Halfway Diner sign and the neon makes this sound, this high-pitched buzzing that's like something about to explode.

"Sweet dreams, ladies," says Gus when he climbs into his seat. "We're bringin it home."

It's dark as pitch and it's quiet, but nobody is having sweet dreams. We're all listening. I don't really know how to explain this, and like I said, we're not exactly the League of Women Voters on that bus but there's a spirit, a way we root for each other and somehow we feel that the way it comes out between Lee and Delphine will be a judgment on us all. Nothing spoken, just a feeling between us.

Fifty miles go past and my stomach is starting to worry. Then, when Del finally speaks, her voice is so quiet I can hardly hear one seat away.

"So," she says. "San Luis Abysmal."

"Huh?" says Lee.

"Mexico," says Delphine, still real quiet. "You were telling me about your honeymoon down in San Luis Abysmal."

"Yeah," says Lee. "San Something-or-other—"

"And he says he speaks the language—"

You can feel this sigh like go through the whole bus. Most can't hear the words but just that they're talking. You can pick up the tone.

"Right," says Lee. "Only he learned his Spanish at Taco Bell. He's got this *deal*, right—"

"*Finalmente*," one of the sisters whispers behind me.

"*¡Qué bueno!*" the other whispers. "*Todavía son amigas.*"

"... so we get to the so-called resort and he cuts open the back seat and all these *cassettes* fall out, which I know nothing about—"

"Course not—"

"Only on account of the heat they've like *liquified*, right—"

"Naw—"

"And this guy who runs the resort is roped off but so are we cause this so-called brand-new resort is so brand-new it's not *built* yet—"

"Don't *say* it, girl—"

"It just a *construction* site—"

"Hah-*baaah!*"

The bus kicks into a higher gear and out of nowhere Gus is whistling up front. He's never done this before, not once, probably because he had Mrs. Tucker talking with him, but he's real good, like somebody on a record. What he's whistling is like the theme song to some big romantic movie, I forget which, real high and pretty and I close my eyes and get that nice feeling like just before you fall to sleep and you know everything is

242

under control and your body just relaxes. I feel good knowing there's hours before we got to get off, feel like as long as we stay on the bus, rocking gentle through the night, we're okay, we're safe. The others are talking soft around me now, Gus is whistling high and pretty, and there's Del and Lee, voices in the dark.

"There's a beach," says Lee, "only they haven't brought in the *sand* yet and everywhere you go these little fleas are hoppin around and my ankles get bit and swole up like a balloon—"

"I been there, girl," says Del. "I hear you talkin—"

"Honeymoon Heaven, he says to me—"

Del laughs, softly. "Honeymoon *Heaven.*"

June 1987

Dog People

SOMETIMES WHEN ALLAN STONNIER DROVE OUT AND THE DOGS WERE there, he revved up and aimed. He had an agreement with them that no matter how disdainfully they stood their ground, they would at the last moment lurch out of range if he went no more than a certain speed. The time he brushed McCoors's brown dog he felt bad about it, but the dog hadn't cooperated. The dog was too cocky. Stonnier had nothing against it. How could a man have anything against a dog? After that, when he revved up he was ready to brake, fast.

McCoors was coming through his woodlot and saw Stonnier drive at the dogs. He said, "If you ever hit one of my dogs, I'll break your fucking head."

"I wouldn't hit your dogs. I just want to scare them. Keep your dogs off my property. You have land."

"I'll break your fucking head."

"I'll be where you can find me."

That was a long time ago, when you could still talk to people about their dogs.

This morning Stonnier was out early, and running. It was a typical Cape Cod spring, more evident on calendars from the hardware store than on the land. A dry northeaster thrashed the roadside picket of unleafed oak,

E. S. GOLDMAN

cherry, and locust. A patch of melting snow, sprawled like a dirty old sheep dog on the lee side of a downed pine, drained toward the dozer cut that had made Stonnier's lane forty years ago. Stonnier's running shoes threw wet sand from the runnels. He took in all the air his chest would hold; he had been a runner since making the mile relay team at Nauset Regional, and had known ever since that even when the air was foul you had to fill up.

The air held the thaw of dog shit banked over the winter by neighbor dogs on his paths and driveway lane, in his mown field and kitchen garden—butts and drools and knobs, clumped grains and hamburgers, indistinguishable except in shape from their previous incarnation in bags and cans. Stonnier couldn't see how a dog took any nourishment from such food. It looked the same coming as going. No wonder they used so much. From time to time deposits were withdrawn on Stonnier's rakes and shoes, were wheeled into the garage on the tires of his Ford hatchback. Verna's gloves gathered the stuff in the seagrass mulch on the asparagus. He would have been better off to have set out a little later, when the sun was high enough to define the footing better.

He looked as if he had seventy or so disciplined years on him: he was a man of medium height, bony, with a cleaving profile—a fisherman before he had the stake to buy The Fish & Chips. He loped along the lane evasively, like a football player training on a course of automobile tires.

When it still was possible to speak to people about their dogs, Verna had said, "You could talk to him. He probably doesn't realize what his dogs do when he isn't looking."

But why not? He knew the dogs ran all day while he and his wife were away in their store. What did he think the dogs did with what had been put in them when they were turned out in the morning?

McCoors said, "I don't think my dogs did it." He said he would keep an eye on them. He tied them. They barked. They barked from eight o'clock, when he left, to six, when he came home and let them run until dark. Stonnier skipped a stone at them a couple of times, to let them know he didn't want them near his house. They stayed beyond the turn in the driveway so he wouldn't see them.

Stonnier encountered McCoors one day when they both were looking for their property bounds. Stonnier mentioned that the dogs barked all day and McCoors might not know it because he was away.

McCoors said, "If you tie up dogs, they bark." He tied them up to please Stonnier. Now Stonnier was complaining again. McCoors broke off the conversation and walked away. McCoors had a tough body, and eyes that quickly turned mean.

Stonnier told Vera that the man reminded him of a prison guard. "I guess there are all-kinds-of-looking prison guards, but McCoors is what I think of. That's nothing against prison guards." Stonnier always tried to be fair.

Deakler, another two-dog man, bought the place on the other side of the hill. His dogs came over to find out about McCoors's dogs at the same time McCoors's dogs came over to investigate the new neighbors. They met on Stonnier's driveway where it joined the Association lane, smelled each other, peed on the young azaleas Stonnier had raised from cuttings in tin cans, and agreed to meet there each day when their food was sufficiently digested. Wahlerson's half chow and Paul's black Newfie heard about the club and came up the Association lane to join.

Stonnier spoke to Deakler.

Deakler was an affable man who had been the sales vice-president of a generator-reconditioning company and knew how to get along while not giving in. "Well, you know how it is with dogs. You don't want to keep a dog tied up all the time. That's why we moved out here."

"I shouldn't have to take care of other people's dog dirt."

"Shoo them off if they bother you. Do them good."

"They scare my granddaughter when she visits. They charge."

"They never bit anybody. People have dogs. She should get used to them."

"That's up to her, if she wants to get used to dogs charging and growling at her. I had dogs. I like dogs. I have nothing against your dogs. They should stay on their own property. Is that a communist idea?"

Deakler looked at him speculatively, as if it might be.

"I don't like to quarrel with neighbors," Stonnier said. "We'll have to see. There's a leash law. I don't like to be talking law."

Stonnier already knew from the small-animal officer that if you couldn't keep a dog off your property, you had to catch it before you called for somebody to take it away.

"You don't have to catch your own bank robbers," Stonnier had said.

The SAO had cut him down. "That's how the town wants it—don't talk to me."

"Laws are one thing," Deakler said. "This is all Association property. Private property. You don't have to leash your dog if it's on private property."

Deakler told him something he hadn't thought about. The leash law didn't even apply to members of the Association, because the Association was made up of private properties, including the beach and the roads that all the private-property owners owned in common.

246

"That's why I came out here," Deakler said. "It isn't all closed in, like it is in town."

STONNIER BROUGHT IT UP AT THE ASSOCIATION MEETING IN JULY. OH, that was twenty-four years ago—how time flies. He remembered getting up to speak to the others on Giusti's patio. He had not in his lifetime before—or later—often spoken in meetings of that size. He thought he could remember every time. Three times at town meeting—about the algae on the pond and the proposed parking ordinance and the newspaper not printing what the Otter River Bank was doing on mortgages—and at the Board of Trade, about extending town water to the new subdivisions. Subjects that affected him. His house. His business. That's how the world worked. You spoke for yourself, and if you made sense, others voted with you even when that went a little against their own interests. That's how he always voted. He didn't sign petitions for things like the new children's park, but he voted for the park. The Taxpayers' Association said the park would put points on the tax bill. That was all right—it still made sense that the kids have a place with a fence around it, where dogs couldn't get in. That was what he would want for his own grandchildren if they lived in town. A few years back he would have asked, "Why don't they fence in the dogs, and let the kids run?" but you couldn't ask anything like that anymore.

Mostly he jogged these days. He paced an easy 120, waiting for his body to tell him how hard he could run. It wasn't his heart, it was his back: were his tendons and nerves lined up so that the jolt passed through like smoke and went off into the air, or would it jam somewhere on his hip or fourth vertebra? He told Verna, "He says it's in the vertebra, but that's not where I feel it." They knew all about hearts, but they didn't know anything about backs except to rest them. They told his father and his grandfather the same thing. He felt secure, and let out to 130.

He had thought his statement—that he had nothing against dogs but that the town leash law ought to prevail in the Association—would appeal to reasonable people. The dogs tramped down the lettuce, shat so that you couldn't trust where to walk after dark, chased cars, growled at strangers. He didn't say "shat," he said "did their business." Somebody said, "They doo-doo on your Brooks Brothers shoes," a reference to a man who at that time was running for President of the USA, and everybody laughed except Morrison and Dannels, who were large contributors to the candidate's committee. Halfway along into the laughter Stonnier caught on and joined to show his fellowship, although he sensed that the joke took the edge off the seriousness of his argument.

He had expected David Haseley would say something. Haseley had several times mentioned to him—or agreed with him—that the dogs were out of hand. As a retired high officer of a very large business in Cleveland, Haseley was usually taken seriously, but he chose not to speak to the motion. Only Larry Henry's widow, Marcia, spoke for it. Verna had been good to Marcia, shopped for her, looked in on her when she was laid up.

Sensing the anger of their neighbors, who spoke of liberties being taken from people everywhere, and now this, the summer people kept quiet or voted with the dog people. The ayes lacked the assertive spine of the nays. Stonnier thought that most members hadn't voted and that a written ballot might have turned out better. But that didn't seem to be the way to press an issue among neighbors.

In a spirit of good will members unanimously supported a resolution that people were responsible for their own dogs. It did not specify how the responsibility should be manifested.

After the meeting Stonnier said to Haseley that he had thought more people would support the leash law. Haseley nodded in the meditative, prudential manner that had earned him his good name and said, "Yes, that's so." He might have meant "I agree with you, that's what you thought." People didn't use words like they used to. "Speak up and say as best you can what you mean, so people know what's in your mind," Stonnier's mother had said to him. Now you had to be sure you asked the right question, or you might not find out what they really thought.

Stonnier hadn't pressed Haseley, toward whom he felt diffident not only because of his bearing but also because the older man was of the management class—as were all the others in the Association but himself. They were vice-presidents, deans, professors, accountants, lawyers; immigrants from Providence, Amherst, Ohio, Pennsylvania; taxed, many of them, in Florida, which the Stonniers had visited in their camper but had not been taken by sufficiently to give it six months and a day every year. The others had all gone beyond high school.

"I still don't know how he voted," he said to Verna.

Allan and Verna Stonnier were second-generation Cape Cod, the only native-born in the West Bay Association, the first to raise children there and see them bused to school in Orleans and then go out on their own. Allan had done well with The Fish & Chips—better than such a modest-looking enterprise had implied—but he remained somewhat apart from the others. His three-acre parcel on the waterfront had cost under three thousand dollars, but that was when you had to bounce a half mile in a rut to get out there. After the fire at The Fish & Chips, ten years ago, a real-estate woman who called about buying the lot asked about the house, too. She had a customer she thought would pay more than a million dollars for it if Allan would consider selling. They thought he would sell his house and get out, but nothing could make him move after the fire. He was so set that Verna had to make it half a joke when she said that with a million dollars and the insurance from the fire they could live anywhere they wanted. By now the house might be worth two million, the way prices were. He knew it as well as she did, and if he wanted to talk about it, he would say so. "It's the whole country," he said. "Everywhere. You might as well deal with it where you are." A million dollars after tax wasn't all that much anymore anyhow.

McCoors's two dogs came out to yap at him. He said, "Yah," and raised his elbow, and they shut up and backed off while he padded on toward the wider, graveled lane that looped through the fifty-three properties in the West Bay Association and carried their owners' cars to the blacktop and town.

Shoeman's black-and-white sort-of spitz bitch met him there and trotted with him companionably. Stonnier considered her a friend. Some mornings she stayed with him past three or four properties, but this morning the collie next door came out and growled and she stopped at the line. "Yah," Stonnier growled back at the collie; he raised his elbow and jogged on.

AFTER ONE SPRING THAW STONNIER DUG A PIT NEAR THE LINE CLOSE TO McCoors's driveway. McCoors was quick to defend the integrity of his property. He had taken his neighbor on the other side to court in a right-of-way dispute. McCoors asked Stonnier what he was doing. He was going to bury dog shit.

"You don't have to do that here," McCoors said.

"It's your dogs,'" Stonnier said.

That afternoon a man from the Board of Health drove up to the house. Allan was down at The Fish & Chips, watching some workmen shingle a new roof. The man told Verna that burying garbage was against the law. He told her about the hazard to the groundwater supply. He said the fine could be fifty dollars a day as long as the nuisance continued unabated. He left a red notice. This unsettled Verna, because she had always thought ways could be found to work things out.

Allan went to the board and said they were off base. A human being

249

had to get a porcelain bowl and running water and an expensive piping system to get rid of his waste, but a dog could leave it anywhere. Their ruling was off base. The health officer said he didn't write the laws, he enforced them, and Allan better close the pit and not open another one. The newspaper carried a story under the headline "PRIVATE DUMP OWNER THREATENED WITH FINE." Stonnier thought it gave the idea that he was trying to get away with something.

He wrote a letter to the editor. Melvin Brate didn't print it. Stonnier thought that Brate was still peeved about a letter he had written earlier, saying that the Otter River Bank was using small type to sneak foreclosures over on people, trying to get out of old, low interest rates into the new crazy rates. Stonnier knew about that because they had done it to his cousin. In his letter to the editor Stonnier gave the names of the man who ran the bank and the men who were on its investment committee and said that was no way for neighbors to act when they had signed their names to a contract. The bank was the biggest advertiser in the paper, so naturally Melvin Brate didn't print the letter. Allan got up at town meeting in non-agenda time and read his bank letter to the voters to let them know what was going on. This was the first time he had ever gotten to his feet to talk to more than a thousand people, and it was no harder than holding your hand in a fire.

Melvin Brate sat with his arms folded and looked hard at the floor while Allan spoke about his newspaper's not saying anything about what the bank was doing. Just that day Brate had published an editorial titled "Your Free Press: Bastion of Liberty," which he counted on for an award from the League of Weekly Publishers, and here was this fried-clam peddler carrying on. It wasn't surprising that Brate didn't print the dog-shit letter either, even though Stonnier called the stuff "scat."

Verna was secretly glad that the letter wasn't published. She thought a way could be found to deal with the problem so that dog owners wouldn't get upset and people wouldn't look at her sideways and stop going to The Fish & Chips. She knew that speaking to Allan was useless unless she could say it in another way, and she couldn't think of any. He had been such a usual man when she married him, and people were getting the idea he was an oddball. She couldn't clearly see why that was, because he had a right to complain about the dogs; nevertheless, he ought to do it a different way for his own sake, and not write to the paper or take it up at town meeting. It irritated people.

ONE DAY STONNIER COUNTED EIGHTEEN DOGS AT THE JUNCTURE OF HIS land and the Association lane.

The Association lane went into the blacktop that wound and rolled toward the town. The houses on either side were on the required acreage and fully suited to their purposes. Once home to cranberry farmers, fuel dealers, printers, boat builders, lobstermen—Stonnier knew the names that went with the oldest properties—they had been bid away in the sixties and seventies by retirement and stock-market bankrolls at stiff prices. The new owners had the means to dormer up and lay on wings and garages. On some properties two and three houses stood where before there had been a single low shingle house, a big garden, and woods. The newcomers followed the traditional styles of the Chatham Road, rendered for art shows on the high school green—saltboxes, houses-and-a-half, Greek revival, all well shrubbed and fenced. One ghost of gnawed and mossy shingles had withstood all tenders to purchase and a siege of trumpet vines, rampant lilacs, and fattening cedars intent on taking it down.

Only the jolly French house looked as though it ought to have been in the old town, along with other houses of the style built by managers of the company that had laid the telephone cable to France; indeed, it had been trucked from town in the deal with the architectural commission that had licensed the Cable Station Motel to be built. To Stonnier, the French house's journey down the Chatham Road at two miles an hour, with outriders from the telephone company and the electric company and the police, was the most memorable event since the passage of the great glacier, which he had not witnessed. Had he not come into money so late, this would have been the house Stonnier built for his family. The French house sat square on the ground and knew how to shed water off its hat. It looked like a toby jug; it was gold and blue, its cornice was striped with purple, and the door was gunpowder red.

"It's different," he said to Verna, who thought it was a rather queer house that would fit in better if it were white. "You just like things one way or another," he said. He liked the moment of coming out on the blacktop around the corner from West Bay and finding himself two weeks further into spring, jogging by the French house with the long hedge of breaking forsythia skirted with daffodils and crocuses. The air here stank too. Some of it was spring rot coming out of the ground. Most of it was dog.

Ahead on the long straight stretch Gordon's basset (that dog must be a hundred years old), carrying his skin like a soaked blanket, turned and turned in the middle of the road, trying to find a way to let his rear end down and create the right precedent for the rest of him. He slept there every morning for an hour or two, unless the snow was a foot deep. Regular drivers knew to watch for him, and the Lord protected Sam the basset against everybody else. That dog was going to get it one day. The driver who did it better have a good head start and not ask around whose dog it was so that he could tell them he was sorry but he had passed another car and there the dog was, in the middle of the road, and he had done his best to avoid him, he was sorry, he knew what it was to lose a dog, he had two himself, don't shoot, please don't shoot. You couldn't know anymore what to expect if there was a dog in it. Juries looked at those dog people out there. If you ran for sheriff, you took questions at public meetings and the dog people heard your answers. Senators wanted some of that dog-PAC money, especially because the dog-PAC people said that what they were really interested in wasn't dogs but good government. If a dog question was coming up at town meeting, you saw people voting you never saw anywhere else. They went home after voting on dogs, and left the rest to find a quorum for the payroll and potholes.

Allan Stonnier was the only human being afoot on the Chatham Road. His red sweatshirt was well known at this hour. Most of the sparse traffic was pickups, with elbows crooked out the windows, wheels crunching and kicking up cans, wrappers, cups, laid down by the pickups that had gone that way earlier, tools and dogs riding behind. He saw Dexter Reddick's green pickup, with the sunburst on the radiator. Without being too obvious, Stonnier adjusted course to the edge of the road. He couldn't be absolutely sure Reddick wouldn't take a swerve at him for the hell of it. He prepared to break from the shoulder for the grass slope. Reddick went by with angry eyes, threw up a finger. Reflexively, Stonnier gave it back. He heard the pickup brake hard behind him and push hard in reverse as it came back. He kept going. Reddick passed, got twenty feet beyond, and put his head out the window.

"What did I see you do?"

"The same as you." By then he was past the truck, and Reddick had to grind back again to talk to him.

"Let me see you do that again, you fuckhead. You old fart. You can't get it up. You firebug. I'll burn your ass." Stonnier kept going. Barricaded behind shovels, rakes, and lawnmowers, Reddick's Labs yammered and spittled at him. Reddick jack-started a groove in the blacktop and went on his way. Stonnier decided to take the side road that went toward the dump.

Pilliard's pack of huskies, brought back from Alaska last year, saw him coming and started their manic racket. Pilliard had one-upped everybody at the Landing Bar with that one. Jesus, twelve huskies, did you ever see such dogs? You could hide your arm in the fur. The strut and drive of those legs. They had Chinese faces as if they were people. Those people fucked their dogs. Pilliard had them in the cyclone-fenced stockade he had put up to hold his cords when he was in the stovewood business. Ten feet high, and ground area about as big as any factory you would find in a place like Cape Cod—lots of room even for twelve huskies.

Pilliard's idea was to take them to fairs and show them, for a good price, pulling a sled he'd fitted with siliconed nylon runners that slipped over turf. Take your picture with a real team of Eskimo huskies. Children's birthday parties. Beats ponies all hollow. Fourth of July parades. He brought Santa Claus to the Mall. Altogether, the bookings amounted to only a dozen brief outings all year. The dogs were used to doing miles of work in cold weather. In the stockade they hung around. At night they could be heard barking for hours for their own reasons, and the sound carried to West Bay.

Verna thought Allan must be running on the dump road, because he would be there about now, and there went Pilliard's huskies. They didn't often see people go by on foot. They acknowledged pedestrians and slow drivers by lunging at the fence, climbing, piling on, snarling, yelping powerfully. Allan had driven her by, and slowed the car so she could hear it up close. It scared her. It was more like mad screaming than barking, all of them exciting each other. Some things Verna wished Allan wouldn't do, and one of them was to run past Pilliard's huskies.

"Run someplace else," Pilliard said. "You don't like dogs and they know it, and they don't like you, so why don't you run someplace else."

What was the use explaining to a man who already knew it that Stonnier was running on a public road, and he was there before the dogs anyhow. And even if he wasn't . . .

Stonnier left them yelping, went over the crest of the rise and around the next corner, running, feeling good, well sweated as he went toward halfway. It was the dumb part of the route, the mall and the file of flat-roofed taxpayers and show-windowed front porches of old downtown; service stations, eating places, clothes shops, music stores, cleaners, laundries, drugstores elbowing to be seen along the old bypassed highway number.

He could have gone around by the marsh road and avoided town, but one thing could be said for Main Street. It smelled better than anywhere else. Better than West Bay behind the dunes, where the ocean lost its innocence; better than Chatham Road and all the lived-on lanes and roads from the bridge to Province Lands. He had never thought he'd live to see the day when downtown smelled better than the countryside. If a stray wandered into the mall, the small-animal officer showed up fast and snared him into the cage mounted on his police wagon. The merchants saw to it. You couldn't let a leashed dog step onto one of those neat rectangles of shrubbery if you didn't want a ticket. If a dog hunched to empty out, you had to drag him to the library lawn. Even the dog people understood the deal. You left the merchants alone, they left you alone.

Soon after dawn old downtown could have been a movie set in storage. The cars and service trucks of early risers were parked in front of Annie O, who opened first, for the fishermen. The overnight lights in the stores and the streetlights watched him go by. Stanchions of sulfur light guarded the plaza of Canine City, with its eleven veterinarians, four cosmetologists, several outfitters; the portrait studio featured the work of fifteen internationally known dog artists; an architect displayed model residences: cape, half-cape, Federal, Victorian, Bauwowhaus, duplex, ranch.

The stoplight turned irrationally against him, as if programmed to recognize a man of ordinary size in a red sweatshirt running in from the west. The wind batted through the open cross street and went back again behind the solid buffer of storefronts until it came to the empty lot on the cove where The Fish & Chips had been. He faced into it, running in place, when he got there.

THE REAL-ESTATE PEOPLE NEVER STOPPED BRINGING HIM OFFERS. HE WAS going to leave that up to his daughter to decide. The land was money in the bank. "That's what everybody needs, Verna—something in back of him so no matter how hard he's pushed he doesn't have to give in to others. That's what it's all about. More people could be like that if they didn't want too much."

The Conservation Commission asked, If he wasn't going to use it, would he consider deeding it to them for the honor of his name in Melvin Brate's paper and the tax deduction? They thought a price might be worked out if he met them halfway. He thought about it. He got as far as thinking about what kind of sign he would require them to put up if he sold them the land, but he could never get the wording right. He knew if he got it right they wouldn't do it. He neatened up the section of burned-out foundation the building inspector allowed, and let the lot sit there with the sign.

SITE OF THE FISH & CHIPS RESTAURANT.
BURNED DOWN BY VANDALS A.D. 2002 IN HONOR OF
THEIR DOGS.

Someone stole the sign the first night. He wasn't going to fool with them; he went right to a concrete monument, anchored with bent iron rods into a six-foot-square concrete pad. They tried to jump it out with a chain but they would have needed a dozer and they never got that far. They hit it with a hammer now and then. They painted out the inscription. He used to go back a few times a year to put it in shape, but he hadn't had to touch it for two years now. The old generations had lost interest, and not even the young Reddicks cared much unless something happened to stir them up.

Coming on their first glimpse of salt water in twenty miles, visitors swung onto the apron and reached for their cameras. Alert to station their wives at the photo opportunity where George Washington watered his horse and the salt water beckoned, they walked over to read the legend about the restaurant and the vandals and the dogs. They would throw up their hands. What's that all about? Stonnier himself wasn't satisfied with the statement, but after so many years the story was boring to anybody but himself anyhow.

He had kept a dozen clipped mallards for his own table in a chicken-wire pen half in and half out of the water, the way you penned ducks if you had a waterfront. He had heard a terrible squawking, and when he looked out from the kitchen door the two dogs that patroled Reddick's garage at night were running wild in the pen, breaking wings and necks, tossing every duck they could get their jaws on. He hollered at them, but you couldn't call a dog off anything like that. He got his shotgun and drove a charge into the side of one; the other ran off, and Reddick came over from his garage, goddamning him.

The paper said that Reddick was there to get his dogs, and Stonnier threatened him with the gun to keep him off, and he shot the dog.

A week later a southerly breeze pulled an early-morning fire out of the rubbish trailer onto the shingle. Flame was all through The Fish & Chips by the time the pumper got there. His was the fourth restaurant that went up that fall, and the arson investigator from the state asked him how his business had been. They went over his records at the bank. The insurance company took two years to pay up.

HE RAN WHERE HE STOOD WHILE HE LOOKED AROUND AND CHECKED out the site. It was as usual. The fresh northeaster gusted at him out of a mist that lay up to the land at the water's edge. A gull stalked the tidal drain looking for garbage. Another, unseen, cried as if lost. On the scrim of fog his memory raised the shed of The Fish & Chips, with the huge lobster standing guard, and then the new Fish & Chips with the Cape Cod roof and the kitchen wing. He was looking out the back window and saw Reddick's dogs in the pen and went after them. A charred beam leaned on a course of cement block that had been the foundation. Ravined and grainy, the blacktop was being worked by frost and roots. Spindly cedars had found footing. He remembered when they had poured the blacktop: four inches, and four of gravel under it, and then sand, and the cedars had found enough to grow on down there. He felt himself already cooling out, and took off at a 120 jog back through town, wiping sweat from his forehead with the flat of his hand.

The last thing he discussed with himself as he went up the rise at the mall and turned again toward Pilliard's was how his daughter and her children could be made to keep their minds on being positioned not to give in to others. All he could do was leave them the land; they had to understand what it was for. If they sold it, they would have the money, and if you had money, you had all kinds of duties to it. You had to see that you didn't lose any of it, and you had to get the best interest for it, and you bought things you didn't need that brought you new duties, like a place in Florida. The land would stay there to back you up. He didn't stop thinking about that until he got into range of Pilliard's huskies and they started in on him again. Pilliard was carrying an armful of pipe, fence posts maybe, and spat a word he couldn't hear. He kept going.

The wind off the bay blew some of the sound away, but Verna heard the pack distinctly again. She threw a last handful of cracked corn for the quail and jays and listened. She wore untied walking shoes for slippers and a nubby white robe over her nightgown. She had brushed her hair but not in detail, and its style was a simple black-speckled gray flare cut off at her earlobe. She took her wristwatch out of the robe pocket but couldn't read it. Her glasses were still inside, on the table. If that was Allan, he would be nine or ten minutes. Then he would shower and she would be dressed and have breakfast on. It wasn't an egg day. He might want tuna on toast.

The dogs went on. She wasn't dressed to stay out, but the dogs kept barking. She picked up a dead branch, carefully positioned it, and flicked a dog divot into the rough. All the deposits over which oak leaves had settled stirred and gave off a tribal odor, as if they were a single living thing giving warning. She threw another handful of corn without noticing exactly what she was doing. Pilliard's dogs sounded louder, but that couldn't be. They were where they were. In the tops of the scratch pines the wind had not changed. Individual voices could be distinguished rising out of the wild yammer of the pack.

Were Pilliard's dogs out? He leashed and ran them sometimes in the back of the dump, but that was farther, not nearer, and never this early. She felt nervous and wished to know something. She started toward the house to look up Pilliard's name and telephone him but knew immediately that was not the thing to do. The thing to do was to get in the car and drive over there.

She was not constrained now by any civilized notion that she should not be seen, even by herself, to overreact. She suddenly wished to act as quickly and as arbitrarily as she knew how and to get over to the dump road. The Ford spurted back out of the garage, skidded while she pulled on the wheel to get it around, and went out the lane faster than McCoors's dogs had ever seen it come at them. They couldn't believe it was going that fast until it kicked the big kind-of airedale into the ditch. She had no time for regret or succor and pushed the gas harder. The wheels jumped out of potholes and ruts, clawing air, and jolted down. She was frightened by her speed. She held on as if she were a passenger. Coming to the fork at the blacktop she judged—willed, rather—that she could beat the blue car, and cut it off. Its horn lectured her past Sam the basset, sitting on the stripe with his back to her, knowing she wouldn't dare, until she lost the sound at the turn beyond the straightaway.

A quarter mile up toward Pilliard's she saw them on the road. She looked for a human figure but could see only the pack and whatever it was they were larking around on the road. She kept her hand on the horn and drove at them, not thinking any longer that he could have possibly gone another way, or got up a tree, or even gone into Pilliard's house. She put the pedal on the floor. She was angry at Allan for getting himself into anything like this. He could have lived his life like other people. But he hadn't, and that's how it was, and, enraged, she owed him as many of them as she could get her wheels into.

August 1988

Two Kinds

MY MOTHER BELIEVED YOU COULD BE ANYTHING YOU WANTED TO BE IN America. You could open a restaurant. You could work for the government and get good retirement. You could buy a house with almost no money down. You could become rich. You could become instantly famous.

"Of course, you can be prodigy, too," my mother told me when I was nine. "You can be best anything. What does Auntie Lindo know? Her daughter, she is only best tricky."

America was where all my mother's hopes lay. She had come to San Francisco in 1949 after losing everything in China: her mother and father, her family home, her first husband, and two daughters, twin baby girls. But she never looked back with regret. Things could get better in so many ways.

WE DIDN'T IMMEDIATELY PICK THE RIGHT KIND OF PRODIGY. AT FIRST MY mother thought I could be a Chinese Shirley Temple. We'd watch Shirley's old movies on TV as though they were training films. My mother would poke my arm and say, "*Ni kan*. You watch." And I would see Shirley tapping her feet, or singing a sailor song, or pursing her lips into a very round O while saying "Oh, my goodness."

"*Ni kan*," my mother said, as

AMY TAN

Shirley's eyes flooded with tears. "You already know how. Don't need talent for crying!"

Soon after my mother got this idea about Shirley Temple, she took me to the beauty training school in the Mission District and put me in the hands of a student who could barely hold the scissors without shaking. Instead of getting big fat curls, I emerged with an uneven mass of crinkly black fuzz. My mother dragged me off to the bathroom and tried to wet down my hair.

"You look like Negro Chinese," she lamented, as if I had done this on purpose.

The instructor of the beauty training school had to lop off these soggy clumps to make my hair even again. "Peter Pan is very popular these days," the instructor assured my mother. I now had hair the length of a boy's, with curly bangs that hung at a slant two inches above my eyebrows. I liked the haircut, and it made me actually look forward to my future fame.

In fact, in the beginning I was just as excited as my mother, maybe even more so. I pictured this prodigy part of me as many different images, and I tried each one on for size. I was a dainty ballerina girl standing by the curtain, waiting to hear the music that would send me floating on my tiptoes. I was like the Christ child lifted out of the straw manger, crying with holy indignity. I was Cinderella stepping from her pumpkin carriage with sparkly cartoon music filling the air.

In all of my imaginings I was filled with a sense that I would soon become perfect. My mother and father would adore me. I would be beyond reproach. I would never feel the need to sulk, or to clamor for anything.

But sometimes the prodigy in me became impatient. "If you don't hurry up and get me out of here, I'm disappearing for good," it warned. "And then you'll always be nothing."

EVERY NIGHT AFTER DINNER MY MOTHER AND I WOULD SIT AT THE Formica-topped kitchen table. She would present new tests, taking her examples from stories of amazing children that she had read in *Ripley's Believe It or Not* or *Good Housekeeping*, *Reader's Digest*, or any of a dozen other magazines she kept in a pile in our bathroom. My mother got these magazines from people whose houses she cleaned. And since she cleaned many houses each week, we had a great assortment. She would look through them all, searching for stories about remarkable children.

The first night she brought out a story about a three-year-old boy who knew the capitals of all the states and even of most of the European countries. A teacher was quoted as saying that the little boy could also pronounce the names of the foreign cities correctly. "What's the capital of Finland?" my mother asked me, looking at the story.

All I knew was the capital of California, because Sacramento was the name of the street we lived on in Chinatown. "Nairobi!" I guessed, saying the most foreign word I could think of. She checked to see if that might be one way to pronounce *Helsinki* before showing me the answer.

The tests got harder—multiplying numbers in my head, finding the queen of hearts in a deck of cards, trying to stand on my head without using my hands, predicting the daily temperatures in Los Angeles, New York, and London. One night I had to look at a page from the Bible for three minutes and then report everything I could remember. "Now Jehoshaphat had riches and honor in abundance and . . . that's all I remember, Ma," I said.

And after seeing, once again, my mother's disappointed face, something inside me began to die. I hated the tests, the raised hopes and failed expectations. Before going to bed that night I looked in the mirror above the bathroom sink, and when I saw only my face staring back—and understood that it would always be this ordinary face—I began to cry. Such a sad, ugly girl! I made high-pitched noises like a crazed animal, trying to scratch out the face in the mirror.

And then I saw what seemed to be the prodigy side of me—a face I had never seen before. I looked at my reflection, blinking so that I could see more clearly. The girl staring back at me was angry, powerful. She and I were the same. I had new thoughts, willful thoughts—or, rather, thoughts filled with lots of won'ts. I won't let her change me, I promised myself. I won't be what I'm not.

So now when my mother presented her tests, I performed listlessly, my head propped on one arm. I pretended to be bored. And I was. I got so bored that I started counting the bellows of the foghorns out on the bay while my mother drilled me in other areas. The sound was comforting and reminded me of the cow jumping over the moon. And the next day I played a game with myself, seeing if my mother would give up on me before eight bellows. After a while I usually counted only one bellow, maybe two at most. At last she was beginning to give up hope.

TWO OR THREE MONTHS WENT BY WITHOUT ANY MENTION OF MY BEING a prodigy. And then one day my mother was watching the *Ed Sullivan Show* on TV. The TV was old and the sound kept shorting out. Every time my mother got halfway up from the sofa to adjust the set, the sound would come back on and Sullivan would be talking. As soon as she sat down, Sullivan would go silent again. She got up—the TV broke into loud piano music. She sat down—silence. Up and down, back and forth, quiet and loud. It was like a stiff, embraceless dance between her and the TV set. Finally, she stood by the set with her hand on the sound dial.

She seemed entranced by the music, a frenzied little piano piece with a mesmerizing quality, which alternated between quick, playful passages and teasing, lilting ones.

"Ni kan," my mother said, calling me over with hurried hand gestures. "Look here."

I could see why my mother was fascinated by the music. It was being pounded out by a little Chinese girl, about nine years old, with a Peter Pan haircut. The girl had the sauciness of a Shirley Temple. She was proudly modest, like a proper Chinese child. And she also did a fancy sweep of a curtsy, so that the fluffy skirt of her white dress cascaded to the floor like the petals of a large carnation.

In spite of these warning signs, I wasn't worried. Our family had no piano and we couldn't afford to buy one, let alone reams of sheet music and piano lessons. So I could be generous in my comments when my mother bad-mouthed the little girl on TV.

"Play note right, but doesn't sound good!" my mother complained. "No singing sound."

"What are you picking on her for?" I said carelessly, "She's pretty good. Maybe she's not the best, but she's trying hard." I knew almost immediately that I would be sorry I had said that.

"Just like you," she said. "Not the best. Because you not trying." She gave a little huff as she let go of the sound dial and sat down on the sofa.

The little Chinese girl sat down also, to play an encore of "Anitra's Tanz," by Grieg. I remember the song, because later on I had to learn how to play it.

THREE DAYS AFTER WATCHING THE *ED SULLIVAN SHOW* MY MOTHER TOLD me what my schedule would be for piano lessons and piano practice. She had talked to Mr. Chong, who lived on the first floor of our apartment building. Mr. Chong was a retired piano teacher, and my mother had traded housecleaning services for weekly lessons and a piano for me to practice on every day, two hours a day, from four until six.

When my mother told me this, I felt as though I had been sent to hell. I whined, and then kicked my foot a little when I couldn't stand it anymore.

"Why don't you like me the way I am?" I cried. "I'm *not* a genius! I can't play the piano. And even if I could, I wouldn't go on TV if you paid me a million dollars!"

My mother slapped me. "Who ask you to be genius?" she shouted. "Only ask you be your best. For you sake. You think I want you to be genius? Hnnh! What for! Who ask you!"

"So ungrateful," I heard her mutter in Chinese. "If she had as much talent as she has temper, she'd be famous now."

Mr. Chong, whom I secretly nicknamed Old Chong, was very strange, always tapping his fingers to the silent music of an invisible orchestra. He looked ancient in my eyes. He had lost most of the hair on the top of his head, and wore thick glasses and had eyes that always looked tired. But he must have been younger than I thought, since he lived with his mother and was not yet married.

I met Old Lady Chong once, and that was enough. She had a peculiar smell, like a baby that had done something in its pants, and her fingers felt like a dead person's, like an old peach I once found in the back of the refrigerator; its skin just slid off the flesh when I picked it up.

I soon found out why Old Chong had retired from teaching piano. He was deaf. "Like Beethoven!" he shouted to me. "We're both listening only in our head!" And he would start to conduct his frantic silent sonatas.

Our lessons went like this. He would open the book and point to different things, explaining their purpose: "Key! Treble! Bass! No sharps or flats! So this is C major! Listen now and play after me!"

And then he would play the C scale a few times, a simple chord, and then, as if inspired by an old unreachable itch, he would gradually add more notes and running trills and a pounding bass until the music was really something quite grand.

I would play after him, the simple scale, the simple chord, and then just play some nonsense that sounded like a cat running up and down on top of garbage cans. Old Chong would smile and applaud and say, "Very good! But now you must learn to keep time!"

So that's how I discovered that Old Chong's eyes were too slow to keep up with the wrong notes I was playing. He went through the motions in half time. To help me keep rhythm, he stood behind me and pushed down on my right shoulder for every beat. He balanced pennies on top of my wrists so that I would keep them still as I slowly played scales and arpeggios. He had me curve my hand around an apple and keep that shape while playing chords. He marched stiffly to show me how to make each finger dance up and down, staccato, like an obedient little soldier.

He taught me all these things, and that was how I also learned I could be lazy and get away with mistakes, lots of mistakes. If I hit the wrong notes because I hadn't practiced enough, I never corrected myself. I just kept playing in rhythm. And Old Chong kept conducting his own private reverie.

So maybe I never really gave myself a fair chance. I did pick up the basics pretty quickly, and I might have become a good pianist at that young age. But I was so determined not to try, not to be anybody different, that I learned to play only the most ear-splitting preludes, the most discordant hymns.

Over the next year I practiced like this, dutifully in my own way. And then one day I heard my mother and her friend Lindo Jong both talking in a loud, bragging tone of voice so that others could hear. It was after church, and I was leaning against a brick wall, wearing a dress with stiff white petticoats. Auntie Lindo's daughter, Waverly, who was my age, was standing farther down the wall, about five feet away. We had grown up together and shared all the closeness of two sisters, squabbling over crayons and dolls. In other words, for the most part, we hated each other. I thought she was snotty. Waverly Jong had gained a certain amount of fame as "Chinatown's Littlest Chinese Chess Champion."

"She bring home too many trophy," Auntie Lindo lamented that Sunday. "All day she play chess. All day I have no time do nothing but dust off her winnings." She threw a scolding look at Waverly, who pretended not to see her.

"You lucky you don't have this problem," Auntie Lindo said with a sigh to my mother.

And my mother squared her shoulders and bragged: "Our problem worser than yours. If we ask Jing-mei wash dish, she hear nothing but music. It's like you can't stop this natural talent."

And right then I was determined to put a stop to her foolish pride.

A FEW WEEKS LATER OLD CHONG AND MY MOTHER CONSPIRED TO HAVE me play in a talent show that was to be held in the church hall. By then my parents had saved up enough to buy me a secondhand piano, a black Wurlitzer spinet with a scarred bench. It was the showpiece of our living room.

For the talent show I was to play a piece called "Pleading Child," from Schumann's *Scenes From Childhood*. It was a simple, moody piece that sounded more difficult than it was. I was supposed to memorize the whole thing. But I dawdled over it, playing a few bars and then cheating, looking up to see what notes followed. I never really listened to what I was playing. I daydreamed about being somewhere else, about being someone else.

The part I liked to practice best was the fancy curtsy: right foot out, touch the rose on the carpet with a pointed foot, sweep to the side, bend left leg, look up, and smile.

My parents invited all the couples from their social club to witness my debut. Auntie Lindo and Uncle Tin were there. Waverly and her two older brothers had also come. The first two rows were filled with children either younger or older than I was. The littlest ones got to go first. They recited simple nursery rhymes, squawked out tunes on miniature violins, and twirled hula hoops in pink ballet tutus, and when they bowed or curtsied, the audience would sigh in unison, "Awww," and then clap enthusiastically.

When my turn came, I was very confident. I remember my childish excitement. It was as if I knew, without a doubt, that the prodigy side of me really did exist. I had no fear whatsoever, no nervousness. I remember thinking, This is it! This is it! I looked out over the audience, at my mother's blank face, my father's yawn, Auntie Lindo's stiff-lipped smile, Waverly's sulky expression. I had on a white dress, layered with sheets of lace, and a pink bow in my Peter Pan haircut. As I sat down, I envisioned people jumping to their feet and Ed Sullivan rushing up to introduce me to everyone on TV.

And I started to play. Everything was so beautiful. I was so caught up in how lovely I looked that I wasn't worried about how I would sound. So I was surprised when I hit the first wrong note. And then I hit another, and another. A chill started at the top of my head and began to trickle down. Yet I couldn't stop playing, as though my hands were bewitched. I kept thinking my fingers would adjust themselves back, like a train switching to the right track. I played this strange jumble through to the end, the sour notes staying with me all the way.

When I stood up, I discovered my legs were shaking. Maybe I had just been nervous, and the audience, like Old Chong, had seen me go through the right motions and had not heard anything wrong at all. I swept my right foot out, went down on my knee, looked up, and smiled. The room was quiet, except for Old Chong, who was beaming and shouting, "Bravo! Bravo! Well done!" But then I saw my mother's face, her stricken face. The audience clapped weakly, and as I walked back to my chair, with my whole face quivering as I tried not to cry, I heard a little boy whisper loudly to his mother, "That was awful," and the mother whispered back, "Well, she certainly tried."

And now I realized how many people were in the audience—the whole world, it seemed. I was aware of eyes burning into my back. I felt the shame of my mother and father as they sat stiffly through the rest of the show.

We could have escaped during intermission. Pride and some strange sense of honor must have anchored my parents to their chairs. And so we watched it all: The eighteen-year-old boy with a fake moustache who did a magic show and juggled flaming hoops while riding a unicycle. The breasted girl with white makeup who sang an aria from *Madame Butterfly* and got an honorable mention. And the eleven-year-old boy who won first prize playing a tricky violin song that sounded like a busy bee.

After the show the Hsus, the Jongs, and the St. Clairs, from the Joy Luck Club, came up to my mother and father.

"Lots of talented kids," Auntie Lindo said vaguely, smiling broadly.

"That was somethin' else," my father said, and I wondered if he was referring to me in a humorous way, or whether he even remembered what I had done.

Waverly looked at me and shrugged her shoulders. "You aren't a genius like me," she said matter-of-factly. And if I hadn't felt so bad, I would have pulled her braids and punched her stomach.

But my mother's expression was what devastated me: a quiet, blank look that said she had lost everything. I felt the same way, and everybody seemed now to be coming up, like gawkers at the scene of an accident, to see what parts were actually missing.

When we got on the bus to go home, my father was humming the busy-bee tune and my mother was silent. I kept thinking she wanted to wait until we got home before shouting at me. But when my father unlocked the door to our apartment, my mother walked in and went straight to the back, into the bedroom. No accusations. No blame. And in a way, I felt disappointed. I had been waiting for her to start shouting, so that I could shout back and cry and blame her for all my misery.

I HAD ASSUMED THAT MY TALENT-SHOW FIASCO MEANT THAT I WOULD never have to play the piano again. But two days later, after school, my mother came out of the kitchen and saw me watching TV.

"Four clock," she reminded me, as if it were any other day. I was stunned, as though she were asking me to go through the talent-show torture again. I planted myself more squarely in front of the TV.

"Turn off TV," she called from the kitchen five minutes later.

I didn't budge. And then I decided. I didn't have to do what my mother said anymore. I wasn't her slave. This wasn't China. I had listened to her before, and look what happened. She was the stupid one.

She came out from the kitchen and stood in the arched entryway of the living room. "Four clock," she said once again, louder.

"I'm not going to play anymore." I said nonchalantly. "Why should I? I'm not a genius."

She stood in front of the TV. I saw that her chest was heaving up and down in an angry way.

"No!" I said, and I now felt stronger, as if my true self had finally emerged. So this was what had been inside me all along.

"No! I won't!" I screamed.

She snapped off the TV, yanked me by the arm and pulled me off the floor. She was frighteningly strong, half pulling, half carrying me toward the piano as I kicked the throw rugs under my feet. She lifted me up and onto the hard bench. I was sobbing by now, looking at her bitterly. Her chest was heaving even more and her mouth was open, smiling crazily as if she were pleased that I was crying.

"You want me to be someone that I'm not!" I sobbed. "I'll never be the kind of daughter you want me to be!"

"Only two kinds of daughters," she shouted in Chinese. "Those who are obedient and those who follow their own mind! Only one kind of daughter can live in this house. Obedient daughter!"

"Then I wish I weren't your daughter. I wish you weren't my mother," I shouted. As I said these things I got scared. It felt like worms and toads and slimy things crawling out of my chest, but it also felt good, that this awful side of me had surfaced, at last.

"Too late change this," my mother said shrilly.

And I could sense her anger rising to its breaking point. I wanted to see it spill over. And that's when I remembered the babies she had lost in China, the ones we never talked about. "Then I wish I'd never been born!" I shouted. "I wish I were dead! Like them."

It was as if I had said magic words. Alakazam!—her face went blank, her mouth closed, her arms went slack, and she backed out of the room, stunned, as if she were blowing away like a small brown leaf, thin, brittle, lifeless.

IT WAS NOT THE ONLY DISAPPOINTMENT MY MOTHER FELT IN ME. IN THE years that followed, I failed her many times, each time asserting my will, my right to fall short of expectations. I didn't get straight As. I didn't become class president. I didn't get into Stanford. I dropped out of college.

Unlike my mother, I did not believe I could be anything I wanted to be. I could only be me.

And for all those years we never talked about the disaster at the recital or my terrible declarations afterward at the piano bench. Neither of us talked about it again, as if it were a betrayal that was now unspeakable. So I never found a way to ask her why she had hoped for something so large that failure was inevitable.

And even worse, I never asked her about what frightened me the most: Why had she given up hope? For after our struggle at the piano, she never mentioned my playing again. The lessons stopped. The lid to the piano was closed, shutting out the dust, my misery, and her dreams.

So she surprised me. A few years ago she offered to give me the piano, for my thirtieth birthday. I had not played in all those years. I saw the offer as a sign of forgiveness, a tremendous burden removed.

"Are you sure?" I asked shyly. "I mean, won't you and Dad miss it?"

"No, this your piano," she said firmly. "Always your piano. You only one can play."

"Well, I probably can't play anymore," I said. "It's been years."

"You pick up fast," my mother said, as if she knew this was certain. "You have natural talent. You could be genius if you want to."

"No, I couldn't."

"You just not trying," my mother said. And she was neither angry nor sad. She said it as if announcing a fact that could never be disproved. "Take it," she said.

But I didn't, at first. It was enough that she had offered it to me. And after that, every time I saw it in my parents' living room, standing in front of the bay window, it made me feel proud, as if it were a shiny trophy that I had won back.

LAST WEEK I SENT A TUNER OVER TO MY PARENTS' APARTMENT AND HAD the piano reconditioned, for purely sentimental reasons. My mother had died a few months before, and I had been getting things in order for my father, a little bit at a time. I put the jewelry in special silk pouches. The sweaters she had knitted in yellow, pink, bright orange—all the colors I hated—I put in mothproof boxes. I found some old Chinese silk dresses, the kind with little slits up the sides. I rubbed the old silk against my skin, and then wrapped them in tissue and decided to take them home with me.

After I had the piano tuned, I opened the lid and touched the keys. It sounded even richer than I remembered. Really, it was a very good piano. Inside the bench were the same exercise notes with handwritten scales, the same secondhand music books with their covers held together with yellow tape.

I opened the Schumann book to the dark little piece I had played at the recital. It was on the left-hand page, "Pleading Child." It looked more difficult than I remembered. I played a few bars, surprised at how easily the notes came back to me.

And for the first time, or so it seemed, I noticed the piece on the right-hand side. It was called "Perfectly Contented." I tried to play this one as well. It had a lighter melody but with the same flowing rhythm and turned out to be quite easy. "Pleading Child" was shorter but slower; "Perfectly Contented" was longer but faster. And after I had played them both a few times, I realized they were two halves of the same song.

February 1989

Author Biographies

ALICE ADAMS
Alice Adams is the author of the novels *Listening to Billie* (1978), *Rich Rewards* (1981), and *Caroline's Daughters* (1991), among others, as well as three short story collections. She lives in San Francisco.

JOHN BARTH
John Barth lives in Baltimore and teaches at Johns Hopkins University. His novels include *The Floating Opera* (1956), *The End of the Road* (1958, revised 1967), *The Sot-Weed Factor* (1960), *Giles Goat-Boy* (1966), and, most recently, *The Last Voyage of Somebody the Sailor* (1991). "Lost in the Funhouse," his first *Atlantic* story, is also the title story of Barth's 1968 collection.

RICHARD BAUSCH
Richard Bausch teaches English and creative writing at George Mason University. He is the author of four novels and two collections of stories, the latest of which is *The Fireman's Wife and Other Stories* (1990).

DIANNE BENEDICT
Dianne Benedict was raised in the Rio Grande Valley and now lives in Maine, where she teaches fiction. "Shiny Objects," her first *Atlantic* story, is the title story in her 1982 collection.

ETHAN CANIN

Ethan Canin graduated from Stanford University, received an MFA from the Iowa Writer's Workshop, attended Harvard Medical School, and now lives in San Francisco. "Emperor of the Air," his first *Atlantic* story, was also selected for *Best American Short Stories 1985*, and is the title story in his 1988 collection. His first novel is *Blue River* (1991).

WILLIAM FAULKNER

William Faulkner, winner of the Nobel Prize in literature in 1949, was the author of *The Sound and the Fury* (1929), *As I Lay Dying* (1930), *Light in August* (1932), *Absalom! Absalom!* (1936), and many other novels and short stories. Born in 1897, he lived nearly all his life near Oxford, Mississippi, where he died in 1962. "Gold Is Not Always" was excerpted from one of Faulkner's early novels, *Go Down Moses*.

E. S. GOLDMAN

E. S. Goldman lives on Cape Cod. He had long careers in advertising and retail sales before turning to writing. "Dog People" was the first story he sold. *Earthly Justice*, a collection of stories, was published in 1990.

SHIRLEY ANN GRAU

Shirley Ann Grau has written five novels, including *The Keepers of the House* (1965), which won a Pulitzer Prize, and three collections of stories. She lives near New Orleans and on Martha's Vineyard.

RALPH LOMBREGLIA

Ralph Lombreglia is the author of *Men under Water* (1990), a collection of stories. A graduate of the writing program at Johns Hopkins University and a former Wallace Stegner Fellow at Stanford University, he now lives in Arlington, Massachusetts. "Men under Water" was his second *Atlantic* story and was selected for *Best American Short Stories 1987*.

BOBBIE ANN MASON

Bobbie Ann Mason, a native of Kentucky, is the author of *Shiloh and Other Stories* (1982), which received the PEN/Hemingway Award for first fiction; *In Country* (1985), which was made into a movie; and *Love Life* (1990), a collection.

MARY MCCARTHY

Mary McCarthy, who died in 1989, was a novelist and critic born in Seattle, Washington. Among her best-known works are the novels *The Company She Keeps* (1942), *The Groves of Academe* (1952), and *The Group* (1963); the short story collection *Cast a Cold Eye* (1952); and the autobiography *Memories of a Catholic Girlhood* (1957).

ALICE MUNRO

Alice Munro has published seven collections of stories, including *Dance of the Happy Shades* (1968) and *The Progress of Love* (1987), as well as a novel, *Lives of Girls and Women* (1971), which won the Canadian Booksellers' Award. She was born in Ontario, where she still lives. "Visitors" was the first of many appearances in *The Atlantic*.

VLADIMIR NABOKOV

Vladimir Nabokov was born in Russia in 1899 and became a United States citizen in 1945, after establishing a literary career as an exile in Berlin and Paris. His most popular novels were written in English and include *Lolita* (1959), *Pale Fire* (1962), and *Ada* (1969). He died in 1977.

JOYCE CAROL OATES

Joyce Carol Oates published her first fiction in 1959 and has since published more than twenty novels, including *Do with Me What You Will* (1973) and *You Must Remember This* (1989), as well as many essays, poems, and stories. "In the Region of Ice" marked her first appearance in a national magazine. The story won first prize in *Prize Stories 1967: The O. Henry Awards* and was adapted for a short-feature film, which won an Academy Award.

EDWIN O'CONNOR

Edwin O'Connor was the author of *The Oracle* (1951), *The Last Hurrah* (1956), and *The Edge of Sadness* (1962), which won a Pulitzer Prize. He was born in Providence, Rhode Island, in 1918, and died in Boston in 1968. "The Gentle, Perfect Knight" was the first of many contributions to *The Atlantic*.

GRACE PALEY

Grace Paley, born in the Bronx in 1922, published her first collection of stories, *The Little Disturbances of Man*, in 1959. Her other collections are *Enormous Changes at the Last Minute* (1974) and *Later the Same Day* (1985).

JOHN SAYLES

John Sayles is a screenwriter, novelist, and short story writer whose books include *Pride of the Bimbos* (1975), *Union Dues* (1979), and *The Anarchists' Convention* (1979). He has written and directed several films, including *The Return of the Seacaucus Seven* (1980), *Matewan* (1987), *Eight Men Out* (1990), and *City of Hope* (1991).

WALLACE STEGNER

Wallace Stegner has received the Pulitzer Prize (1972) and the National Book Award (1977), among other literary awards, for his novels, short stories, and articles. His books include *The Big Rock Candy Mountain* (1943), *Angle of Repose* (1972), *Crossing to Safety* (1987), and *Collected Stories* (1989). Also a naturalist, he lives in California and Maine. A longtime *Atlantic* contributor, Stegner first appeared in the magazine in 1940.

AMY TAN

Amy Tan has published two novels, *The Joy Luck Club* (1989), which she is adapting for a motion picture, and *The Kitchen God's Wife* (1991). She lives in San Francisco. "Two Kinds" was her first story in a national magazine.

EDMUND WILSON

Edmund Wilson was a novelist (*Memoirs of Hecate County,* 1946), literary critic, and social commentator. He was also editor-in-chief of *The New Republic* from 1926 to 1931 and chief book reviewer for *The New Yorker*. He died in 1972 at the age of 76.

Acknowledgments

"Gold Is Not Always" from *Go Down Moses* by William Faulkner. Copyright © 1940 by William Faulkner. Reprinted by permission of Random House, Inc.

"Two Rivers" by Wallace Stegner. Copyright © 1942 by Wallace Stegner. Copyright renewed © 1970 by Wallace Stegner. Reprinted with permission of Brandt & Brandt Literary Agents, Inc.

"Mademoiselle O" from *Nabokov's Dozen* by Vladimir Nabokov. Copyright © 1958 by Vladimir Nabokov. Reprinted by permission of Vintage Books, a division of Random House, Inc.

"The Man Who Shot Snapping Turtles" by Edmund Wilson. Copyright © 1943 by The Atlantic Monthly Company. Reprinted with permission of Hippocrene Books.

"The Unspoiled Reaction" by Mary McCarthy. Copyright © 1946 by The Atlantic Monthly Company. Reprinted with permission of Brandt & Brandt Literary Agents, Inc.

"The Gentle, Perfect Knight" by Edwin O'Connor. Copyright © 1947 by Edwin O'Connor. Reprinted by permission of William Morris Agency, Inc., on behalf of the author's estate.

"The Man Below" by Shirley Ann Grau. Copyright © 1960 by Shirley Ann Grau. Copyright renewed © 1988 by Shirley Ann Grau. Reprinted by permission of Brandt & Brandt Literary Agents, Inc.

"In the Region of Ice" by Joyce Carol Oates. Copyright © 1966 by Joyce Carol Oates. Reprinted with permission of Joyce Carol Oates.

"Lost in the Funhouse" by John Barth. Copyright © 1967 by The Atlantic Monthly Company. From *Lost in the Funhouse* by John Barth. Used by permission of Doubleday, a division of Bantam Doubleday Dell Publishing Group, Inc.

"Distance" from *Enormous Changes at the Last Minute* by Grace Paley. Originally appeared in *The Atlantic Monthly*. Copyright © 1967 by Grace Paley. Reprinted with permission of Farrar, Straus & Giroux, Inc.

"Alternatives" by Alice Adams. Copyright © 1973 by The Atlantic Monthly Company. Reprinted with permission of International Creative Management.

"Shiny Objects" by Dianne Benedict. Copyright © 1982 by Dianne Benedict. Reprinted with permission of Dianne Benedict.

"Visitors" from *Moons of Jupiter and Other Stories* by Alice Munro. Copyright © 1982 by Alice Munro. Reprinted with permission of Alfred A. Knopf, Inc. Reprinted by permission of Macmillan of Canada, a Division of Canada Publishing Corporation.

"The Retreat" by Bobbie Ann Mason. Copyright © 1982 by Bobbie Ann Mason. Reprinted with permission of International Creative Management.

"Emperor of the Air" from *Emperor of the Air* by Ethan Canin. Copyright © 1988 by Ethan Canin. Reprinted by permission of Houghton Mifflin Co.

"Men under Water" by Ralph Lombreglia. Copyright © 1986 by Ralph Lombreglia. Reprinted with permission of Liz Darhansoff Agency.

"The Man Who Knew Belle Starr" by Richard Bausch. Copyright © 1987 by Richard Bausch. Reprinted with permission of Harriet Wasserman Literary Agency.

"The Halfway Diner" by John Sayles. Copyright © 1987 by John Sayles. Reprinted with permission of John Sayles.

"Dog People" by E. S. Goldman. Copyright © 1988 by E. S. Goldman. Reprinted with permission of E. S. Goldman and Another Chicago Press/TriQuarterly Books.

"Two Kinds" by Amy Tan. Copyright © 1989 by Amy Tan. Reprinted with permission of G. P. Putnam's Sons.